Jessica Blair grew up in Middlesbrough, trained as a teacher and now lives in Ampleforth. She became a full-time writer in 1977 and has written more than 50 books under various pseudonyms including *The Red Shawl*, *A Distant Harbour*, *Storm Bay*, *The Other Side of the River*, *The Restless Spirit*, *The Seaweed Gatherers*, *Portrait of Charlotte*, *The Long Way Home*, *The Restless Heart*, *Time & Tide*, *Echoes of the Past*, *Secrets of the Sea*, *Yesterday's Dreams*, *Reach for Tomorrow*, *Dangerous Shores*, *Wings of Sorrow*, *Stay With Me*, *Sealed Secrets* and *Secrets of a Whitby Girl* all published by Piatkus.

For more information about the author visit:
www.jessicablair.co.uk

D0378190

The Locket

Jessica Blair

piatkus

'PIATKUS

First published in Great Britain in 2000 by Judy Piatkus (Publishers) Ltd
This paperback edition published in 2011 by Piatkus

3 5 7 9 10 8 6 4 2

A CIP catalogue record for this book
is available from the British Library.

ISBN 978-0-7515-4556-2

Typeset in Sabon by Action Publishing Technology Ltd, Gloucester
Printed and bound by CPI Group (UK) Ltd, Croydon, CR0 4YY

Papers used by Piatkus are from well-managed forests
and other responsible sources.

MIX
Paper from
responsible sources
FSC
www.fsc.org FSC® C104740

Piatkus
An imprint of
Little, Brown Book Group
Carmelite House
50 Victoria Embankment
London EC4Y 0DZ

An Hachette UK Company
www.hachette.co.uk

www.piatkus.co.uk

For Joan
With love and grateful thanks for happiness

Chapter One

Emily ran her gaze from the waters of the Humber to the ridge on the southern edge of the Yorkshire Wolds where she sat quietly on her horse after the exhilarating ride from home.

It had been along familiar paths and she always halted at this point for she enjoyed the view across the river to the Lincolnshire countryside. Today, however, her attention was drawn more to the roof and chimneys of a house just visible beyond a small stand of oaks and she turned her horse along the ridge in its direction. She gave a little frown, puzzled as to her action. She had known that it was there, ever since she had visited it on two occasions with her father five years before when she was fifteen. She had had no cause to return. Had her curiosity been raised by the fact that she knew it had stood empty for eight months since Mrs Harriet Walton's death last December? But why now? A feeling of compulsion? Was something drawing her to it? She half-halted her horse, chiding herself for entertaining such foolish ideas, but almost at once allowed her thoughts to revive with speculation and rode on towards the silent house. Had she known the outcome of that decision maybe she would have turned back.

She rode past the oaks to stop where the ridge curved to form a natural backdrop to a small hollow in which the house, protected from the north, gazed southwards over fields sloping to the river bank some two miles distant.

But Emily had no eyes for the view, they were riveted on the house. She was mesmerised by its loneliness, emphasised by the silence which only an unoccupied house can convey. She could feel its longing to be loved even though she was still nearly a quarter of a mile away.

Emily sat for a few minutes, compelled to absorb the atmosphere. Then she sent her horse forward at a slow pace, her eyes concentrated on the house. As she slipped away from the ridge down the slope to a path which would take her to the front of the building she was struck by the appearance of neglect which was starting to take its toll. Some stonework was flaking, window frames needed a coat of paint, the windows were marked by rain, dust and bird droppings, the garden was beginning to run wild, the grass was long and at the edges brambles sent their shoots to choke the plants and flowers that had once received tender care. Her progress was hampered by undergrowth, but she encouraged her horse to force a way through and finally she reached the bottom of the slope. She rode to the front of the house

2

and dismounted. Knowing the animal would not stray far she left it free to champ at the grass.

She looked at the building. Silence assailed her ears. She felt like an intruder, trespassing on privacy, until she recalled that no one was living there. She sensed an empathy with the house as if it wanted her to share what it had to give.

'Hello, Shaken Hall,' she whispered.

She remembered asking her father, on the first of her two visits, when he was drawing up a will for Mrs Walton, why the strange name, and being told, 'In 1750 a previous house was struck by lightning and people commented that it had been shaken. It was a name that stuck and was still used when a new house was built in 1760.'

Now she saw the date plainly visible above the front door. She started, for it also bore the day and the month – 12 August. Today. Her own birthday. Surprised, she wondered why she had not noticed it five years earlier, but then a young girl had eyes for other things. She smiled at the coincidence. 'A happy hundredth birthday,' she said warmly as if she was congratulating a friend. 'Sorry you won't have a party like me.'

Her ice-blue eyes sparkled at the thought. There would be about thirty friends and family for an evening buffet and dancing. The Sutcliffes, Thomas and Meg, with their son Simon and daughter Grace, their lifelong friendship unmarred by the friendly rivalry of Thomas and her father, Jonas, both attorneys in Hull. Simon and Sylvia, her elder sister by two years, would, no doubt, have most of the dances together. But who will I dance with? The Eburys? The Masons? The Chadwicks? In all probability there would be a surprise or two. Birthdays had always been special occasions in the Thornton household and she knew this would be no exception. Wondering what lay in store, her lips broke into a smile, for she had been pestered into taking a ride this morning. To get her out of the way? Not that she had protested very much, with fine weather beckoning.

She had removed her hat shortly after leaving home, for at full gallop she enjoyed the wind blowing through her hair. Now its copper tint shimmered in the sunlight as she ran her long fingers through it.

She surveyed the front of the house. Four wide steps led to a terrace, with a waist-high balustrade, which ran the width of the building. Two simple columns supported a frieze surmounted by a triangular pediment forming a porch over the front door. Situated in the centre it had a six-paned window on each side. Beyond these were two matching windows making six in all to the ground floor. The first storey had identical windows giving the whole front a symmetrical look, and an impression that a precise orderly household had existed here. There were two attic windows allowing light into the roof space, which Emily thought must have been used as servants' quarters.

As she walked up the steps her imagination drew her back into the past, seeing this as a happy family home, full of life. Elated by the feeling, she danced a few steps, twirling as much as her long, tight riding skirt would allow. She laughed at her own exuberance as she came to a halt.

The laughter died on her lips and the brightness in her eyes was driven away by concern. The lower east window was partially open. It shouldn't be.

Since Harriet Walton's death the house had been shut up on the instructions of James, her adopted son. She remembered her father reading Mrs Walton's will. She had been present in her capacity as her father's assistant. She had always had a thirst for knowledge, a spirit which looked beyond the confines of following her mother's example of running a household with several servants, organising and attending tea parties, practising needle-work and outwardly the gentle art of conversation, though she knew it contained more gossip than opinion. Sylvia was more suited to that, in fact she liked it. But Emily thought there was more to life and that this was a time for women to exert their influence and not sit dormant under male dominance. Though she gave in half-heartedly to her mother's wishes, Emily, knowing she could twist her beloved father round her little finger, slowly influenced his thinking.

At eighteen she was bereft by her mother's sudden death and for six months a sombre atmosphere prevailed in the Thornton household. With the support and love of his two daughters, Jonas settled into his new home life with Sylvia taking over the role of running the house, though her father did not want that to dominate at the expense of a social life among her friends. Emily, not wanting to be under the eye of her elder sister, took to visiting her father's office more frequently. Though strict with his instructions that she should not interrupt his work he had welcomed her visits, for she lightened the atmosphere of office routine. She absorbed the work of an attorney and it came as no surprise to him when one day she suggested that she should help him.

He had pondered her proposal before he said, 'You have a nimble brain, you are sharp, intelligent, you get on well with people and one day maybe I could train you fully in the intricacies of my profession.' Excitement had come to Emily's eyes but he tempered it when he held up his hands to calm her. 'I only said one day. It would be very unusual for a lady to take up this profession. It would be frowned upon, but I will risk disapproval. Until that day I will employ you, because of your excellent copperplate script, as a writer and copier of documents.' His eyes twinkled with merriment as he added,' No doubt you will allow your-self to learn much more.'

So Emily had copied out Mrs Walton's will and could recall its contents when her father started to read it to the beneficiaries in his office the day after the funeral. A meticulous man, he had straightened papers on his desk, fidgeted with some envelopes, and checked once more that he had all the necessary documents. James, eager to know how his mother had disposed of her wealth, which had come from her husband through the family import business, had pressed him with anxious impatience to 'get on with it'.

Jonas had pulled him up sharply. 'Young man, there are certain procedures to follow and follow them I will.'

Emily had smiled to herself when he started by reviewing Harriet's life as he knew it, which was confined to her early years, for since her husband's death in 1839 when he was only 40 and James was four, she had lived a very reclusive life. Emily knew he was deliberately being verbose, repaying James's rudeness.

He paused, cleared his throat and said, 'Now to the will.' He picked up a sheet of paper and started to read, '... to my faithful housekeeper and companion, Mrs Sugden, for all the care and attention she lavished on me without one word of complaint, I leave the sum of three hundred pounds. I also bequeath to her the figurine of the flower-seller which she so greatly admired, the silverware which stands on the sideboard in the dining room, the gold necklace I wear every day of my life, for I know she will treasure it as I do, and the five gold and sapphire rings which are in the wash-leather purse in the jewellery drawer of my dressing table.' He paused and glanced at Mrs Sugden who sat straight-backed, her gloved hands folded neatly on her lap. There were tears in her eyes, but she held them back. This was not the time for her to weep. It would not be right in front of people. It could wait until the privacy of her room, where she would also offer a silent thanks to Mrs Walton for her generosity.

Jonas did not notice the look of annoyance that crossed James's face but Emily did. She knew he saw those bequests as money slipping out of his hands. Her father coughed and started to read again. 'To the servants in my employ at the time of my death I leave the sum of twenty-five pounds each, provided they have been with me for a year or more.' Again Jonas looked at the housekeeper. 'You will let me have their names, Mrs Sugden?' She nodded. He looked at his paper, picked up

7

another sheet and, much to James's chagrin, checked that it was the right one. 'Now I come to the main beneficiary.' He read, 'I leave to my son, James, an annual sum of five hundred pounds—'

'What?' James had sprung to his feet. 'A pittance! With all she had! Is that all the thanks I get for being a devoted son?' There was disgust in his voice. His eyes blazed with anger, his face reddened quickly revealing the fury which boiled within him.

'Pittance?' Emily had seen annoyance and disgust in her father's expression. 'Young man, you should think yourself lucky. There's many a person who would give an arm for what you call a pittance. You will be able to live comfortably on what your mother has allowed you until the rest of the will can be fulfilled.' His tone hardened. 'Now sit down and let me get on with the reading.' He shot a glance of apology to Mrs Sugden, who looked embarrassed by James's outburst.

Rebuked, James scowled, said nothing and sat down.

'I leave to my son James an annual sum of five hundred pounds,' Jonas restarted. 'That should see him comfortable until he is twenty-five by which time I hope he will have curbed what I would describe as irresponsible ways, which he sometimes exhibits. Though I disapprove of these, he has often brought much happiness since my husband and I adopted him at birth. In view of this, at the age of twenty-five I leave him my house and land, the residue of my fortune and the rest of my possessions.' Jonas paused then added, 'Signed Harriet Walton on this day 12 July 1855, witnessed by Jane Sugden and Martin Geary.' He looked up, straight at James. 'Young man, I hope you will live up to your mother's expectations. I know you broke her heart when you were arrested for the murder of John Ainslie. It is a great pity that she did not live to know Simon Sutcliffe was able to get an acquittal.'

'I don't need reminding of that episode,' snapped James. 'Standing in the dock, wrongly accused, was not a pleasant experience.'

'It might be as well if you do remember it from time to time,' replied Jonas icily. 'It might keep you out of trouble. I must say I think you are a very lucky young man to inherit what you will in November. See that you don't squander it.'

So Mrs Sugden had taken her rights and, after the house had been cleaned, the furniture covered, James had paid off the staff and closed it down. He had moved into a house in the best part of Hull so that he could more easily entertain his friends and indulge in his favourite pastimes.

Emily was uneasy as she stared at the open window. It spoke of a friendly house having been desecrated by intruders. Vagrants? Itinerant workers? Gypsies? Thieves? Oh, why hadn't James thought more about the house, which after all had been his home, and continued to live there? She glanced around. Silence hung on the building. The only sound came from the soughing of the breeze high in the branches of the oaks, elms and chestnuts.

She stepped to the window and looked in. Dustcovers had been scattered from two high-back chairs and the table, which held two cups, two plates, a jar, a jug,

9

knives and spoons, the remains of a pie and some bread. Anxious, Emily stooped to the opening and listened intently. Were there people still in the house? No sound reached her. She hesitated. Should she leave? Report it to her father? Say nothing? She stood still, trying to decide. She glanced along the terrace. The house seemed to be wanting her to do something. She thrust the riding crop she was carrying into the top of her calf-length riding boot, then gripped the bottom of the window frame and slowly pushed it upwards, hoping it would move noiselessly.

It was half open when it squeaked. In her anxious mind it sounded as if it would wake the dead. She stopped and listened. Silence reigned. She pushed again until the opening was wide enough for her to climb through. She was irritated by the tightness of her skirt, but managed to swing herself over the sill.

She stood a moment surveying the room. The dustcover had been removed from the sideboard and the drawers were open. She crossed the room, careful to make as little noise as possible. This must be the dining room, for the drawers contained cutlery. The bread and pie were mouldy. It seemed that whoever had been here had gone. She felt some relief at this supposition and also at the fact that no damage had been done. But what about the rest of the house?

She went to the nearest door, opened it cautiously and looked into the hall. No sound reached her. She took her bearings. Across the hall there was a corresponding door which, from five years before, she remembered, gave access to the drawing room where her father had talked with Mrs Walton. Beyond it a fine oak staircase, its rail surmounted at intervals with beautifully carved birds, gave the hall a majestic air. She had a feeling of being watched and glanced upwards to the landing, but there was no one. She shivered and shook off the sensation, chiding herself not to be so imaginative. Beyond the staircase was a door which she remembered led to the kitchen, for it was there, five years ago, that the smell of baking had been too much for her curiosity when she had slipped out of the drawing room, leaving her father and Mrs Walton to discuss matters which, at that time, were beyond her. She recalled the rosy face of the cook who had tempted her with a scrumptious jam tart and a piece of Victoria sponge.

Now, she wondered if anything had been disturbed there. Much to her relief, there was only a mess left by someone who had used it to prepare food without any thought of clearing up afterwards. After returning to the hall a quick glance into the drawing room revealed little upset.

She looked up at the landing again and then started up the stairs. A step creaked. To her it was like a clap of thunder. Her heart beat faster. She heard a rustle below, and spun round, her eyes wide with apprehension. Nothing. 'Emily Thornton, get a grip on yourself, there's no one here,' she whispered sharply. She drew some confidence back, but, even so, there was still caution in her progress to the next floor.

She glanced along the landing. All the doors were closed. There were rooms in the roof space so she decided to go there first. Holding the rail attached firmly to the wall, she eased her steps as she moved in gingerly fashion up the narrow staircase. Nothing had been disturbed in the rooms, which had been used by the staff.

Returning to the landing she found that the beds in two rooms had been slept in and the bedclothes left scattered. Another showed no signs of use, but when she went into the room at the other end of the landing she saw chaos. It was the largest bedroom and no doubt from its bed and decorations had been used by Mrs Walton. The bed was in disarray, every drawer was open, the contents scattered on the floor. Ornaments were broken and papers were strewn around the desk. It was obvious that a search had been made for anything the intruders had thought valuable. They must have used the house as a refuge and then moved on.

Emily looked round the room, sighed with disgust at the mess and then instinctively hunched down to tidy the papers, an automatic reaction of one used to having documents and correspondence stored neatly. She put them on the leaf of the bureau which had been left open and started to straighten them into organised piles. She would have to contact James Walton about this and tell him what she had done. As she brought some order to them, words impinged themselves on her mind. Suddenly she stopped. 'Will.' No, she must have been mistaken. But was she? Cautiously she looked back through the last few papers. There it was. She stared wide-eyed at the neatly folded paper in her hand. 'The Last Will and Testament of Harriet Walton.' The fluttering in her stomach heightened when she read the date, '12 December 1859.' Two days before Mrs Walton had died!

This wasn't the one her father had drawn up and read out after the funeral. That had been signed nearly five years before.

Her thoughts were wild as she unfolded the paper. Had James known about it? Surely not? But who had written it, and was it officially signed?

Her eyes scanned the writing. She did not recognise it. There were two signatures, both dated with the same date. Jane Sugden, Mrs Walton's housekeeper and companion who had witnessed the original will, the other, Thomas Laycock, unknown to Emily. Who was he? He had signed on the same day as Mrs Sugden, so she could have told them, but not now. She had died two months after Harriet.

She must get this piece of paper to her father quickly.

Chapter Two

Once in the saddle, Emily urged her horse up the slope to the ridge and then put it into a gallop for home.

She usually took her homeward ride at a gentle pace in order to enjoy the view of the Humber towards Hull. The movement of craft on the river always fascinated her, from small boats plying to and from Lincolnshire, to merchantmen heading for the sea and the far corners of the world. It was from some of these that her father gained his income. Apart from being an able attorney he was also a shrewd investor.

Emily appreciated his acumen for she knew it gave them an enjoyable lifestyle, not wealthy but comfortable, able to indulge themselves in luxuries and pursue their interests without too much restraint. Without it she would not own two horses apart from the two her father used as carriage horses. Their staff would not consist of groom, housekeeper, cook, butler and several maids. They would not have moved three miles into the country, from their modest house in Hull to a more salubrious abode, only a little smaller than Mrs Walton's.

But now she had no eyes for the activities on the river. She needed to see her father urgently.

The groom, hearing the beat of a horse's hoofs, came to meet her as she rode into the stableyard. He saw that the horse had been ridden hard, but he made no comment. Something had spooked Miss Emily for she was out of the saddle and rushing into the house without speaking. He raised his eyebrows. It was most unusual for her not to have a word with him and pat her horse as if thanking it for the ride.

Emily flung the doors open along the passage leading from the back of the house to the hall. Sylvia, her curiosity raised by the noise, came from a room on the right.

'What's going on?' The question was immediately followed by an admonishment when she saw her sister. 'Emily, your hair! You know it should be—'

'I haven't time for niceties,' snapped Emily, who, after she had been riding, always readjusted her hair to suit decorum before arriving home. 'Where's Father?'

'In his study.'

Emily rushed across the hall without any explanation for her hurry.

'I hope you're calmer by the time of the party.' Sylvia couldn't help making a parting comment about her younger sister's behaviour.

Emily burst into her father's study where he was sitting behind his desk, which occupied one corner of a book-lined room with the light coming from a window on his left. He looked up from the newspaper he was reading to see who had perpetrated this sudden intrusion into his calm world. He had been enjoying a quiet time, for he knew that later that day he would have to help his daughters entertain their guests. Earlier he had approved Sylvia's organisation and then left her to carry it out with Mrs Wentworth, the housekeeper, and Mrs Harvey, the cook.

'Emily.' The pleasure at seeing his younger daughter turned to concern when he saw her agitation. 'What's the matter?'

She drew the will from her skirt pocket, held it out to him, saying, 'I found that this morning.'

As she dropped on to the chair beside his desk, he glanced at the paper she had given him. He took in the words quickly and looked up at her with a startled expression, for the date had pierced his mind like a spear.

'Where did you get this?' he asked with an overtone of disbelief that he was handling such a document.

She told her story in a few short sentences as he was unfolding 'The Last Will and Testament of Harriet Walton.'

'You've read this?'

'No. When I saw the date I only opened the paper to see if it had been witnessed by two people. It had, so I brought it to you straight away.'

He nodded. He read a few words silently and, immediately grasping their significance, started again, reading them aloud. 'I Harriet Walton being of sound mind, write this will to revoke my previous will drawn up on 12 July 1855. I leave to my housekeeper and companion the money and items mentioned in my first will. I also leave to my servants the money as stated in that will. It is now that this will differs. I leave to my son James, five hundred pounds a year for five years only. My hope is that this will provide him with the means to establish some way to make his own living. The rest of my moneys, my house and my possessions I leave to Elizabeth Ainslie.' He paused. 'Signed H Walton. Witnessed by Jane Sugden and Thomas Laycock. Dated, 12 December 1859.'

Dumbfounded, father and daughter stared at each other. Emily broke the momentary silence. 'Is it legal?'

'I can see nothing wrong with it. It is clear in its content. It is signed by two witnesses. There can't have been any coercion. Mrs Sugden would have gained no more by this will than the first. The staff get the same. This Thomas Laycock is not mentioned in it, so he gained nothing. But I would have liked some confirmation about Harriet's frame of mind.'

'Unfortunately Mrs Sugden is dead, so that leaves only this Thomas Laycock, whoever he might be,' commented Emily.

'You've never heard of him?'

She shook her head.

Jonas tightened his lips in frustration. 'We'll have to try and find him. This will is going to raise a furore with James. He'll challenge his mother's soundness of mind especially as she died only two days after making this will.'

'I suppose in the aftermath of her death the second will was forgotten.'

'It's a pity Mrs Sugden didn't remember it, but in all the upheaval and with James closing the house so quickly she must have overlooked it.'

'Maybe she thought Mrs Walton had sent it to you,' said Emily. 'No doubt she wouldn't know the contents of the wills and therefore thought the will you read out was the second one.'

'That is plausible and the most likely explanation,' agreed her father.

'It's a wonder James didn't find it.'

'That young man wasn't bothered about the house or its contents; all he wanted was to close it down and move into Hull.'

'As far as this will is concerned,' mused Emily, 'it will be easy to implement. The only bequest to be altered is that which concerns James. What he would have got at twenty-five now goes to Elizabeth Ainslie.'

'Why to her?' Jonas's brow furrowed. 'Why to the wife of the man James was accused of murdering?' He continued in a thoughtful voice as if he were reminding himself and enlightening Emily to what had happened. 'It was a strange case, with James also accused of robbery in order to clear a gambling debt. He denied it, but the prosecution found a witness who said he had seen James running away from the scene of the crime. Thank goodness Simon managed to keep the case going until it was shown that the debt had been paid before the murder and therefore he had no motive for killing Captain Ainslie.'

'And where is Mrs Ainslie?' pondered Emily. 'It is said she left Hull immediately after the trial. Who can we ask? She led such a quiet life and appeared to have no friends.'

Jonas shook his head. 'I wish I knew. We need to find her and Thomas Laycock quickly.' He picked up the paper and put it in a drawer which he locked, depositing the key in his pocket. 'That will be safe. Say nothing of this to anyone. We'll give it more thought tomorrow. It is your birthday today and that is what we'll concentrate on now. Sylvia has put a lot of hard work into it, as have Mrs Wentworth and Mrs Harvey. Nothing must spoil their efforts, nor your enjoyment.' He came from behind his desk and together they walked out of the room.

Sylvia was crossing the hall when they left the study. She stopped and asked, looking from one to the other. 'Is something the matter? Emily, you were flustered when you came in.'

'A legal matter,' returned her father. 'Nothing for you to worry about. Some problem Emily thought she had an answer to.'

'And had she?' Sylvia always tried to be interested though legal matters bored her.

'Partially. We won't know yet for a while,' replied Jonas. 'Now,' he went on quickly. 'Are the party preparations in hand?'

'Yes,' replied Sylvia, thankful that neither he nor Emily wanted anything to do with the organisation of such events. She was grateful that, in entertaining friends the arrangements were always left to her. She liked the responsibility and enjoyed organising, though she was the first to acknowledge the help and support she got from Mrs Wentworth and Mrs Harvey and from all the staff. Indeed they put their whole effort into making social occasions at Bramwell House a huge success.

They had been bustling about the house all day and would do so throughout the afternoon until four o'clock when everything would be ready for the first arrivals at five, when all the maids would be dressed neatly in black ankle-length dresses, trimmed with white lace at the collar and cuffs. They would be wearing a small white apron tied at the waist and their hair would be tucked into a small white muslin cap, leaving only traces showing around the edge.

'Neither of you must go into the dining room until this evening,' warned Sylvia, her hazel eyes glinting in mischief in the knowledge that she knew something they didn't. She liked keeping up the tradition in the Thornton family of springing surprises, something her mother had instigated. 'But I will tell you that, as it is such a pleasant day, which bodes well for the evening, I plan to open the doors on to the terrace and have the musicians there.'

'Dancing outside,' cried Emily, anticipating that pleasure with excitement. 'Sylvia, you are so thoughtful.'

'And guests will be able to stroll on the lawn and around the garden while still hearing the music.'

'Splendid, my dear. Your mother would have loved it.'

'Oh, thank you so much.' Emily hugged her sister. 'I know I'm going to enjoy it immensely.'

Jonas beamed. It pleased him to see his daughters with a close bond. They were different in their outlook.

Emily was so interested in his business that he had already made up his mind to train her in its more serious and complicated aspects. A son would have inherited that side of the family assets but, as he and his wife were not so blessed, it would now be Emily. Other people might ridicule the idea but Jonas was forward-looking and appreciated that women could take roles in a world which had once been the sole province of men.

Sylvia on the other hand showed only the slightest interest in his work, and that merely when it came up in conversation at home and it would be with just a passing comment. She was much more interested in the household, running the family home, overseeing the garden and everything that this entailed. She reminded him so much of his late wife, not only in this respect but in looks too. She had the same oval face, thin arched eyebrows and high cheek-bones. Her skin was smooth, a delicate shade of pink. Her hair matched the colour of her eyes and, unlike her sister, she wore it cut short to her neck allowing the natural wave to sweep away from her forehead. Her fingers were long, those of a piano player, an accomplishment that Jonas and his wife had insisted both their daughters achieve.

Sylvia started towards the dining room. 'Remember,' she called over her shoulder, 'no going in, not even a peep.'

'We won't. Promise,' Emily called after her. She turned to her father. 'Sylvia told me James is coming with Simon. Will you mention the will to him this evening?'

'No. Don't breathe a word about it to anyone. I want

to try to discover who this Thomas Laycock is, and hope to contact him for verification of Mrs Walton's state of mind. But until then, not a word.' Jonas was emphatic about this attitude.

With the dining room unavailable, Jonas and his two daughters took a light lunch in the small drawing room, after which Jonas retreated to his study and Emily to her room to relax with one of the new magazines which were becoming available to women, leaving Sylvia to oversee the final preparations for the party.

But Emily could not concentrate on the words. Her mind kept drifting to the second will. She was puzzled as to why Mrs Walton should change the first one and cut James out of it apart from the provision of £500 which had been in the first. Could it have been because of his arrest? She must have seen this as a disgrace and inflicted her own punishment. But she had admitted in the first will that James had brought her much happiness, so why this rebuke?

She knew James had his wild side and he had grown fond of gambling. There were rumours that he sometimes frequented inns in the less salubrious parts of Hull and had been known to participate in wild parties thrown by the rich young gentry at certain country houses.

She knew there was some truth in these rumours, but like all rumours she expected they lost nothing in their telling and probably even were enlarged out of all proportion. She herself knew him as a pleasant young man who moved easily in her own circle of friends, something she admired in him for he had, after all, in his early years, led a secluded life in the company of his reclusive mother. The widening of his outlook had to be attributed to the governess his mother had employed. She had not only detected a nimble brain, thirsting to be stimulated by knowledge, but she had seen that the boy had a charm which could hold him in good stead in adult life. This had been the case, but what she had not seen was that knowledge and charm would combine to take him into undesirable company ever ready to cultivate a young man who had money and one day would, to their expectations, be wealthy. Use him right and they had much to gain.

Emily, gazing from her window across open fields where cattle grazed, wondered if any of his associates could be behind James's arrest. Had he been the victim of a conspiracy? If so why? Had he angered someone who wanted revenge? These were all aspects which might have a bearing on Mrs Walton's making another will. But why had she left her wealth to the widow of the murdered man?

Time had drifted away and she realised with a start that she should be getting ready to receive her guests.

As she began to prepare and to choose her dress the thoughts which had occupied her were banished to the far recesses of her mind. She hummed lightly as she opened the wardrobe and tried to make the right choice between two dresses. She held each in turn in front of herself and viewed its appearance in the cheval mirror. After a little uncertainty she cast them both aside and without further thought dressed in a red Garibaldi linen

23

waist-shirt with a small turned-down, embroidered collar and small black velvet bow. It had a tailored bosom with four pale blue buttons and its long sleeves were gathered to a wristband. She chose a pale blue skirt, tight at the waist with a broad waistband, pleated at the front, its ankle length giving a glimpse of stockings which matched her waist-shirt. She slipped her feet into highly polished light leather shoes with a semi-high heel, chosen specially with dancing in mind. Her hair, which earlier she had given a meticulous brushing, she swept upwards from her ears; allowing it to lie free on top, but brought tight at the back of her neck where she tied it with a pale blue ribbon, allowing the remainder to fall tail-like from the bow.

She surveyed herself in the mirror and decided one more item was needed. She went to the bowl in the window where fresh roses had been placed while she was having lunch. She chose a deep red blossom, perfectly shaped without being too big, and fastened it in her hair on the right-hand side of her forehead. One more glance in the mirror and she left her room.

She crossed the landing, but her step faltered at the top of the stairs. She glanced at her bright red sleeves. She would make a few heads turn, eyes widen and lips part, exchanging hushed comment. But why not? Hadn't she purchased this outfit for the sensation it would cause? Wasn't she making a protest against convention? She hoped people would see it as an emphasis for female liberties, that women should be taken more seriously, that they had a place in the world other than running a house, and that they should be able to express their opinion without censure from their male counterparts.

She took a deep breath and started down the stairs. There was no one in the hall, but when she entered the drawing room she found her father and Sylvia taking a glass of Madeira, a fortifier before the hectic time ahead.

'Emily, my dear.' Her father spoke from his favourite wing-back chair. His immediate reaction was one of surprise, but that vanished in a look of admiration. 'You do look smart, you'll certainly catch the eye in that outfit.'

'You certainly will,' agreed Sylvia. She showed no criticism, no envy. The sisters recognised each other's freedom of choice in their dress, something their mother had encouraged as a development of their individuality, provided it was not garish and completely against propriety. Though she stuck more to convention, Sylvia recognised and agreed with change in the female role in society, but in her view it needed to be a slow process, a careful evolution.

'That's new too,' commented Emily, eyeing her sister's dress.

'Especially for today, for you.'

'Thank you. The stripes suit you, and the colour?' She cocked her head and nodded. 'I like it.'

Sylvia smiled. She was pleased, for she had made a careful consideration of what she should buy and had finally decided, with the help of Simon's sister Grace, on a pink silk muslin dress flared slightly from the waist. The pale pink and white stripes gave it a delicate touch and the trimmings of white ribbon, net and lace brought a feminine look. The neckline came from off the shoulders and the pointed waistline still held sway, though, as with the flare, it was not as prominent as it used to be. With the short lace-trimmed sleeves leaving bare arms, Sylvia had decided to wear white kid gloves and had draped a muslin shawl around her shoulders.

Emily poured herself a glass of Madeira and sat beside her sister on the sofa. She glanced at the clock, set in marble, standing on the oak mantelpiece. 'Half an hour to relax,' she said, letting the excited tension drain from her. She sipped her wine and looked at her sister. 'Thank you for all you have done to make this party—'

'You haven't been into the dining room?' The touch of alarm caused Emily to laugh.

'Of course not. I wouldn't want to spoil your enjoyment of the surprise.'

Sylvia felt relieved. She looked at her father. 'Should we give Emily our present now?'

'A good idea.' He put down his glass and went to the table standing between the two windows through which there were views towards the Humber. He opened its one narrow drawer and drew out a small box which he handed to Emily with a proud paternal smile. 'A happy birthday, my love, from Sylvia and from me.' He kissed her fondly on the cheek.

Sylvia came to Emily and hugged her. 'A happy birthday.' She then added a whispered, 'You look very attractive,' close to her ear. She also pressed a small package into her hand. 'Just a little something you might like to try.'

26

'Oh, thank you both so much.' Emily's eyes were damp with happiness as she looked from one to the other.

She sat down and started to open the packet her father had given her. The flowered wrapping was removed to reveal a royal blue rectangular box. She raised the hinged lid and gasped at the sight of the string of pearls shimmering in the light from the windows.

'Oh, they are so beautiful. Were they Mother's?'

Jonas nodded. 'Yes. Sylvia agreed that you should have them.'

Emily looked at her sister with deep appreciation. 'Thank you, so much.' She drew them from the box and held them out to her sister. 'Please.'

Sylvia fastened them round Emily's neck. Emily crossed the room to the mirror on the wall between the two windows.

'Perfect,' she said. 'So beautiful.' Her red waist-shirt emphasised the beauty of the necklace. She swirled round and hurriedly kissed them both before sitting down to open Sylvia's present. Impetuously she tore the paper off to find a bottle of her favourite French perfume and a copy of *A Tale of Two Cities* by Charles Dickens. 'Sylvia!' The tone of her cry expressed all her thanks and excitement. She jumped to her feet and hugged her sister again.

At five o'clock the first guests arrived and Emily was in the hall with her father and sister to receive them. Maids stood by to take coats and hats, and presents, which would be put separately in the small drawing room to be opened later when Emily could give them her full attention and savour them without rushing. Guests were ushered into the main drawing room where they were offered drinks to their particular taste.

Apart from birthday wishes, snippets of news or comment were exchanged.

There were two extra people with the Mason party and after greeting Emily with a kiss Mrs Mason said, 'I know it was always a tradition with the Thornton parties that there should be surprises, well, I'm afraid I played on this.'

'What Mother is trying to say,' broke in her daughter Adelaide, knowing her mother would go into a long roundabout explanation, 'is that we have brought along my two cousins, Sabina and Fanny. She was worried that we shouldn't do so. I tried to convince her that it would be perfectly all right.'

'Of course it is,' cried Emily. 'I am pleased to see them. Think nothing more about it, Mrs Mason.' She gave her a reassuring smile and turned her attention to Adelaide and the newcomers, expressing a welcome that made them feel at home.

By half-past five all the guests, with the exception of James Walton and the Sutcliffes, had arrived. Five minutes later Mr and Mrs Sutcliffe and Grace were apologising that Simon was not with them.

'I hope he is coming,' commented Sylvia.

Meg smiled. She was pleased the childhood friendship between Sylvia and her son had blossomed into a closer relationship. 'Oh, yes, he wouldn't miss a party. He's gone to pick up James.'

'Of course. I thought he might have done that first.' Sylvia was relieved. She had been looking forward to dancing with Simon for not only was she fond of him but he was a good dancer.

'We needn't wait for the two young men,' said Jonas. 'We can greet them whenever they come. Let us join everyone else in the drawing room.' He fell into conversation with Thomas and they followed Emily who exchanged the latest gossip with Grace while Sylvia escorted Mrs Sutcliffe.

Conversation flowed between friends, personal news was exchanged, comments made about the liberation movement in Italy, the election of Abraham Lincoln as President of the United States, and the latest fashions. The glass doors were open on to the terrace and the warm evening air attracted some of the guests outside where they enjoyed their drinks while admiring the garden. The Stodart piano, manufactured in London, had been taken on to the terrace and placed at one end where four musicians started to play softly, the notes drifting through the still air, bringing a sense of peace and tranquillity.

The opening of the door into the drawing room from the hall drew Emily's attention. She saw Simon Sutcliffe enter followed by James Walton. Both were impeccably dressed in single-breasted swallow-tail coats, Simon's being black and James's grey. Both wore silk waistcoats of the same colour as their coats. Simon's trousers were also black, a colour which suited him for it enhanced his athletic figure. James's trousers were of small yellow checks, the colour matching his shirt highlighted by a

29

red silk neckcloth. As smart as they were it was the third person to enter the room who really caught Emily's attention.

Six foot tall, he seemed taller for he held himself erect, but was perfectly relaxed. He was no smarter than his companions. He wore a claret swallow-tail coat and matching trousers. His waistcoat was silk, pale blue, with pearl buttons and two points at the front. He wore a pale blue shirt and claret neckcloth. But it was his demeanour which immediately attracted Emily. There was a certain presentation, not deliberate, of personal pride and dignity. There was a leanness about him, not a weakness for there was a sense of a tough quality too. He seemed to be a man who had his wits about him, alert, always taking in information as if he thought that at some time in the future it might be useful. His jaw-line had a rugged, handsome appearance that she found attractive. His lips were full, a perfect bow, but Emily thought they could harden with determination. But there was one thing she felt sure would never do that – his pale blue eyes. They were smiling eyes and would always counteract his attempt at hardness.

Emily went to greet the new arrivals. 'Simon.' She held out her hand, which he took gently between his fingers.

'Emily, a happy birthday.' He bowed and kissed her hand.

'And from me too.' James said with sincerity and warmth.

'Thank you both for coming.'

'Knowing tradition, I thought I would surprise you by

bringing a guest whom I'm sure you will enjoy talking to. He has recently returned from America. Emily, may I present Thomas Laycock?'

Chapter Three

Though the chatter was no less noisy around the room it faded from Emily's mind. The name she had just heard forced her concentration on the young man standing in front of her. She was only dimly aware of Simon making his excuses on seeing Sylvia across the room and James turning to answer a greeting from Grace.

Thomas Laycock! It couldn't be true. This couldn't be the same man who had witnessed Harriet Walton's signature, whom she and her father were desperate to find.

'I am pleased to meet you, Miss Thornton.' He bowed slightly, but never took his eyes off her. His voice was gentle and gracious. 'I hope your look of surprise does not mean that I am not welcome. Simon assured me it would be perfectly all right.'

Emily was sorry that she had expressed her astonishment for she had tried hard to subdue it. 'Indeed, Mr Laycock, you are most welcome. Simon did right to invite you. It is the tradition of Thornton parties that there are surprises and Simon no doubt was keeping up that tradition. I welcome you.'

'Then I am most fortunate,' returned Thomas. 'To meet such a charming hostess as you gives me enormous pleasure.'

Emily blushed. 'You flatter me, sir. You do not know me.'

'From what I have observed in these few moments I am sure that you are a kind and generous person and from your most admirable and eye-catching dress that you are not afraid to be noticed and voice your opinions.'

'Thank you for the compliments. I am pleased you admire my outfit.' Emily felt a little uneasy that he had summed her up so quickly, for it meant she had come under close scrutiny. 'But already I am neglecting my duty as a hostess. Would you care for a glass of Madeira or would you prefer something else?'

'A glass of Madeira will be to my taste, thank you.'

Emily signalled to the maid, who had been hovering close by with a tray of drinks. She came to them and they both selected a glass.

'Should we stroll outside?' Emily suggested. 'And you can tell me about yourself.'

As she led the way on to the terrace she caught a questioning look from her father and knew he was wondering about the identity of this stranger, but she made no move to introduce the two men. She would come to that later. She wanted to know a little more about Thomas first.

'Your home is in a pleasant situation,' he observed as they stepped outside.

'Yes, we like it. We used to live in Hull until Father decided that we would enjoy somewhere out of town. This property came up for sale. We liked it and so here we are.'

'Such good views.'

'I never tire of them.'

'Nor would I. I wish I had similar ones.'

'You live in Hull?'

'I do now.'

'Now? You're not Hull born?'

'No. I was born in Whitby. Raised there.'

'A man of the sea?'

Thomas gave a little chuckle. 'No. A lot of Whitby men are, but I never had the inclination. I worked for a merchant.'

'And you are in Hull in that capacity?'

'Again, no. It's a long story.'

'I am a good listener.'

They had strolled along the terrace and down the steps into the garden while they had been talking.

'Shall we take a seat and you can tell me,' Emily invited.

'But your other guests, Miss Thornton?'

'I shall not neglect them, you can be sure. We have time. The buffet will not be served for about another half hour.'

'Very well then, but on one condition; you stop me if I am boring you.'

'Considerate of you, Mr Laycock, but I am sure you are never boring to young ladies, and I sense you have an interesting story to tell.'

'Well, we shall see. As a matter of fact the recent turn in my life is one reason Simon invited me here.'

Emily raised a surprised eyebrow. 'Indeed, Mr Laycock.' So there was more behind Simon's invitation than springing a surprise, it also had a purpose. Emily wondered what it could be. 'Have you known Simon long?'

'About two months. I met him two weeks after I came to Hull.'

'Newly acquainted then?'

'Indeed. It was fortuitous that I met him.' He paused a moment and then appeared to change his mind about what he was going to add. Instead he said, 'For it has meant that I have met you.'

'You flatter me again, Mr Laycock.' She eyed him with a twinkle of pleasure at his words. She felt so at ease with him, it was as if they had been friends for a long time. There was about him an aura that spread interest and confidence, that exchanges would never become gossip and that there was sincerity in his words. He would not offer compliments lightly.

'Miss Thornton, let me assure you that the main purpose of my visit this evening has paled on meeting you.'

Emily had no reply to that so she sipped her wine and waited for him to continue.

He knew she had taken his statement seriously, but he recognised that she was waiting for him to recount his story. 'Simon, in his capacity as an attorney, put some work my way. He suggested I come this evening to meet your father whom I may be able to help through my work.'

Emily nodded. This was getting more intriguing every minute. 'How might that be?' She did not let the question stand on its own, but quickly confirmed her interest by adding. 'I help my father with his work.'

Thomas smiled. 'I have heard that too.'

'You are amused!' Emily showed a little annoyance.

'No. No.' He denied her accusation quickly. 'I meant it as a smile of admiration. I am a great believer in ladies participating much more in today's world.'

'Then you are a man of perspicacity I am pleased to say. But how can you help my father's firm?'

A smile came back to his eyes. 'Maybe we should say your firm, meaning both of you. And maybe it should have been put round the other way, that your firm can help me.'

'You mean by putting work your way as Simon did? If so, what work do you do, Mr Laycock?'

'I think to continue my story might explain things better. As I said, I was Whitby born and bred. I worked for a merchant, but it wasn't what I really wanted to do. Sad to say at that time I had nothing fixed in my mind. I was restless. My parents died four years ago. I had nothing to keep me in Whitby but I didn't know where I wanted to be.'

'You had no relatives?'

'Only one. An aunt, my father's sister. She lived near here at Shaken Hall.'

Emily's heart leaped. She felt a strange tightening in her stomach. Shaken Hall. But Harriet Walton had no relatives?

Thomas was going on. 'She was housekeeper-companion to a Mrs Walton, who, my aunt told me, was something of a recluse, but Aunt Jane stayed with her until her death.'

Emily's mind was racing as she put her query, 'Her surname was—?'

'Sugden.' Thomas finished for her.

'I met her once, five years ago when I went to Shaken Hall with my father. She was crossing the hall when we arrived. She spoke only briefly.'

'She was a nice lady.'

'She must have been to be so faithful to Mrs Walton. Did you visit your aunt there?'

'Yes. Twice. About six months after my parents died and also one day last December'

December! The month the second will was signed and witnessed! She wanted to ask him question after question, but she held back, allowing him to finish his story.

'On my first visit she recognised my restlessness. She was a shrewd woman. "Emigrate," she told me. "Go to America. If you like it, stay. If you don't, come back. You'll have got your uneasiness out of your system and you'll then find something you want to do."'

Emily's attention was riveted on him. 'But you are back, so didn't your aunt's advice work?'

'It did. When I was in America I got involved with the Pinkerton National Detective Agency. It was interesting work and I learned a lot from them. As I said I came to England briefly last December, when I saw my aunt for a day. That visit made me realise that I couldn't settle permanently in America so when I reported to the agency I gave my notice and here I am setting up on my own.'

'You've done that?'

He nodded. 'I was inclined to do so in London, where I thought there would be more opportunity, but I couldn't have lived there. I was Yorkshire through and through and although I was brought up in Whitby I was never far from open spaces. I would have missed them in London. So I looked for a likely place to establish myself in the north and finally settled on Hull. I'm hoping that your father will be able to put some work my way.' He smiled. 'I've stated my case. I hope I haven't bored you.'

'Not in the least. It has been most interesting.' More than you know, she thought. She had a vital question she wanted to ask him, but she curbed her enthusiasm. Her father should be the one to do that. 'I think you had better meet my father.' She rose from the seat and they went back on to the terrace.

The musicians were playing a waltz and Sylvia and Simon were one of three couples taking the opportunity to dance. She admired them and wished she danced as gracefully as her sister.

They were making for the door when Jonas came out. 'Ah, my dear, I was wondering where you were. I think it is time to start the buffet but, as you know, we cannot enter that room until your sister says so.' He glanced at Thomas. 'My eldest daughter, who runs the house, insists that it must be a surprise. She's kept Emily and me out all day.'

'Father,' Emily put in quickly before he got carried away. His eyes turned on her and she held them as she said, 'I want you to meet Thomas Laycock.' For one moment there was no reaction to the name, but then Emily saw it come and she flashed a warning to say nothing.

'Sir, it is a pleasure to meet you.' Jonas held out his hand and he felt it taken in a warm friendly grip.

'The pleasure is all mine, sir.' Thomas knew he was coming under the scrutiny of a man of shrewd judgement. Anyone interested in his youngest daughter, especially a stranger, would be thoroughly vetted. 'I have just spent a little while in the delightful presence of your charming daughter.'

Flattery, thought Jonas, but there was sincerity in the man's tone.

'Mr Laycock is starting a detective agency in Hull,' Emily explained. 'Simon has put some work his way and Mr Laycock wonders if there might be some forthcoming from you?'

Jonas saw his chance. 'Indeed. A very interesting proposition.' He smiled. 'Young man, come and see me at my office in the morning. Bowlalley Lane. It runs off Lowgate towards The Land Of Green Ginger. Do you know it?'

'I'll find it, sir. And thank you for your time.'

'I hope I can be of help. A detective agency might be very useful in Hull. Shall we meet at ten-thirty?'

'Very good, sir. I'll be there.'

The waltz was coming to an end. Jonas turned to Emily. 'Let us get Sylvia and start the buffet; I'm sure our guests are ravenous.' He glanced at Thomas. 'Excuse us.'

Thomas bowed. His eyes smiled at Emily and, as she accompanied her father along the terrace, she could feel the eyes of the stranger on her.

'Is he—' Jonas had no need to complete the question he made in a low voice. He knew his daughter would realise what he was asking.

'Almost certainly. He was Jane Sugden's nephew and was at Shaken Hall last December.' Emily's reply came swiftly and in the same quiet tone.

There was no time for more. Sylvia was there with Simon at her side.

'I think it is time to open the dining room,' Jonas suggested.

'Very well,' replied Sylvia. She indicated to the band not to start another tune. The leader nodded his understanding. Sylvia went into the hall and signalled to the butler, who was standing beside the dining-room door. He picked up a hand gong and beat it twice. Silence descended on the guests.

'Friends.' Sylvia addressed them with a firm voice. 'You are most welcome and we thank you for coming to celebrate Emily's birthday. A buffet is laid in the dining room. Please help yourselves, the maids will be there to assist you. But I would like my sister to see the room first. Enjoy the rest of the evening.' She turned to Emily. 'Ready?'

She nodded, the excitement of anticipating something nice shining in her eyes.

Sylvia crossed the hall, followed by Emily and her father. Guests were charged with curiosity, for they knew by Sylvia's tone that a surprise awaited Emily. The

Thornton tradition was being maintained. Sylvia opened the door to the dining room, and stepped inside. Emily moved past her sister and stopped, taken aback by the presentation.

The central table was laden with food for the main course. Smaller tables on all four walls held the first course and the sweets. As Emily took it all in with one encompassing glance she saw that the food was artistically and appetisingingly presented. But her attention was drawn to the decorations on all the tables. They were special. She saw that Sylvia had excelled her talent for flower arranging on this occasion.

The decoration which held the centre of the main table reflected the banks of the Humber. Stones had been arranged in an oblong dish, at one end of which was a bowl of water. Mosses and small green plants had been woven among the stones and around the lip of the water bowl. At one corner rushes rose, trimmed to keep them in perspective. Cuttings from a weeping willow trailed in the water, which glistened in the light and seemed to move as if flowing downstream. A typical reminder of the river which dominated the lives of so many at this southern edge of Yorkshire.

The decorations on two of the smaller tables had been inspired by the beach, a reminder of the days when they were young and the family would visit the coast at Hornsea and Withernsea. Pebbles and sand were strewn with twisted driftwood, a frond of seaweed and a few links of a fisherman's net.

It was not hard to imagine light filtering through a wood in the two remaining decorations. Leafy branches had been arranged above a carpet of twigs, bark and moss through which there was the hint of tree roots. It brought a lump to Emily's throat for it reminded her of the days walking in the woods with her mother.

Emily was transfixed, then suddenly she turned to her sister and hugged her tight. 'Oh, Sylvia, it's wonderful. Thank you so much for your time and thought.'

'I enjoyed doing it,' she replied. 'Now come and start the buffet, you're keeping the guests waiting.'

Jonas had been equally struck by the attractive displays. He squeezed Sylvia's hand and silently mouthed the words, 'Thank you,' for he was too full of emotion to voice them aloud. He thanked God that he had been blessed with two wonderful daughters, who, so different in many ways, complemented each other and got on together so well.

The exchanges of the guests centred on the eye-catching interpretative decorations and on the tempting food. Sylvia had discussed the menu with Mrs Wentworth and Mrs Harvey, and the result catered for all tastes. There was white soup or appetisers to be followed by a wide choice on the main table. Cold roast beef, ham, mutton, chicken, duck, game pie could be accompanied by potato salad, peas, green salad, mushrooms, pickles, carrots and spinach. Dishes of salmon and trout tempted appetites further and the sight of the sweets had already set many mouths watering – compôte of fruit, almond pudding, marbled jelly, apple pie, meringues and Coburg Pudding. Home-made cheese biscuits were there to accompany Stilton, Double Gloucester and Wensleydale. There were wines to complement each dish and coffee or tea available as required.

Emily could not express her thanks enough to her sister. 'I wonder how you managed it all,' she exclaimed. 'I certainly couldn't.'

'You could,' Sylvia reassured her, but Emily shook her head.

'But the planning and organisation—'

'I had Mrs Wentworth and Mrs Harvey to help me.'

'I must thank them, and of course all the staff.'

Sylvia knew her sister to be a considerate person who was never slow to show her appreciation to the staff of Bramwell House.

Kind wishes came her way as the guests filled their plates and circulated with friends, some taking advantage of the warm evening by moving on to the terrace. It gave Simon much pleasure to hear considerable praise for Sylvia. Throughout the meal Jonas kept turning his attention to Thomas Laycock. He seemed a likeable young man. He was certainly presentable and had an attractive aura which Jonas could see was not lost on some of the young ladies. He noted that, while Thomas appeared to be giving them his every attention, his eyes kept drifting in the direction of Emily. He would need to know more about this young man.

Thomas's plate was empty. He had enjoyed the food and the temptation to partake of some more meat gave him the opportunity to excuse himself from the two people with whom he was conversing.

As he was choosing more delectable meats he noticed Emily strolling on to the terrace. He had been taken not only by her good looks but by her ease of charm, and the spirit and zest for life which he judged lay below the outward appearance of calm. He hoped she too would be at her father's office tomorrow. Now might be a good time to get to know more about her before then.

But his immediate intention to join her was thwarted by a voice close to his side. His mind had been so occupied with Emily that he had been unaware of someone coming to the table beside him.

'Thomas, enjoying yourself?'

He half-turned to see a friendly smile from James. 'Yes. This is an unanticipated pleasure. I'm glad Simon suggested I come and explained I would not be intruding. A nice house with a wonderful outlook, but don't you agree it's the people who make a house a home and that it's certainly the case here?'

'You've never met the Thorntons before?' James knew nothing about Thomas. When Simon called for him as arranged he had been surprised to find him accompanied by a stranger.

'No. I've only just come to live in Hull. Have you and Simon been friendly long?'

'I suppose I've known him all my life, but we have only become friendly during the last five years. He's the best.' There was no doubting his conviction.

'Then I take it that you've always lived in Hull?'

'Yes, well, just outside, at Shaken Hall.'

'Shaken Hall? James Walton. Then you must be Mrs Harriet Walton's son?'

James nodded. 'Yes.' His answer was tentative as he wondered how this stranger knew these facts.

As some other guests came to the table to help themselves to the buffet, the two men moved away.

'Then you would know my aunt, Jane Sugden.'

'Of course. A wonderful woman.' He stared at Thomas in amazement. 'Good Lord. You're Jane's nephew? I didn't know she had any relatives. She never talked about them.'

'She and my father were brother and sister. She met a Hull whaleman when his ship, badly damaged in the Arctic, put into Whitby. She married him later, came to Hull and never returned to Whitby. He was killed on a whaling expedition. My father wanted her to come back to Whitby but she would not. We lost touch, though I did visit her after my parents had died. I was restless at the time and on her advice went to America.'

'America?' James's expression showed interest. 'What did you do there?'

'Took a few odd jobs but then spent most of my time with the Pinkerton National Detective Agency.'

'Detective agency? Now there's something different.'

'It was founded by a Scotsman, Allan Pinkerton, who had emigrated to America in 1842 and eight years later founded the agency. It was an interesting experience for me.'

'So you're just on a visit here?'

Thomas shook his head as he forked some pickle. 'No, I'm back for good. I prefer England to America. I decided I'd like to have my own firm, and thought there'd be an opportunity to establish a detective agency in Hull.'

'Rather than London?'

'I like the north. Here you are soon out into the country and open spaces and the sea's not far away.'

'So you're just finding your way around. I know Hull pretty well. I left Shaken Hall after Mother died and moved into the town, well, just on the outskirts. You'll have to let me show you Hull.'

'That is kind. I'll take advantage of your offer.'

'Splendid,' said James, forking his final piece of pie. 'It's good to have new friends, and a detective at that. A pity you weren't here last year.'

'Why?' Thomas glanced up from his plate.

'I was tried for murder.'

'What?' Thomas's eyes widened in disbelief.

James gave a small smile. 'It's true. As you see I was acquitted, thanks to Simon. He was brilliantly eloquent. But there are those who still think I was guilty.'

'What were you supposed to have done?' Thomas's curiosity was aroused, but he was careful how he phrased the query.

'I was accused of killing a ship's captain as he was returning to his ship, the *Fauconberg*, with wages for the crew.'

'For the money?' Thomas was astonished.

James gave a half laugh. 'Imagine it?' he answered with derision.

There were lots of questions which sprang to Thomas's mind, but he had no chance to put them as Grace Sutcliffe came towards them.

'That was a deep conversation, but can I break it up and invite a gallant gentleman to help me choose from this delightful array of food?'

46

Both men apologised for their inattention. James took a plate and said, 'I can recommend the game pie.'

'Then game pie it shall be,' she said coyly.

'A slice of this succulent ham?'

'Why not? And a dash of pickle.' Grace started to look around at the other dishes.

Thomas, noting James's gentlemanly attention to her, said, 'Please excuse me. I'm sure I leave you in good hands, Miss Sutcliffe.' He bowed to her and, with a glance at James, said, 'We must talk another time.'

'Call on me at my club, the Curzon, in Whitefriargate, tomorrow morning eleven o'clock.'

'I have a morning appointment. Could we meet during the afternoon?'

'Very well. Three o'clock.'

Thomas paused in the doorway leading to the terrace. The quiet melody drifted through the air. Several groups were enjoying the soft summer evening and one another's company.

Emily, who was talking to four friends, glanced along the terrace and saw Thomas was alone. She excused herself and left them. Catching her movement he stepped towards her.

'Alone, Mr Laycock?'

'Not any longer, Miss Thornton. I now have the pleasantest of company.' His voice was caressing in its sincerity.

'You flatter, Mr Laycock,' she answered with a demure inclination of her head.

'If I do, it is deserved.' He made a slight pause and added. 'If we are to be friends, and I hope that will be so now that I am permanently in Hull, please use my Christian name.'

She gave him a gracious acknowledgement and said, 'I too hope we will be friends, so Thomas and Emily it shall be.'

He greeted her consent with pleasure.

'I hope you are having an enjoyable evening?' she queried.

'Most delightful. Excellent company in pleasant surroundings and good food, what more could a stranger to Hull ask?'

'I am pleased that my party is the cause of your early introduction to our social life and that of our friends. I hope we shall have the pleasure of your company on more occasions.'

'Tomorrow, at your father's office? Will you be there?'

'Most certainly.'

'A business meeting, which I presume it is, will be all the more pleasurable.'

'Maybe I should not divert your attention from what my father has to say,' she replied with a demure smile.

'My dear Miss Thornton, let me assure you that while your presence will be distracting in a pleasing way, I will, nevertheless, pay a great deal of attention to what your father has to say. It may affect my future in Hull.'

'Indeed it may.'

'So you know what it is about?'

'Yes.' Emily offered no more.

'Then your father won't be merely assessing my credentials?'

Emily smiled a warning. 'Don't ask, Thomas. But I will say he'll certainly do that, though he has probably come to some conclusion by observing you this evening.'

'I have noticed him doing so.'

'As behoves a detective.'

'True.'

'And what conclusions have you come to about some of the people you see here this evening?' There was a challenge in her eyes.

'Ah,' he replied cautiously. 'Should I really reveal those to my hostess?'

'She promises to keep them to herself, but it would be interesting to see if, even in this short time, you get near the truth.'

'Truth? Do we ever know the truth about people? Aren't there secrets we never know? Aren't our opinions only of the surface?'

'Surely we know more about a person than what we see?'

'Only after a while and then hardly ever the whole person.' He glanced around. 'At this moment my opinions can only be made from surface observations.'

'Tell me, I wonder how near you will be to what I know of them.'

He gave a wry smile. 'Well, first, you are testing me so you can report to your father.'

'So, already I can tell him you are shrewd, someone who cannot be tricked easily.' A slight flicker of alarm that he might have misunderstood her crossed her face. 'Though let me hasten to add, I had no intention of developing this conversation this way.'

'I didn't think you had, but it is an interesting turn.' He paused and gave her a questioning look. 'Well, should I begin?'

Emily's inclination of her head was accompanied by a smile which told him she was enjoying his company.

'I haven't spoken to everyone—'

'Do you need to speak with a person? Can't you make an assessment without exchanging words?'

'Of course.' He decided to rise to that challenge first. He glanced along the terrace at a young lady who was holding the attention of three men. Conversation flowed briskly between them and brought smiles and laughter.

'Those four,' he indicated the group discreetly. 'The young lady—'

'Adele.'

He nodded. 'Adele. I'd say twenty-five. From her clothes, her pearl necklace and diamond brooch, I'd say she comes from a wealthy family. She wears no rings, so is not married, nor even engaged. Surprising for one so pretty and lively with an attractive personality. Why not? I ask myself. Is there a flaw in her character? That I cannot tell by this surface examination. The young man to her right must be her brother. He is so much like her they could be twins. From his actions and expressions, while there is joviality about them to match that of their companions, he is protective of his sister. So, are the other two predators? Interested in her because of the wealth she has in her own right or what she is likely to inherit? Or don't your guests entertain such thoughts? Maybe? We don't know what goes on in people's minds. However, I would put those two men in about the same age category, good friends, out to enjoy themselves, maybe indulged in by their parents who are possibly—' He pursed his lips in judgement '– ship-owners.'

Emily put down her plate on the small table beside her and clapped her hands silently. 'Splendid. You are not far wrong. Indeed Adele and her brother David are twins. They are wealthy – their father, a merchant, was killed in an accident and their mother, who was devoted to him, died of shock.'

'So that is why David is so protective?'

'Yes.'

'And the other two?'

'George Geary and Albert Megson. Very rarely apart. A bit wild at times, like a bit of a gamble – will bet on anything. Sometimes they'll indulge in a hard drinking session, but they generally know how far to go and are able to keep out of trouble.' She gave a small pause. 'Now, who else? Someone you have talked to.'

'Simon. Solid, dependable. Enjoys everything he does. A good friend. Your sister, home-lover and good organiser as is evident from the preparations for your party. Loves her family. I think she and Simon are in love. A good match.'

'And do I need someone solid and dependable too?'

'Not in the same way as your sister. You'd want to be sure, safe, but you would not be averse to risks, excitement and adventure with the man who would be privileged to have you as his wife. I can see it in your eyes and your dress.'

'And who would you recommend?' she asked coyly.

'Well, from the people I have met since returning to

Hull, I would have said James Walton.' He hesitated then quickly added. 'That was from my visual assessment, but having spoken with him since arriving here I'm not at all sure that he would be the right person for you. You might have some excitement but I don't believe he would have the dependability that you would seek in marriage.'

'You've spoken with him?'

'Yes, and learned that he is the adopted son of Mrs Walton for whom my aunt worked.'

'You said nothing about your visit to your aunt at Shaken Hall?' Her words came quickly with a sharp edge to them.

'No.' He eyed her with curiosity. 'You seem concerned?'

Emily was annoyed that she had reacted with disquiet, but still did not bring her reaction under sufficient control. 'No, no.' Her voice was still abrupt.

'I believe you are worried about something connected with my conversation with James,' he said, watching her closely.

'Please don't ask me any more. What has to be said will be said by my father tomorrow.'

He detected that she was worried in case he pressed her further. He knew better than to do so. It would be discourteous to go against this young lady's wishes; besides, he did not want to offend her. He inclined his head in acknowledgement of her request and said, 'Then let us enjoy the rest of the evening together. May I get you something else to eat?'

'I would rather dance first.'

'My pleasure.' He stood up and held out his hand.

She took it and immediately all thoughts of the next day were banished as they floated gracefully into the waltz.

Chapter Four

Emily was disturbed by the light filtering past the curtains half-drawn across the windows, which looked over the fields to the Humber. Her eyes flickered open then closed again against the brightness. Feeling the comfort of the feather bed, she relaxed and slowly came awake. She stretched sensuously as thoughts of the previous evening came flooding back. It had been such a good party. Thomas Laycock had been so charming and attentive that she had regretted having to play the hostess and circulate among her other guests. Nevertheless she had managed many dances with him, a fact remarked upon by Sylvia in a teasing way.

Emily smiled to herself. She had experienced the companionship of many young men in her circle of friends, attending the local balls, the races at nearby Beverley, excursions to the coast, to Hull Fair, but there was not one of them who had had the same effect on her as Thomas Laycock.

She looked forward to seeing him again that day even

though it would be in the course of business at her father's office.

She took care with her dressing, choosing a plain but fashionable dress which fitted to perfection. The only decoration she allowed herself was a marcasite lizard pinned at the front of her left shoulder below the narrow lace collar which matched the lace around the cuffs of her full-length sleeves. Her fresh complexion needed no enhancing, but she paid extra attention to her hair, making sure that not one strand was out of place.

Sylvia raised an eyebrow when Emily entered the dining room for breakfast. A faint smile twitched her lips and her eyes sparkled with teasing amusement. 'I thought you were going with Father to the office?'

'So I am.'

'You're rather smart for routine.'

'There's nothing to say I shouldn't look my best for work,' replied Emily haughtily.

'Nothing at all,' agreed Sylvia and added with a knowing smile, 'especially when an eligible young man, who paid you particular attention last evening, will be there.'

Deciding not to rise to her sister's teasing Emily said, 'He was rather handsome, wasn't he?'

'I suppose he was.' Sylvia played down her opinion. 'Simon tells me he's settling in Hull.'

The course of the conversation was diverted with the arrival of their father, who bade his daughters a pleasant 'Good morning.'

'Mr Thomas Laycock.' The clerk in the offices of Jonas

Thornton, Attorney, announced the visitor with a certain superior air, relishing his role of momentary authority. It was a fleeting instant and he always made the most of it and then looked forward to the next arrival.

'Thank you, Dillon.' Jonas rose from behind his desk to extend a hand to Thomas. 'Welcome, young man.'

'Good day to you, sir, and thank you for seeing me,' he said with a compelling smile. He turned to Emily, who had risen from her chair. 'A pleasure to see you again, Miss Thornton.' He made a slight bow. 'And thank you for a most pleasant party.'

'It was our pleasure to have your company.' She inclined her head and her eyes smiled with a little more than friendliness.

'You all made a stranger feel at home. I am indebted to you both and of course to your other daughter, sir. I am most grateful to Simon Sutcliffe for this introduction and I hope you may be able to make use of my role as a detective.'

'Do sit down.' Jonas indicated a chair and took his own place behind his desk as Emily resumed her seat. 'I think we can be of service to each other.'

'I can assure you of my attention to detail no matter how trivial the case.' He put his hand into his pocket. 'I have references here from the Pinkerton National Detective Agency in America.'

'Leave them.' Jonas waved his hand dismissively. 'I don't think I need peruse them.'

'If you're sure, sir. Thank you for your trust and confidence.'

'I pay great heed to what my daughter tells me.' Jonas gave a small knowing nod.

'Then I owe you a debt,' said Thomas, glancing at Emily.

She met his gaze. 'I think you might be able to clear up a matter of some importance to us.'

'Me?' Thomas was mystified.

'Yes.' Jonas unlocked a drawer in his desk and took out some papers.

Thomas noticed they had been folded together with extreme care so that when Jonas pushed them across his desk to him all he could see were two signatures.

'Is that your signature?' asked Jonas, without diverting his serious gaze from Thomas's face.

He gave the paper a quick scrutiny. That was all he needed to verify the authenticity of what lay before him. He looked up to meet the attorney's eyes without flinching. 'Yes.'

'You recognise the other?'

'My aunt's.'

'Do you remember the occasion?' put in Emily.

'I visited my aunt at Shaken Hall in December last year. While I was there she asked me to witness Mrs Walton's signature on a document.'

'Did you know what that document was?'

'No. Nothing was explained to me.'

'It was Mrs Walton's will,' said Jonas. 'Do you know what happened to it after you left Shaken Hall?'

'You have it, so I suppose it was deposited with you.'

'It wasn't.'

'So is there some trouble about it?'

Jonas glanced at his daughter. 'You had better explain, Emily.'

She quickly related how she had discovered the will and then added, 'But the problem is that Mrs Walton made a will five years ago and that one was deposited with my father and has been implemented.'

Thomas gave a little whistle. 'And this is the one which should have been followed.'

'Exactly,' said Jonas.

'But only if we can verify that Mrs Walton was of sound mind when she made it,' put in Emily. 'And you are the only one who can do that.'

Thomas nodded his understanding and pursed his lips thoughtfully as he recalled his visit to Shaken Hall. He knew he was under close scrutiny and that a lot might hang on his opinion. But he only took a moment to come to his conclusion. 'Without a doubt, when I saw Mrs Walton her mind and reason were as sharp and clear as any of ours are right now.' His delivery left Jonas and Emily in no doubt about the sincerity of his statement.

But Jonas had to be cautious. 'And that would be at the moment of her signature?'

'Yes.'

Jonas heaved a sigh of relief, though in some ways he judged the opposite might have saved him a lot of bother and possible unpleasantness. But he was an attorney and must see that all proper procedures and disposals were observed.

'If you want verification of her state of mind over the period immediately before that time you could contact people who were her servants then,' Thomas suggested.

'We will do that if necessary.'

'I take it this document drastically alters the first and therefore will take some sorting out?'

'The two wills are identical except for one clause,' explained Jonas. 'Because I need your help I must disclose what that is, but first, before I go any further, I have to insist that what I am going to tell you about the contents of this will' – he tapped the papers in front of him – 'are kept a secret until I think the time is right to disclose them.'

'You have my solemn word that nothing of what you tell me will pass my lips until you think it appropriate or there is need for me to do so.'

'You will have to judge if and when it is necessary to reveal your knowledge in the course of the work I want you to undertake. That will become apparent when I tell you how the two wills differ.'

'Thank you for your faith and of course for the opportunity to help you. You have my assurance that whatever you require I will do my utmost to fulfil.'

'Thank you,' replied Jonas. He had held this young man under his scrutiny and searching judgement ever since he had entered the office. Linking it with Emily's reaction and observations from the previous night he had come to the conclusion that this young man would be trustworthy, dependable and his desire to succeed would hold him to a quest until he could determine a satisfactory result.

As the attorney looked down at the papers in front of him, Thomas glanced at Emily, who smiled her own thanks and pleasure that he had accepted to work with them.

'As I say,' resumed Jonas, 'the wills differ in only one clause. The bequests to your aunt and Mrs Walton's staff remain as in the first will so they present no difficulties as there are no alterations to be made. The clause which I expect will raise the most consternation is that which deals with Mrs Walton's bequest to her son, James.'

Thomas's thoughts and concentration were latched firmly on to Jonas's words.

'The amount of money which he is allowed until he is twenty-five remains the same in the second. It is only the deposition of the bulk of Mrs Walton's fortune which is altered. It was to go to James on his twenty-fifth birthday, but now goes to someone else.'

Thomas raised his eyebrows, but merely said, 'That was Mrs Walton's prerogative. I don't expect it will be easy breaking the news to James. He isn't going to like it.'

'He certainly won't,' said Emily. 'He's going to lose a fortune.'

'The beneficiary is Elizabeth Ainslie, the wife of the sea captain whose murder took James into the dock,' Jonas revealed.

Thomas could not control his surprise.

'You know about James's trial,' put in Emily quickly.

'Not in any detail. He merely mentioned that I might have been of use when he was accused of murder, but yesterday evening was not the time for sordid stories. But tell me, why should Mrs Walton leave her wealth to Mrs Ainslie?'

'That surprised us and it puzzles us too,' said Emily. 'We had nothing to do with the trial. We did not know Captain Ainslie nor his wife. She did not attend the court as she was not called upon by either the prosecution or the defence. She is said to have left Hull after the trial, and I suppose that is understandable.'

The reason for his presence here was beginning to dawn on Thomas. 'You want me to find her?'

'Yes,' said Jonas.

'You are interested?' Emily wanted any doubt casting from her mind.

'Most certainly. It promises to be an intriguing case.'

'You see it as more than tracing Mrs Ainslie?' Jonas raised an eyebrow.

'I am curious as to why Mrs Walton should change her will to the detriment of her own son and to the benefit of the widow of the man he is supposed to have murdered. Did she know something no one else knew? Maybe there are facts which need uncovering.'

'You think James did commit the murder?' Emily looked shocked.

'No,' Thomas hastened to reassure her. 'But maybe Mrs Walton was in possession of knowledge which made *her* think that her son was a murderer.' He paused a moment and added thoughtfully, looking quickly from Emily to Jonas. 'If I uncover unsavoury things do you want to know?'

Emily's gaze held on to her father. Thomas had put him in a difficult position. After all he had engaged Thomas only to find Mrs Ainslie.

Jonas steepled his fingers together and looked

61

intently at Thomas. 'Young man, I want you to find Mrs Ainslie first and foremost. If in the pursuit of that aim you discover other things we will judge each one on its merits and then assess the action to be taken.'

'Sir, you have my total understanding.' Thomas paused a moment to let the frankness of his statement sink in. 'When will you be contacting James? I ask because I would prefer it if that could be delayed.'

'Well, there isn't a lot of time. James will be twenty-five on 10 November. As you realise from my explanation of the wills, James's money will continue as it is until he is twenty-five, then he will expect his fortune, so the sooner I can clear the future with him the better.'

'I realise that sir, but it might be better if we locate Mrs Ainslie first.'

'True,' agreed Jonas. 'I hope you can do that quickly. I don't want a long delay before I see James.'

'I'll do my best, sir. I'm seeing James this afternoon. Maybe some discreet enquiries would not be amiss.' He saw doubt come to Jonas's eyes. 'They will only be in the course of natural conversation, nothing of what has been said in this office will be revealed. I have an easy lead as he mentioned his trial to me. It would help if you can tell me something about him. I met him for the first time yesterday and that was only briefly. He seemed pleasant enough.'

'Oh, he is,' replied Emily. 'He is a good mixer.'

'Has he any special friends?'

'Not as far as I know. I suppose Simon is the nearest.'

'Because he got him off a murder charge?'

'They were friendly before that.'

'What was his relationship with his mother?'

'Good, I believe. She was something of a recluse after her husband died, which was not good for a growing boy. Fortunately his governess saw him through that and he turned out well.'

'Mind you, how much does heredity play in shaping a person?' put in Jonas. 'James has a wild streak and sharp temper which occasionally surface. There have been rumours of bad company, gambling, wild parties.'

'But we don't know how much James has been involved.' Emily made a defence.

'Bad company can be found in all strata of society. Which was James involved in?' Thomas threw up his hands in apology. 'I shouldn't be questioning you like this. Forgive me. I can learn from James, but there is one more question which, because of the change of will, I'd rather you answered than for me to put it to him. Would he have known Mrs Ainslie personally?

'Not that I know of,' replied Emily.

'Highly unlikely,' agreed Jonas.

'Good day, sir.' The footman at the Curzon Club greeted Thomas brightly as he strode through the doorway into a large impressive hall with a divided staircase swinging round from either side to unite at the final six steps to the first landing. The floor was white marble with black symmetrical patterns, several of which were designed as imitation pathways to heavy oak doors.

'Your coat, sir.' The footman indicated an open door

to Thomas's right which led to a cloakroom. As he moved towards it, another footman appeared to take his outdoor attire.

The first footman, who was standing by, had been sizing up this stranger. He prided himself on first appraisal and judged this good-looking young man to be self-assured. He held himself well without a shadow of haughtiness or self-importance, but he had the air of one who knew what he wanted and would be assertive in a nice way to get it.

'I am to meet Mr Walton,' Thomas explained.

'Very good, sir. He warned me he was expecting a visitor. He is waiting in the lounge. This way, sir.'

Thomas followed the man across the hall to the second door on the right. The footman opened the door. 'He's over there by the second window,' the man said in a hushed tone.

As he crossed the carpeted floor, Thomas was aware of a large spacious room furnished with several sofas and wing-chairs with small tables conveniently placed near them. The walls were papered; the small geometric patterns set against a pale pink background did not divert the attention from the landscape and seascape paintings. Light came from four large windows.

James rose from his chair. 'Pleased to see you, Thomas.' His greeting was friendly as he extended a hand. Thomas felt a firm grip. 'Do sit down.' James indicated a wing-chair which had been drawn close to the one he had occupied, with a small round table between them.

'It is good to see you too,' returned Thomas. 'Most

kind of you to invite me here.' He glanced round the room and added, 'It's such an elegant place.'

'It is,' replied James, keeping his voice low so as not to disturb the other occupants of the room who were either reading newspapers, snoozing, or engaged in their own quiet conversations. 'A drink?' he offered.

Thomas had noticed a glass with a drop of whisky still in it. 'Is tea possible?'

'Of course, but wouldn't you prefer something stronger?'

Thomas shook his head. 'Not at this time of the day, thank you.'

'Ah, keeping the clear head as befits a detective.' James gave a little smile but Thomas saw that it contained admiration rather than contempt, and he recognised a man who respected the attitudes and convictions of other people. 'Tea it shall be.' He glanced round and signalled to one of the two footmen standing close to a door on the far side of the room. He drained his glass before the man arrived and ordered tea for two.

'Scones, sir?'

James raised a questioning eyebrow at Thomas who indicated that he would enjoy scones.

'So you are intending to stay in Hull?' queried James, relaxing in his chair.

'If things work out for me.'

'In business you mean?'

'One has to make a living somewhere. I would prefer it to be in Hull.'

'So you need connections, people who might be able to put work your way?'

'Exactly. Simon has been kind enough to give me a couple of jobs and of course the party last night was an introduction to Mr Thornton who says he will employ me whenever something merits it. I hope then that word of mouth will gradually expand my work.'

'You'd investigate anything?'

'Of course, so long as what I had to do was not illegal.'

The flow of the conversation was interrupted momentarily when the tea arrived.

'Those look scrumptious,' commented Thomas indicating the eye-catching scones with the accompanying butter and jam.

'Best in town. Do help yourself.'

'Thanks,' returned Thomas and spooned some sugar into his tea.

When they were both contentedly settled, James took up the conversation again. 'It could help you to be a member of this club. You'd get to know people, and they are all in some position of authority, be it merchant, ship-owner, ship's captain and so on. Who knows what any of them might want when they know they have a detective in their midst?'

'But would I be eligible? And then there's the cost. I detect wealth here and no doubt the membership fees match that.'

'True,' replied James. 'And you do have to be recommended, but that will be no problem because I could do that. You have to have a seconder. Simon will agree to stand for you. So it is only the cash. Again that can be arranged. Sorry, I'm assuming from your observations about expense that you anticipate it to be beyond your means. I apologise, I should not conclude so.'

Thomas gave a little shake of his head negating the apology. 'That's perfectly all right. Your assumption is correct. I have little money, I make no secret about it. I have enough to maintain my present lifestyle for a while and I hope I will have the income to maintain it, if not enhance it.'

'You can help those by borrowing,' James pointed out.

'Go into debt?' Thomas looked shocked by the suggestion.

'James laughed. 'Don't look so startled. See it this way. You borrow, you become a member here, there's more chance of work so you are more likely to have a greater income.'

'Sounds easy,' said Thomas thoughtfully.

'It is. And I have a friend, George Geary, whose father is a banker.'

'And you'd get him to persuade his father—?'

'Exactly.'

James saw doubt on Thomas's face, but what he could not detect were the thoughts which were revolving in his mind. Joining this club would give him the opportunity to get closer to James, come to know him better and, since his interview with Mr Thornton and Emily, he had a feeling that he needed to do this, though why he could not define. It was one of those instincts which he preferred not to ignore. And this club could take him into the circle of James's friends. Hadn't he said that some members were sea captains?

They would have known Captain Ainslie, and talking about him might give him a lead as to the whereabouts of Mrs Ainslie.

'We've got to take bold steps in this life if we want to get on,' pressed James. For a moment he wondered why he was making all these suggestions to someone who was really still a stranger to him. But he had liked what he had seen when they met for the party and had felt an immediate empathy with Thomas. Besides, he was a detective, and James was still unsettled about the way he had been set up. Maybe now there was a chance to get to the bottom of it.

Thomas nodded thoughtfully and swallowed a piece of scone. 'Why not?' His answer came with enthusiasm. 'One thing I learned in America – take a chance, it might come off.'

'Good man,' replied James, his face broadening into a wide smile. 'Leave everything to me. I'll see Simon and arrange with him to second my proposal, which I will put forward to the committee so that they'll have it on the agenda for their next meeting.' He paused as if making a calculation. 'That will be a week today. And I'll see George to set up an interview at the bank with his father. Let me have your address so that I can let you know when that will be.'

'You are being most solicitous of a comparative stranger, but I thank you.'

'Think nothing of it. I liked you from the moment Simon introduced us and after our short talk at the party I thought you needed friends in Hull, and I can introduce you around.' He gave a slight pause and then added, 'There is one thing you can do for me, though let me hasten to add this was not my motive for befriending you, I would have done that in any case.'

'Name it. If at all possible I will do what I can.'

'I would be grateful if in the course of your work and social activities you could make any discreet enquiries which might lead to uncovering the person or persons who put me into the embarrassing and ignominious position of having to stand in a court accused of murder.'

'Certainly I will do that, but first let me ask you, do you really want to know? You have been acquitted, would it not be better to let the matter rest? Aren't you likely to stir up more trouble if you pursue this?'

'I'm not averse to facing trouble if it comes, and it may well do so if ever I find out who attempted to get me at the end of a rope. But more than anything, I want to know for my own peace of mind, otherwise the query will haunt me for the rest of my life.'

Thomas nodded his understanding. 'I will do what I can, but I will have to have some information from you. Are you prepared to give it to me?'

'Ask. I'll tell you what I can.'

Thomas noted that the reply seemed to be a little guarded but he made no comment. Instead he said, 'Tell me what happened the day of the murder.'

James lingered over a sip at his tea as if he was trying to decide where he should begin, and how much to tell.

'Captain Ainslie?' Thomas prompted.

'I never met him.'

'But you knew of him?'

69

'Oh, yes. He was well known as an able mariner. He had been sailing out of Hull for many years. He was fifty when he was murdered and I believe he had been a captain for twenty years.'

'Was he a member of this club?'

'No. He was a reserved and very private man, not one to socialise.'

'Married?'

'Yes. His wife also kept very much to herself, so I'm told.'

'The murder?' Thomas prompted again when James seemed to hesitate.

'The *Fauconberg*, a merchantman under Captain Ainslie, had docked late afternoon—' As James continued using his first-hand knowledge and what had been revealed at the trial the whole episode became alive for Thomas.

Satisfied that his ship was secure, the captain was thankful that another voyage had been completed successfully. His run from America with tea, sugar and tobacco had been uneventful. His crew, who liked their captain, knowing him as a fair, just man but a strict disciplinarian with whom they knew where they stood and exactly what was expected of them, had worked the ship well. They looked forward to disposing of the cargo, receiving their pay and bonuses and taking a week's leave before signing up again with Captain Ainslie for the next voyage.

'No one knew him any better no matter how many times they had sailed with him. He was a likeable man, always ready with an encouraging word when it was deserved, but never coming to the edge of friendliness. Even his first mate, Wesley Burns, who had sailed with him for fifteen years, was not close to him, though a deep understanding existed between them where matters of the sea were concerned.

'His marriage, when he was fifty, had surprised everyone. He had announced it to his crew when they were mustered an hour before sailing on a second voyage to Spain, and they knew he expected no congratulations, except from the mate in the name of his men, and that had to be only one word. It was not until after their return home that they learned his wife was called Elizabeth and was twenty-five years younger than their captain. No one, not even their wives, girlfriends and acquaintances learned anything about her except that she was not a Hull girl. In fact it was rumoured that on the previous voyage he had smuggled her on board at one of their ports of call and that he had taken her ashore at Hull under cover of darkness to a house in a secluded area on the outskirts of the town. She kept very much to herself, made no friends, maybe complying with her husband's wishes. She ventured out only at odd times on brief shopping expeditions.

'As usual Captain Ainslie handed over command of the ship to Wesley Burns while he went to collect the money.

'It was late afternoon. There was a bleak wind blowing from the Humber. Darkening clouds were threatening rain and hastening night. The mate said the captain was wearing a thick thigh-length jacket and a peaked cap when he left the ship and that was the last he saw of him.

'The manager of Smith's and Thompson's bank in High Street, Henry Smith, gave evidence that Captain Ainslie was known to the clerks, who were under instructions to announce him immediately whenever he appeared in the bank. He agreed that it was men like Captain Ainslie who made money for the bank, for as master mariners they were in positions from which they could build up extensive overseas connections.

'When questioned he stated that Captain Ainslie appeared to be in good spirits, but said that in all the years he had known John Ainslie he had never broken down the barrier of formality. He could offer him a glass of Madeira, just as he did on the fatal day, and the captain would enjoy it while the conversation was kept to the business outcomes of the voyage, but all invitations to social activities in and around Hull were always politely refused.

'On this occasion there was more business than usual to attend to, for Captain Ainslie knew of another vessel coming up for sale which would fit in well with the trading which he and the bank shared. He laid the facts without any frills before Mr Smith who knew that Ainslie's judgement would be sound, for his analysis of the situation would be thorough.

'Mr Smith told Captain Ainslie he would see the man selling the ship, a Mr Harrington, the following day. They agreed a price to put before the owner hoping it would be acceptable and high enough to avoid all the trouble of an auction.

'The banker agreed, when questioned, that Captain Ainslie was a great asset to the bank having made it money from their agreement about trading arrangements. This vessel would have been the fifth sailing under their flag. He wanted the captain to come ashore and run the company. He had pointed out that if he was in direct control of the sailings of all the ships, rather than leaving the planning of their voyages to individual masters, it would widen the objectives. He told him that he had had a long time at sea and suggested that he and his wife should enjoy some of the fruits of that now, pointing out that he might as well use his money as he had no family to leave it to.

'Captain Ainslie's reply was that he and his wife were happy with their life. He wanted to continue in his capacity as captain of the *Fauconberg* and shareholder in the shipping side of the bank's enterprises. He was pleased with the way things were and did not wish to disturb his way of life.

'That was the end of their conversation and on returning to the main office Captain Ainslie found that the wages for the crew were ready for him in a brown leather bag.

'The bank manager agreed that when he saw the captain leave the bank the gloom had deepened, the wind had strengthened and a steady rain was falling.

'It was stated in court that there were few people about; work along the dockside had finished and the quay appeared deserted. Nobody could be certain about what exactly happened, but this is what was suggested in court. Somewhere between the bank and the quay the

73

captain was followed. He was keeping close to the side of a warehouse seeking extra protection from the rain, which was developing into a downpour, when a blow behind the ear pitched him to the ground. His assailant pounced, kicked him repeatedly in the head until he was dead, took the money from the bag, dragged the captain to the quayside and pitched him into the water.'

Thomas nodded as James paused in his story. 'Was the bag found?' The answer to this question was vital at this moment, for it could prove to him whether there was substance in what he had just heard.

'The bag was found close to the wall of the warehouse. That is why the authorities assumed Captain Ainslie had been murdered there and that his body must have been dragged across to the quayside and thrown into the water.'

Thomas was satisfied with the explanation. If the bag had been found elsewhere who would have known the site of the killing but the murderer?

'And you? Where were you at this time?'

James hesitated. 'I cannot answer that.'

'You mean you won't answer it.'

James shrugged his shoulders. 'If you like.'

'I suppose if you had said where you were and had been able to prove it there would have been no trial?'

'That is correct.'

'Then it must have been something important for you to risk being sentenced for a crime you say you did not commit.'

James stiffened. His eyes darkened with a flash of anger. 'What do you mean? Don't you believe me?'

Thomas gave a small smile. 'A trick, James, to see your reaction. I'm sorry, I had to do it. Yes, I believe you are innocent. So why were you accused?'

'Someone came forward to say that they had seen me running away.'

'And you were nowhere near that area?'

'No.'

'Who said they saw you?'

'Nobby Carson. Unsavoury character from the rough side of Hull.'

'Why should he want to accuse you? Do you know him personally? Does he bear a grudge against you?'

'The word should be did – did he bear a grudge? He died the day after my acquittal. Fell, supposedly in a drunken stupor, and hit his head against a stone pillar. Split his head open.'

'Was that death investigated?'

'No. Who cared about Nobby Carson? No one.'

'But you'd had personal contact with him prior to your trial?'

'Yes.' James hesitated, but he saw Thomas was waiting for an explanation. 'Oh, you may as well know. I had my wild moments. I won't deny it. But let me say that having seen where it can lead me – the trial – I've been more careful what company I keep.' James shook his head. 'Nobby hadn't any reason to bear me a grudge. I've bought him many a drink and he was always grateful.'

'So I take it that you believe Nobby was put up to it?'

'It's possible.'

'And a further conclusion could be that someone was

frightened he might talk after your acquittal and made his death appear an accident.'

James raised his eyebrows at this suggestion. 'You certainly are thinking as a detective. You could be right, though I never thought of that aspect of it.'

'But why would someone want to set you up, because that is what it appears to be?'

'Well, I was supposed to have murdered Captain Ainslie for the money to pay a gambling debt.'

'And were you in such a debt?'

'Yes, but I had paid it the day before Captain Ainslie was murdered.'

'Therefore the person to whom you owed the debt could have cleared you?'

'Yes and he did, but not until the trial was well under way. In fact it looked as if it would be concluded before he could do so.' Thomas was looking a little puzzled so James explained. 'The person to whom I owed the debt was in London when I paid the money – leaving it, as I had done before, in a sealed envelope with his attorney who knew nothing of what was in that envelope.'

'Before we go any further, James, are you going to name this person to whom you were in debt?'

'No reason why I shouldn't. Jeremy Loftus. If you like a flutter, a good time, you'll be meeting him. He has a nice estate west of Hull.'

'No connection between him and Nobby?'

'Hardly likely. Knowing Jeremy, he wouldn't want to be seen conversing with the likes of Nobby or his cronies on that side of Hull. No, Jeremy is for the easy, safe life.'

'Whereas you like a tinge of so-called adventure at times? Right, back to the trial.'

'I came up for trial, but Jeremy hadn't returned. I said there was someone who could prove I had paid the debt, and I gave his name. The authorities tried to trace him in London, but he had gone to the Continent. The law here took it that I was lying and put me in the dock. Simon was brilliant. He got connections in London to keep a look-out for Jeremy's return and also here in case he sailed directly to Hull. He called witnesses, asked long questionings, made long speeches, all to prolong things until Jeremy returned and I did not get a taste of the horrible conditions in jail. Right at the start he had obtained bail for me and he saw that the authorities honoured that throughout the whole time.'

'Then Jeremy came back and you were cleared. The fact that you had paid the debt before the murder gave you no reason to kill Captain Ainslie.'

'Right.'

'So whoever involved you must have known of your debt,' mused Thomas. 'Tried to make that the reason for the murder whereas the real reason was something else. Any idea what that might have been?'

'No.'

'Maybe revenge?'

'If that is so I have no idea what that could be, or who would want to harm me.'

Chapter Five

'Good day, sir.' Dillon sprang lightly to his feet when Thomas entered the Thornton offices the following morning. There was a slight sign of disappointment on his face and the reason was revealed when he announced, 'I'm sorry, sir, but Mr Thornton is out this morning.'

'It's Miss Thornton I would like to see.'

The disappointment evaporated as he anticipated the pleasure he would have in announcing the visitor. He came from his desk. 'Follow me, sir.' He knocked on a door further along the corridor; after a pause he opened it and stated with bright authority, 'Mr Laycock to see you, miss.'

With a nod of thanks Thomas strode past him into the room. Emily showed surprise, which did not disguise her pleasure when she looked up from the paper on which she was writing. 'Thomas.' She rose from her chair and extended her hand in greeting. His touch was gentle as he took it and she did not mind when he held it a little longer than suited etiquette. 'Please do sit down. I'm sorry Father is meeting an old client who cannot get into the office.'

'I have some regret that he is not here,' said Thomas as they sat down, 'but it was you I really wanted to see.'

'Now I am curious,' replied Emily.

'You shouldn't be, for it is my pleasure to be in your company once again.'

'And what excuse have you for engineering this meeting?' she asked with a coy expression which nevertheless revealed that she was flattered.

'I need your help.'

Emily raised her eyebrows in surprise. 'My help?'

'Yes. I believe that you will be able to make some enquiries more easily than I, questions which might help us towards finding Mrs Ainslie.'

'I don't see how. I know nothing of her, nor would I know where to make them.'

'Ladies gossip over tea.'

Emily threw up her hands in horror. 'You are not asking me to take tea with gossipy matrons?' The mere thought of the boredom sent a shudder through her.

Thomas laughed. 'I knew tea-parties wouldn't be on your social calendar, but, for the sake of our investigations, I thought you might just be able to bear them for a week or two. After all, if we are to work as a team—' He left the rest of the implication unsaid for he saw that the horror of having to attend those gatherings had been dismissed by a look of excitement at the thought of what could lie behind his suggestion.

'A team? But I know nothing of detective work.'

'I can teach you. I can tell you'll be a quick learner. Besides most of it is routine enquiries from which, when they are all gathered together, deductions are made and followed up.'

'And sometimes there could be an element of excitement, possibly danger,' Emily suggested, her eyes brightening at the thought.

'I'll not disguise that there could be, but I would hope that danger would not come your way. In fact I would do my utmost to see that it didn't. I need someone who knows Hull, who can enter company I could not enter, and I believe you are of a mind to enjoy the subterfuge and risks which may arise.'

Emily smiled. 'You have talked me into it, though my first assignment sounds rather mundane.'

'You might like it.' A teasing smile twitched his lips.

'And become as domesticated as Sylvia? Never!'

Thomas spread his hands. 'There you are, the perfect introduction to that world of ladies' gossip – your sister.'

'And she'll wonder why I've become interested in something I've tried to avoid.'

'You'll think of some excuse.'

'All right. But there's one other thing we should set straight – my father is not to know, at least for the time being, that we are collaborating. I don't think he would approve. Not,' she hastened to add, 'because of you, but he is rather protective, though he is liberal in his attitudes.'

'Your wishes will be observed to the letter.' Thomas gave a little bow setting a seal on their arrangements.

'So you want me to listen for any words about Mrs

Ainslie that might fall from the tongues of the ladies with whom I take tea?'

'You may have to direct the conversation, though of course you must do that subtly without raising suspicion as to what you are really about.'

'And that is your first lesson in detective work?' she said with a smile and a knowing glance.

'Precisely,' he returned, amused by the tone she had adopted. Instantly he became more earnest. 'Seriously, Emily, I don't know that you are going to learn a lot, but you just might pick up a crumb of information which could be useful. I had a long talk with James yesterday. He told me what led to his trial. He wants me to keep my ears open for any information which could lead him to discover why he was accused and who was behind it. He also told me what he knew about Captain and Mrs Ainslie, but that was very little.'

'Surely the murder can have nothing to do with our need to find Mrs Ainslie?'

Thomas hesitated.

Emily gave him a look of surprise. 'You think it might?'

'I don't know,' he said doubtfully. 'I just have a feeling there might be a connection. We do have one, even though it seems tenuous. Mrs Walton left her fortune to the murdered captain's wife. Why? It puzzles me. It appears Captain Ainslie was well-off. I'm sure Mrs Walton would surmise this, so it would seem that her intention was not to see an impoverished widow comfortable. She must have had some other reason for changing her will.'

Emily agreed with his reasoning but, realising that it could not be pursued at the moment, asked, 'What will you be doing while I'm making polite conversation?'

'I'll follow up some of the introductions James is going to open up for me,' he replied, and went on to tell her of James's suggestion that he should join the Curzon Club.

Two days later at breakfast Sylvia said, 'I don't expect you two will be home for tea today.'

Jonas looked up from his bacon and egg. About to ask why, he suddenly realised what was behind his daughter's statement. 'I'd forgotten. A good job you reminded me or I'd have walked right into a chattering clutch of gossiping women.'

Sylvia smiled. She knew her father meant no malice.

'I'll be here,' said Emily casually.

Sylvia's eyes widened in disbelief.

'Don't look so surprised, sister. I'm quite capable of helping to entertain your circle of tea-friends without upsetting anyone,' said Emily. 'I have no need to be in the office and Father will no doubt find conversation in his club. So I may as well join you.'

At three o'clock she and Sylvia greeted five ladies who all arrived within a few minutes of each other in their carriages driven by their grooms. Each gushed with praise for the others' dresses while secretly thinking none was as good as her own. Keeping up a flow of welcome, the sisters shepherded their guests into the drawing room where seats had already been placed in a

82

rough circle so that conversation could pass easily between everyone.

After ten minutes Sylvia rang the bell and a few moments later two maids appeared with trays of sandwiches and cakes which were placed on a table next to Sylvia. A third maid appeared with two teapots and began pouring tea at the sideboard. As the cups were filled they were handed to the guests.

Emily joined in the polite conversation which ranged across the new developments in Hull, the latest play at the theatre and the books they were reading, before it turned to gossip about friends and acquaintances. Emily, remembering the reason she had agreed to attend this boring afternoon, looked for an opportunity to turn the conversation to the question of Mrs Ainslie's whereabouts.

'I hear that Westfold is coming up for sale.' She seized the opportunity during a slight lull in the chatter to make a statement she could not corroborate, but hoped that no one would want absolute proof.

Her statement brought a stop to any other tittle-tattle. All eyes turned on her.

'The Ainslie house?'

'Yes.'

'Where did you hear that, my dear?'

'Overheard a conversation. Not that I was evesdropping,' she added quickly. 'Whoever it was was talking so loudly I could not help but hear.'

'Is it to be auctioned?'

'I don't know. Are you interested, Mrs Sackville?'

'Well, we had been thinking of moving.'

'It is in a nice secluded position.'

'Do you know what the house is like?'

No one could shed any light on that.

'Very much the quiet ones, the Ainslies,' snorted Mrs Featherstone, peeved at the number of times her invitations had been rejected and her curiosity about Elizabeth Ainslie never satisfied.

'Well, it's a good job it's being sold. It would only fall into rack and ruin and that would be a pity for a house which was newly built by Captain Ainslie for his bride.'

'Does anyone know where she came from?' asked Emily.

'No,' replied Mrs Sackville. 'Nor where she's gone.'

'Disappeared immediately after James Walton's trial.'

'Strange to leave so soon.'

'Maybe she just wanted to get away from the place where her husband was murdered,' Emily suggested.

There was a nodding of heads.

'Maybe you are right, my dear.'

'Well, wherever she is I hope she has settled and found some happiness.' Emily hoped the prompt might bring some reaction. She sharpened her attention when it did.

'I heard tell she went to London.'

'London? To relations?'

'Relations? No one knew if she had any. You could never get to know anything about her.' Mrs Carnet was irritated that her probing curiosity had never been satisfied.

'Well, I understood she'd gone to France.'

'France? That's unlikely.'

'Why? My husband had it on good authority that Captain Jameson had taken a woman on board bound for France.'

'He'd have her name on the passenger list.'

'He didn't have a Mrs Ainslie, only a Mrs Brown.'

'Common enough name, so that looks suspiciously like a ruse to cover her real identity.'

'Why should she want to do that?' asked Emily.

'Who knows, my dear? No one knew the woman.'

'And did Captain Jameson recognise her?' Emily pressed.

'Doubtful. I don't know of anyone who had seen her. Captain Ainslie installed her in that house and as far as I know she never went out.'

'Oh, she did.'

All eyes turned on Mrs Featherstone who had made this emphatic announcement. A tension came to the room as they waited for her to go on. There was an expectancy that they were going to hear something which had eluded them for some time.

'I have ridden past the house a number of times,' Mrs Featherstone went on. 'Call me an old nosy-parker if you like. I'll admit I was curious. I noticed that there were carriage tracks through the main gateway. I thought that if I kept riding that way I might see the mysterious Mrs Ainslie and engage her in conversation.'

'And did you?' asked Emily in quiet tones as if anything louder would shatter the expectancy which everyone was hanging on to.

'I saw her, only a glimpse. I called but she took no notice and hurried into the house.'

'But you saw her?'

'Yes. A young woman. She was well dressed. A beautiful full-length cloak. The hood had slipped from her head to reveal shortish hair with a natural wave which would have been the envy of you all. I only caught a glimpse of her face, but she was beautiful, with an ethereal air about her, and she seemed to glide with grace as she went into the house.'

'You saw this from the main gate?' There was a little doubt in Mrs Sackville's voice.

'Yes. The main gate is not far from the house,' she replied and added sharply, 'and my eyesight is excellent.'

'A beautiful woman just disappears completely,' mused Emily. 'What a pity no one knows where she is. She might have an intriguing story to tell.'

'She might at that.'

'I have no doubt she would.'

'Mysterious women always cast a spell.'

The comments drifted away thoughtfully, and Emily knew she would learn no more.

Had she really gained anything which would be of use to Thomas? She doubted it, but she had enjoyed this first mission for him and was pleased with the way she had steered the conversation to Mrs Ainslie, though she hoped none of these ladies made further enquiries about the sale of the house. But did it matter if any of them did? She had said she only overheard a conversation.

At the moment when Emily and Sylvia were greeting their guests, Thomas received a call from James. Within half

86

an hour they were both shaking hands with Ralph Geary in the manager's office of the Pease and Liddell bank in High Street. By the time they left an hour later, Ralph, on the recommendation of James, backed by that of his own son, had opened an account in the name of Thomas Laycock, credited it with an agreed loan, and knew that if ever the bank had need of the services of an investigator it need look no further than Thomas.

'Before I came to take you to the bank I had obtained Simon's signature as seconder to my proposal that you be admitted as a member of the Curzon Club, and I lodged it there,' said James as they turned into Scale Lane. 'It will be posted in the Committee Room where members of the committee can see it and give it consideration before their next meeting. They'll quietly ask other members if they know you so it will be as well for you to be seen in the club several times before then as my guest. I'll introduce you to people who matter and to some who don't appear to, but whose opinions might be sought by committee members.'

'You are going to a lot trouble, James, and I thank you for it.' They continued along Silver Street and into Whitefriargate.

'Think nothing of it. I am sure you will be a friend in return. And don't forget anything that might throw light on why I was accused of the crime will be appreciated.'

'I'll not forget.'

They reached the club and as they walked into the lounge James gripped Thomas's arm, bringing them to a halt. 'Just right,' he whispered as he quickly surveyed the room. He indicated a man, whom Thomas judged to be in his mid-sixties, who was sitting in a chair beside a window reading a newspaper. 'Ben Hobson, ex-ship's captain. Recently retired from the sea. He could have done so long ago as he had made his money as a merchant trading from his own ships, but he loved the sea – it had been his life. Very influential here. Let me introduce you.'

He led the way across the room. 'Excuse me, Captain Hobson,' he said politely in a quiet voice. 'May I introduce my friend, Thomas Laycock, recently come to Hull. I think you may be interested to meet him.'

As James had been talking, Captain Hobson had laid his paper down on his lap. Thomas saw a kindly face which bore the leathery features of a man who had spent a lifetime buffeted by the wind, battered by the sea and scorched by the sun. His blue eyes were still young and bright, revealing his probing interest in everyone and everything. Behind those eyes Thomas knew there must be a nimble brain.

'Good day, sir. It is a privilege to meet you,' said Thomas with a friendly smile.

Ben nodded, weighing up the newcomer. Well dressed, tall, lean, athletic, he filled his clothes well. He reminded him of himself at that age and he sighed for years that were gone, but there was no real regret, life had been good to him, he had made it so. 'Please sit down.'

'I'll leave Thomas with you if I may, sir, I have a little business to attend to with the steward.' James leaned a little closer to Ben. 'Incidentally, sir, I have recommended Thomas for membership.'

Ben shot James a glance with a wry smile. 'So, you

want me to run my judgement over him? Favourably, no doubt?'

James straightened, gave the captain a conspiratorial smile and walked away.

'Don't be embarrassed, young man,' said Ben, noting that Thomas had been uncomfortable with that exchange. 'This is not going to be an inquisition. If I am going to see you around the club we may as well be friends right from the start.'

Thomas relaxed. 'I'd like that, sir.'

'No more formality, please.' He gesticulated with his hands as if brushing away an irritation. 'Ben, it is.'

'Or Captain?' Thomas knew an old sea-dog, as the one who sat before him, would relish being reminded of his authority at sea.

Ben's eyes brightened a little. 'Either, my boy, either. I take it you are new to Hull?'

'Yes. I originated from Whitby.'

'Seafaring family?'

'Yes. Whalemen.'

'Ah, brave men.' Thomas detected a deep admiration in the captain's voice. 'I never did go whaling myself. I was always on merchant ships. But I invested in some of the whalers sailing out of Hull. They brought me a good return. And you?'

'I worked for a merchant, but I got restless three years ago, after my parents died. I went to America.'

Ben raised his eyebrows. 'No desire to stay?'

'None. I worked with the Pinkerton National Detective Agency and thought I might set up a similar organisation here.'

89

'Well, that's something different for Hull. I hope you make a success of it. You've found a good friend in James. He'll spread the word about you. Likeable young fellow. A pity his early childhood was restricted because of his mother.'

'You knew her?'

'I certainly did. Fine woman, lit up any social gathering. Devoted to her husband and to James when they adopted him. Then her husband's tragic death changed everything. She became a recluse. My wife and I had been particularly friendly with the Waltons so we tried several times to get her to break the barrier which she had thrown up around herself, but to no avail. It became obvious that she wanted no company. It was bad for young James but thank goodness his mother had the sense to see it and engaged an excellent governess who saw that James was capable of moving into the outside world.'

'If you knew Mrs Walton, you'd know my aunt, Jane Sugden?'

'Harriet's companion – your aunt?'

'Yes.'

'Never really knew her. Met her only once. Harriet did not want contact with anyone, not even her old friends. Did you visit Shaken Hall?'

'Twice. My aunt was really a stranger to me, she left Whitby when I was a youngster, but it was she who suggested I try America.'

'She was good to Harriet I believe.'

'James's trouble must have worried his mother.'

'I'm sure it did, but I remember her as a strong woman, always in control of herself and her feelings.'

'Some parents would have been very depressed under similar circumstances, maybe even become deranged.' Thomas watched Captain Hobson intently for his reaction.

'My dear boy, you're not suggesting that Harriet succumbed that way,' said Ben indignantly.

'No, sir, of course I'm not.' Thomas was quick with his apology. 'I meant no aspersions on her character. I was merely making a general observation.'

'I'm sure you were,' said Captain Hobson with a calmer voice. 'I'm sorry I got tetchy. She wasn't that type of woman.'

Thomas saw this as some support for his own opinion that Mrs Walton had been of sound mind when she signed the second will.

The captain changed the subject. 'So you're interested in becoming a member of the Curzon?'

'Yes.'

'It could be an asset to you through the people you'll meet. And from what I've seen of you I'm sure you'll be approved.'

'That's kind of you to say so, sir.'

They fell into conversation about Hull and Thomas began to see even more possibilities for his services.

Twenty minutes later James returned expressing a regret for being so long.

Captain Hobson waved away the apology. 'Not at all. I've enjoyed Thomas's company. I look forward to it again.'

'Thank you, sir,' replied Thomas, rising from his chair. 'I too have enjoyed our chat.'

'Next time you must tell me more about Whitby and your family's experiences whaling.'

'I'll look forward to that.'

The two young men took their leave and as they left the club James commented, 'You've made a good impression there, and that will help your application. The day after tomorrow I'll introduce you to some people at a place I go to out of Hull, that is if you're not averse to visiting the gaming tables.' He gave a merry laugh when he saw Thomas's expression. 'That shocked you after the trouble gambling got me into? Don't worry, Thomas, that's behind me and I have learned my lesson. I got in deep then but not any more. Now I keep to a modest flutter. So, are you against going?'

'No. I don't mind small stakes.'

'The fellow who runs this place is from a well-to-do family. He's the youngest son of four, and a bit of a black sheep. Keeps this side of his life hidden from his family, who have an estate north of the Wolds. He goes by the name of Jeremy Loftus. Only three of us know his real identity.'

'How did you find out?'

'An accident. That's all you need know. He swore me to secrecy. And that I'll always observe.'

Thomas could tell he had a genuine admiration for Loftus, but he had to put the question, 'You're sure he wasn't behind what happened to you?'

'Never! I told you I'd paid what I owed. Someone learned of the debt but didn't know I'd honoured it and thought they were using it against me.'

'But you also told me that this Jeremy Loftus was

abroad, so he couldn't know you had paid the debt. Maybe, thinking he was not going to be paid, he instigated action against you before he left this country.'

Anger rose on James's face. 'He and I are friends – he wouldn't.' He broke off when he saw Thomas's hands raised in protest. His eyes softened. 'Sorry. I see you are in the role of detective.'

Thomas shrugged. 'You asked me to explore possibilities. I have to try to gain knowledge, reactions and attitudes and then sieve them all.'

'I know, I'm sorry I lost my temper.' James looked contrite. 'You'll see Jeremy in two days' time. You can make your own judgement.'

That same evening over dinner Sylvia received a note from Simon saying that he and Thomas were going riding the following morning and suggesting that she and Emily join them. 'We'll arrive at Bramwell House at ten if you care to join us,' was the final sentence.

'Why not?' agreed Jonas. He glanced at Emily and guessed the brightness in her eyes had come from the expectation of seeing Thomas again. 'The documents you are copying can wait another day or so.'

Emily was thankful that the morning was bright with only a slight breeze blowing from the west. She and Sylvia were ready when Simon and Thomas arrived. They left Bramwell House at a gentle pace, moving along the bridleway to the top of the rise behind the house.

'I didn't know you rode,' commented Emily to Thomas as they paired off.

'I learned in America and was pleased when Simon suggested this outing.'

'So was I,' returned Emily.

'Good. I hope it will lead to many more pleasant times together.'

'I see no reason why it shouldn't,' said Emily, delighted at his suggestion.

'And it will give us the perfect opportunity not only to get to know each other better but also to exchange notes on our progress to find Elizabeth Ainslie.'

Emily smiled knowingly. 'So it will.'

They turned along the ridge following the bridleway taken by Sylvia and Simon.

Thomas breathed deeply on the sharp air. 'I know I'm going to be pleased that I chose to come to Hull. Nice countryside not far out of the town and a delightful young lady to share it.'

Emily was flattered by Thomas's ease of charm which came naturally without any presumption that he would not be rejected. She knew from his attitude that if she had not agreed to a continuing relationship he would have respected her wishes. But she had no intention of doing that.

Emily inclined her head graciously. 'And I am happy to share it.'

'I thank you for the privilege,' he said, not only with his voice but with his eyes. They held hers in a look filled with admiration and the expectation that their future would be entwined.

His horse tossed its head and broke the spell. Thomas steadied the animal then turned to Emily with a teasing twinkle in his eyes. 'I suppose you'll be looking forward to your next tea-party?'

'No I'm not,' Emily snorted, 'but for the sake of Laycock's Detective Agency, I'll put up with another.' She went on to tell him what she had gleaned from the first one.

He looked thoughtful when she had finished. 'I hope Mrs Ainslie hasn't left the country. Finding her in London might be a problem, but it will be even more difficult if she is abroad. However, it is useful to know that she sometimes left her house. Someone must know where she went, if she met anyone and if so, who? We need to find out who her staff were, particularly a groom if she had one, he would know where he took her. Do you think you could make some enquiries along those lines?'

'I'll see what I can do.'

'Good.' Thomas was pleased with the interest she was showing. He went on to tell her what James had been doing for him and what Captain Hobson had said about Mrs Walton. But when he mentioned where he was going with James the next day a look of concern crossed her face.

'Do be careful, Thomas. I've heard some unsavoury stories about that place,' she warned.

'You can't believe everything you hear,' he replied. 'And remember, this man Loftus sent word to the court, immediately on his return from Europe, to verify that James had paid the debt before the murder, so he can't be all that bad. But I'll make a judgement after my visit tomorrow.'

Emily said nothing. She hoped that Thomas wasn't a gambling man who could be swept up in the urge to win. Gambling had brought trouble to James and, although he seemed to have reformed since the trial, Emily wondered if he was slipping back into his old ways. If so, she hoped he was not taking Thomas along the same path, but she had no right to interfere. Besides, Thomas looked as if he could take care of himself. If he couldn't he shouldn't be following the profession of a private detective.

'Now, let's wipe away that glum look. Race you to the others!' Thomas yelled.

'Right!' shouted Emily and put her mount into a gallop. Thomas was ready for her and the earth pounded with thundering hoofs. The exhilaration of the ride swept her gloom away. It was a laughing exuberant couple who pulled their horses to a halt on reaching Sylvia and Simon, who entered into their enjoyment.

The rest of the ride went agreeably and when they returned to Bramwell House the two men had a pleasant surprise to find a meal ready for the four of them. Mrs Wentworth and Mrs Harvey, following Sylvia's instructions, had excelled themselves in their preparations, for they felt sure that the two young ladies would want to create an impression with the two young men.

And so it was that they all enjoyed an excellent meal and a lazy afternoon of chatter in the garden.

'Good to see you again, James.' The welcome was hearty, accompanied by a prolonged handshake and a few slaps on the back.

Thomas stood back so that he could better observe the man who gave James such an enthusiastic greeting. He saw a man impeccably dressed. His clothes, of the very best material, fitted to perfection. They spoke of money. He was tall, slim, his figure athletic. His face was long, his chin pointed. Dark eyebrows arched deep-set, piercing eyes, but there was nothing fierce about them as Thomas had expected from his first glance. A more leisurely study revealed that in their darkness there was laughter and pleasure mingled with an ability to make shrewd judgements.

Thomas reckoned that here was a man who could show kindness, be a loyal friend but a vicious enemy should anyone dare to cross his path – and he was in a 'game' where people could do just that if they tried to outsmart him.

'Jeremy, I've brought a friend, Thomas Laycock.' He turned to Thomas, 'Thomas, meet Jeremy Loftus, owner of Briar Manor where you can enjoy good food, good wine and try to increase the money in your pocket.'

'Welcome.' There was warmth in Jeremy's voice and eyes and friendliness in his handshake. 'Any friend of James is welcome at Briar Manor.'

'I'm pleased to meet you,' returned Thomas, aware that he had come under swift but searching scrutiny.

'You must be new to Hull otherwise James would have brought you here before now.'

'I originated in Whitby. I've been in America where I worked for the Pinkerton National Detective Agency. I decided to return in England and start my own agency in Hull.'

'Well now, there's something different for Hull,' said Jeremy with a laugh. 'I hope you are not questioning the legality of my operation?'

Thomas smiled as he shook his head. 'That's the job of the police and I'm not in league with them unless whatever I'm investigating leads to an arrest being necessary. Besides I like to play the tables now and again.'

'Then you are more than welcome.' He queried more seriously: 'Are you a good detective?'

'Yes.'

'There's confidence for you.' He smiled his approval. 'I've had debtors and thieves who've needed tracing, so, if those situations arise again, you might be useful to me.'

'I hope I can be if the need arises.'

'Good. James, you can introduce Thomas to our offerings, but,' he gave a precautionary pause, 'don't teach him your foolish ideas. They don't work. You've learned your lesson, I hope. Remember what I advocate, enjoy a gamble, don't get in too deep and don't chase your losses. Now, you must excuse me. Enjoy your evening.' He turned his attention to four new arrivals.

While they had been talking, liveried footmen had taken their outdoor clothes. Feeling more relaxed, James led Thomas to a room on the left. Four tables were laid with an assortment of sumptuous-looking food, both savoury and sweet, and wine to suit all tastes. Footmen and servant girls stood with their backs to the wall ready to serve.

'That is available until midnight. Guests,' he gave a wry smile, 'or should I say customers, partake whenever they want.'

'Free?'

'Oh, yes. Jeremy says he gets it all back through what the gamblers lose.'

'But if it's free don't people over-imbibe?'

'No. Everyone knows Jeremy will not tolerate drunkenness. A little merry, happy, maybe, but to be the worse for drink is taboo here. Anyone who over-drinks will never be allowed in again. Few do, for they know they receive fairness in whatever form of gambling they choose and they can have a good time. So, let's go and see if we can win.'

He crossed the spacious hall to double doors on the right. When he opened them they were met with an excited buzz of conversation as gamblers anticipated wins or bemoaned their bad fortune before getting ready to place their bets again.

Thomas took in the scene. The large room was panelled in light oak to a height of five feet with heavily patterned wallpaper above. The ceiling and frieze were painted a brilliant white which reflected the light from the oil lamps, placed in metal brackets on every wall, and from the three chandeliers each holding thirty lighted candles. The floor was thickly carpeted, helping to subdue noise. Three tables occupied the centre of the room, the middle one of which was offering roulette while at both of the others dice games were in progress. At several tables around the room various card games held the attention of players and spectators.

'The police turn a blind eye to all this?' asked Thomas in a subdued tone.

'Yes. It's out in the country. Who bothers? If there's any query, inspection or whatever, it's a dining club – you've seen the array of food.' He gave a little chuckle. 'And there's another thing: some of the police officials like a flutter.'

'I didn't expect to see ladies here?' whispered Thomas, noting that there were about fifteen females among the company.

'This is not exclusively a male club as are those in town which of course are of a different type. Apart from retreats from the cares of domesticity they are primarily for the discussion of business and trade, a common meeting ground where there is privacy for such transactions and exchange of the latest trends. Here the main object is to enjoy a gamble. Jeremy's liberal-minded and realises there are ladies who have the desire to gamble, who like a bit of excitement and don't want to be sitting around every evening with needle and thread plying their way across a tapestry canvas. But there is another room similar to this, though not quite as large, for those men who do not see things his way.'

'The club is strictly for gambling, is it not?'

'And the enjoyment of food and wine.'

'Nothing else?'

'No. Jeremy would not tolerate, never mind provide for, any other, what we might call, the broader aspects of entertainment.'

'But there is every opportunity to form liaisons?'

'Undoubtedly, but assignations beyond that must not

take place here. No one gossips about who or what they have seen here. To do so would reveal where they have been and people tend not to want that known.'

'What about the servants?'

'Loyal to Jeremy. Hand picked. They know there would be serious repercussions if they talked about Jeremy's clientele. Besides, they would lose a well-paid job with good food provided.'

Thomas assimilated these facts and added to them as he played the tables and enjoyed all the amenities. He stored his observations in his mind in case of future use. It appeared that the conspiracy against James had not originated here, but where else? This was where his debt had formed. Had someone a careless tongue? Or had James an enemy here? And Thomas wondered why he still harboured the feeling that James's implication in murder was connected to Elizabeth Ainslie's disappearance when there seemed to be no link between them?

Chapter Six

Emily had pondered the information she had gleaned at the tea-party. It was little, and it would appear to be of no use, but the fact that Mrs Featherstone, to allay her curiosity, had ridden to Westfold on several occasions stuck in Emily's mind.

Could she not do the same? But what was the point if Mrs Ainslie was not there? Could she not have said the same about the ride she had taken to Shaken Hall? But look where that had led. Might a visit to Westfold yield something?

She ordered the groom to have her horse ready for a ride after lunch. She told no one of her intended destination, but with an objective in mind lost no time in negotiating the lanes to the north of Hull until she reached a rutted track which she knew would take her to Westfold.

A tall beech hedge surrounded the house, with a double wrought-iron gateway at one corner the only means of access to the grounds. The ideal place for a reclusive life thought Emily as she slipped from the saddle and tied her horse to the hedge close to the gate. She paused and surveyed the house.

It was of two storeys each with six large windows, three on either side of the front door which was centrally positioned. The windows on the ground floor were covered with black wooden shutters while those on the first floor had curtains drawn across them, giving the air of a dead place. That feeling strengthened as Emily walked tentatively along the short gravelled drive which swung past the door into a loop back on to itself.

The breeze moaned in the tall oaks at the back of the house. It was low and lilting, creating the impression that voices were warning her that she was trespassing, voices of the dead, of the departed, born to the desolation of the sea and loneliness even though close to the activity of a bustling seaport. Emily shivered. Her steps faltered. She stiffened her back, took a grip on her nerves and allowed her curiosity to carry her closer to the house.

She had expected the garden to be overgrown, a jumble of plants and grass running wild, but here there was order and neatness. The garden showed the touch of a caring hand. Someone must be visiting the place regularly. Who? And did they care for the inside of the house? Did Mrs Ainslie intend returning? Or had the house been sold and the new owners not moved in yet?

She searched for more signs which might give her a clue to these questions. Were there answers at the back of the house? The side revealed nothing. She paused at the corner. The spreading branches of the oaks seemed to be attempting to shut out the light, and the ground which ran away from the house towards them wore a damp musty smell as if the sun had been prevented from exerting its natural drying warmth.

The back of the house showed no more signs of occupation than the front. Emily shivered. A sudden sharp clatter startled her and brought her swinging round towards the two stone outbuildings across the cobbled yard. Her eyes were wide with fright. But there was no one, nothing, only a door unfastened and swinging in the wind.

She should leave. She had no right here. If the house held secrets they were not hers to know. She half-turned then stopped, thinking, 'Wouldn't I impress Thomas if I did find something? Surely I have the right to know if there is anything here which might lead to the discovery of Mrs Ainslie's whereabouts. But what clue could there be behind the swinging door of an outhouse?'

Drawn towards it she was almost there before she realised that she had automatically adopted a stride of stealth and caution, as if she was afraid of disturbing whatever lay beyond the door.

She pushed it open and stepped gingerly inside. She saw that the building had once been a stable but was now a store for garden implements.

A noise. Faint. A scuffle. Rats? She shuddered. There it was again. Was someone there? She tensed. Her heart beat harder. Again. Over in the corner where there was less light. A movement. Behind the big wooden chest. A mutter. Words. Indistinguishable. Louder. 'Damn the wind. Have to shut the bloody door again.' A form rose

104

slowly from behind the chest. A head, shoulders. The person turned and light fell across features which sent a shiver down Emily.

The face was heavy with an annoyance which emphasised the grim set of the angular jaw. The skin, yellowish, was pockmarked. The black hair was matted, but strands drooped across a broad forehead. The eyebrows were thick and shielded dark eyes, fearsome in their deep setting.

Her heart raced faster. She wished she hadn't come. She could turn and run but she was frozen to the spot. She tightened her lips and tried to dismiss the terror which gripped her as she reminded herself of why she was here. Maybe she could find some answers if she faced this man unflinchingly. The dread which gripped her heart in a cold vice tightened when the figure stepped from behind the chest and she saw the power in the huge frame.

It seemed for a moment that he had not seen her. Then he stopped and she came under a penetrating gaze, full of suspicion.

'What's thee doing here? Thee has no right.' The voice came deep from a broad chest. It seemed to make his presence fill the stable.

'I was looking for Mrs Ainslie.' Emily tried to speak without faltering, but the words died away as she became aware that the man carried a hedge slasher.

'She ain't here.' The words were gruff.

'Do you know when she will be back?' Emily swallowed, forcing her voice to be as normal as possible.

'Nay.'

'Can you tell me where she has gone?'

'Nay.'

'Are there any servants here?'

'Nay. Place is all locked up. They've left only Matt.'

'Is that you?' asked Emily tentatively.

'Aye.' There was a snap of hostility in his reply.

'So Mrs Ainslie might be away a long time.'

'Don't know.' The man looked at her with a deepening suspicion. 'Who is thee? What d' thee want?'

'An old friend of Mrs Ainslie. I haven't seen her for a number of years.'

'Well, she's gone.'

'And you don't know when she'll be coming back?'

'How should I? They tell me nowt. Just here t'keep t'garden tidy.' His voice was morose, his attitude disgruntled. 'That's all. So off w' thee. I does me job an' I don't want any more of thee snooping around.'

'You've had someone else?'

'Aye.'

'Who?'

'How should I know? He didn't tell me his name.'

'A man?'

'I said he, didn't I?' There was irritation in the man's tone and Emily knew that she should go.

'When was this?'

'Soon after Mrs Ainslie had left.'

'Did he know Mrs Ainslie had gone?'

'Nay. Don't think so. He was snooping, trying to get into the house, but I soon sent him off. Like I'll do with thee if thee doesn't get thissen away. And don't come back!' He ambled a step forward and Emily sensed menace in the set of his body.

'I'm going,' she said backing through the door. Outside she paused for only the time it took to end on a polite note in case she ever wanted to return with further questions. 'Thank you. Goodbye.' She turned and hurried down the path to her horse.

'Thomas, good day to you and thank you for coming.' Simon's instant smile of welcome when his friend entered his office, in Bishop Lane, was then marred by an expression of apology. 'But I'm afraid I've got you here for nothing.' He indicated a chair and returned to his own. 'I had hoped to tell you that I had an investigation for you but the matter has been amicably solved.'

Thomas gave a resigned look. 'It can't be helped. It's regrettable for me but I'm glad a solution was forthcoming. I'm grateful to you for thinking of me.'

Simon leaned back in his chair. 'Well, are you finding Hull to your liking?'

'Yes, and I've much to thank you for.'

'Not the least, introducing you to Miss Emily Thornton?' Simon raised an eyebrow in teasing query.

'A charming lady. I'm pleased you took me along to her birthday party. I look forward to meeting her again soon.'

'Right, we'll arrange that. You and I will take Miss Emily and Miss Sylvia to the theatre.'

'Splendid,' agreed Thomas. His immediate enthusiasm was not lost on Simon.

'I'll arrange it, possibly for Friday.'

'That will suit me admirably.'

'Good, I'll let you know the arrangements.'

'Thanks.' Thomas's expression turned serious. 'If you have a few minutes I'd like you to tell me more about James Walton.'

'You look concerned, is something troubling you?'

'No.' Thomas was quick to lighten the moment. 'Since you introduced us on the way to Miss Thornton's party he has been extremely friendly. He's taken an interest in my work and as you know has proposed me for membership of the Curzon Club.'

'I was pleased to be able to second his proposal. It was a good idea of his. You'll make more contacts.'

'But why should he do this for me?'

'That's James. Generous with his friendship.' Simon concentrated his gaze on Thomas when he put the question, 'Are you suspicious of something?'

'No. No.' Thomas was sharp with his denial. 'When James learned that I was running a detective agency he asked me to keep an ear open for any information which could prove that he was conspired against for the murder. You know him, you defended him, so I thought you could tell me something about him, something about the trial which might help me to know what I should be looking for.'

'How much has he told you?' asked Simon cautiously.

Thomas gave Simon the facts quickly.

'There is little more I can tell you about the murder or what went on in court. He insisted that a plot must have been hatched against him, but the authorities disbelieved him in the face of identification, or so-called identification, especially as James would not say where he had been at that time. He would not provide an alibi, no matter how much I begged him to say where he had been. So he was accused of murder and robbery, but fortunately Jeremy Loftus returned home in time to clear him by showing that the gambling debt had been paid and therefore James had no motive for murdering Captain Ainslie.'

'Has he never told you where he was, not even as a friend in confidence?'

'No. Believe me, I am not being loyal by keeping a secret.'

'Could he be protecting someone?'

'It's a possibility but I know of no one whom James would want to protect.'

'Do we really know everything about a person, even a very close friend?' suggested Thomas.

'I suppose not.' Simon had to agree though Thomas detected a reluctance at having to admit that he didn't know everything about James.

'Would you tell me what you know of his past? He admitted to me that he had had his wild moments.'

Simon gave a small smile as if he was recollecting certain incidents. 'That's true. He got carried away with gambling, but since the trial he's seen it in a different light.'

'I thought so. He took me to Briar Manor.'

'Did he?' There was surprise behind his words.

'He laid a few bets, but nothing large, and I could sense a cautious attitude. He was there to have a pleasant evening and I think he took me to let me meet the man with whom he had incurred his debt.'

'Jeremy Loftus. And your opinion was?'

'Likeable and I think genuinely concerned that James shouldn't get as deeply into debt as he did before.'

Simon nodded. 'I take that as a fair assessment.'

'I knew about James's gambling, the place he went to and the sort of people who were there, but what about other sides of his life? Had he any other haunts?'

'As you say, we can't know everything about someone, but James was not averse to visiting some of the less salubrious districts of Hull.'

'Why?'

'I think he looked upon it as a bit of an adventure.'

'Wasn't he taking a risk?'

'Of course, but let me tell you James is quite capable of looking after himself. I went with him once and he was alert every second.'

'Did you go anywhere in particular?' Thomas leaned forward, his attention riveted on Simon.

'He took me to the Seafarers' Arms in Dagger Lane not far from Prince's Dock. We went on a circuitous route through an area I'm not particular to see again. I think he did it on purpose because he said he was educating me. Between the main thoroughfares of the old town, such as Market Place, High Street, White-friargate which links up with Silver Street and Scale Lane, all respectable streets of offices, shops, traders and so on, the hub and spokes of Hull's prosperity, there are warrens of ill-assorted overcrowded streets, where the filth and poverty are unbelievable. Though

I shouldn't say it, there are men on the town council who would rather develop parks than improve the living conditions of the poor. James was amused by my embarrassment especially when we were approached by beggars, some of them mere children, and were made offers by prostitutes.'

'Did he know any of them?'

'Most of them, because they acknowledged him in a friendly way, but nothing more than that. I believe they knew they would get no further with him.'

'Tell me about the inn you visited.'

'Reasonably respectable. A sailors' inn.'

'Was he known?'

'Yes. Very friendly with Dick Farrar, ex-sailor who now has the inn.'

'That seems to imply that he had been there several times.'

'Without a doubt. He was greeted most amiably by everyone else; well, I suppose he would be, he bought everyone a drink.'

'Did he go there to meet anyone in particular?'

'Not that I was aware of.'

'Did he engage in any specific topics?'

'Mainly about ships and sailings.'

'Any female company?'

'None that he spoke to.'

'But there were some women there?'

'Only four and they were accompanied by husbands or sweethearts and were respectable in their class.'

'Was that the only place you visited?'

'Yes.'

'Do you think he frequented other inns in that area?'

'Although he never mentioned anywhere else, I remember, as we were leaving that evening, someone called, "Bound for the Golden Hind?" I couldn't swear that it was directed specifically at James but I believe it was.'

'He never took you there, nor mentioned it?'

'No.'

Thomas gave a knowing nod. 'All very interesting.'

'Do you think by frequenting that part of Hull James could have got involved in something which led him to court?'

'Anything's possible. If he made an enemy or enemies in that quarter who can tell what they could do?'

'But how would anyone from there know of James's gambling debt? That was central to the case against him and put forward as the motive for the killing.'

'And the witness, Nobby Carson, came from that area of Hull and was killed in a fall the day after the acquittal.'

'If I understand correctly what you are implying, Thomas, then there were two murders.'

Two evenings later a carriage, driven by the Sutcliffe coachman, brought Simon and Thomas to Bramwell House. The two men were admitted by a maid who showed them into the drawing room.

'You've just time for a glass of my best whisky.' Jonas rose from his chair in greeting and directed the maid to pour two measures for the newcomers. 'My daughters will be down in a few minutes.' He waved his hand

112

towards some chairs. 'Are you going to the Palace?'

'Yes, sir,' returned Simon settling himself with his glass. *The Rivals.*'

'I remember seeing that some years ago.' Jonas chuckled at the memory. 'You'll enjoy it. Lots of fun.'

They passed a few pleasant minutes discussing the merits of the decision to lay out a new park, until Sylvia and Emily arrived, excited by the prospect of an evening at the theatre.

Their anticipation was fulfilled with seats in a box giving them an excellent view. The theatre was full, and, though the production of the play left something to be desired, it raised lots of laughter and ribald comments shouted from the gods.

Seated as they were, Emily took the opportunity, before the start of the performance, to acquaint Thomas with her visit to the Ainslie property, keeping her voice trained to his ears alone while Simon was devoting his attention to Sylvia.

'Emily, what you have learned could be useful, but I don't want you taking any risk on my behalf.' His concern, which showed in his troubled expression, did not disguise the fact that he thought highly of her enterprise.

She was pleased she had gained his admiration. 'There was no risk. Matt was a bit frightening, but I think that was only put on to protect himself because he's only ten to the dozen.'

'Well, no going there on your own again.' Thomas pressed her hand in a gesture of concern. 'You're too precious to run unnecessary risks.' She appreciated his

113

solicitude but merely smiled. He went on to tell her briefly of his visit to Briar Manor, but he said nothing of Simon's information for he had decided that it might be worthwhile making some investigations of his own in the quarter of Hull which had been visited by James.

The audience were in a good mood as they left the theatre and chatter and laughter flowed freely.

'Hello, there, you four.' The call brought the friends turning to see the light from the gas lamps outside the theatre casting their glow across the faces of Captain Hobson and his wife.

'Hello, sir, pleased to meet you again.' Thomas was the first to react. He bowed to Mrs Hobson. 'And I'm delighted to make your acquaintance, ma'am.'

Friendly greetings were exchanged all round.

'This is the young fellow I was telling you about, Martha,' said the captain to his wife.

Thomas knew her eyes, though gentle, were making a piercing assessment as they would of all newcomers. 'I am pleased to meet you, young man. I was curious and looked forward to meeting you after my husband's glowing report following his talk with you at his club. Live up to it and you'll go far. I like your idea of a private detective agency for Hull.'

'Thank you, ma'am,' returned Thomas. 'I hope you will never be in need of my services but, if you are, rest assured I will give your problem one hundred per cent of my attention.'

Martha gave a light laugh. 'Now that would be something to set my lady-friends' tongues wagging – "Have you heard the latest scandal, Martha Hobson's

had to employ the services of a private detective."'
Everyone laughed at her mimicking.

'Did you all enjoy the play?' asked the captain.

As they were exchanging comments a group of six people in a raucous mood emerged from the theatre. There was some horseplay going on as they swept past Captain Hobson and one of them, a slim red-headed young woman, cannoned into him as she swung out of the clutches of her companion.

'Midge, leave off,' she snapped, her eyes blazing. 'Keep yer hands off my tits.' She looked up at the scowl on the captain's face. 'I'm sorry, sir. Boyfriend's hands are too big an' he thinks he has a right.' Her white smile flashed across the ladies. Emily and Sylvia were embarrassed in front of their escorts and Mrs Hobson showed disgust mingled with a haughtiness at someone she thought below her. 'Don't look like that, ladies. We all have 'em.' She glanced back at the captain and winked before hurrying after Midge who was shouting, 'Come on, Annie.' She caught him up and was heard to say with a laugh as she gave him a playful dig, 'I'll let you when we get to my room.'

Captain Hobson gave a puzzled frown as he stared after the couple, who were rejoining their theatre companions.

'Something wrong, sir?' asked Thomas.

The captain started as if he had interrupted deep, concerned thoughts. 'Er ... No. Nothing.' He quickly regathered his composure.

As farewells were being made, Captain Hobson managed to get a whispered word to Thomas. 'See me in the club, eleven tomorrow morning.'

Before Thomas had a chance to find a reason for the captain's request his attention was drawn back to Emily, who was making her goodbyes to Mrs Hobson.

Thomas arrived at the Curzon Club a few minutes before eleven and ordered hot chocolate to be brought as soon as the steward saw Captain Hobson arrive. With greetings exchanged the two men settled themselves in chairs, the captain choosing two in a corner away from those occupied by other members. It was a gesture not lost on Thomas who thought it would possibly have something to do with a slight agitation he recognised in the captain's demeanour.

A few minor pleasantries were brushed quickly out of the way and, with the drinks served, Captain Hobson leaned forward in a confidential attitude.

'You remember you asked me if something was wrong when we were talking outside the theatre last evening?' Thomas nodded. 'Well, something did trouble me.'

'I thought so.'

'You may be able to help.'

'Me?'

'A chance to exercise your detective ability.'

'In what way?'

'You remember the girl who bumped into us?'

Thomas gave a small wry smile. 'Who could forget?'

The captain let the implication pass without comment. 'She wore a locket.'

'Yes.' Thomas had noticed it but had not taken in any details.

116

'It was unusual. A very delicately painted ship with its mainmast broken, its sails tumbling.'

'As you say, unusual.'

'I have only ever seen one like it before with the painting framed by the same finely worked silver.'

'And where was that, sir?'

'Mrs Walton wore it. You remember I told you we were very friendly with her and her husband. We visited them on one occasion and Harriet showed us the latest present from her husband.'

Thomas's interest heightened with the mention of Mrs Walton. 'You are sure it was the same?' he asked with a tone of caution.

'Yes. I remember it distinctly because I remarked on the broken sail. Mr Walton explained that it was in commemoration of his father, a whaling captain out of Hull, who suffered a storm in the Arctic which broke his mainsail, but by skill he brought his ship and crew back safely. The ship was the *Harriet* which he had named after his son's wife for whom he had a great affection. But how did that hussy get it?'

'Maybe more than one was made,' Thomas suggested.

'But it was made especially to Mr Walton's order.'

'The craftsman may have liked the idea and made some copies.'

The captain nodded, but there was doubt in his expression.

'I wonder if Mrs Walton left it as a bequest in her will?'

'To that hussy?'

Thomas smiled at the thought. 'Whoever it was left to might have sold it or lost it. There are all sorts of possibilities.'

'I know, but it bothered me and I've spent half the night awake trying to find an answer to why it should be round that girl's neck. I'd like you to investigate, but discreetly. Just between you and me.'

'Certainly, sir. I will do my best.'

Thomas had many things to ponder on his walk home. He tried to draw a connection between them all, the murder of Captain Ainslie, the disappearance of his much younger wife who nevertheless had led a reclusive life, the trial of James on what appeared to be a trumped-up accusation, his gambling debt, the change in Harriet Walton's will, and now a necklace worn by an attractive but uncouth girl. Were all of these connected in some way? If he could find the solution to one question would he discover the answers to the others? But first and foremost he had to learn the whereabouts of Elizabeth Ainslie and yet he could not dispel the feeling that the solution might lie somewhere among the other problems.

As he turned things over in his mind he recalled Simon's information about accompanying James to the Seafarers' Arms. Deciding that he needed to verify a point he turned in the direction of Simon's office. He learned that his friend was engaged in discussions with a client but might be free in ten minutes. He decided to wait.

'I regret having to keep you waiting, Thomas,' apologised Simon once his client had left.

Thomas brushed the apology aside and made one of his own. 'I'm sorry for pestering you again, but there is something I want to ask you in the light of what you had told me about your visit with James to the unsavoury side of the old town.'

Simon leaned back in his chair and with his elbows resting on the arms steepled his fingers in front of his mouth. 'Ask away. I hope I can help.'

'When you were with him did you hear any mention of the name Annie?'

Simon looked thoughtful for a moment, then gave a little shake of his head. 'No. But wasn't that the name of the girl who bumped into us after the theatre,' he gave a little smile, 'the one whose tits seemed to be attracting her boyfriend's attention? I recall him calling her Annie.'

'It was,' confirmed Thomas. 'She was pretty, a redhead.'

Simon snapped his fingers. 'That's it.' Excitement had come to his eyes. 'You've just broken the spell. I thought I'd seen her somewhere before but I couldn't remember. I cast it from my mind thinking I must be mistaken. But you have jolted my memory with that word redhead. She was present at James's trial every day.'

'Are you sure?'

'Yes. There are few redheads about. Do you think she might be involved in the accusations against James and attended the trial to see what happened?'

'I don't know, but someone has asked me to look into a certain matter which might have something to do with her.' He saw curiosity rising on Simon's face. He held up his hands as if to stop what he thought was coming.

'Please don't ask me any more. This new enquiry is in the strictest confidence at the moment.'

Simon nodded. 'I understand.'

Is this one more link in the chain? wondered Thomas as he left Simon's office. Was the fact that Annie had been present every day at James's trial significant? Why had this young woman, who wore a locket which had more than likely belonged to James's mother, been so interested? As he tried to reason a way to a solution he decided he had a request to make of Emily.

Chapter Seven

When Thomas reached Bramwell House that same afternoon he was shown into the drawing room.

'Thomas, this is an unexpected pleasure,' said Emily, rising from her chair.

'I hope you'll forgive me for calling without an invitation.'

She held out her hands, which he took in his as she said, 'You are welcome here any time, and I'll look forward to your visits.'

'I hope as much as I'll enjoy coming.'

As they sat down she asked, 'Is this more than a social call?'

'Yes. Before we parted after the theatre last evening Captain Hobson asked me to meet him at his club this morning. I have done so and what he requested of me was in the strictest confidence but, as I regard you as helping my detective agency in the matter of finding Mrs Ainslie, I think you are entitled to know.'

'Has it something to do with her?' asked Emily eagerly.

'Well, not as far as I know, but I have this feeling, as I voiced to you before, that all the events leading to James's trial are connected with my pledge to your father to find Mrs Ainslie.'

'Then it has something to do with the murder?'

'Not that I am aware of and yet I am wondering if it could.' He went on to acquaint Emily with the information that Captain Hobson had given him.

'I noticed that locket,' she commented. 'It was very beautiful, but how had that girl come by it if it was Mrs Walton's?'

'That's the mystery Captain Hobson wants me to solve.'

'And how do you propose to go about it?'

'I will try to trace the girl.'

'That might be risky considering the part of Hull you will have to visit.'

'Simon told me James used to go there.'

'Mrs Walton must have given the locket to James as an heirloom so surely you don't think he parted with it to her?' There was strong doubt in Emily's tone.

'If he gave it to anyone I think he would only do so to someone he thought highly of.'

'We've got to find the girl, but what do we know about her? Only that she is pretty, a redhead, her name is Annie and her boyfriend, as she called him, though he looked much older than her, is Midge.'

Thomas smiled. 'You are observant. You'll make a detective yet.'

'You know no more?'

'No.'

'And we don't even know if it has any connection with our main purpose of finding Mrs Ainslie.'

'True. Regarding that, you told me that the gardener, Matt, said there had been a man snooping round the Ainslie house.'

'Yes.' Emily anticipated Thomas's request by adding. 'You want me to try to get Matt to tell me who it was?'

'Yes, but I'll accompany you, I don't want you meeting him alone. He told you not to return so he might turn nasty when you do.'

'All right, but I think it might be better if you keep out of sight and I face him alone. I detected hostility in his voice when he mentioned a man had been snooping around the house. I think he would be less antagonistic to a female.'

Thomas saw sound reasoning behind her words. 'Very well,' he agreed, 'but I will be close at hand in case of any trouble.'

'Shall we go now?'

'The sooner the better. We must try and get a lead on Mrs Ainslie's whereabouts as soon as possible. Your father won't want to delay too long before he informs James of the second will.'

'And we don't want him pushing us.' Emily rose from her chair. 'I'll get ready. You've come by carriage?'

'Yes. I thought it easier to hire one.'

Within ten minutes they were driving away from Bramwell House. The track they followed took them through open spaces of meadows unmarred as yet by the threatened expansion of Hull. Daisies, buttercups, cow parsley and poppies gave colourful touches at the edges of the track. Beyond the fields the waters of the Humber glistened in the sunshine.

As they chatted any remaining barrier that might have existed between them was broken. She was flattered that he had taken her fully into his confidence and regarded her as a partner in his enterprise. The empathy he felt for her was different to that he had experienced with any other woman. He had come close to marriage with a Swede who had emigrated to the United States, but the final measure of understanding had not been there. Even in their short acquaintance he thought he knew Emily better than he had ever known anyone before and this was in no small measure to the response he sensed coming from her – a desire to be together, an enjoyment of being in his company.

She relaxed in the easy atmosphere and wished the ride could go on without the prospect of an unpleasant encounter at the end of it.

With the house in sight Thomas pulled the horse to a halt.

'I think we'll leave the carriage here. It will attract attention if we go too close.' He helped Emily alight and they walked the rest of the way to the gate where they paused.

A concentrated gaze came to his eyes as he studied the building and its surroundings. 'Substantial. Not cheap. The captain must have had money, but he was in the right trade to make shrewd investments. No family. Mrs

Ainslie, not known around Hull, must have led a quite inexpensive life. So why leave all this behind? Does she intend returning?'

'Maintaining the garden would seem to indicate she does.'

'Or she's keeping it respectable to sell.'

'But why not do so immediately she decided to leave?'

'Maybe she just hadn't made up her mind about what she should do. Maybe she just felt she wanted to get away from the town where her husband was murdered, at least for a while until she had come to terms with his death.'

'If I had been Mrs Ainslie,' mused Emily, 'I would have wanted to return to any family I had. I wonder where she came from?'

'Captain Ainslie brought her here newly married?' Thomas glanced queryingly at Emily.

'Yes, so we cannot get anything from the local church registers.'

'And he could have married her in any port he visited.'

'Would his crew know where that was likely to be?'

'Brilliant, Emily. That's the next enquiry I'll make. Now let's see if we can find out about the stranger who visited this house after Mrs Ainslie had left. And it might be as well to see if Matt knows anything about her servants. I'll wait here. If you meet trouble give a shout.'

Emily walked steadily towards the house and, seeing no sign of Matt, moved on to the back. She paused at the corner of the house. There was no sound from the old stable. She shivered. She felt as if eyes were watching her, but she could see no one. She had an urge to run but, remembering Thomas, she drew new strength and approached the stable. She pushed the door open. No sound. She sensed someone was behind her. She spun round, her eyes widening in startled expectancy, but there was no one. She let out a deep breath and looked across the stableyard to the wood. Only the breeze stirred the grasses and the leaves. The light filtering through the branches revealed no human presence. She started to turn away, but froze at seeing a bulk rise from behind the waist-high stone wall at one edge of the yard.

Matt swung his legs over it with ease, an action which seemed to make him more formidable. 'I thought I told thee not to come back,' he growled, his bushy eyebrows adding to the fearsome look which he directed at Emily.

'I know,' replied Emily.

'Then what's thee doing here?' he snarled. Seeing Emily drawing herself up and taking it as a sign of authority he adopted a meeker attitude. 'I want no trouble. I only want leaving alone to do the gardening. I don't want to lose my money. It's all I get.'

Emily seized her chance. 'Matt,' she said gently. 'No one wants to take your job away. I don't want you to lose your pay. You are doing good work here keeping the place tidy.' She saw him relax a little and his chest swell with the praise, but he still regarded her with some suspicion.

'You ain't just saying that to get round me? 'Cos I'll not be got round.' He shuffled on his feet.

'No, Matt. I mean it. All I want is to ask you a few

126

questions relating to what you told me the other day. May I do that?'

He hesitated. His eyes seemed to be searching for her sincerity. Then slowly he nodded. 'All right, but I may not answer.'

'That's your right,' she agreed, hoping he would see that she did not mean to press him. 'You told me there had been a man snooping around after Mrs Ainslie had left.'

'Yes.' A deep chuckle came from his chest. 'I showed him my fists.' He held them up in a menacing attitude for her to see. Clenched, they were enormous, formidable weapons and Emily could imagine any man backing down when threatened by them. 'He went.' There was a note of triumph in his voice as he recalled the incident. 'I had to get rid of him again.'

'He was here more than once? You're sure? You didn't tell me that before.' Emily was suspicious that Matt might be exaggerating.

'I've just said he was.' A little snap had come back into his voice. 'Matt don't lie.'

Emily realised she had done wrong to show doubt. 'I believe you, Matt. You told me you didn't know him. Can you remember anything about him? What he looked like?

'Like a man.'

'What clothes did he wear?'

'Coat and trousers.'

Emily knew it was hopeless to try to get a description so she asked him, 'Did he say what he wanted or why he had returned?'

Matt grunted. 'Asked if I knew when missis was coming back and where she'd gone.'

'Could you tell him?' She hoped his answer would be different to their first confrontation.

'Nay. If I could it would be more than my job's worth to tell him or you. Now I think thee'd better go.'

'Just one more thing, Matt, do Mrs Ainslie's servants still look after the inside of the house?'

'How can they?' he replied, a touch of derision in his voice as if he thought her ignorant. 'They was all paid and told they weren't wanted any more.' A low chuckle of pleasure came from deep in his chest and his eyes widened with glee as he said, 'Serves 'em reet, they nivver had a word for Matt, thought I was light in the head, but I was the one missis kept on.' He paused as if he was troubled by a thought. 'One would speak t'me. Robert Walsh, the groom.'

Emily seized on this information but toned down the feeling of elation as she asked, 'Do you know what happened to him?'

'Aye. He was t'only one to bid me farewell. He told me he'd got a job with a family called Sleightholme at Riplingham Hall.'

She saw his lips clamp tight as if that was the end of the matter. She deemed it wise to leave. 'Thank you for talking to me,' she said gently. Almost at once she wished she had not adopted such an appreciative tone in her voice.

She saw his eyes soften, with a spark of admiration. Before she realised what was happening, he reached out and took her hands in his. Alarm surged through every nerve. She felt revulsion at being touched by this unkempt man. What was he going to do? The instinct to shout for Thomas was strong but she knew she must not show alarm. She urged herself to relax. Then she felt gentleness in his broad fingers and massive hands and she sensed that this big, ungainly man was trying to show that he had never meant her any harm and that he had an almost childlike innocence.

'Yes, Matt?' she queried firmly.

'I like thee.' He gazed at her and in that moment she sensed he meant her no harm and she crushed the impulse to tear herself free. 'So I'll tell thee, something else about the man who came here.' Then, frightened, he said quickly, 'Thee won't tell anyone I told thee will thee?'

'No, Matt, I won't. I give you my word.' To emphasise her sincerity her gaze never left his eyes.

'He was a gent. I saw him once when he didn't see me.'

'Here? Did he come a third time?'

'Nay, it weren't here.'

'Where was it?' Excitement gripped Emily but she tried not to sound too pressing.

'In the streets near the docks. Not the place for the likes of him.'

'Anywhere particular?'

'He was going into the Seafarers' Arms.'

'By himself?'

'Aye.' He released her hands.

Sensing that he could tell her no more and not wanting to force the issue, Emily thanked him again and walked quickly out of the stableyard.

*

Reaching the gate she was thankful that Thomas had not come forward to greet her, for she sensed that Matt had come round the corner and was watching her. She was relieved to pass from his gaze and find Thomas a few yards away hidden by the high wall.

'Are you all right? I was getting worried. I nearly came looking for you.'

She was touched by his concern. 'Just as well you didn't. If he'd seen you he would have shut up like a clam. As it is I think I have learned something useful.'

He took her arm by the elbow and hurried her towards the carriage. Though he was anxious to know what had transpired he did not ask until they were seated and driving away from the house.

She told him what she had learned. He listened intently without interrupting, his mind attempting to interpret and assess the information, trying to slot it in with all the other disconnected facts he had at his disposal.

'And one other thing,' she added with exuberance. 'I know Mr Sleightholme, he's a client of my father, so we'll have no opposition to talking to Mrs Ainslie's ex-groom.'

'This might just be what we want.' Thomas was elated. 'He'll be able to tell us where he drove Mrs Ainslie when she left. Another thing, the man Matt described as a gent, could he be James?'

'What?' Emily was startled by the suggestion. 'No, that's not reasonable.'

'Think about it. We know from Simon that James has sometimes frequented that part of Hull.'

130

'But that had nothing to do with that house or Mrs Ainslie.'

'Matt said the man visited after Mrs Ainslie left. If he was James couldn't he have been seeking Mrs Ainslie to offer his sympathy and reassure her that the verdict of the court was the correct one?'

Emily looked thoughtful. 'I suppose so. We can ask James.'

'No.' Thomas was hasty. 'Not yet. If we do he'll wonder why we are trying to find Mrs Ainslie and we certainly don't want that to happen until after your father has revealed the second will to him.'

'So what do we do next?'

'We'll have to contact the groom, but there is something I want to do first. In the meantime you keep attending tea-parties – you could pick up a piece of gossip which might help us.'

Emily pulled a face. 'And I suppose you'll be doing all the exciting things?'

Thomas laughed. 'If you want to call routine gathering of information and trying to make sense of it exciting, then yes, I will be.'

Emily made no comment. She recalled that earlier he had hinted at what he might do but she was not going to remind him that she knew.

Two days later Emily appeared in the hall dressed in a black skirt and magenta merino jacket edged with black velvet. She wore a tan-coloured Glengarry which added attraction to her copper-tinted hair.

Sylvia, who was equally smartly dressed for visiting,

gave a wry smile as she commented, 'So you accepted the invitation from Mrs Hardy? My, you are becoming the little lady.'

'I thought you might like me to accompany you,' replied Emily.

'You've never considered that before. Who's brought this change of heart?' She gave a slight pause and added with sisterly teasing, 'Practising for being the lady-wife to Thomas?'

Emily's face reddened. Instead of rising to the taunt she said with a little haughtiness, 'I think it's time we were going.'

Emily was pleased to find that there were three ladies at Mrs Hardy's who had not been at Sylvia's tea-party, for she was able to bring up the topic of Mrs Ainslie again.

'I did see her once,' Mrs Hardcastle informed them with something of a gleeful note that she was the only one who had some information, slight though it might be. All ears were attentive, eager to learn something of the lady who had assumed an air of mystery in their conversational exchanges. 'I was in Kenyon's the drapers when this young woman came in. She quickly chose some material, cotton and buttons, spoke only to the assistant. She kept her voice low as if she wanted no one else to hear, but I did catch her instructions for the account to be sent to Captain Ainslie.' As she spoke the last few words she cast her eyes around her audience and, seeing that their attention was full of curiosity, she went on. 'Hearing that name I concluded that she must be Mrs Ainslie and was about to introduce myself, but she turned quickly from the counter and was gone before I could speak.'

'So it seemed even then that she wanted to keep very much to herself?' commented Emily.

'That is exactly the impression I got,' agreed Mrs Hardcastle. 'She did not want contact with anyone. She knew precisely what she wanted, obtained it and left before she could be drawn into even the shortest conversation.'

'What did she look like?' asked Sylvia.

'Extremely pretty, petite, attractive and she seemed to glide out of the shop with a sort of graceful sweep.'

'Exactly my impression,' agreed Mrs Featherstone, reminding them of the information she had passed on at Sylvia's tea-party.

'You were lucky to have even seen her,' said Mrs Hobson. 'The story is that she very rarely left the house.'

'I wonder why?' mused Mrs Hardy. 'You would think a young thing like her would have wanted to get out and meet people.'

'Her age might be the answer,' said Mrs Hobson. 'Remember, her husband was twenty-five years older than her, and between us,' she let her voice sink as if she were going to reveal something in confidence, 'I believe he was a bit of a tartar. Kind enough, she wanted for nothing, adored her, but, according to my husband who had a few dealings with Captain Ainslie, he was very possessive. So maybe he did not want her mixing with other folk.'

'And she, knowing she was well off, complied with his wishes,' mused Emily. 'I wonder if she felt devastated by his murder or whether she felt liberated?'

'I accompanied my husband to the funeral,' said Mrs Hobson. 'She was heavily veiled, you could not see sufficient of her face to tell how she was reacting. She hurried away immediately after the vicar's final words without speaking to anyone.'

'I did hear she left Hull immediately after James Walton's trial,' said Mrs Featherstone. 'Locked the house up and went.'

'And no one appears to have heard anything of her since,' added Mrs Hardy.

'I wonder if she intends coming back,' said Mrs Hobson.

'There's a man keeping the garden tidy, so maybe she does,' put in Emily, and immediately realised she had made a mistake when she saw her sister shoot a mystified glance at her, but before Sylvia could query the information she added quickly, 'I've seen him when I've ridden past there a couple of times.'

When Emily visited Thomas at his office the next day and informed him of the conversation concerning Mrs Ainslie which had passed between the ladies, she concluded by showing her disappointment. 'I'm sorry I've learned nothing.'

'On the contrary,' he said, 'you may have gained something of importance.' The seriousness behind his expression told her that he was not just trying to placate her.

'But I don't see what?' She was puzzled. Nothing that had been said at the tea-party had struck her as significant to their quest to find Elizabeth Ainslie.

'The piece about Mrs Ainslie buying material for a dress could be helpful. She must have had a dress made for her. Maybe the dressmaker knows where she went.'

'But we don't know who her dressmaker was.' She saw Thomas looking at her with a disarming smile and she was immediately thrust into knowing what he was going to say next. 'Oh no—' she gulped. 'You can't want me to go round all the dressmakers asking if they—'

'I'm sure you won't have to visit them all. Remember at your first tea-party, Mrs Featherstone told you that she had seen Mrs Ainslie and that she was well dressed and I gathered from what you said that that was praise indeed. So if Mrs Ainslie had such good taste in clothes, and they appeared to be impeccably made, then she must have engaged a top-class dressmaker. Do you know those who would come into that category?'

'Some.'

'Start with them. One thing can lead to another. But you need patience and don't be disappointed if you appear to be getting nowhere. Something will come out of your enquiries just as this possible lead has come out of your tea-partying.'

Thomas pulled a thick jersey over his collarless shirt. His trousers, which came over rough leather boots, were held up by a broad belt with a heavy buckle. He tied a neckerchief, emblazoned with the American flag, around his throat. He placed a dark cap with small peak on his head, viewed himself in a mirror, and, satisfied, picked up a cudgel. He eyed it for a moment, wondering if it signified he was expecting trouble. He slapped it against his left palm and decided that, where he was going, it was better to go forearmed. As he opened the door of the small house he had rented he wondered what Emily would think if she could see him now.

The evening was dull with thick clouds bringing darkness sooner. The air, drawn in from the river, was damp. He headed for the docks at a brisk pace. He left the newly tarred streets recently constructed under the innovated process of McAdam, for the less fortunate area which was still cobbled. The main thoroughfares in the old town were lit by coal gas, but side streets still exuded an air of mystery and menace with their darkness.

Reaching the more crowded streets he slowed his pace so as not to draw attention to himself when there became more people about. Dockers drifted home from their work or found their way to the nearest tavern, barefooted urchins raced in chase or played ball near a light. At the corner of one street two sisters, no more than ten years old, their clothes in rags, sang 'Home Sweet Home' to the music rendered from a concertina played by the taller girl. The sweetness of their voices contrasted with the squalor and dirt around them, but their nostalgic words drifted over the heads of those making their way to places other than those of the song. Thomas dropped a coin into the tin mug held by the shorter girl. Their plaintive notes faded and were lost on the night air as he weaved his way past women clutching their precious purchases of bread and fish to feed families they wished were smaller, past drunks who called lewdly at the females or were too far inebriated to care, around sailors who were discussing where they should go for their evening entertainment.

Houses were dark and silent or by flickering candle-light showed they were inhabited. Lamps gave a weary light to shops as their owners tried to bring a few more coppers to their paltry incomes. Raucous noise flowed from the inns as if celebrating that the night had come alive.

He found the Seafarers' Arms and, on pushing open the door, was surrounded by a blast of sounds each indistinguishable from the other but together forming a harsh intrusion on the ears. The smoke rising from numerous pipes, most of them churchwardens, acted like a fog which needed penetrating to find the bar. The long mahogany counter was crowded with customers, reluctant to move from their advantageous positions even after they had received their foaming glasses from the four barmen who tried to keep pace with shouted demands. The tables around the room were all occupied by sailors and those engaged in work allied to the shipping trade.

Thomas crossed the floor, only just avoiding colliding with a stubbled sailor carrying four tankards of ale to his thirsty companions who had shown their muscle to commandeer a table from two youngsters on their first visit to the world of ale. He inched his way into a corner of the bar from which he could keep most of the room under observation. He called for a drink and had to make his presence known a couple more times before the tankard was thrust at him slopping ale on to the counter.

He sat quietly allowing the activity and noise to have no effect on him. The man next to him was bleary-eyed and well on the way to a raging headache in the morning. He was morose, only mumbling a few words now and again of which Thomas could make no sense. He wondered how James found any pleasure in coming here. These were not his type of people and yet according to Simon he had a sort of empathy with them. Maybe it was an hereditary trait – a throwback to his real parents or even his grandparents. Who knew where James had been born and to whom? That was the past and though the past might help with answers this was the present and Thomas had to work from here and now.

The man beside him called for another beer, but his slurred voice did not carry authority. He tried again but in the bustle of customers further along the bar he was ignored once more. When he was overlooked a third time he brought all the curses he could on the Seafarers' Arms, slid from his stool and weaved a grunting path to the door.

Thomas glanced at the man who had taken the vacated stool. He saw someone whom he judged to be in his late twenties, though a lined and weather-beaten face made it hard to judge. He was broad-shouldered with an air of toughness about him. His chin was angular with a determined thrust. His hair was almost black and matched his eyes which had the alertness of one used to observing, maybe scanning distant horizons. His long-fingered hands resting on the bar had been broadened with a life of hauling ropes and handling cargoes.

He called loudly for a beer. His deep voice must have had a familiar ring about it because Thomas saw one of the barmen look quickly in the direction of the newcomer. A surprised look of recognition broadened into a smiling welcome as he came to the sailor.

'Good to see thee back, Ed,' he said enthusiastically as he shook hands. 'What is it, nearly a year?'

'Nearer eighteen months, Dick,' grinned Ed with a confirming nod. 'And I'm looking forward to some good Yorkshire ale again, after that American dishwater I've had to drink, so let's have a big foaming tankard.'

Dick laughed. 'First one on me, welcome home.' He slipped away to fulfil the order.

Ed cast a glance at Thomas. 'No disrespect to thee.' He indicated Thomas's neckerchief.

'None taken,' replied Thomas adopting the American accent he had cultivated when he was with the Pinkerton National Detective Agency. 'And I know what you mean, this sure is strong liquor.'

Ed thrust out his hand. 'Ed Berriman. What's an American doing in Hull?'

Thomas shook hands. 'Thomas Laycock. I came into London. Friend of mine sailed on the *Fauconberg*. He said it was a good ship, so I thought I'd come to Hull and see if I could join him.'

Dick returned with the ale and Ed asked him, 'Is the *Fauconberg* in port?'

Dick shook his head. 'Sailed for Australia and had no schedule for immediate return, if there were profitable cargoes to be picked up out there. Owners left that to the discretion of the captain.'

'Still John Ainslie?'

'No.' He slapped his fist into his palm. 'Of course, you won't know. Ainslie was murdered.'

'What?' Ed looked aghast.

'Aye, last year. Fished out of the dock.'

'Not one of his crew? I know he ruled his ship with an iron fist but he was generally fair and you couldn't find a better sailor. But I guess there's always someone who will bear a grudge.'

Dick shook his head. 'Wasn't one of his crew. Least I don't think so. A gent stood trial, you might remember him, came in here occasionally, James Walton. Nice fella, though what he saw in the likes of this lot I don't know.' He gave a gesture towards the rest of the room.

'What happened?' Ed prompted Dick to continue.

'Got off. Ainslie was returning with the crew's wages when he was killed.'

'Robbery?'

'Aye. It was said that Walton had a gambling debt and Nobby Carson said he'd seen him running away.'

Ed gave a snort. 'Who'd believe that drunk and liar?'

'That's what I thought. Walton said he'd paid the debt but wasn't able to prove it. Then just before the verdict Jeremy Loftus appeared with proof of the payment. He'd been out of the country and knew nowt about it until he had returned the previous day.' He leaned forward conspiratorially, but Thomas, who had been listening intently, caught the words. 'If you ask me it was all put up and for some reason the blame laid on Walton.'

'But why? Who would want to do that?'

Dick shrugged his shoulders and pulled a face. 'Don't know. But it was very suspicious to me when Nobby was found dead the day after the trial. I reckon someone paid him to give that evidence and was frightened he might talk.'

Dick moved away to dispense some more ale.

'Gruesome deeds,' commented Thomas.

Ed gave a small laugh. 'Little better than New York.'

'Does Dick own the Seafarer's Arms?' asked Thomas, having noted throughout the conversation how he had kept a supervisory eye on the barmen and a wary watch on his customers.

'Aye. Runs a tight ship as you might say. Was a sailor himself once. He'll stand no nonsense in here. If you want to know what's going on in Hull, he's a mine of information. He'll be able to advise you on another ship. Do you want one now?'

'I think I'll hang around for a while but thanks for the suggestion.'

Dick, judging that Ed might want bringing up to date with other happenings, wandered back to them.

After a few exchanges, Ed asked, 'How's Annie?'

Dick smiled. 'Still got a soft spot for the redhead?'

Thomas sharpened his hearing. This must be the same girl they had seen at the theatre, the one whom Simon had seen in the court throughout James's trial, the one who wore the locket. It would be too much of a coincidence if there were two Annies whose hair was red.

Ed nodded. 'We were close.'

'Thee shouldn't have gone away when thee did.'

'It was too good a chance to miss. Good pay

141

operating down the American coast. I offered to pay her passage out, but she wouldn't leave England. She said if I went I needn't expect her to wait. Is she still in Hull?'

'Aye. I haven't seen much of her. I think she regarded the Seafarers' Arms as the place thee shared and didn't want to be haunted by memories of thee and looked for somewhere new.'

'And where would that be?'

'Well, she disappeared from all the usual haunts for a while and reappeared at the Golden Hind.'

'Midge Whitley's place,' hissed Ed with disgust as if it held poison. 'She didn't take up with that louse?'

'Aye. It appears so.'

Ed tossed his head in disgust. 'She's sunk to associating with that conniving bastard.'

'More than that.'

'She hasn't married him?' There was a touch of alarm in Ed's voice.

'No, Midge wouldn't want that, but it's almost as good. You know Midge, what other folk has he wants and God help anyone who gets in the way.'

Ed's eyes narrowed. 'I fancy she needs rescuing. I wonder how she'd take to me reappearing in the Golden Hind?' He glanced at Thomas whom he knew could hear every word of the exchange. 'Do you think the lady should be saved?'

'Is she pretty?'

'Startling.'

'A firy temper goes with red hair.'

Ed chuckled as memories flitted through his mind.

'Aye she's firy all right but that makes her all the more tempting.'

'And he's a louse?'

'Aye. A rat, who'd skin his grandmother for a penny. Annie ain't for the likes of him.'

'Then there's only one thing for you to do.'

'Stranger, I'm glad you agree.' He drained his tankard, slipped from his stool and paused. He slapped Thomas on the back. 'Best of luck, America. I might see you here unless Dick advises a ship soon. Maybe I'll be able to introduce you to Annie.'

Thomas watched Ed move through the crowd. He went out into the night. Thomas's venture into this area of Hull had proved valuable; he might be no nearer discovering the whereabouts of Elizabeth Ainslie but he was close to a certain redhead who wore an unusual locket. He left the inn in time to see the tall figure of Ed before it disappeared into the mist swirling up from the river.

Thomas sharpened his step. He must not lose him for he had no doubt that Ed was making for the Golden Hind.

Chapter Eight

The mist swirled, thickened then parted only to close again as if attempting to obliterate the sailor from Thomas's gaze. He concentrated his attention on the figure ahead, only dimly aware of the folk moving around him, some with steps which showed where they wanted to go, others shuffling, hunched in the desultory posture of the drifter. Street lamps tried to penetrate the gloom, their light lost on the writhing haze.

Someone bumped into him. Automatically his hand grasped a wrist in a movement he had learned against the pickpockets of New York. His vice-like grip brought a yelp of pain from the youth who had dared to dip his fingers. Thomas felt the hold on his purse slacken. His inclination was to teach this would-be thief a lesson, but he had a more important item on his mind. He gave the wrist another vicious twist as he thrust the pickpocket away, sending him sprawling across the cobbles. The youth stiffened in momentary retaliation but thought better of it even though his intended victim appeared to be paying him no attention.

Thomas cursed. He had lost sight of the sailor. Impatient with annoyance he hurried forward, his eyes straining to penetrate the fog. The flow of people thickened, holding back his haste. He had almost given up hope when he heard a creaking sound and, after a few more steps, he saw an inn sign swinging under the impact of stones thrown by two urchins who laughed and ran on. The light from a close-by lamp revealed paint peeling from a board on which there was the picture of a ship under full sail and a name which announced that this was the Golden Hind.

The Golden Hind – the inn where Ed expected to find Annie, the girl who might be wearing a locket that once belonged to James's mother. He was sure he had heard the name before. He thought hard then slapped his cudgel into his palm, got it – in relating his only venture to the Seafarers' Arms with James, Simon had said someone had called out "Bound for the Golden Hind?" From what he had heard in the Seafarers' Arms the Golden Hind was an unsavoury place run by a worthless character. So why had James visited it?

He stepped towards the door but stopped before he reached it. Was it wise to enter the Golden Hind now? If he did so it could look as if he had followed Ed and his purpose might be questioned with suspicion. Instinct warned him that it would be better to visit the Golden Hind another time when he could see Annie alone.

Ed pushed open the door of the Golden Hind and

paused inside. His gaze swept the room which was filled to near capacity. The air was stale with smoke and the smell of beer and spirits. Oil lamps did their best to pierce the haze. The noise of gabbling tongues mingled with raucous laughter and the loud demands for orders to be fulfilled. Ed started towards the long wooden counter, weaving between tables swimming with spilt beer. Boisterous comments and cat-calls passed between seated seamen and labourers and a few scroungers who moved from table to table trying to elicit a free drink. Prostitutes tried to catch the eye of a customer, quietly made offers of a night's entertainment, or laughed loudly at some lewd comment given in return.

One released herself from the arms of a drunk as Ed passed and said, 'He won't be any good tonight but thee'll do for me, big man.'

He pushed her away and she collapsed on to the knees of the drunk, who grabbed her thigh.

Ed ignored the curses thrown after him, thankful that he patronised the Seafarers' Arms where Dick would not tolerate the likes of that girl on his premises. He wondered why on earth Annie had taken up with Midge who encouraged prostitutes to ply their trade in the Golden Hind on condition that they paid him a slice of their takings. This really wasn't Annie's environment. She had respectability. Surely she couldn't have sunk into the morass of the underword in which Midge Whitley operated. The Annie he remembered was too level-headed for that unless Midge had got a hold over her. She was tough and uncompromising and pretty, but with a fire to match her red hair. Sometimes that could

146

be her undoing, and Ed knew that Midge Whitley was just the man to exploit it for his own ends.

He had almost reached the bar when he cast his glance to a corner of the room. He saw Midge engrossed in a card game with one opponent, and there was no mistaking the flaming hair of Annie who, with her back to him, was standing casually among the ring of spectators behind the card player facing Midge.

Ed's lips tightened. He knew the arrangement, one in which the Annie he remembered would have had no part. She was in the ideal position to see the stranger's hand and, with prearranged signals, transfer the information to Midge. It certainly looked as if Midge had got a hold over the girl he had once regarded as his. She needed rescuing before Whitley cast her into the pit of nonentity when she had served his purpose.

Ed pushed his way between two men until he was standing at her back. He eyed the game a moment, judged the situation, saw the stranger receive a card which changed his hand to a winning one provided his opponent had no knowledge of the new card. 'Hello, Annie.' He timed his greeting so she had no time to make her signal to Midge.

The shock of hearing someone who had had a special place in her heart, whom she thought was thousands of miles away, shattered her concentration. She swung round, her eyes widening with surprise and excitement. 'Ed!'

'Good to see you, Red.'

They heard a curse and, directing their gaze to the table, saw Midge, his face a mask of fury, throw down his cards and the stranger, with a smile of triumph, rake in his winnings. Midge's chagrin flooded his face with colour which deepened when he saw that the obstruction to his win had been perpetrated by Ed Berriman. He knew immediately that Ed had seen through his method of cheating and had deliberately timed his intervention to prevent Annie passing the vital information he needed. His eyes went cold with hatred.

Realising the game was over, the ring of spectators started to break up.

'Hello, Midge,' said Ed with a mocking smile. 'I'm taking Red out of this hole for good.'

'Oh, no you ain't.' Midge rose to his feet. He was a man of medium height with a tense air of authority, one which could command men with much more physical ability than himself. And they dare not cross him for they knew there lay behind his outward appearance a ruthless and sadistic streak which could bring them more than just trouble from those who would obey Midge without any conscience. 'You walked out on her once. She ain't yours any more.' His dark eyes burned with a warning which did not bode well for Ed.

'I'm taking her back.' He glanced at Annie. 'All right by you, sweetheart?'

She nodded.

'There you are, Midge. You ain't got any say in the matter.'

Midge tensed. His sign was almost imperceptible as he said, 'You're taking her nowhere. After what I've done for her she's staying.'

But Ed's attention was not held exclusively to this statement for he realised Midge's intention.

'Back door!' he hissed quietly close to Annie as he leaned slightly forward. He had noted that the way to that door was clear.

As Annie moved instantly at his bidding, he pushed hard at the card table, pinning Midge back against the wall. In the same movement he spun round and met the first of Midge's henchmen with a blow which sent him reeling backwards. He would have fallen but for the crowd. The second man was upon him but Ed brought his knee hard into the man's groin and with a cry of pain he doubled up. The first man launched himself at Ed who sidestepped and drove his fist hard into his assailant's face. He pitched forward across the table, which helped to hold a struggling Midge tighter.

Ed, prepared for another assault, took in the situation instantly, and, realising one was not coming, moved quickly after Annie who was already through the door. He found her tense and anxious. He did not stop but grabbed her hand and hurried down the alley to turn on to the street away from the Golden Hind to be lost in the thickening mist.

Annie had to take two paces to Ed's one to keep up with him. She did not know where they were going nor did she care. She hoped this was an escape from Midge's clutches which had been tightening around her with claustrophobic effect, except for one brief escape which had collapsed around her driving her back to a life at the Golden Hind which she had hoped to forget. Now with Ed's return she saw a rekindling of the light which she should never have extinguished by refusing his offer of a passage to America. But she knew that she should not be over-optimistic; Midge's influence throughout the low life of Hull was tentacle-like and could venture beyond it when he so desired.

They passed out of the old town and she was gasping for breath by the time Ed stopped outside a terraced house in Bourne Street. He flung open the door, bustled her inside and, after a quick glance along the street in both directions, followed her, slammed the door and bolted it. Annie, her body tense, her eyes still filled with disbelief at what had happened, leaned against the wall breathing deeply.

Ed straightened. Tension drained from him. He gave her a reassuring smile as he said, 'Relax, Annie, you're safe here.' He took her hand and led her down the short passage to a room at the back of the house. It was a small square room with a black range on an inside wall. A fire burned with little life in the grate. A small oak table occupied the opposite wall, a cupboard had been fitted in an alcove beside the fireplace. A wooden settle was positioned under the recess formed by the staircase, which turned from the hall and ran upwards to two bedrooms. A large sash window looked out on to a small yard with a door in a high brick wall giving access to an alley, beyond which was another row of identical houses. The room was furnished with two Windsor chairs, one on either side of the fireplace, and two wooden chairs at the table. Three clip rugs covered most of the flagstone floor.

'Not the greatest of places, Annie,' apologised Ed.

She looked at him with appreciation and admiration. 'It will do for me, Ed. Oh, it's so good to see you.' Her eyes were filling with tears.

He held out his arms and she sank her head against his chest feeling comfort and safety in his presence as he enfolded her with strength and tenderness. They stood like this for a few minutes, she hoping that this was the start of a new life for her but fearing there might be repercussions, he seeing the eighteen months he had been away fading as if they had never been. He had loved Annie then and he knew he still did.

He eased her gently away so that he could look into her eyes. 'You haven't changed,' he said.

She gave a wan smile. 'You are seeing what you want to see.'

He shook his head. 'I carried your image in my mind wherever I went and it is what I am seeing now.'

'I was a fool. I should have come with you, but I—'

He placed a finger on her lips. 'Don't say it. The past has gone, we've the future to think of.'

'And that means Midge,' she said with a tremor in her voice.

'He doesn't know where to find us.'

'He soon will. And you know him. He'll not stand by and let you take me from him. We'd better think of leaving Hull.'

'We'll not do that.' Ed put determination into his voice, trying to instil confidence in her. 'And I'll make him see that he has no right to you.' He noticed her locket and fingered it. 'Did he give you this?' He pulled

151

at it, tightening it at the back of her neck as if he would pull it free if she answered Yes. She shook her head.

'It's a pretty piece, skilfully made. Where did you get it?'

'That's another story, I'll tell you some time, but please not now.' Annie did not want to reveal the truth so soon after this reunion for fear of losing him again. She turned away, sank on to one of the chairs and diverted his attention away from the locket. 'Is this house yours?' she asked.

He went to the fire and started to poke life into it. 'No. I only got into Hull yesterday and was lucky to find this partially furnished house to let.' He straightened and looked down at her. 'Here I am and here I mean to stay.' He paused a moment then said, huskily, 'It's good to see you, Annie.' He bent forward and kissed her.

Emily sighed with frustration. She had visited ten dress-makers whom she knew or had been told were the best in Hull. None of them had ever had a client by the name of Mrs Ainslie. Wondering if she had used a false name, she posed the question, 'Have you ever delivered a dress to Westfold?' No one had.

It was in this discontented frame of mind that Emily met Thomas the following day when he called at Bramwell House.

'I know there are other dressmakers in Hull but these ten are the best. From the descriptions of Mrs Ainslie's dress by Mrs Featherstone and Mrs Hardcastle, slight though they were, I felt sure that her dresses had been made professionally and assumed one of those ten must have been her dressmaker.' As she was speaking a thoughtful look had come to her face. 'Maybe she made her own dresses.'

'In that case it's no good pursuing that line of enquiry any more,' said Thomas. 'Now let me brighten you up with my news.' He told her of his visit to the Seafarers' Arms and of following Ed to the Golden Hind.

At the beginning she expressed alarm for his safety, but he brushed it aside. When he had finished his story she reminded him, 'But this gets us no nearer finding Mrs Ainslie and that is the prime concern of the Laycock Detective Agency.'

'I know,' agreed Thomas. 'I still have this feeling that there could be a connection between that locket, the murder and the missing Mrs Ainslie.'

'Then I suppose you will be visiting the Golden Hind again?'

'This evening.'

'Thomas, is what wise?'

'It is the only way I'll find Annie to ask her about that locket.'

'Oh, do be careful. That is a very rough area.' There was worry not only in her voice but in her eyes also.

'I appreciate your concern, but risks are sometimes part of a detective's work. I saw that in America. I can take care of myself.'

'I know, but I should hate anything to happen to you.'

He fixed his eyes firmly on hers and she saw them express a wish for her not to worry. There was kindness and consideration and she saw something else, an interest

153

in her as a woman. She felt his fingers reach out to hers. She did not pull away but let her fingers respond to his.

'I will take great care, for I hope that I have more to come back to than my solitary life. May I say how much pleasure I am getting from having you help me with these enquiries.'

'It's my pleasure also,' she replied. 'And you need never think of a lonely life. You will always be most welcome at Bramwell House.'

'Thank you for those kind words, Emily.' His eyes had never left her and he leaned forward to kiss her on the lips. As their lips parted he looked down as if he had overstepped the bounds of decorum, 'I'm sorry I—'

She placed her fingers under his chin and gently eased his head upwards until their eyes met. 'Don't apologise, Thomas. If I judge you correctly that is not what you really mean. And I don't want an apology because I wanted you to do that and I want you to kiss me again.'

Their lips met and this time they lingered, sealing a bond which Emily hoped would deepen in the days ahead.

When Thomas left there was joy in Emily's heart, but a sense of frustration started to grow when the problem of finding Mrs Ainslie began to exert itself. She felt so hopeless. She wanted to do something to further Thomas's investigations. He was having the action and she wanted to play her part. She had an urge to try to push the enquiries forward for she wanted to show what she could really do before her father needed to know the results of Thomas's work.

She went over the facts they had uncovered so far, but they did not sign the way to Mrs Ainslie's whereabouts. Her mind turned to Thomas's theory that there might be a connection between her disappearance and her husband's murder.

There had been an attempt by someone to link the murder to a gambling debt which James owed to Jeremy Loftus. Could the clue to the false accusation have come from his establishment? It was a question she was to wrestle with for a couple of days before she elicited a possible course of action.

Thomas sensed antagonism when, after a couple of pints of ale in the Golden Hind, he casually enquired if anyone knew a redhead called Annie. He noted that while the barman, to whom he was speaking, kept the query open, another man made for a door at the end of the long counter. He saw him knock, pause and go inside. A few moments later a man of medium height, tough-looking with an air of authority, appeared.

'Who's asking for Annie Newmarch?' he growled.

'I am, if that's the redhead's surname,' replied Thomas.

'And what might thee want with her?' he asked, appraising the stranger who spoke with an American accent.

'To give her a message from a friend.'

'Who's the friend?'

'That's for Annie's ears.'

'I give her any messages.'

'Not this one.'

Midge's eyes narrowed. He did not like the attitude of this stranger. He was suspicious at the lack of real information he was receiving. Here was an American saying he had a message for Annie. Could it be from Ed Berriman? If so was Annie not with him? 'How do thee know Annie?'

'I don't know her. I was asked to pass a message on to her personally. I was told I would find her here with someone by the name of Midge Whitley. You're showing a lot of interest, is that you?'

'Aye. And whether Annie should see you or not is my decision.'

'Like hell,' snapped Thomas. 'It's her choice. So let me see her.'

'She ain't here.'

Thomas eyed him, doubting the veracity of that statement. Was this a ploy to get rid of him? Or was that the truth? 'I'll wait.'

'Thee'll have a long wait.'

'Why?'

'She walked out yesterday.' This seemed genuine.

'Where to?'

'I don't know. She left without a word.'

'Have you any idea?'

'None.'

Thomas felt perplexed. His mind was racing with possibilities. He had seen Ed enter the inn. If he had waited would he have seen him leave with Annie? He cursed himself for not thinking of that possibility and for expecting to find Annie still here.

He nodded. There was nothing more to be gained.

'Thanks,' he muttered, drained his tankard and left the Golden Hind. He walked a few yards down the street and stopped, casual in his attitude but with his attention on the door of the inn. A figure emerged, paused as if searching among the people on the street. Thomas moved into a steady walk and after a couple of hundred yards felt sure he was being followed. He tested out this idea three times in the next quarter of a mile, at the end of which he was certain he was right.

Midge had had him followed. Was he interested in him as a person? Thomas realised he must not let Midge discover his true identity – certainly not yet. Or had Annie really left the Golden Hind and was Midge hoping that Thomas might lead him to her? Whatever the reason he must lose his shadower. Thomas found that easy enough when he brought the skills he had learned in America into play.

But he returned to his house in Portland Place disappointed that he had not found Annie. He could only assume that she had left the Golden Hind with Ed, but he did not know where Ed lived. His only link was Dick at the Seafarers' Arms. But his next two visits there proved negative. Dick had not seen Ed. By his third visit he had become more friendly with Dick and told him of his visit to the Golden Hind. Dick expressed surprise when he was told that Annie was no longer with Midge Whitley. 'If Ed took Annie away from the Golden Hind, they had better be extremely careful,' he warned. 'Midge is not one to give up easily and he doesn't like being outsmarted. Annie would know that and may have persuaded Ed to leave Hull.'

157

'You look a bit doubtful about that suggestion,' Thomas commented.

'Well, Ed was never one to avoid trouble. He never looked for it but if it came his way he'd meet it head on. I don't think he'd leave Hull.'

'Do you know where he's living?'

Dick shook his head. 'No. He'd only just arrived in Hull the day before you met him.'

'So he could be in hiding for a while hoping that Midge will lose interest?'

There was a touch of derision in Dick's low laugh. 'Midge lose interest? Not likely. He needs to be seen to be top dog in order to keep the influence he wields among his own sort and the hangers-on who think he's God's gift to them. But Ed might deem it wise to keep out of sight for a while. However, he can't do that permanently.'

'Is he likely to come in here again?'

'I can't say for definite but I think it's highly likely. He was a regular customer before he went to America and he and I became good friends.' Although he thought Thomas likeable, a note of suspicion tinged his voice as he asked, 'Why do you want to see him?'

Throughout the conversation Thomas had been studying Dick. He had shrewd eyes used to seeing and absorbing, not just looking. His cheeks still showed the marks of wind and sun and Thomas judged he had once been a man of the sea who had given it up to serve the thirst of sailors. He had the sincerity of a man who could be trusted, so Thomas decided to take him into his confidence.

158

'First I must make a confession.' He dropped the American accent he had favoured for his forays into this area of Hull.

Dick started. 'Hi, where's the American accent?' he snapped, annoyed at the deception.

'Sorry about that. And I must tell you it isn't Ed I want to see, it's Annie. It was her I was looking for when I first came in here and by chance overheard that conversation between you and Ed when her name was mentioned. That night I followed Ed out of here so that I could locate the Golden Hind and know where it was in order to find Annie later, but when I returned there Midge said she had gone. He never mentioned Ed, but I calculated that she may have left with him.'

'That doesn't tell me why you want to see her nor why you adopted the disguise of an American seaman,' returned Dick, still with a hint of suspicion.

'The answer to your second question leads to the first. I wanted to hide my true identity when I came into this part of Hull. To pose as an American seemed a good idea. You see, I have spent some time in America with the Pinkerton National Detective Agency and on returning to Hull recently I set up my own agency.'

'A detective!' Dick was taken aback. Some of his customers, if they knew, would not take kindly to this. He controlled his reaction and asked, 'It's in that capacity that you are looking for Annie? What's she done?'

'She's done nothing wrong.' Thomas was quick to reassure him. 'I was asked to investigate a case and I think she might be able to help me.'

159

'And what case might that be?'

Thomas smiled. 'You can't expect me to tell you that. A client's wishes are strictly private.'

Dick noted that Thomas had not revealed that his employer was male or female and he admired him for his discretion.

'You're sure she's not in trouble?' Even as he put the question Dick held up his hands in apology, 'Sorry. You've already said she had done nothing wrong. I shouldn't have doubted you.'

'You have every right.'

'No, you've been open with me and I like folk who are that way.'

'Then I can ask you to let me know where she is if you find out?'

'Yes.' There was a promise in Dick's tone which Thomas knew he would not break.

'Can you tell me something about her?'

'She walked in here about three years ago. A young lass who looked lost, but there was a confident air about her and something which told me she wasn't from around these parts and that her background was a bit better than you find around here. I can tell you no more, for she never spoke about it even though I came to know her quite well. The first time she appeared a few heads turned. A pretty girl will do that, but that red hair was sure to attract attention. She was looking for lodgings and a job. Ed was in here at the time. I could see he was smitten by her. He heard what she wanted and was able to offer a room with his mother. She seized the chance and I could see she had quickly sized Ed up as someone

160

who was not merely taking advantage of her. She settled in well with them, went through a variety of jobs and was good company for Ed's mother when Ed was at sea. He switched from large merchantmen sailing the world to coastal ships so that he was home more often. I believe it was because of Annie. They came in here regularly when he was ashore.

'Then his mother died and about that time he got this offer which would take him trading along the American coast. It was too good to miss. He took the job and sold the house, expecting Annie to go with him, but she refused.'

'Do you know why?' asked Thomas as Dick paused.

'Only that she didn't want to leave England.'

'So what happened to her when he had gone?'

'She was devastated. Disappeared from my sight. Then I heard she had taken up with that louse Midge Whitley. I knew he'd be no good for her, he'd drag her down to his ways. Then I heard he was looking for her. It seemed she had disappeared again. I don't know why or where she was, but I'll tell you it was no secret that Midge was roaring mad.'

'But she came back to him?'

'Aye. One day out of the blue she walked back into the Golden Hind and has been there until now. She came to see me one day, cried her eyes out. I took it that it was for Ed but I have wondered if there had been someone else or whether it was for the life she knew before coming to Hull. I did not see her again, but I kept hearing talk of the life she was leading with Midge and I didn't like it, but it was out of my hands. I was glad to see Ed the other day and hoped it might mean a change for Annie.' He looked hard at Thomas and added, 'I hope that might be of help to you when you find her. Keep calling on me and I'll try to get some knowledge of her whereabouts.'

'Thanks. What you have told me has given me a picture and that will help when I meet her. I'd rather you said nothing about me being a detective nor about my enquiries.'

Chapter Nine

Emily hurried up the stairs to the first floor where, at this time of the morning, she knew the maid Meg would be tidying the bedrooms. Her father had gone to the office, and Sylvia was discussing the needs of the kitchen with the housekeeper and the cook, so Emily seized the opportunity to have a word with Meg without interruption.

She looked into her father's room but Meg was not there. She stepped lightly to the next door, her own room, and found Meg tidying the dressing table.

The maid looked round and was surprised to see Emily, for when the bedrooms were being attended to the family generally kept out of the way. She showed a little embarrassment as she bobbed a curtsy, grabbed her duster and in a fluster started for the door. 'Sorry, miss. I'll come back later.'

'It's all right, Meg,' said Emily gently, closing the door with an almost inaudible click. 'It's you I want a word with.'

'Oh, miss, have I done something wrong?' A troubled look clouded her face.

Emily's smile was reassuring as she tried to put the eighteen-year-old at ease. 'No, Meg, nothing is amiss. I just want to ask you something which might be of help to me.'

'Me? Able to help you?' Meg was curious, for she did not see how that was possible.

'Yes. Do you know anyone who works at Briar Manor, owned by Mr Loftus?'

Emily thought the immediate response was going to be a denial, but in Meg's slight hesitation and expression of "should I tell the truth?" she knew the real answer to be "yes".

'If you do, Meg, I really need to know. It is a matter of some importance.' Emily emphasised her words carefully.

The girl still hesitated. She looked nervously at Emily. She saw no rancour, only a desire to have any information she might be able to offer. If she denied knowing anyone who worked at Briar Manor she knew there would be no recriminations, but Miss Emily would be hurt that she had not helped. She liked Emily who was always ready to express her thanks and offer words of kindness and encouragement. Meg was happy working for the Thorntons and she did not want anything to ruin that. She looked down at the carpet and fidgeted with the duster.

'Well, Meg. I do believe you know someone who works for Mr Loftus,' prompted Emily.

Meg bit her lips and mumbled, 'Yes, miss.'

'Who?'

The maid raised her head and Emily saw that she was still having doubts about revealing the information. She knew she must encourage her. 'What you tell me could help me with an enquiry I am making. It is very important to me.

Meg wetted her lips, nodded and said reluctantly, 'It's my sister.'

Emily couldn't believe her luck, though there was still no certainty that she could capitalise on this information. 'Your sister?'

'Yes, miss,' Meg confirmed and, now that the information was in the open, her words flowed quickly to clarify the situation. 'Mum and Dad don't like her working there. They say it's no place for a good girl. But Patsy, my sister, says they've got the wrong idea, it's not a place like that. They know there is gambling but they believe other things happen.' Meg blushed as she added, 'You know what I mean, miss?'

'Yes.' Emily smiled to herself at the girl's discomfort.

'Well, Patsy refuses to leave. Mr Loftus looks after his staff and pays them well, though they do work until the early hours of the morning. Unfortunately Mum and Dad won't have her in the house, but I keep in touch with her for the sake of the family. We meet every Tuesday afternoon, my afternoon off as you know.'

'So you'll be meeting this afternoon?' Excitement gripped Emily.

'Yes, miss.'

'Where do you meet?'

'One of the grooms from Briar Manor comes into

Hull daily for supplies and on a Tuesday Patsy gets a lift with him. She has about three hours before he leaves the town. We meet in Mrs Jenkins's cake shop in Lowgate. We can get a cup of tea there and she doesn't mind how long we stay.'

'How do you get into Hull?'

'Walk, but more often than not I manage to get a lift from a carrier.'

'Well, Meg, if you'll take me to meet your sister this afternoon I'll take you by pony and trap.'

'You want to ask her about Briar Manor?'

'Just a few simple questions.'

'Oh, miss, I don't know. Mr Loftus's staff are not supposed to talk about it, especially who goes there. If they are found out they lose their job immediately.'

'I assure you that your sister will not get into trouble.'

Meg, trying hard to come to a decision, looked worried.

'Just let me meet her and let her decide if she should talk with me. She may not be able to tell me what I want to know.'

'In that case I can see no harm in you meeting her,' agreed Meg.

Emily felt an immediate relief. She had surmounted one barrier, the next would be convincing Patsy.

Emily viewed the cake shop with a critical eye. It was neat, tidy and spotlessly clean. The smell of new baked bread and the array of tempting cakes was enough to whet anyone's appetite. They passed into the room at the rear of the shop. It was well appointed with six

166

small round tables, covered in white tablecloths, at each of which were four square-backed chairs. Emily thought it an admirable enterprise to attract people in need of refreshments when about their shopping or business.

One table was occupied by a young couple. Meg indicated a corner where a young lady was sitting. 'My sister,' she whispered to Emily.

Emily saw that she was neatly dressed, a little more elegantly than Meg which seemed to indicate that Patsy had extra money to spend on her clothes. Her dress was dark blue, its plainness relieved by a lace collar and pink ribbon tied at the throat. She had removed her small bonnet, revealing straight dark brown hair parted in the middle and tied in a bun at the nape of her neck.

She looked surprised to see her sister accompanied by the younger Miss Thornton, whom she knew only by sight. She looked questioningly at Meg as she rose to her feet.

'Hello, Patsy.' Meg give her sister a quick kiss on the cheek. 'I've brought Miss Thornton because she wants a word with you.'

'Miss Thornton.' Patsy inclined her head respectfully, wondering what Meg's employer could want with her.

'Do sit down, both of you,' said Emily as she drew up a chair for herself. 'I'm sorry to intrude on your time with your sister, Patsy, but I believe you might be able to help me. First let me order some tea.'

Patsy eyed Meg quizzically as Emily signalled to a waitress who took her order for tea and cakes, but Meg shrugged her shoulders in a gesture of ignorance.

'Your sister tells me that you work at Briar Manor,' said Emily, her tone soft and casual.

'She had no right,' snapped Patsy, shooting a sharp look of annoyance at Meg.

'She only told me when I enquired if she knew anyone working there, so please don't blame her. I then asked her if she could arrange a meeting with you. She was reluctant and only agreed when I told her how important it was for me.'

Patsy gave a curt nod as if she accepted the explanation but only with some reservation. 'But what can you want with me?' she asked, a wary look in her eyes.

'I need to know something about one of Mr Loftus's customers.'

Patsy tensed. Her guard was up. 'It's more than my job's worth to talk about them.' She looked sharply at Meg. 'You know that. You shouldn't have agreed to this.'

'I didn't—' started Meg at the same time as Emily offered an explanation, 'Meg didn't know why I wanted to see you.'

An awkward silence came over them as tea was brought to the table and set for their convenience.

As soon as the waitress moved away, Emily took up her point before Patsy had time to intervene. 'Your sister did tell me that you might be reluctant to say anything about Briar Manor as Mr Loftus is such a considerate employer.'

'He is that. And I'm not about to risk losing my job!'

'You won't do that.' Emily was quick to reassure her but she saw doubt lingering in Patsy. 'What I need to know is of vital importance to an enquiry I am making.'

'I don't care how important it is – I ain't talking.' Patsy's firm tone was tinged with irritation.

'Have some tea,' said Emily gently, indicating the cup of tea which Meg had placed in front of her sister. She took up a plate of cakes and held them out to Patsy, who hesitated, as if she saw the offering as an attempt to persuade her to talk.

'Go on, sis, I know you like those with the icing,' Meg cajoled.

'Come on,' Emily encouraged with a smile, 'and then hear me out.'

Patsy took a cake and studied it carefully as if it could help her make up her mind. She looked up slowly and met Emily's watchful gaze. 'If I hear what thee has to say it don't mean I'll tell thee anything.'

Emily nodded. 'I know. If I tell you that the information I require may help to clear someone's name of a crime I don't believe they committed, would you be willing to answer my questions?'

Patsy was silent, a little on edge. She did not want to jeopardise her job, yet she didn't want to disappoint her sister whom she knew was trying to be helpful to a kind and respected employer.

Emily was about to speak again when she caught a signal from Meg to remain silent. Realising that Meg would know her sister's attitudes, Emily waited.

Patsy pulled a face covered in doubt. 'I dunno, miss.'

'Drink your tea and think about it,' suggested Emily.

Patsy said nothing. She bit at her cake and sipped her tea. Emily, who was silently urging Patsy to agree, nibbled at her cake without knowing what she was eating. Meg, who was neutral in this situation, was not going to give up the opportunity of having more than one cake.

'Another?' said Emily offering the cakes to Patsy.

'Why not?' she said amiably, seeing her sister having a second. On other occasions they could only afford one, so why not take the opportunity now when someone else was paying?

Emily hoped Patsy's attitude was a good sign.

Patsy looked thoughtful while she finished her second cake and then looked up at Emily. 'Tell me, miss, is it as vital as you say?'

'It is if you know the answers.'

'And if I don't?'

'Then I will have to look elsewhere.'

'Why come to me first?'

'Because at the moment I really don't know where else to go. Some information I had led me to think that Briar Manor might be the place to start, but I needed to know someone who worked there. When I asked your sister if she knew of anyone who did she mentioned you. I could not ignore the chance that you might be able to help me.'

'And it is really important for you to know?'

'It certainly is.'

Patsy had been studying Emily. She knew that Meg thought highly of the Misses Thornton, especially the younger one, and she liked what she had seen in these few minutes. Miss Emily was pleasant, not pushing but earnest in her conviction. She would like to help but if word got out that she had imparted information which she should have kept to herself, she would be in deep trouble.

She glanced round the room. No one else had come in and the young couple, their heads close together, were lost to the rest of the world in their conversation. 'What do you want to know?' she asked tentatively, her voice low.

'James Walton was a frequenter of Briar Manor. You would know him?'

'No, miss, I did not know him, but I knew which was him.'

Emily smiled to herself. The girl was sharp. She would have to be careful how she phrased her questions. She nodded. 'As you say. Now, he ran up a debt with Mr Loftus and because of it stood trial for murder.'

'Yes.' Alarm flickered for a moment in Patsy's eyes and Emily saw that as a sign that she knew more.

'Someone must have known about that debt. Do you know if Mr Walton made any enemies at Briar Manor?'

'Not that I know of, but how could I?'

'I suppose not,' agreed Emily. 'Would the staff know of his debt?'

'We know most things that go on but Mr Loftus trusts us not to divulge what we see and hear.' As she made this statement Patsy was reminded that she was near betraying a confidence. 'Maybe I should say no more.' She started to rise from her chair. 'Meg, we should leave.'

'Please, just a few more minutes,' said Emily. 'I assure you your name will be safe.'

Patsy hesitated.

'Sit down,' said Meg. She reached for the teapot, a gesture which Patsy read as meaning that her sister thought she should answer more questions from Miss Thornton.

She sat down slowly, her lips tightening in doubt.

'Thank you,' said Emily softly. 'Do you know if any of the staff might have talked about Mr Walton's debt to anyone outside Briar Manor? It was a considerable amount.'

Patsy did not answer. The words pounded deeper and deeper into her mind, thundering there with accusation, as if the questioner already knew the answer. Her mind burst with confusion which brought a heightening of her colour.

Emily, seeing the girl's face redden, knew the answer. 'You?' she whispered. 'You talked to someone.'

'Patsy!' Meg gasped at the significance. Her sister, indirectly, had been the cause of Mr Walton's trial and might even have been the cause of his hanging if Mr Loftus had not returned to Hull when he did and was able to cast doubt on Mr Walton's guilt.

Patsy stared unseeingly at her empty plate and nodded. No one spoke. She looked up slowly and met Emily's gaze, which sought more answers.

'Miss, I didn't know what it would lead to. I didn't know there would be murder.' She went on quickly hoping to exonerate herself. 'But I don't think Mr Walton did it, he's too nice a gentleman, though I have seen his temper flare sometimes, but generally when he has been annoyed with himself, but he wouldn't kill anyone.'

'Whoever you told – would they be capable of murder and trying to put the blame on Mr Walton?'

'Certainly not!' Patsy's voice rose with convincing indignation.

'You seem positive.'

'I am. She wouldn't do that.'

'She?'

Patsy gulped and her lips tightened as if she was annoyed with herself for letting slip something which she had intended to keep to herself.

'Who was it?' pressed Meg, deeming it was for her to put the question to her sister.

Patsy hesitated, poised on the brink of a revelation but not knowing whether she should make it.

'You've gone this far, sis, you might as well tell Miss Thornton who it was.'

Patsy wetted her lips as if to draw courage. 'Annie Newmarch,' she whispered.

For one split second Emily couldn't believe her ears, but then the significance of this information burst upon her. Annie! Annie knew of James's debt! She wore a locket belonging to James's mother. Had James given it to her? If so then they must have had a close relationship. Had Annie's presence every day at the trial been because of this? Or had she used the information to get back at James for something which had happened between them? Was she capable of arranging a murder to implicate James? There were so many questions pouring into Emily's excited mind. If only Thomas had been here. Now they really did need to find Annie!

'Who is Annie Newmarch?' Emily tried to keep the eagerness out of her voice.

'A friend of mine.'

'Why tell her?'

There was reluctance to answer in Patsy's hesitation, then she said, 'I don't think I should tell thee,' she mumbled. 'It's over and done with, finished. It doesn't matter any more. And it's best kept quiet now.'

'I think I should be the judge of that,' said Emily calmly, keeping friendliness in her tone. She recognised the delicacy of the moment; one harsh word, even a wrong word, could put a barrier between them. 'The reason you told Annie Newmarch might be vital to my enquiries.'

Patsy looked embarrassed, her eyes downcast as she fiddled with the handle of her teacup. Emily waited. She recognised that Patsy was trying to reach a decision. Once again she caught a warning in Meg's glance to say nothing.

Patsy ran her tongue round her lips and slowly lifted her eyes to Emily's. 'If you'll pardon me, miss, I don't think it's my decision to tell you. I think Annie should decide. After all it is her private affair.'

Emily nodded. 'I understand,' she said slowly, with disappointment mounting. 'If you won't tell me that then please just tell me why you revealed Mr Walton's debt to her?'

'A warning, miss.'

'Warning? Against Mr Walton?'

'I've said more than I should, miss.' Patsy stood up quickly. 'I must go. Goodbye, miss.' She walked from the room with a determined step.

'I must go after her, miss. I'll try and persuade her—'

Emily cut Meg's words short as she laid a hand on the girl's arm. 'Leave her, Meg. She'll say no more.'

Meg pondered a moment. 'Maybe thee's right.' She looked apologetically at Emily. 'I'm sorry my sister wasn't more helpful.'

'On the contrary, Meg, she has been most helpful. I have no doubt that what she has held back would have been more so but I respect her right to withhold it. Tell me, Meg, is this Annie a friend of yours?'

'No, miss. I know her through my sister but that is all.'

'Do you know where I might find her?'

Meg frowned. 'You don't want to know that, miss.'

'Why not? And I certainly do. After what your sister has said it becomes even more important that I talk to Annie. So if you know, tell me.'

Meg felt awkward. She wanted to defy her mistress, but at the same time she wanted to help her. 'It's no place for you to be going, miss.'

'I'll decide that.'

Meg pondered, then said. 'Very well. The last time I heard of Annie she was with a man called Midge Whitley, a right blackguard, miss, who owns the Golden Hind in an area of the old town where you shouldn't be going.'

Emily nodded. 'Thank you, Meg. That is a great help.' She was not going to let on that she knew this already. Meg was obviously unaware of Ed's return and the subsequent disappearance of Annie. But one thing was certain: Annie must be found.

175

Emily, eager to tell Thomas what she had learned, went to Portland Place, but was disappointed to find that Thomas was not at home. She left a note asking him to contact her as soon as possible. Her impatience was not alleviated until four o'clock that afternoon. As soon as he was announced she told the maid to show him in and to bring tea for two.

Thomas, who had been speculating about the reason behind Emily's urgent note, hurried into the room.

'Is something the matter?' he asked with concern as he took her hands in his. He searched her face, trying to deduce an explanation to his question.

Her placating smile allayed his immediate fears. 'No,' she replied calmly, 'but I thought you should know, as soon as possible, what I learned earlier this afternoon.'

He was all attention as they sat down and Emily started to tell him about the course of action she had taken. 'Your theory that Mrs Ainslie's disappearance could be linked to her husband's murder set me thinking. The murder supposedly arose from James's debt to Jeremy Loftus, so I wondered if the accusation had come from someone at Briar Manor or someone who visited that establishment, and if that information would give us a lead of some sort to help us discover Mrs Ainslie or Annie.' She paused when the maid brought the tea and then, while they enjoyed scones and cakes, she imparted the information she had gleaned from Patsy.

When she had finished her story she added with regret, 'I'm sorry we've gained no more about their whereabouts.'

176

'Don't worry about that,' replied Thomas confidently. 'This is important information. It links Annie more strongly into the mystery and I feel sure we'll discover a connection when we find her. I wonder why Patsy revealed James's debt to her?' He leaned forward and grasped Emily's hands. She did not resist his touch and felt a thrill when he squeezed them as he added, 'You've done so well and shown initiative. You'll be a fine asset to our detective agency.'

His use of the word 'our' did not escape her and she saw that his smile of appreciation was also one of admiration. The light in his eyes gave her joy and she felt that working together towards the same end was bringing them closer on a personal level.

'I wish I could have gleaned more but I had to respect Patsy's point that any further information should come from Annie.'

'Quite right,' agreed Thomas. 'We must find her. I'm sure she's with Ed. They can't stay hidden forever. I'll keep visiting Dick, he's the most likely one Ed will contact.'

'Thomas, you must be careful. No doubt Midge will be on the lookout for them. From what you told me he's not a man who takes easily to being outdone.'

'I know. But don't worry. I'll be all right. Now, we can't just sit back until we find Annie, so I propose that tomorrow we visit Riplingham Hall and question Mrs Ainslie's ex-groom. Will it suit you if I call for you at ten o'clock?'

'I'll be ready,' replied Emily eagerly. 'Let's hope he can tell us something. Father is beginning to ask questions about your progress towards finding Mrs Ainslie.'

The ride was enjoyable, with Thomas handling the horse with an expertise she admired. His conversation drew responses from her as he swung through a variety of topics. She recognised it as an attempt to let each of them get to know the other better. He kept away from the investigation on which they were engaged and she realised he was wanting to make this outing pleasurable along with its professional connotations. Her attraction to him when they first met had deepened during subsequent meetings and now she found herself having to admit that her admiration for him was turning into something much stronger.

A remark he had made the previous day had haunted her during the night and when she was getting ready to accompany him to Riplingham Hall she made up her mind to ask him what lay behind his words. Now she hesitated, fearing that his answer might not be the one she wanted.

Their chatter died into a silence, which only two people who feel close can share. There was no need for words. Their two spirits were locked in a common bond. The clop of hoofs and the creak of the trap did not intrude on the empathy between them.

Shortly after leaving the main highway, Thomas brought the horse to a halt. He shifted on the seat so that he was facing her.

'Emily, yesterday I used the words "our agency".' There was a slight hesitancy as if he was making a quick

178

search for a way to express the real meaning behind them. Emily, her gaze intent on him, remained silent. She did not want to break the spell. 'It implied that I hope we will continue to work together, but I meant more than that. I hope it conveys that I have very deep feelings for you and that I nurture a hope that our friendship will develop into something much, much stronger.' As he was speaking he had taken her hands in his and he drew confidence from the fact that she did not resist his hold. There was a wistful, searching look in his eyes and the expression on his face not only spoke of love but also a desire for her to feel the same.

Emily met his gaze. 'Thomas.' Her voice, quiet, sultry, caressed him. 'I'm sure I'm in love with you.'

Before she could say any more he swept her into his arms. 'And I love you.' His lips met hers, gently.

Her heart soared. She responded to his kiss. Her whole being thrilled at the excited tension which surged through her. Her pulse raced at his touch as his arms, strong, protective, held her tight. She felt almost over-whelmed by the love which surged between them as his kiss lengthened with a passionate desire.

'Emily, Emily, I love you so much,' he gasped as their lips parted.

'And I you,' she returned huskily. 'Dear, sweet Thomas, how grateful I am that you came into my life.'

'And I hope it's there that I shall remain.'

A little caution raised itself in Emily. 'I hope so too, but,' she went on quickly stopping the words which she saw coming to his lips, 'we have not been friends for very long. There are sides of me that you do not know.'

'Whatever they are they will be of your sweet nature so can't be bad.'

'Don't be blinded by seeing what you want to see. Let us get to know each other better and what better way than working together to find Mrs Ainslie? That is if you want me to go on helping?'

'Of course I do, but as a partner, not a helper.'

She smiled. 'Thank you for that confidence.'

'We'll make a good team.' He kissed her again.

Though she wanted to linger in these cherished moments, the purpose of their outing thrust itself upon her. 'Maybe we should be getting to Riplingham Hall,' she said reluctantly.

'I'd like nothing better than to stay here for ever, but I suppose you are right.' He leaned forward and kissed her again.

She held his kiss when he would have broken it and in that gesture he saw that all his hopes for the future might materialise.

Ten minutes later Thomas turned the trap into a long drive lined with oak trees. He had already noted the healthy-looking cattle feeding on lush grass amidst well-kept parkland dotted with chestnuts and more oaks.

'Mr Sleightholme appears to be a man who knows his farming and who is prepared to put his profits to good use.' His latter observation was aimed at the well-kept hedges which showed the use of plenty of trained employees, and of the immaculate condition of the farm buildings and of the house which, though not pretentious in size, was of such proportions that it indicated it had been built for someone with a family who enjoyed their comfort and were prepared to entertain friends.

'You're a shrewd judge,' returned Emily. 'Mr Sleightholme is indeed a successful farmer. He inherited the estate from his father who followed his own father. He was not content to benefit solely from their hard work. He developed a fine herd of cattle, and drained some poor land to grow more crops. He also redesigned the house, making it much more comfortable and homely even though he added two wings during the renovation.'

The house had come into full view as Emily had been speaking.

'Whoever the builders were they have done a good job of matching the original stonework.'

'Mr Sleightholme was very particular about that.'

'As he is about the gardens,' added Thomas, noting the well-kept lawns and the formal rose and herb gardens which were being attended to by four gardeners.

Thomas pulled the horse to a halt in front of the house, helped Emily from the trap and gently supported her elbow as he escorted her up the five steps on to the terrace, which ran the full width of the house, and then up three more to the front door. He tugged hard at the metal bell-pull and a few moments later the door was opened by a young maid neatly dressed in black with a small white apron tied around her waist.

'Miss Emily Thornton and Mr Thomas Laycock would like to see Mr Sleightholme if he is at home.'

'Please step inside. I know Mr Sleightholme will be going out soon but I'll see if he has time to see you.'

181

Within a matter of seconds of the maid's leaving them a red-faced portly man hurried into the hall.

'My dear Miss Thornton, it is a pleasure to see you.' He took her hand and bowed politely. 'And this young man?' he added as he straightened and turned to Thomas, who knew he had come under close but friendly scrutiny as he waited for Emily to make the introduction.

Thomas had been making his own assessment and judged Mr Sleightholme to be a man who loved good living, whose rounded cheeks and twinkle in his eyes spoke of a man of good humour. Behind that Thomas saw a sharpness that would be difficult to outmanoeuvre.

'Mr Sleightholme, this is Mr Thomas Laycock. Thomas, this is the gentleman of whom I was speaking.'

'Flatteringly I hope, my dear.' He beamed, showing a row of bright white teeth, as he shook Thomas's hand.

'Nothing else, sir,' returned Thomas. 'Her words about you were all that were good.'

'Your father's not with you?' Mr Sleightholme turned to Emily again. 'I hope he is not indisposed?'

'No,' she replied. 'He's in remarkably good health.'

'Then I take this is a social call and not business?' Mr Sleightholme turned to a door on the right of the hall and led the way into an elegantly furnished and comfortable drawing room.

'We seek your help,' said Emily.

'Indeed?' He inclined his head in surprise. 'And how am I able to do that?' He indicated chairs to his visitors.

As she sat down Emily continued, 'I had better

182

explain that Thomas is newly arrived in Hull to establish his own detective agency.'

'Detective agency?' His raised eyebrows added to his surprised expression. 'Now that is something different for Hull.'

'I'd better let Thomas explain,' Emily concluded.

'I spent some time with the Pinkerton National Detective Agency in America. When I realised I couldn't settle there I decided to return to my native Yorkshire.'

'No place like it, my boy. You chose wisely.'

'I thought Hull might be a likely place to follow my profession. I met Simon Sutcliffe who was helpful and also introduced me to Mr Thornton.'

'And he has employed you on some investigation?'

'Yes, sir.'

'If this involves me I cannot for the life of me think how?'

'You are not involved directly, sir, but I need your permission to interview one of your employees here and now.'

'Has one of them been up to no good?' Mr Sleightholme expressed annoyance at the thought that he might be harbouring a rogue. 'Give me a name and I'll drum him out of here.'

'No, sir, that's not the case. We are trying to trace Mrs Ainslie, the widow of Captain Ainslie, and would like to talk to her ex-groom.'

Mr Sleightholme looked serious. 'A very sad affair. Robert Walsh came to me when Mrs Ainslie closed the house. She had given him good references. An excellent man. I couldn't wish for a better groom.' He stood up.

'Certainly, talk to him. I hope he can be of help. I'll take you to him now. No doubt he'll have my horse and trap ready. You just caught me before I left for Market Weighton on business.'

'Thank you, sir. You are most kind.'

'Not at all. I've done nothing. I hope your visit will be of help.' He turned to Emily. 'Give your father my best wishes and tell him I'll call on him next week. Wednesday afternoon. I'll be in Hull and there are some transactions I'd like to discuss with him.'

'Very well,' Emily smiled. 'Apart from business, I know he'd love a chat.

On their way across the hall Mr Sleightholme collected his overcoat, hat, stick and leather document case. As he led the way to the stables Thomas noted how neat and tidy everything was. The stableyard had been recently swept and two young men were busy cleaning out some stables. A third, an older man, was meticulously brushing down a handsome chestnut. Hitched to a post, a horse stood quietly between the shafts of a black-painted trap.

'Ah, Robert, all ready for me?'

'Yes, sir.' The man's words were crisp. He left the horse he was brushing and stepped smartly towards his employer. His own appearance was one of neatness, of a man who cared how he looked even when working. There was hardly a hint of an unwanted mark on his dark blue shirt and sand-coloured jodhpurs. His calf-length black boots were highly polished, and a yellow cravat was tied neatly at his throat. Thomas judged him as a man who would not want to let his employer down.

'Robert,' Mr Sleightholme continued, 'these two good people, Miss Thornton and Mr Laycock, would like to have a few words with you.'

'Miss.' Robert touched his forehead with his right forefinger. 'Sir.' He glanced at Thomas.

'They sought my permission to approach you and have given me a hint of what it is about so I agreed they could speak to you.'

'Very good, sir.' He turned to Emily and Thomas. 'If you'll excuse me for a moment, I'll just see Mr Sleightholme away.'

'Certainly,' agreed Thomas in an amiable tone.

Mr Sleightholme said goodbye and followed Robert to the trap.

'Let's hope Robert can help us,' whispered Emily. 'If Mr Sleightholme is going to see Father next week he's sure to mention our visit here. We must have some information before then.'

Robert watched the trap until it had left the stable-yard and then returned to Emily and Thomas.

'It's a pleasant morning, may I suggest we sit outside? There are some chairs under an oak.'

'A good idea,' agreed Thomas.

'And you, miss?' Robert inclined his head enquiringly.

'I will enjoy the fresh air,' she smiled. She had taken a liking to this open-faced man whose features spoke of an outdoor life. His blue eyes were alert, but at this moment showed some caution and curiosity.

Robert led the way outside and left the path to cross the grass to a huge oak tree underneath which were several wooden chairs. 'I like to spend time out here when I can,' he commented. 'It is a pleasant view.'

'Indeed it is,' agreed Emily, taking in the panorama of fields and woodland sloping gently southwards towards the distant Humber with views across the water to Lincolnshire.

When they were seated, Robert turned his gaze on his two visitors. 'I am curious. What can I do for you?'

Thomas made the explanation. 'I had better tell you that I am a detective – no, not the police,' he added quickly to reassure Robert that he and Emily were not here as the result of some law-breaking. 'We are making some private enquiries for Miss Thornton's father, who is an attorney, and you might be able to help us.'

'Me?' Robert gave a puzzled frown.

'Yes. Before you came to your position here as groom you served in that capacity with Mrs Ainslie, the wife of the late Captain Ainslie.' Robert gave a little nod of verification though he knew it wasn't really necessary. 'It is of the utmost importance to her for Mr Thornton to get in touch with her as soon as possible. We wonder if you might know where she is?'

Robert shook his head slowly. 'I'm sorry, I have no idea.'

Emily had noticed a wary look flick across Robert's eyes at the mention of Mrs Ainslie. 'Her house, Westfold, is all shut up, giving the appearance that she does not intend to return. Do you know if that is so?' she asked.

'No, I don't.'

'But you have left her employ with good references, I

hear. Do you not think that is a sign that she won't return?'

'I don't know, miss.'

Thomas frowned. The man was not very forthcoming. Answers were going to have to be coaxed from him. 'Matt is keeping the garden tidy; do you think that might mean she is coming back?'

'I don't know.'

'Maybe she intends selling the property?' suggested Emily.

'Mrs Ainslie never confided in me, miss, I was only her groom.'

'And well thought of I understand,' put in Thomas. 'As groom you would probably drive her to various destinations?'

Robert replied hesitantly. 'Ye...s, but she only left Westfold occasionally.'

Emily had the feeling that it might have been more often than he was appearing to admit.

'Where did you take her?' pressed Thomas.

Robert stiffened a little. He still felt loyalty to his late employer and he did not like the way the questions were shaping. 'I don't think I am at liberty to disclose that, sir. After all, whatever the visits, they were Mrs Ainslie's private affair.'

'Robert,' said Emily gently but with emphasis, 'it is very important that we contact Mrs Ainslie quickly. She has much to gain. Any information, no matter how trivial it may seem, could help us. We must locate her. Did you take her to friends in Hull?'

'No, miss. Those times were for her to do some

shopping. As soon as that was done we would return to Westfold.'

'And she spent no time with anyone other than the shopkeepers?'

'That is so.'

Emily was wary of this answer. She had a feeling that Robert was holding something back. 'Did you drive her anywhere else, maybe outside of Hull?'

'Oh, I would sometimes take her into the country or by the river so that she could have a walk and enjoy the fresh air.'

The answer came a little too glibly for Emily's liking and she sensed he had seized on a chance to explain away something he was not prepared to divulge. 'Did she meet anyone on those occasions?'

'No, miss.'

Again Emily thought the reply came a little too quickly. It was as if Robert wanted to get this line of questioning out of the way.

When Thomas moved in with a question she sensed that he had got the same impression as herself and that he deemed it wise not to press this line of enquiry for fear of making Robert too cautious and quietening him altogether.

'Do you know where Mrs Ainslie came from?' he asked.

Robert felt some relief that the questioning had taken another tack. 'No.'

'Nor where Captain Ainslie met her?'

'No. I was engaged after Captain Ainslie returned to Hull with his bride, as were all the staff.'

'Were they local people?'

'No. Only Matt and I were from local parts. The rest were from London.'

'And no doubt returned there when Mrs Ainslie left?'

'Yes.'

'So we are not likely to trace them quickly?'

'I'm afraid not, sir. But they would know nothing of Mrs Ainslie's whereabouts.'

'Robert,' Emily put in quietly, thoughtfulness in her tone, 'Mrs Ainslie would require to be taken somewhere when she left and no doubt you would take her. Where was that?'

Robert gave a half-smile. 'You are shrewd, miss. Yes, I did take her somewhere when she left but I do not know where she went.'

Emily looked puzzled. 'What do you mean?'

'Well, miss, I took her to the station. That is all I know. I do not know where she was going.'

Emily looked a little crestfallen. It seemed the possibility of learning something of importance had been snatched from them. But with Thomas's next question she realised that he still had a glimmer of hope that something could be salvaged from what she had viewed as a dead end.

'What time of day was that?'

'Two o'clock,' replied Robert automatically. Then, realising that he should not have disclosed that information, he added, 'But that won't help you. You may be able to check which train was leaving near that time but remember you can change trains and reach many destinations.'

189

'I am well aware of that,' replied Thomas. 'Did anyone meet her at the station?'

'No.'

Emily decided that maybe a different approach was merited at this point and that names should be mentioned. 'Did you ever hear her mention Mr James Walton, the man who stood trial for the murder of her husband and was acquitted?' When she saw Robert hesitate over his reply she added quickly. 'This may have a bearing on the reason my father wants to contact Mrs Ainslie and it is important that he gets any help possible, no matter how slender. If you know anything at all please help us. In doing so you will be helping her.'

Both Emily and Thomas sensed an uneasiness come to Robert. Then he said slowly, 'I never heard her talk about him nor about the murder. She was very distraught about the whole affair.'

'Did she know Mr Walton personally?'

Robert shook his head. 'Not that I am aware of.'

'You told us you sometimes drove Mrs Ainslie out of Hull.'

'Yes, so she could take the air and some exercise.'

'And she met no one?'

'Not that I am aware of.'

'You were with her all the time?'

'Of course not. I respected her need for privacy.'

'So she could have met someone, and you wouldn't know?'

Robert looked doubtful but then had to admit somewhat reluctantly, 'I suppose so.'

Emily, who was expecting Thomas to continue this line of questioning, was astounded when he drew the visit sharply to a close. He stood up. 'Thank you, Robert, for your time. You have been most helpful.'

Taken aback, Robert said, 'I don't see how.'

'Oh, but you have,' smiled Thomas. 'Don't you think so, Miss Thornton?'

Emily hid her surprise at the question and answered readily, 'Yes. Certain facts have emerged which I am sure will be helpful.'

Once the horse was trotting briskly down the drive Emily revealed her doubts. 'Do you really think we gained much from that interview?'

'You are pessimistic?' Thomas gave a wry smile. 'I thought you questioned brilliantly and I surmised that you thought we were gaining valuable information.'

'Oh come, Thomas, what did we really glean?'

'Well, we know that Mrs Ainslie left Hull by train about two o'clock. I suggest we go to the station and find out where that train was going and therefore where the good lady might be heading.'

'But that could be anywhere.'

'Let's wait and see what we learn at the station. It might narrow our area of search.' He paused thoughtfully then added, 'You know I'm not at all sure that we got the full truth about Mrs Ainslie's trips outside Hull. I don't think Robert was telling us everything.'

'You suspect she was meeting someone?'

'It is a possibility.'

'And he was a bit wary when talking about James.'

'You noticed that too?'

'It was feeling I got. You don't think she was meeting James?'

'Again, anything is possible, but so far we have no real connection between the two.' Thomas gave a little shake of his head. 'If only we knew where she came from.'

His words sparked off an idea in Emily's mind. Her eyes brightened as she put it to him. 'The shipping firm for whom Captain Ainslie worked should have a record of his voyages. If we could get a look at the one when he brought his bride to Hull—'

'It might indicate when she came aboard,' Thomas finished excitedly. 'Link that to the possible places she could reach by the train on which she left and presuming she has now returned to her origins—'

'We might find her!' completed Emily, grabbing his arm in her enthusiasm. 'We did do well coming out here.'

'In more ways than one,' smiled Thomas knowingly, and turned to kiss her on her lips.

'This has been a good day,' she agreed after she had returned his kiss, sealing more strongly the bond which was growing between them.

'And now,' he said, 'we have some more enquiries to make, and the sooner the better.' He urged the horse faster. 'We need some answers for your father before he learns of our visit to Riplingham Hall from Mr Sleightholme.'

Chapter Ten

On reaching the outskirts of Hull Thomas kept the horse to a brisk pace, drawing glances of admiration for the animal and its handler from some, while others showed disapproval of the speed. He slowed as they neared the station and entered the forecourt at a walking pace.

He helped Emily down, tossed a coin to two eleven-year-olds eager to provide a service of looking after the horse and trap, and escorted her to the booking office.

Enquiries soon elicited the information that someone, arriving at the station just before two on the day of Mrs Ainslie's departure, would most likely have left on the train for Selby as there was not another leaving for an hour and a half and that would be going to Bridlington. They also learned that the Selby train had several stops between the two towns and that it was timed to reach Selby to connect with two trains arriving at that station five minutes after the train from Hull. One was heading south to London and the other north to Newcastle. There were connections for other places provided the passenger did not mind waiting.

'So she could have gone anywhere,' commented Emily somewhat despondently as they left the station.

'True,' agreed Thomas, 'but I think it most likely that she caught one of those two trains.'

'That still leaves her with a lot of options.'

'I think we may be able to narrow those down.'

'How?'

'Come on, you'll see.' He took her hand and guided her to their trap.

Ten minutes later they were being shown into the office of Henry Smith in the premises of bankers Smith and Thompson in High Street.

'Good day, sir,' said Thomas brightly as he came towards the desk behind which Henry Smith was rising from his chair.

'And to you, sir.' The manager extended his hand which Thomas took firmly. 'My clerk said, Mr Laycock. I haven't had the pleasure. Nor have I had the delight of meeting you, Miss Thornton.' He turned towards her and bowed graciously. 'But I do know of your father through his impeccable credentials.'

Emily smiled as she inclined her head acknowledging his compliment. 'A pleasure to meet you too, Mr Smith.'

'Please do sit down.' He indicated two chairs, and returned to his own behind the desk. 'Now, what can I do for you?' he asked, interlacing his fingers as he rested his hands on his desk.

Thomas knew he had come under the close attention of a man who had developed the art of judging quickly customers who sought favours from the bank or made propositions in which they expected the bank to be interested. He, for his part, had judged the manager to be perspicacious, a man who would listen, making assessments as he went along and then, a decision made, would stick firmly to it. Any deal made with a customer would always be to the benefit of the bank, though the client or partner in any joint venture would not lose out.

'Well, sir, I'm making enquiries on behalf of Miss Thornton's father,' said Thomas, 'trying to ascertain the whereabouts of Mrs Ainslie, Captain Ainslie's widow. I believe that he worked closely with the bank in trading ventures. Therefore, I wondered if you had any knowledge of what happened to Mrs Ainslie after she left Hull. Mr Thornton has some important news for her and it is imperative that he should get in touch with her as soon as possible.'

Henry Smith gave a half-smile and a little shake of his head. 'I wish I knew, Mr Laycock. There are a number of matters which I need to clear up with her and several documents to be signed.'

'I understand she was a very reclusive lady. Did you have any contact with her after her husband's unfortunate death?'

'None. As a matter of fact I only ever once met the lady. That was when Captain Ainslie brought her here to legalise some transactions which would become effective in the case of his death. I have tried to contact her through Captain Ainslie's attorney, but even he does not know where she is. We are both anxious to be in touch with her in order to clear up the captain's estate.'

'Would I be right in thinking that Mrs Ainslie was not left impoverished?'

Henry Smith laughed as he sank back in his chair. 'Mr Laycock, Miss Thornton, you both know that I am not at liberty to disclose private matters unless it is essential in the course of justice, but I can say that Mrs Ainslie is well cared for.'

'Surely she has been in need of money and she must have drawn from the bank and therefore that could give you a clue as to where she is?'

The manager spread his hands in a gesture of despair. 'Alas, she has made no transactions since her husband died.'

'Which means,' put in Emily thoughtfully, 'that she either has a source of income elsewhere or is supporting herself by some other means.'

'Work, you mean?'

'Yes. Or an investment that was not made through your bank.'

Henry nodded. 'Both are possibilities. The investment I doubt. Captain Ainslie always gave me the impression that he dealt nowhere else but here.'

'Suppose she had money in her own right?' suggested Emily.

'Hardly likely, Miss Thornton. Captain Ainslie gave me to understand that she had nothing when he met her. She was of reasonably good stock, but the family had hit hard times and when he met her she had nothing and no one. He did not want her ever to be in that position again and, through me, he drew up the necessary provisions so that that would never happen. But I do need to discover her whereabouts to clear up some investments.'

'Obviously from what you have just said, Captain Ainslie talked to you about her. Did he ever say where he had met her?' asked Thomas.

'No. He was a very private man. He would never discuss anything personal. Every conversation here was channelled on business. I have known him many years, but I never knew him. I am afraid I'm not being of much help, nor will you find out any more from his attorney; he and I have an agreement that whoever hears anything will immediately inform the other. Now, Mr Laycock, I hope we can come to the same arrangement?'

'Certainly,' agreed Thomas. 'It is in both our interests and I believe we both have the lady's welfare at heart.'

'Good. I suppose I can always contact you through Miss Thornton.'

'Yes, but I will also give you my home address: 7 Portland Place.'

'Excellent.'

'It might help if we could trace Mrs Ainslie's origins. As you and the captain were partners in a trading enterprise, would you have the details of his voyages?'

'Of course. We have a summary of every voyage listing the ports of call and we also keep the relevant log books.'

'Would it be possible for us to see those relating to the voyage undertaken by the captain when he returned to Hull with his bride?'

'Certainly.' He rose from his chair. 'Excuse me a moment.' He left the office to return to tell them the clerk would have the necessary items in a few minutes.

Perusal of the summary showed that the voyage had been to Spain for a consignment of wine and that on return to England the ship had called at London, Newcastle and Middlesbrough before returning to its home port of Hull.

Seeing those names Emily immediately linked them with her knowledge of the train Mrs Ainslie had apparently caught from Hull, a train which could have resulted in a journey north or south. She hoped that Captain Ainslie had put more detail in the log book through which Thomas was searching.

'Was that a usual voyage for the *Fauconberg*?' she asked Mr Smith.

'No. It was rare that Captain Ainslie did not bring the full cargo to Hull from where it would be distributed. He had called at London before, but Newcastle and the comparatively new town of Middlesbrough had never been included before. He suggested it this time because of the quantity of the order placed by merchants in both those places. He thought it would save time, but after this experiment he was not in favour of doing it again. He reckoned he could do more good by getting off on another trading voyage and letting coastal vessels distribute the cargo when necessary.'

'Had he mentioned meeting Mrs Ainslie before this voyage?' she asked.

'No, but he may well have done. As I said he was a very private person.' A thoughtful look had come to his face as he was speaking. 'Although – and this is only an impression for what it is worth – I got the feeling that this was the first time he had met her.'

'Interesting,' said Emily with a nod. She turned to Thomas. 'Any reference to Mrs Ainslie and his marriage in the log book?'

Thomas shook his head. 'I can't see anything.' He looked up at Mr Smith. 'I thought a captain was supposed to log everything that happened on a voyage?'

'That is true,' agreed Mr Smith.

'And from what I see Captain Ainslie was very meticulous about it, yet there is no mention even of Mrs Ainslie coming aboard.'

'Then it seems he wanted to forgo that for the sake of privacy.'

Thomas nodded, closed the book, placed it on the desk and thanked Mr Smith for his time and trouble. 'I hope one of us will have some news before too long, as my time to find her is getting short.'

'You have a time limit?'

'Yes. I'm sorry I am not at liberty to divulge why at this stage of my inquiries.'

Henry raised his hands as if to stop any more information. 'I understand.'

The two men stood up and shook hands. Mr Smith made his goodbye to Emily and she and Thomas left the premises.

'Well?' she prompted, eager to know Thomas's conclusions as they walked along High Street.

'London, Newcastle or Middlesbrough,' he said. 'You can take your pick.'

'Or even Spain,' returned Emily.

Thomas nodded and repeated her words then added, 'But I think that is the place we should look only as a last resort.'

'I agree. I think it more likely to be one of the others and she could have reached any of them conveniently by the train she took.'

They went on discussing the relevant facts, unaware that a small stocky man, his clothes a little worn, had crossed the street and was close behind them. His head was half-turned as if he was trying to catch their words with his left ear. His ferret-like eyes kept darting at Thomas, appearing to be trying to verify an identification which had flashed in his mind when he had seen Thomas from across the street.

He followed them down Church Lane and into Bowlalley Lane where he walked past them when they paused outside the Thornton office. He continued a little way before stopping on the pretext of fastening his shoe. Looking back he saw them part and the young lady enter the building. The young man was his main concern and when he saw him start in his direction he straightened and continued his walk at a pace which would enable Thomas to pass him. Thereafter, keeping at a discreet distance, he eventually saw Thomas enter the Curzon Club in Whitefriargate. All the while he kept having doubts about the conclusion he had reached regarding Thomas's identity, but then he would dismiss them and convince himself that he was right.

Now, settled in his mind, a tremor of excitement ran through him. He rubbed his hands together, gleefully anticipating passing his news to Midge Whitley. He had always wanted to win Midge's favour from which could come an easier life than humping ships' cargoes. He had frequented the Golden Hind for some time but had only

200

been on the periphery of Midge's cronies. Now he hoped the information he had would make him one of his trusted aides.

His short muscular legs carried him quickly through the streets to the Golden Hind.

'Shorty,' the barman acknowledged him without any enthusiasm. 'Usual?' He was used to Shorty Marsden's visits, and held in contempt his attempts to curry Midge Whitley's favour. Secretly Midge had had Marsden's background checked.

He had learned that he was a Hull man born into poverty in the unsavoury streets of the old town. He had risen only a little above them through not being afraid of hard work, but now saw Midge as a possible escape from that and the drudgery that went with it. But he had also learned that Shorty had a nimble brain and an alert mind, that even in his casual attitude he was absorbing information from people and the situations around him and that he was not averse to reaching conclusions, which were often right.

'Usual? Nay. Might have something a bit stronger as a celebration.' His grin, at the barman's questioning look, revealed a row of broken teeth. 'Is Midge in?'

'Aye.' His voice was clipped.

'Can I see him? I have some information which I don't think he'll want to miss.' He gave him a knowing wink.

The barman made no comment but went through a door behind the bar. When he reappeared a few moments later he still did not speak but, with an inclination of his head, indicated that Shorty was to follow him.

Shorty scuttled round the end of the counter and tagged along behind the barman down a passage to the second door on the left. The barman knocked, hesitated, then opened the door and gestured to Shorty to step inside.

Shorty found himself in a square room, the light coming from two windows on the right though even that was fighting against the grime for admission. Two oil lamps helped to illuminate the room and the dancing flames of a bright fire aided the light as well as providing warmth. Several easy chairs were spread around the room, two of which were occupied by men whom Shorty recognised as Midge's closest henchmen. One was honing the edge of a vicious-looking knife with tender care, the other had his head in a newspaper and did not drag his attention from it when Shorty came in. He knew they had a low opinion of him but they would soon change their attitude. Midge would see to that once he had absorbed his news.

Behind a desk, placed across one corner, Midge was examining a sheet of paper full of figures. He looked up and eyed Shorty as he crossed the room in a subservient shuffle. Midge flicked a finger towards a chair facing him across the desk. Shorty slid on to it.

'Well, what information have you that you think I'd be interested in?' The voice was harsh with contempt and indicated a doubt that Shorty would have anything which would be of interest.

'You know me, Mr Whitley, I wouldn't waste your time if it wasn't something you'd want to know.' Shorty made his voice subservient but nevertheless imparted the impression that he was doing Midge a favour.

'You'd better not waste my time and it had better be important.' Midge bunched his fists as a threatening gesture implying what could happen if Shorty had nothing worth his attention.

Shorty's eyes darted here and there trying to avoid Midge's piercing gaze, but he could not help being drawn back to the demanding authority sitting opposite him.

'What I have to tell you,' Shorty simpered, 'will be worth your time.'

'And I suppose you're expecting it to be worthwhile for you?' Midge, in a swift movement, leaned forward on the desk, seeming to leap at Shorty who involuntarily made a backward movement. Midge's eyes were even more darkly piercing, emphasising the threat to the small man.

'I ask for nothing, Mr Whitley, nothing, really.'

Midge gave a snort of disbelief. He hated simpering men but revelled in their subservience. He had sometimes wondered if Shorty could be an asset. Shifty individuals had their uses especially as information-gatherers. Maybe he would be able to make a better judgement of Shorty's possible uses when he had heard what information he had now.

'Oh, I think you'll be looking for some sort of reward otherwise you wouldn't be here,' said Midge, leaning back in his chair, his eyes never leaving Shorty. 'But we'll deal with that after I hear what you have to say. So get on with it.'

Shorty swallowed hard and fidgeted with his fingers.

Tough he might be around the docks, but here in the presence of a domineering, ruthless man he felt weak, afraid of the consequences should his information prove useless, yet feeling a sense of power at knowing something which Midge did not.

'I was in the Golden Hind the night the American sailor came in inquiring about Annie. You remember him?'

At the mention of Annie, Midge straightened. His eyes narrowed, hooded by thick eyebrows. It offended him that someone of Shorty's background should even mention her name. 'Yes,' he snapped.

'Well, he ain't an American and he ain't a sailor!' Shorty smirked, seeing Midge startled by the news.

Incredulous, Midge stared at him for a moment. 'What do you mean, he ain't an American?' he demanded testily, doubt in his tone. 'If this is some kind of joke—'

'No joke, Mr Whitley. No joke. He's as English as we are.'

Midge saw that he was in earnest. 'Explain!'

'I was in High Street and saw this man walking with a young lady. They were both well dressed but there was something familiar about his face. Curious, I got closer and I am certain he was the American who came in here. I got near enough to catch fractions of their conversation and, though I did not know what they were talking about, he had no trace of an American accent. Oh, he's English all right.'

Midge rubbed his chin thoughtfully. 'I wonder why he adopted the disguise of an American seaman and why he was interested in Annie?' he muttered to himself. Then he looked sharply at Shorty. 'Did you follow them?'

'Aye. I was curious. She left him at the offices of Thornton, attorney, in Bowlalley Lane. I then followed him to the Curzon Club.'

Midge raised surprised eyebrow. 'And?'

'That's when I came here.'

'So we know no more about him, nor where he lives?' The exasperation in his voice startled Shorty. He thought he had done well, but realised now that he could have done even better had he kept watch for the reappearance of the so-called American from the club.

'I'll get back to the Curzon Club. Maybe he hasn't left yet.' Wanting to oblige, desiring Midge's favour, Shorty was out of his chair and hurrying to the door.

'Shorty!' The snap in Midge's voice brought him up short. He turned, half-expecting disapproval for his shortcoming. Instead he heard Midge say quietly, 'You did well, Shorty. I'll overlook the fact that you could have done better. You can retrieve the situation. The identity of this man is important. If you don't pick him up again today keep watch at the Curzon Club. Only members are admitted alone so, as he was by himself when you saw him, he must be a member and therefore likely to return again.'

'Leave it to me, Mr Whitley.' Shorty, euphoric that he had pleased the man who was a law to himself in the seamier side of the old town, scurried quickly out of the room and out of the Golden Hind.

He lost no time in reaching the Curzon Club and took

up a position from where he could view the entrance without attracting attention to himself.

His patience was rewarded. Forty minutes later his body tensed when he saw Thomas emerge from the club accompanied by James Walton, a fact which startled him. Had it been a casual meeting of club members or were they known to each other? If the latter, how deeply were they connected? He could not remember the man in whom Midge was interested being in Hull when James Walton stood trial. Yet, now, as he followed them, they appeared to be on good terms. But this was not a time for speculation. His job was to learn what he could about the man who had posed as an American sailor.

When the two men turned into Portland Place Shorty held back and watched them from the corner. He saw them go to a house where Thomas pulled a key from his pocket, opened the front door and they both entered the building.

Shorty punched his left palm with his right fist, a gesture of pleasure in triumph. He knew where the man lived and that he appeared to be friendly with James Walton. This was indeed news for Midge and would no doubt raise him in Midge's estimation.

His return to the Golden Hind was swift and within moments he was sitting in front of the man he wanted to impress.

'He lives in Portland Place.' He imparted his knowledge with zest. 'And he appears to be extremely friendly with James Walton.'

Midge was startled by this piece of information, but

listened patiently to Shorty's explanation as to why he had come to this conclusion.

When he had finished, Midge sat silent and thoughtful. Shorty knew better than to interrupt the intense concentration.

Midge idly tapped his fingers on his desk as if this helped him to think. Who was this man who was interested in Annie and now appeared to be friendly with James Walton? This latter fact could make him dangerous and as such ... Midge let the consequences drift away. That might come later, but in the meantime there was the possibility that this man could lead him to Annie. His own efforts to find her had failed, but maybe this man knew something he did not.

He looked up at Shorty. 'You've done well. Now you can continue with this job. I want you to keep an eye on this man who passed himself off as an American sailor. Follow him wherever he goes and report his every movement to me.'

'Very good, Mr Whitley. Leave it to me.' Shorty was bursting with pride that Midge had entrusted him with an important job.

Midge opened a drawer and threw two sovereigns across the desk to Shorty.

'Thanks, Mr Whitley, thanks,' gasped Shorty as his broad fingers closed round the coins.

'Whatever you find out about this man is important to me,' Midge reminded him. 'Don't let me down.'

Little knowing what his encounter with James in the Curzon Club had led to, Thomas had informed James

207

that he had made little progress in finding out who might have implicated him, but that he had certain suspicions which he was not prepared to divulge at this moment. He persuaded James to accompany him to Portland Place to go over the events which had led to the trial. He had hoped that James was ready to explain where he had been when Captain Ainslie was murdered, but to no avail. James was as tight about that as he had been at his trial, and no amount of pleading or cajoling would persuade him to be otherwise. Even when Thomas had voiced his suspicions that James was shielding someone, he received no inkling that he might be right.

While at the Curzon Club, Thomas had also managed to have a private word with Captain Hobson to tell him he had so far failed to locate Annie to question her about the locket. Recalling that brief meeting made him resolve to make another search in the old town for Annie whom he was certain must be with Ed Berriman. Accordingly as evening fell he changed into his sailor's clothes and adopted his American persona.

It was dark when he locked the house in Portland Place and he failed to notice a man some distance away who became alert when Thomas hurried towards Prospect Street. Darkness had been hastened by low clouds, driven by a chill wind blowing from the river. He turned up the collar of his waist-length jacket, hunched his shoulders and lengthened his stride, hoping that this foray would produce something to tell Emily and her father at the meeting Mr Thornton had called him to the next morning.

The inclement weather had kept some people indoors and it was not until he reached the warren of streets, alleys and buildings in the old town that his progress was slowed. He became alert to the pickpockets, the beggars, and the would-be entertainers among the folk seeking home, or dubious entertainment, heading for their favourite inn, or merely wandering with nothing to urge them to more enlightening pastures. Alleys took on sinister countenances, buildings seemed to crowd in as if to seize and make their victim vanish without trace. His gaze swept around him as he hastened to the Seafarers' Arms in hopes that Dick might have some news for him.

'I haven't set eyes on Ed,' Dick informed him as he placed a tankard of beer in front of him. He gave a puzzled shake of his head. 'If Ed is still in Hull I'm sure he'd have contacted me.'

'What are his possible haunts? Where is he likely to be living?'

'Who knows? Remember he's been out of the country for eighteen months, and he'd have had to make new arrangements when he returned. And since it looks as though he whisked Annie from under Midge's nose he'd lie low. Midge has cronies everywhere, and there are no-gooders who'd sell their souls to curry his favour.' He lowered his voice and inched a little nearer Thomas. 'And you be careful. Your enquiries for Annie at the Golden Hind will have brought suspicion on you. You may well have been followed here.'

'I don't think so,' Thomas returned, but Dick's remark had made him wonder if he had been careless.

'I hope you are right, but I'm not so sure. Fellow by

the name of Shorty Marsden just put his head round the door as if he was looking for someone. He didn't take his time about it. His first glance was at you and then he went out again.'

Thomas tensed. If Dick was right then someone had been keeping an eye on him. For how long? He tossed speculation aside as he asked, 'And who might this Shorty be?'

'He works on the docks, but he's shifty. He'll try to run with both the hare and the hounds, but I know he hangs out in the Golden Hind a lot, hoping to gain Midge Whitley's eye. He could have set him on to follow you.'

Thomas nodded. 'Thanks for the warning.'

'When you leave here I'll take you out of the back door, then you can give him the slip.'

Thomas stayed another hour and Dick had his suspicions about Shorty confirmed when he looked into the inn on two more occasions during that time.

Thomas was sorry that Ed had not shown up and he was feeling somewhat despondent when Dick took him through the back of the inn which gave on to a narrow alley. Dick motioned to the left. 'Down there will get you on to Bishop's Lane and then on to Lowgate. Best way then is on to the south side of Queen's Dock.'

Thomas gave him a grateful tap on the shoulder and moved quickly into the darkness.

As he walked into Lowgate he became alert to the people around him. In this frame of mind he reached the end of the street where he pulled up sharply. For a moment he did not comprehend what had made him do this, but his gaze had been caught by a figure passing through a pool of light at the junction with Salthouse Lane.

Though the head was bowed and a hat was pulled down as if to shield the face, the way the body was held and particularly the walking gait reminded him of the person he had followed to the Golden Hind.

'Ed!' He stifled the word before it was uttered. Better not to give his presence away. If they met would Ed be open about any question relating to Annie? Wouldn't he be more likely to deny any knowledge of her whereabouts? Besides, Ed would not want to linger in the open. Far better if he used his luck and followed him. That way he would find out where Ed was living, and Annie if she was still with him.

He saw him head for Queen's Dock and followed at a discreet distance. He crossed the bridge over the inlet from the River Hull. The darkness seemed to intensify as the buildings closed in on one another. Thomas narrowed the gap between them, careful not to betray his presence. Ed hurried along North Street and turned into Bourne Street. Nearing the corner Thomas held back a little before moving cautiously round it. Ed was still in sight but only as a shadowy figure. Thomas started to quicken his pace again but slowed when he saw Ed stop. He saw him take something from his pocket and insert it into a door.

As Ed pushed it open, Thomas rushed forward calling as he did so, 'Hi, Ed!'

Ed, startled by the unexpected shout, half-turned and looked over his shoulder, but quickly gathered his composure. 'America, what are you doing here?'

'Visiting you.'

'How did you know where to find me?' Ed's voice was full of suspicion and he cast anxious glances in both directions along the street.

'I didn't. I've been looking for you ever since we met in the Seafarers' Arms. I've kept in touch with Dick who thought you might call there. Tonight I got lucky. I spotted you shortly after I left the inn. So I followed you.'

Suspicion deepened in Ed. If this American had merely wanted a word with him why not stop him when he saw him? Why had he followed him? To know where he was living? If so why? 'Why did you follow me?' he demanded angrily.

'It's a long story. Please let me come in and I'll explain.'

Ed hesitated only a fraction. He wanted to be off the street. Besides, he believed in meeting trouble head on when it presented itself and if America spelt trouble then he wanted to know about it. He stepped inside and gestured to Thomas to follow. He struck a match and applied it to a candle conveniently placed on a small table near the front door. He picked it up and led the way down the dark passage to a room on the right. 'Come in,' he invited. Suspicion still smouldered in his voice.

Thomas noted that the invitation was delivered in a much louder tone, and he judged the reason why when he saw a light showing beneath a door at the far end of the passage. Someone had been warned that Ed was not alone. Once inside the room Ed applied a spill to the candle flame and lit an oil lamp. He turned the wick until he was satisfied with the illumination, snuffed the candle and then turned to face Thomas.

'Well?' he snapped tersely, annoyed that his whereabouts had been discovered. Who else might know? His eyes bored into Thomas, seeking an explanation.

Thomas met his gaze unflinchingly. 'When you left the Seafarers' Arms, the night we first met, I followed you!'

'What? You're always following—' His words ended abruptly. He stared at Thomas with incredulity in his eyes. 'Hold on! Your accent?'

Thomas gave a wry smile. 'I'm not American. I'm as English as you are, but I didn't want to come into the old town in my true role of private detective.'

'Detective!' Ed's tone not only showed his surprise but also anger at being misled. 'You've a lot of explaining to do. You'd better sit down.'

'I must apologise for all this,' Thomas started amiably, only to be interrupted by Ed.

'Have you been following me in your capacity as a private detective?' he demanded.

'Partially.'

'What? You can't have anything on me.'

Thomas made a calming motion with his hands when he saw Ed's temper rising.

'I'm sorry I was unable to reveal my true identity when we first met. I liked you, but, not really knowing you, I couldn't explain what I was doing.'

'Get on with it,' snapped Ed, his eyes flaring.

Thomas went on to explain how he came to be a

private detective and why he had come back to Hull.

'That's all very well but you haven't offered any explanation as to why you're interested in me,' said Ed.

'Three different people have engaged me to make enquiries into what appeared to be three different cases, but certain facts have emerged which led me to think there might be a connection between all three.'

'But what has this to do with me?' asked a mystified Ed. 'I've been out of the country.'

'They have nothing to do with you, but you know someone who may be vital to all three.'

'Who?' Ed eyed him suspiciously.

'Annie Newmarch!'

For a moment Ed did not speak. He was tempted to deny that he knew the girl but then he realised it would be useless. 'You heard me talking about her with Dick that first night.'

Thomas nodded. 'From that conversation I knew she was with someone called Midge, verifying the knowledge I accidentally gained when leaving the theatre one evening. I followed you to the Golden Hind and returned there the next evening to have a word with Annie, only to be told she had left. I put two and two together and judged she must have left with you.'

'And that's why you were looking for me – really to find Annie. Why do you want her?'

'I was asked to find Mrs Ainslie, the wife of Captain Ainslie for whose murder James Walton stood trial.'

'But what could Annie know of either of those matters?'

'I'm not sure she does, but James Walton suspects

that he was set up. That is my second assignment – to prove that he was. From other enquiries I have a thought that Annie may know something which could help me.'

Ed made no comment and Thomas concluded that, though Ed wanted to believe his girl could not be the holder of such knowledge, an element of suspicion had been sown in his mind.

'My third enquiry arose from that visit to the theatre I just mentioned. As we were leaving the theatre a friend noticed a girl, a redhead. She was with a group, but appeared to be with one person in particular and he called her Annie and she in her reply called him Midge. My client was struck by the locket she was wearing. It was unusual and the last time he had seen it it was in the possession of Mrs Walton, James's mother.'

'I noticed Annie was wearing a locket the night I took her out of the Golden Hind,' said Ed, 'but I hadn't time to examine it. It meant nothing to me and I haven't seen it since.'

Thomas acknowledged the information and went on, 'My client wondered how the girl came to have it and asked me to find out. So you see there are links between all three cases though they don't necessarily have a bearing on each other. I discovered who Midge was and that he came from somewhere in the old town.'

'And that's where you started?'

'Yes. The night we met in the Seafarers' Arms, but that night I was really working on the case for James Walton. I had learned that James Walton used to visit the old town and that one of his special haunts was the

Seafarers' Arms. I was hoping to find some information which would lead me to discovering if and why and by whom he could have been set up. But when I heard you and Dick mention Annie and he told you she was with Midge my line of enquiry was diverted to finding out about the locket.' He paused then added, 'Now you know my story I hope you realise that I mean you and Annie no harm.'

'So, you want to see her?'

'Yes, if you will allow it. I think she is here with you, in the back room. I saw a light under its door and I believe you warned her that you were not alone.'

Ed smiled. 'The loudness of my voice. They trained you well in America. Yes she's here, but it is up to her how willing she is to cooperate. My concern is that she is safe from Midge.'

'I hope I'll not compromise her with him through anything I do.'

Ed saw sincerity. He hesitated only a moment before saying, 'I'll fetch her.'

Chapter Eleven

When Thomas had seen Annie outside the theatre, briefly though it was, he had seen that there was something different about her which, at that moment, had been overshadowed by uncouth behaviour. The aura he had sensed had made him speculate that her coarse actions had been put on because of the man who accompanied her whose open fondling of her mocked the etiquette of other theatregoers.

Now he was having that feeling verified. In the light from the oil lamp her red hair shone like the smooth clear water of some untainted stream. Her features were accentuated by shadow and Thomas saw a quality that would make men look twice. But it was her demeanour which outshone everything else. She was no longer the cheeky, brazen girl he had previously encountered. Midge's influence had gone. Her act for him had vanished. Here was a demure girl who showed a reluctance to meet a stranger, but he had no doubt that behind it lay a spirited person.

Her eyes were downcast while Ed closed the door. When she looked up it was straight at Thomas as if she wanted to verify the authenticity of the stranger. Her expression changed to one of questioning curiosity. Her eyes narrowed slightly as she said, 'Haven't I seen you somewhere?' Her voice trailed away, but, before Thomas could answer her, she said with the sharpness of recognition, 'The theatre. Outside the theatre.' Her face became a mask of contrite horror as she remembered. 'Oh, my goodness!' Then the words poured out. 'Oh, I'm sorry for my behaviour towards your friends that night. I meant nothing by it.' She blushed. 'That wasn't the real me. Please, please apologise to your friends, I meant them no insult.'

Thomas chuckled. 'I'll tell them, but no apology is necessary. I did wonder about you that evening. I thought maybe it wasn't the real you.'

'It certainly wasn't and I'm glad Ed has rescued me from that life.'

Ed who was looking bewildered asked, 'What's this all about?'

Annie explained quickly then gave a little smile. 'Though our paths have crossed it wasn't a time for introductions, you had better put that right now, Ed.'

He nodded. 'This is Thomas Laycock. He would like to ask you a few questions.' He glanced at Thomas. 'I have told Annie nothing, only that you are a friend.'

She looked from one to the other. 'What haven't you told me? Why do you want to question me?'

'I will be perfectly honest with you,' said Thomas, 'I am a private detective.'

Annie looked startled. 'You mean the police?' There was hostility in her voice.

'No. I work for private clients, work which has nothing to do with the police.'

'What do you want with me?'

'You may be able to help me with three cases I am investigating.'

Annie stiffened. 'I don't think so,' she replied crisply. 'What have you told Ed?' She demanded, but before he could reply she swung round on Ed. 'Why have you agreed?' she snapped angrily.

'Annie, I haven't agreed to anything. I heard what Mr Laycock had to say and only said I would let him meet you. What you decide is up to you.'

'I want nothing to do with him.'

'Just listen to me, please,' said Thomas. 'Then you can make up your own mind. It is important to me.'

Annie tossed her head, sending her red hair shimmering in the light. 'So possibly you can enhance your reputation,' she said with sarcasm.

'No. So that my clients will be satisfied and if necessary see justice done.'

'So the police would be involved?'

'Only if it was necessary to make someone pay for a crime they may have committed.'

Annie suddenly changed the tack of the conversation by once again swinging round on Ed. 'How did he find us?'

'He saw me and followed me.'

Her lips tightened angrily. 'If he can do it so can Midge and if he finds us you know what that will mean. Someone may have followed him, or he may even be working for Midge.' Her statements were getting wild.

'I assure you I was not followed this evening,' said Thomas quietly. 'And if I was working for Midge I wouldn't be standing talking to you now. I would be back at the Golden Hind telling him where Ed lived. Please, Miss Newmarch, let me tell you what I know and what I want to know.'

'No. I want nothing to do with you. You will only bring us trouble.'

'Please. I assure you nothing will happen to you.'

'You can't be certain.' She turned to Ed. 'See him out, now!' She turned quickly and left the room before any more could be said.

Ed turned to Thomas. He shrugged his shoulders and raised his hands in a helpless gesture. 'I'm sorry.'

Thomas gave a smile of regret. 'It's not your fault. Maybe the confrontation was too abrupt. Maybe after she has had time to think she'll come round and agree to help. See how she feels in the morning. A new day may bring a change of mind.'

Ed shook his head doubtfully. 'I'm not sure it will but you never know.'

'Have a chat with her. You can tell her what I've told you and then maybe you can persuade her to talk to me.' Thomas clicked his fingers as an idea struck him. 'Maybe she'd rather talk with another woman. So tell her if she likes I can arrange that.' He paused only a moment. 'Better still, if she agrees to that, bring her to my house, 7 Portland Place, tomorrow afternoon at two,

I'll have someone there whom I'm sure she will like and who will be the height of discretion.'

Ed nodded. 'I'll see what I can do.' But there was little hope in his voice.

When Thomas reached Portland Place he carefully patrolled the area but found no sign of anyone watching his house. As he let himself in he had no doubt that the person about whom Dick had warned him, would have the house under surveillance. He would not want to report to Midge that he had lost his quarry. The situation could be tricky if Ed arrived with Annie, but, as he considered it, he had an idea that it might be turned to advantage.

When he had seen Thomas from the house, Ed went straight to the kitchen where a bright fire burned in the black range. An appetising smell of stew came from the side oven and steam puffed from a kettle on the reckon. Two oil lamps illuminated the room adding to the cosy atmosphere. Ed appreciated Annie's efforts to make his house homely and in some ways he regretted that he had subjected her to meeting the detective.

'Annie—' he started.

She swung round on him, her eyes blazing. 'Don't you Annie me! Why did you bring that man in? He's no right to be questioning me.'

'Annie, please calm down. He's a nice bloke.'

Annie tossed her head and grunted with contempt. 'How can you know? You've not been long back from America and most of that time you've been in hiding.

221

How can you know him? How can you know what he's really up to?'

'I admit I have only met him once. That was in the Seafarers' Arms the night I took you from Midge.'

'There you are, one meeting and you trust him! That's ridiculous.'

'I liked what I saw that night and from what he has just told me I think you should have listened to him.'

'Why? What can I tell him?'

'Probably a great deal that would be helpful and clear up some questions his clients are asking. Will you listen while I tell you what he said to me?'

Annie said nothing, but took the teapot to the kettle and poured water on to the tea. She went to the table and sat down. She put a drop of milk into two cups without speaking. Ed knew the signs, said nothing and sat down opposite her. She filled a cup with tea and pushed it towards him.

'Thanks,' he said quietly and watched the liquid swirl as he stirred it.

Annie looked at him. Her annoyance softened. This was Ed, the man whom she had loved before he went to America, the man she had pined for, the man who had returned and rescued her from an alien life with Midge, the man who now wanted her to listen to a stranger's requests. If she did, she knew she would have to reveal things she had kept secret, things which might wreck their relationship. Dare she risk that? Had Ed a right to know?

Ed felt her eyes on him. He looked up slowly and met her gaze. For a moment a shared silence stretched

222

between them and in it their love drew them closer. Regrets were cast aside.

'If you think it right that I should listen to you then I will,' she said quietly.

He did not answer immediately. She waited. Then he gave a little nod. 'I think you should. From what Thomas Laycock told me there are matters involving people I suspect you know and which I think need clearing up.

'All right I'll listen, but I don't promise to do any more than that.'

'That will be your decision and yours alone.' Ed started on his story.

'That is all he told me,' Ed concluded. 'There is one thing more, he said that if you decide to help he will be at his home in Portland Place tomorrow afternoon at two o'clock and that if you would rather talk to another young lady there will be someone there tomorrow.'

She made no comment. She had been startled by the three enquiries Mr Laycock was making and was disturbed by the fact that he assumed all three were connected. She understood she would be dealing with a shrewd man. Should she cooperate, tell him everything? If she did, maybe he could help her escape the knowledge which bound her to Midge, but if ever Midge found out that she had talked she would be looking over her shoulder for the rest of her life.

She rose from her chair and carefully removed a stew-jar from the oven and placed it on a square of metal so that its heat did not burn the table. She ladled some stew on to two plates and placed one in front of Ed. He thanked her but said no more. He waited for her decision.

It did not come until she had eaten half her plateful. She raised her eyes to Ed. 'If he made arrangements for tomorrow he must be expecting me to agree.' It rankled a little that he had made such an assumption.

Ed sensed it. 'He needs to know quickly and set up this meeting in case you agreed.'

'You honestly trust this man?' she asked.

'I do.'

She paused a moment thoughtfully then said, 'All right, so long as you are with me.'

'Of course I'll come with you.'

She wetted her lips nervously. 'Ed, if I am going to talk to these people then there are things you should know, happenings which took place when you were in America, in fact sparked off because you went there and I turned down the chance of coming with you.'

'That was your life. There is no need for me to know.'

'I am going to tell these people certain things which I would rather you hear from me.'

'Very well. As you wish.'

Ed did not press her but waited patiently until they had finished their meal for he knew that she was sorting things out in her mind. With crockery washed and put away Annie settled to her story.

'It all began when you left for America. I was devastated. I did not think you would go and it was only later that I realised the magnitude of my mistake in not going with you. I suppose I was so depressed I little cared what happened to me. I was in that state when Midge showed me kindness and told me he could help me face life and that it could be better than what I had had. I learned later that he had lusted after me ever since the first time he saw me with you. Now he saw his opportunity.'

She shrugged her shoulders resignedly and continued. 'I suppose life wasn't all that bad. Though he was a boor in many ways, ruthless in his dealings if anyone crossed him, he did treat me kindly provided I stayed in his favour, and at that time that was all I asked.

'All went well for a while until I met someone else. I was getting sick of Midge's growing demands and coarse ways. This new man was more of my own breeding.' She paused and met Ed with a frank gaze. 'You never knew my origins nor questioned from where I had come when you kindly took me to your mother's home.'

Ed shook his head. 'It was no concern of ours. We liked you and I put great store by my mother's judgement. She always said that in the fullness of time you would explain who you were. Is this now that time?'

She nodded. 'You deserve that much. I came to Hull from Whitby. I am the daughter of a ship-owner in Whitby. We were very comfortably off. Father was a shrewd judge of trading conditions and everything he turned his attention to seemed to bring its rewards. Unlike my brothers and sisters I was a rebel. Not for me the simpering daughter who followed the convention of tea, sewing and polite conversation. There was a big changing world outside Whitby and I wanted to be part of it so, after a disagreement with Mother and Father, I walked out thinking I could find what I wanted in Hull.'

'And did you?' asked Ed as she paused.

'Not what I expected, but I did find you and then foolishly threw our relationship away.'

'This man you met?'

'James Walton.'

Ed stifled his surprise. The man who had engaged Thomas to try to prove positively that he had not killed Captain Ainslie. Could Annie be mixed up in that crime? Never! his mind screamed at him. Then he was aware that she was continuing.

'James was of good stock. He had been adopted when a very young child. Sadly Mr Walton died when he was still young but his adoptive mother brought him up successfully with the help of a very good governess. But he had a wild streak and occasionally came into the old town looking for a bit of adventure in its seamier side.'

'A risky business for someone who came from the—' Ed's observation was cut short.

'He was capable of looking after himself and did so more than once so that he became known and respected by the folk in the old town. It was on one of these visits that we met. I liked him a great deal. He respected me, never tried to take any advantage and we met more and more frequently outside the old town.' She saw a question rising on Ed's lips. 'It doesn't matter where, so don't ask.'

Ed switched his question. 'Where did Midge fit into this?'

226

'We kept it a secret from him, at least for a considerable time. James wanted me to leave him. I knew Midge would wreak revenge some way or other, but James was persuasive. He gave me a locket and I took it as a symbol that one day we would marry.'

'I told you Mr Laycock is trying to trace a locket that his client believes once belonged to Mrs Walton, James's mother. Is this it?'

'Yes. It was specially made for her, a present from her husband. She gave it to her son as a family heirloom, that is why, when he gave it to me, I assumed it to be a gesture of betrothal.'

'Did he ever ask you to marry him?'

'No.'

'You were wearing it when I rescued you but I've not seen it since.'

'I took it off once we got here. I wanted to forget James Walton and I did not want you asking about it. I was frightened it might destroy our relationship if you knew about him and how close we had been.'

'That would never have happened, Annie. I love you too much for that. I came back from America because of you.'

Her eyes were damp as she said, 'I don't deserve you.'

'We deserve each other.' He kissed her on the lips, a kiss she returned with joy and all the feeling she could muster to confirm her love for him.

'So what happened between you and James to drive you back to that louse Midge?' asked Ed as their lips parted.

'I had left Midge telling him that I was going away for

a while to Whitby, whereas I was actually going to James. But two months after I left Midge I discovered that James was seeing someone else. I followed him on two or three occasions and realised his meetings with Elizabeth Ainslie were serious.'

Ed stared at her in amazement. 'Captain Ainslie's wife?'

'Yes.'

'Then the murder—?' His voice trailed away as he appreciated the different inference that could be drawn.

'I had also learned that James was deep in debt through gambling, and to me that implied he was probably after her money, though I thought that out of character. By the time of the murder I had drifted back to Midge and I must say he was forgiving. However he had learned the identity of the person I had been with, and I believe I let it slip that James had a big gambling debt.'

'So you think Midge arranged the murder, made it look like robbery to pay this debt, and fixed a witness to say that James was seen running away?' said Ed, eagerly picking up a possibility which could get Midge off their backs.

Annie gave a little smile. 'I can't prove it. I was not partner to his plans. But when James was acquitted I did overhear Midge instructing someone to get rid of Nobby Carson, the witness who said he saw James leaving the scene of the crime. Midge's words were, "I can't afford for him to blab his mouth off and get me strung up."'

'How did Walton come to be acquitted?'

'The person to whom he owed the debt had been

abroad and had only returned during the trial. He came forward immediately to say that, unknown to him because he was out of the country, James had paid his debt before Captain Ainslie docked in Hull, so the robbery motive did not hold good.'

'But,' put in Ed thoughtfully, 'his motive could have been to clear the way for him to marry the widow.'

Annie shook her head. 'No, not possible.'

'How do you know? There's every reason to think—'

Annie held up her hand to stop him. 'No. You see I had followed James that afternoon and I saw him with Mrs Ainslie at the time of the murder.'

'And you never came forward to clear him?' Ed showed his amazement.

'I attended the trial every day. If the verdict had gone against him I would have spoken, but it didn't and I saw no reason to cause a scandal for a man I admired even though he had ... well, jilted me.'

'You still have his locket.'

'Yes. I've treasured it because it's so beautiful and, from what he told me, it meant so much to his mother. But I shall never wear it now I know you love me and hold me no grudge.' She was watching him carefully as she made this promise.

He took her hands in his and drew her to her feet. He looked deep into her eyes, drawn by the sheer depth of the hope he saw there.

'Annie, my love,' he whispered. 'I have always loved you, and always will. What you have told me will not influence that. In fact it heightens my admiration of you for being strong enough to survive. And I must share

229

some of the blame for what happened to you. If I hadn't gone to America—'

She raised her fingers to his lips and brushed them lightly. 'Hush. Forget that parting. It happened and what followed will soon be a memory once we have spoken to Mr Laycock.'

'You'll do that?'

'Yes. It has felt good to talk about it and I know I would be wrong in holding back if people's problems can be solved and justice can be done.'

'Good!' He hugged her tight. 'You'll not regret it.' He met her upturned gaze. 'I love you, Annie Newmarch.' He bent and kissed her lips lightly. He felt a tremor run through her and as he crushed her closer she responded with all the passion she knew.

'No doubt you'll enjoy the meeting this morning,' teased Sylvia with a twinkle in her eyes as she and Emily crossed the hall to the front door.

'I always do,' replied Emily in a noncommittal tone.

'Ah, but this morning will be special with Thomas there.'

'Of course,' agreed her sister, giving Sylvia no opening to tease further.

They reached the door and stepped outside to find their father just driving the horse and trap to the front of the house. Emily climbed into the trap and when she had taken her seat, she and her father bade Sylvia goodbye saying they would see her that evening.

It was a pleasant morning, the air refreshingly warm, the countryside bright in its mantle of greens and the birds singing as if they had found the world to their liking. Jonas always enjoyed his ride into Hull on such mornings and having left Bramwell House early he drove at an easy pace.

'Are you bringing Thomas back for an evening meal?' he asked.

'Sylvia suggested I should.'

'And you readily agreed,' said Jonas with a sly glance at his daughter.

Emily caught her father's look and gave a little smile as she said, 'Naturally.' She knew there was no denying otherwise. Her father was a shrewd and observant man, whose interest was for his daughters' welfare. He noted their friendships without comment unless it was to warn, or show his approval.

'You get on well with Thomas?'

'Yes.' Emily recognised his query as a parent's concern rather than a probing curiosity. 'I enjoy being with him.'

'I wish your mother was still here with her wise guidance.' A catch came to his voice. Emily knew a deep love had existed between her parents and she was aware of how much her father missed her mother. She and Sylvia tried to ease the loss for him, but knew they could never fill the huge gap in his life.

She hugged his arm. 'You do very well,' she commented, 'and I know Mother would approve.'

'Thank you for those kind words.' He smiled and patted her hand.

They drove in silence for a little while, Emily respecting her father's wish, for she knew he was lost in his memories. This picturesque section of the drive into Hull, with its views across the Humber, had been a particular favourite of her mother and one where Jonas always slowed so she could enjoy it. He did so now and did not speak until he increased the horse's pace again.

'Do you think Thomas will have any more news about Mrs Ainslie?' he asked.

'I don't know,' she said.

'I hope so, because I can't hold back much longer about the will you found. As a matter of fact I have set up a meeting with James for a week today, Wednesday.'

'So soon?'

'I must get things settled.'

Emily hid the alarm she felt. She could only hope that Thomas would have uncovered something of help by then.

Reaching the office there was half an hour before Thomas was due and they settled down to clear routine work from their desks.

When Thomas left his house for Jonas Thornton's office he was aware that he was observed and followed. It gave him cause for thought, as he walked quickly to Bowlalley Lane, and he reconsidered how he could turn it to his advantage if Annie and Ed came to Portland Place that afternoon.

As he was expected the clerk showed him straight to Mr Thornton's room where he was pleased to find Emily already there.

Jonas greeted him warmly and offered him a seat

across the desk from himself. Emily drew a chair alongside her father, from where she could better see Thomas.

'I asked you to come here as I am getting concerned about James's position. It really is time I revealed the existence of the second will. It would be most improper to spring it on him just before his expected implementation of the only will he knows about. It is only right that I give him time to adjust to what it means to him. So I do require to know if you have discovered anything about the possible whereabouts of Mrs Ainslie.'

Jonas was surprised when Emily spoke before Thomas. 'Father, before Thomas explains the situation, I think there is something you should know.' Jonas frowned at her intervention and he shot his daughter a questioning look. 'I have been helping Thomas with his enquiries.'

'Have you indeed?' Jonas's tone was sharp and touched with annoyance. He looked severely at Thomas. 'Did you encourage her in this, young man?'

'Sir,' replied Thomas, 'may I say that your daughter and I seemed to get on well from our first meeting at her party and—'

'I noticed that, and I am not a fool. I also know that you have seen each other several times since then but . . . detective? That is hardly a lady-like occupation.'

'Let me say, sir, that your daughter has a gift for the work. She is an excellent interviewer with a sharp enquiring mind and an ability to draw answers from the person being questioned. I believe there are many occasions when a female can be an asset in this type of work.'

'There could be awkward situations, even danger and I don't like my daughter being exposed to the unsavoury things you may uncover.'

'Father, I am no longer a little girl. This modern age is changing and with it we change too. I like helping Thomas and working closely with his agency can be an advantage to you as an attorney.'

'I know, Emily, but—' he said rather doubtfully.

'Sir, I would not expose your daughter to any danger. I think too highly of her to do that. She is a great help in what we are doing now.'

Jonas gave a little grunt. Though his natural instinct was to protect his daughter, secretly he admired her tenacity and forward thinking. If she was as good as Thomas indicated he could see why she would be enthusiastic about detective work, but he hoped that her future, as he saw it, would not be marred by her new interest.

He half-turned in his seat and looked seriously at her. 'Very well,' he said gently, his eyes expressing the loving concern he had for her, 'but I do hope this will not supersede the plans we have for you to take over my business.'

'It won't, Father,' she reassured him with firm conviction. 'I can see it will be of benefit.'

Jonas nodded. 'Very well.' He looked hard at Thomas. 'See she comes to no harm.'

'You can depend on me, sir.'

'Now, the business we are here for. What progress have you made in tracing Mrs Ainslie?'

'It has proved difficult. We know she left Hull but we have no definite knowledge of her whereabouts.'

Jonas's lips tightened in exasperation but he made no comment, allowing Thomas to continue.

He explained what they had found out from Matt, their visit to Riplingham Hall and the interview with Mrs Ainslie's ex-groom.

'We think he wasn't telling us everything because of his loyalty to Mrs Ainslie, so we might have to interview him again,' put in Emily. 'We did learn when Mrs Ainslie left Hull.' She glanced at Thomas and he took up the story again, explaining about the trains.

'So she could be anywhere in the country, or even out of it,' said Jonas, disheartened by the news.

'Don't look so despondent, Father.' Emily gave a little smile of encouragement. 'All is not as bad as it seems. We are trying to find out where she came from, as we think she may have returned there.'

'And we have some other lines of enquiry,' put in Thomas quickly, for he did not want Emily to reveal too much at this point. 'I have an important interview this afternoon which may have some bearing on our enquiries.'

Emily, surprised by this revelation, darted a glance at him, but he avoided her look by watching Jonas closely. She felt let down. It rankled that he had seen her as a partner, yet had acted on his own without even consulting or telling her what he was arranging.

'May I know who this is with?' asked Jonas.

'With respect, sir, I don't want to disclose that now. If it brings us any nearer solving our quest you will know quickly. Also I would like Emily to be present at this interview.'

'Very well,' agreed Jonas. He did not want to force the young man's hand. 'But I insist I must inform James next Wednesday, a week tomorrow.' His eyes took on a warning look. 'And I won't be turned away from this arrangement.'

'I understand, sir. We will do our best to have more information for you by then.' He looked at Emily. 'The meeting is arranged for two o'clock at my house in Portland Place.'

'Very good, I'll be there,' she replied a little coldly.

Thomas left the office and the opportunity to voice her irritation and ask him who she would be seeing at his house had gone too. With her mind occupied in speculation, she could not concentrate on her work and was pleased when it was time to leave the office.

She arrived at Portland Place half an hour before the appointed time.

When Thomas greeted her she turned away from his kiss. He grimaced and said, 'What's wrong with you?'

'As if you didn't know,' she replied haughtily and swept past him into the room. 'I thought we were supposed to be partners,' she flung at him as he closed the door.

'So we are.'

'Then why didn't you consult with me about this meeting, whoever it's with?'

He raised an eyebrow and gave a little smile. 'Emily, you've got to understand that there are times in this detective business that we have to act on our own. We can't always consult together before we act. Didn't you do just that when you interviewed Meg's sister, Patsy?'

236

With the obvious pointed out to her, Emily looked contrite. 'I'm sorry,' she mumbled, her eyes downcast. 'I shouldn't have reacted as I did. It just took me by surprise.'

He smiled and laid gentle hands on her shoulders. 'Come here, my love.' He pulled her gently to him.

She looked up to meet his loving gaze. 'Forgive me?' she asked huskily.

'There's nothing to forgive.' He kissed her and she returned the kiss with a passion which begged him to erase her accusations from his mind.

When their lips parted he held her a moment longer looking into her eyes, assuring her that all was forgiven and that there was depth to his love and the special feelings he had for her.

'Now,' he said as they sat down, 'I think you will find what I have to tell you exciting.'

Her eyes brightened. 'What is it? Who are you expecting here?'

'Annie Newmarch!'

'What?' Emily was astonished. 'You found her. How?'

Thomas related his story and she hung on every word.

'Splendid!' she cried when he had finished. 'This may be the breakthrough we want.'

'I hope so, but it is by no means certain that she will come. I think Ed wants her to, so I hope he has strong persuasive powers. Emily, you can probably play an important part.'

'I? How?'

'She may be more willing to talk with you present.'

'Ed, I'm still not really sure about this meeting,' said Annie doubtfully, as the time approached for them to go to Portland Place.

She had been agonising about the situation all morning. Ed had tried to make her see it would be for the best, but he was not sure he had done so; however, he would keep trying.

'Ed, we'd better leave Hull,' she said tentatively.

'I don't like running away,' Ed objected. 'Besides we'd be letting people down, especially when what you know could be important to them.' Troubled thoughts furrowed his brow. Annie recognised the signs from way back when he had wrestled with the conflicting options after he had told her he was going to America and she had pleaded with him not to. He was doing the same now.

'But we must go. We could go to America. I'm sure you could get a job there,' she urged, trying to influence the battle.

'I'd have no trouble doing that,' Ed agreed.

'Then let's do it,' she cried eagerly. 'I'd willingly come with you this time.'

'But, Annie, if we don't help these people we'll have them on our conscience for the rest of our lives.'

'We won't! There's no need to.'

'How do you know?'

'There's only James we can help. And he's free. What good would it be for him to know I saw him at the time of the murder?'

'It would clear him completely, and maybe from what

238

you have to say Mr Laycock might find something to help him bring the real culprit to justice.'

'But I don't owe James anything. He walked out on me.'

'And if he hadn't would you have been free for me? We wouldn't be together now. Your love for me, which I think you never destroyed, would still have been strong but you wouldn't have been able to do anything about it. And I think, though I know it's me you love, you still have a special regard for James Walton. I think you need to help him and in so doing you might destroy Midge who has wrecked many lives in the past and will do so in the future unless he is dealt with by the law. You can provide proof that he was the instigator of Nobby's murder and in so doing was involved in Captain Ainslie's death.'

Ed was being persuasive. Annie was distraught. Her movements were agitated as she moved around the kitchen doing nothing in particular. Tears welled in her eyes.

Ed came to her and gripped her firmly by the arms. He looked down at her with tenderness. 'Annie,' he said softly. 'I love you. I would not want to force you into anything you didn't want to do, but, knowing you, I don't think you will live easily if you fail to talk to these people and tell them what you have told me.'

'Oh, Ed,' she sobbed, 'please help me.' She sank her head against his chest. He held her tightly and knew she was drawing strength from him. They stood like that for a few minutes, then he eased her from him, brushed the tears from her eyes and said quietly, 'It's time we were going.'

She gave him a wan smile, but it told him that she put all her trust in him. She took his hand and turned to the door.

Chapter Twelve

The loud rap of a door knocker brought a quick exchange of looks between Emily and Thomas. They had been on tenterhooks for the last quarter of an hour hoping that Annie would not let them down.

Thomas shot out of his chair and hurried to the front door. Relief surged through him when he saw who was standing on the doorstep.

'Come in, come in,' he said eagerly, ushering them inside and closing the door behind them. 'Thank you for coming.'

Neither Ed nor Annie said anything as they followed him.

Emily rose from her chair as they came into the room. 'Miss Newmarch,' she greeted, extending her hand with friendliness which she hoped would break down the wary barrier which she sensed Annie had set up around herself.

Annie nodded and felt a warm comfort in Emily's grip.

'And Mr Berriman, so pleased you have come.' Ed felt comfortably at ease with this lady as he shook her hand.

'This is Miss Emily Thornton,' said Thomas. 'I thought she might be of help this afternoon.'

'Please do sit down.' Emily indicated two chairs on one side of the fireplace. She had judged that Annie might like Ed to be beside her.

'Thank you,' said Annie and took her seat with a glance at Ed as he sat down next to her. He gave her a reassuring smile.

Thomas took one of the chairs opposite them while Emily went to the sideboard where, a minute or two before the appointed time, she had brought a teapot, its warmth held in by a floral tea-cosy, to join the scones and cakes.

'You will take some tea?' she said over her shoulder.

'That is very kind of you, Miss Thornton.' Ed spoke for them both.

'Emily, please,' she said. 'Miss Thornton is far too formal among friends.'

Annie breathed a sigh of relief. This was not going to be a stiff and starchy encounter with someone looking down her nose at her. She heard Ed breaking down any barriers even further when he said, 'Emily it is and in that case it must be Annie and Ed.'

'Milk for both of you?'

'Please,' returned Annie.

Emily went about serving them quickly and once she had settled in her own chair with a small table, holding the scones and cakes, placed conveniently between the two couples, she said, 'I am so glad you have agreed to tell us what you know, Annie. It might be of the utmost importance to our search for Mrs Ainslie.'

Annie wetted her lips and cast an anxious glance at Ed who returned it with a slight nod and a smile of encouragement. She then went on to tell Emily and Thomas what she had told Ed the previous evening.

They listened intently without breaking in with questions. They feared that to do so might stop the flow as Annie warmed to her subject and felt more and more at ease.

'Well, I think that is all I can tell you,' she concluded. 'It can't help you with Mrs Ainslie's whereabouts but maybe it will in other ways.'

'It clears up how you come to have the locket,' said Thomas as Emily went to make some fresh tea. 'It was the request from a client that I try and trace it. Now I see no reason not to divulge his name now. Captain Hobson was a great friend of Mr and Mrs Walton and he noticed it the night you left the theatre. He recognised it as one specially made for Mrs Walton. His curiosity was aroused because he did not think there would be another like it. That locket led me to looking for you with the results you know.'

Emily returned with the tea and once everyone was relaxing, Thomas took up the facts again. 'When I met James Walton and he knew I was starting a detective agency in Hull he asked me to keep my ears open for any evidence of who might have set him up for the murder of Captain Ainslie. From what you say it seems to have been Midge Whitley. I think we can take that further. The robbery motive was thrown out of court. I must admit that, just now, when you disclosed James's association with Mrs Ainslie, I was thinking that he might have done it because he loved her and faked the robbery so he could be cleared of the murder, and I thought that Nobby Carson's evidence of seeing him running away from the scene of the crime might be true, but of course that idea is proved wrong by you seeing James with Mrs Ainslie at the time of the crime.'

'I wouldn't want to give that evidence in public unless it was absolutely vital,' said Annie.

'That won't be necessary if we can show Midge was behind the murder because he regarded James as a rival for your affections. Having heard about the debt he saw an opportunity to get rid of James through a charge of robbery to clear the debt which Midge did not know had been paid.'

'Don't you think James Walton ought to know his name can be completely cleared by Annie's evidence?' put in Ed.

'It only need be a private matter,' suggested Emily.

Annie smiled her appreciation of her concern to spare her any public embarrassment. 'Thank you, Emily. I would like to do that privately with James.' She turned to Ed. 'Do you mind?'

'Of course not,' he replied, giving her an understanding smile.

'I shall arrange it,' said Emily, 'but it may not be for a little while as there are other matters in which James is concerned which probably should be cleared up first.' She saw the curious glances cast by Annie and Ed and hastened to add, 'I can say no more about them now, and it may not be necessary to, but let me assure you they have nothing to do with what you have been telling us.'

'I am sorry that I have been no help in aiding you to locate Mrs Ainslie,' said Annie.

'We hardly expected you to be able to do that, but it is extremely helpful to know that there is a link between her and James Walton. I had only a weak suspicion that that could be the case. Now you have confirmed it,' said Thomas appreciatively.

'You've done well, Annie,' said Ed with admiration. 'It wasn't too bad was it?'

She smiled. 'Not when I was talking to two such nice people.'

'Then I think we should be getting home,' said Ed, starting to rise from his chair.

'Just a minute,' said Thomas. 'There is something else.'

Ed was taken aback by the solemn expression which had replaced Thomas's easy manner. It seemed to spell trouble. Annie had sensed it too and suddenly she was wishing she hadn't come.

'I regret to tell you that this house is being watched and I have been followed.' Thomas's stark announcement brought a momentary silent tension to the room.

It was shattered by Annie's scream, 'Ed!' which held a powerful plea for help.

Ed's face had darkened. 'Why the hell didn't you tell us before we came here?'

'If I had you wouldn't have come,' said Thomas.

Emily only half-heard the question and answer. She was trying to find a good reason why Thomas had withheld this information from Annie and Ed and why he hadn't told her. Then her mind was penetrated by Ed's angry words.

'We certainly wouldn't. You've tricked us. You've betrayed us for your own ends.' There was a deep antagonism, filled with distrust, in his words, and disgust in his look. 'And to think I was fool enough to trust you.' His eyes hardened. His lips settled into a grim tightness but they spat the question, 'Who's watching this house?'

Thomas shrugged his shoulders. 'I don't know. I was aware of someone the night I followed you.'

'Oh my God! You swore you weren't seen that night,' snapped Ed, his fists clenched tight trying to hold back the mounting anger which threatened to erupt into violence.

'I wasn't when I trailed you. It was before that when I went to the Seafarers' Arms. How they got on to me I don't know. But Dick warned me that it was one of Midge's men and let me out of the back of the inn so whoever it was couldn't have stalked me after that. But at some stage they must have followed me here and have been keeping a watch on me since. Why, I can't be certain, but I thought you ought to know.'

'What is this person who's watching you like?' asked Annie in a voice which trembled, expecting the worst.

Thomas described him.

Annie's flesh crawled and the colour drained from her face. Her words were low as she gasped, 'Shorty Marsden!'

'That little runt.' Ed's lips tightened.

'One of Midge's men?' asked Thomas.

'Always hanging around in the Golden Hind,' said Annie, her voice a little firmer. 'Wanting to get in with Midge. He must have done so and for some reason

Midge has become suspicious of you and put Shorty on to watching you.'

'Someone must have seen through my disguise as an American seaman,' said Thomas thoughtfully.

'The day we had been to see Mr Smith,' put in Emily, her words coming with a quick sharpness, 'we walked back to Father's office, I remember a shortish man being near us for some of the way. I thought nothing of it at the time. Maybe it was him.'

'If he saw you in the Golden Hind and then at the time you mentioned—' said Ed.

'That must be it,' agreed Thomas.

'But if you knew this you shouldn't have brought us here.' Anger was rising again in Ed.

'I thought we might be able to turn this to advantage, but it will need your agreement and maybe courage to go through with it. But it could be the means of trapping Midge.'

'What are you getting at? I'm not exposing Annie to any more danger.' Ed's eyes smouldered.

'If Midge is looking for Annie, Shorty is sure to follow you home, and you could be trapped. What we need is somewhere which will give you more space, and allow us a position from which to watch Annie if she is willing to act as bait to catch Midge.'

'Oh, no. Annie's life could be at risk,' rapped Ed.

Annie's eyes had been on Emily and she saw that she was mystified by Thomas's proposal. Was this a spur of the moment decision or had he a plan which he had thought through? She battled her way through a battery of confused emotions. 'Just a minute, Ed,' she said. 'I'd like to hear what Thomas is suggesting.' She knew she was voicing Emily's desire too. 'If it can make Midge pay for what he has done then I'm for helping.'

Ed shrugged his shoulders. 'If that's what you want,' he said, but there was no mistaking the disapproval in his voice.

Annie turned her attention to Thomas. 'I'll hear what you have to say, and you must understand that the decision to go ahead with your plan will rest with me.'

'It will be your choice,' agreed Thomas. 'And I apologise most sincerely for any offence and distress I have caused you and Ed.'

'Where do you propose the trap should be set?' she asked.

'You can't return to Bourne Street, it would not be suitable, and this house is little better. Until I can arrange somewhere, and it must be soon, I suggest you stay here.'

Emily, though still peeved that Thomas had not revealed the presence of Shorty before Annie and Ed had come to Portland Place, knew she had to help all she could. 'If you want somewhere with more open space, where it would be easier to observe any action taken by Midge, why not Bramwell House?'

Though surprised by the suggestion Thomas hesitated only fractionally. 'It would be ideal.' Pleased that the idea had come from Emily his eyes brightened with enthusiasm for the idea, but he went on cautiously. 'That could put your family, the servants, even the house in jeopardy for there's no telling what Midge might do. I won't accept your offer without your father's permission.'

'Then the sooner we have that the better,' said Emily, rising from her chair. 'I'll go to see him now. He'll still be at the office.'

Jonas looked up from the letter he was writing when the door of his office opened.

'Emily.' He smiled, it was always a pleasure to see his daughter. 'Is the meeting over?'

'Not exactly.' She crossed the floor and sat down opposite him.

'Something wrong?' He was concerned by her serious expression.

'Not exactly.'

'You seem uncertain; want to tell me all about it?'

'That's what I'm here for.'

He raised an eyebrow. 'Can I help?'

'I hope so. I have a request but you'd better hear the whole story first.'

'It's generally best to begin at the beginning.' He leaned back in his chair prepared to listen and then make judgement.

Emily told him about Thomas's quest to find the truth about Captain Ainslie's murder in order to completely vindicate James; of how this had led to finding Annie and Ed and how he had hoped Annie would help him trap Midge and how this had been discussed at the meeting she had just left.

Jonas's frown had darkened as her story revealed all the facts. 'This young man is playing with people's lives.

He's over-stepping the bounds of behaviour.'

'Even if it will bring a murderer to justice?'

'He does not know that Whitley is a murderer.'

'Not even with Annie's evidence?'

'No. He is assuming too much.'

'But if he gets Midge to admit it and he has witnesses?'

'That would be different. I suppose he intends to use Annie as bait but that would put this young lady into great danger and that can't be right. I don't like what Thomas is doing. I thought he would have more sense than to play this sort of dangerous ploy. I must say that I am surprised at you supporting him.' He eyed his daughter shrewdly. 'You are, aren't you?'

Emily hesitated. 'Well, I suppose so.'

'You are uncertain. Emily, you cannot adopt such an attitude. You must be for it totally or truly against it. To be unclear could jeopardise the whole plan, if indeed he has one. You've told me nothing about what he proposes to do.'

Emily looked a little nervous as if she was afraid to disclose something.

'Come along, Emily. There's something about this you don't like.'

'Well, first of all Thomas wasn't straight with Annie and Ed.' She went on to recapitulate about the knowledge he had withheld.

'That I can't condone,' said Jonas whose lips tightened into a grim line. He was hearing things about a young man he had taken a liking to. 'I don't like the way he deceived these two people. It's as if he wanted to put them in a position from which they could not refuse to help.'

'That is exactly what I thought,' agreed Emily. 'But when I thought it over, on the way here, I think it was all done with the best intentions of finding the truth for James.'

He smiled to himself behind his stern features. His daughter was softening towards Thomas. She had been hurt by him but she still thought highly of him, seeing the rift as something she could get over. 'All right, we'll give him that benefit. So tell me about his plan to trap Whitley.'

Emily moistened her lips. 'He hasn't disclosed it in detail yet but obviously, as you said, he wants to use Annie as bait, and therefore needs somewhere with space so that any approach by Whitley could be observed.'

'And I suppose because you are here he has Bramwell House in mind?' Fury flared in Jonas's eyes.

'Fath—'

'The impudence of the man. Daren't he come himself? He has to hide behind you, thinking I'll give in to my daughter.'

'Fa—'

'How dare he assume he can play with other people's lives and now their property?'

'Father—'

'When I think I consented to you helping him with his agency . . . I must need my head examining.'

'Listen—'

'It must stop immediately. He promised me he would

251

see you were never in danger and now this. Well, that young man will feel my tongue. I might be mild-mannered, genial, but I tell you when it comes to my daughter's safety I draw the line at helping him.'

'Father!' This time Emily raised her voice in order to break into his tirade. 'Father, listen to me. Don't go on so. Thomas did not suggest Bramwell House, I did!'

Jonas's look of astonishment banished his rage and indignation. 'You?'

'Yes, me. In fact it was Thomas who said we would need your approval.'

Annoyed with himself at displaying a loss of temper Jonas set his lips in a tight line. 'Well,' he grunted, 'justify your decision.' He looked hard at her.

'I don't know exactly what Thomas has in mind, but when I suggested Bramwell House he said it would be excellent.'

Jonas grunted again. 'And you would go along with whatever he has in mind?'

'Yes.'

'In spite of the fact that he withheld his knowledge that Portland Place was being watched?'

'That is something which is a personal matter between us, and something I will certainly tackle him about. There must be trust between us.'

Jonas was pleased with his daughter's attitude. Her upset was something she would put right, there was no need for him to interfere. 'Good,' he approved. 'But there is something I will take him to task about – he was engaged first to find Mrs Ainslie, now he seems to have got sidetracked into clearing James's name. I've been tolerant in not pressuring him but the time has come for more concentration on that case. As I told you both in my office I have a meeting with James next Wednesday and I am not prepared to put that off.'

'Thomas believes there may be a connection between the two cases,' said Emily.

'I don't see how. Do you?'

Emily screwed up her face. 'I'm not sure. Maybe it will be clear if we are able to bring Whitley to justice. So what about Bramwell House, may we use it?'

Jonas did not answer immediately. He rested his elbows on the arms of his chair and steepled his hands in front of his mouth, tapping his lips thoughtfully. Emily knew this attitude and its significance. The situation and personalities were being considered very carefully and it was better not to interrupt her father's train of thought.

A decision made, he lowered his hands slowly and rested them on his desk. 'Very well, Emily, this is what I suggest. You take these people to Bramwell House and I will give you my final decision when I come home and I have met them and heard what Thomas proposes. That is the only way that I can tell if anyone is going to be endangered.'

'There's bound to be some danger, Father. From what I hear of Midge Whitley he can be a dangerous man.'

'I know. And that is a fact I will take into consideration. Now I think you had better get back to Portland Place.'

'Thank you, Father. We'll see you at home.' She rose from her chair and started for the door. Her hand was on the knob when he stopped her.

253

'Emily. Going to Bramwell House does not mean that I have given approval to whatever scheme Thomas has. Make that quite clear to him. I will decide later.'

'Very good.' Emily left the office and hurried back to Portland Place. There she quickly informed them of her father's verdict.

'Quite right of him to reserve judgement until he knows my proposals,' said Thomas. 'We'll leave right away and that will give me time to make some plans before he arrives. Knowing the house and its grounds from my previous visits, I have something in mind, but I need to check the possibilities.'

'What about Shorty?' asked Ed.

'I've been giving that some thought too while Emily was away. We need Midge to know where we are going, so I suggest that we leave here quite openly and when we do we are discussing Midge, and Annie says reasonably loudly that she heard him plotting to implicate James Walton in a murder and that when he was acquitted he had to get rid of Nobby in case he talked.'

'You want Shorty to overhear this so that he will take that information back to Midge who will then seek to get rid of Annie?' said Ed.

'You think he'll come looking for her at Bramwell House?' asked Emily.

'If Annie shows no signs of moving from there then I believe he will.'

'She can't run the risk. Midge is cunning and vicious,' protested Ed.

'You can't put Annie in danger.' Emily's objection added to Ed's disapproval.

'Keep calm everyone,' Thomas interjected firmly. 'We've all agreed to go to Bramwell House, so let's wait until we get there and I'll show you what I have in mind. Now we must plan carefully what we say when we go from here in full view of Shorty.'

Knowing that they would have to leave Portland Place whatever the agreement Thomas had hired a horse and trap, which was waiting in the street. Now, with their conversation prearranged, the four of them emerged from the house. From his cover, a short distance away, Shorty became alert. He checked them against those he had seen enter the building. Annie, Ed, the man Midge was interested in and the young woman who had accompanied the unnamed man as far as the attorney's office in Bowlalley Lane. Shorty was tense as he watched them pause when they reached the pavement. In a few moments he might have a big decision to make – follow the occupier of the house as Midge had instructed, or follow Annie?

He had almost reached a decision when a snatch of conversation brought his attention sharply on to what was being said.

'I tell you that's what I heard,' said Annie. 'Midge planned Captain Ainslie's murder.'

The group appeared shocked by this statement.

'That's dangerous talk, Annie, better kept to yourself,' chided Ed.

'But it's true,' she insisted. 'And he planned Nobby's murder in case he talked.' Shorty saw her turn to the unknown man. 'Shouldn't he pay, Mr Detective?'

Shorty was startled. The man he had been told to watch was a detective! And Annie was naming Midge as the instigator of two murders. He had no doubt that when he carried this news to Midge she would have condemned herself from her own mouth. He strained his ears to learn more.

'He certainly should,' agreed Thomas. 'Does Midge suspect that you know?'

'I don't think so. I don't see how he could.'

'I still think we had better get you out of Hull, somewhere where he'd never think of looking for you.'

'What about Bramwell House?' suggested Emily, following their agreed exchange. 'He'd never expect Annie and Ed to be staying at the home of an attorney.'

'A good idea,' said Thomas. 'Are you sure your father and sister won't mind?'

'In the cause of justice, no,' replied Emily firmly.

'Are you two agreeable?' asked Thomas, turning to Annie and Ed.

'How long will we have to stay?' asked Ed.

'Until I can get all the evidence sorted out and arrange for Annie to take her story to the police. It shouldn't take me too long.'

Ed looked questioningly at Annie. 'Is it all right with you?'

'It seems the safest course to take,' she agreed.

'Good. That's settled. To Bramwell House we go.' Emily sealed the decision.

The four of them climbed into the trap, Thomas taking the reins.

Shorty watched them until they turned out of

Portland Place. No need for him to follow. He knew where they were going. Midge must be told immediately. He set off for the Golden Hind.

Shorty was breathing hard when he reached the inn. He went straight to the room at the rear where he knew he would find Midge.

A game of cards was in progress. Midge looked up from his hand when Shorty burst in. He frowned at the sudden intrusion. 'You look as though you've been rushing. Something on your mind?'

'News, boss, news.' Excitement gleamed in his eyes. He was relishing imparting his knowledge for he was certain it would boost his standing with Midge.

Midge caught Shorty's glance at the bottle of whisky standing on the card table ready to replenish the tumblers. 'Glass over there.' He nodded towards a table next to the door. 'Help yourself.' He judged from Shorty's attitude that he had something important to tell him. A drop of whisky would help loosen his tongue.

Shorty lost no time in slopping some of the liquid into a glass and draining it in one gulp. He caught his breath, wiped his lips with the back of his hand and said, 'That's better. Thanks, boss.'

'Now get on with it,' snapped Midge, his eyes boring into Shorty, warning him that this had better be good to listen to.

Shorty started his story and, in a few moments, Midge had dropped his cards on to the table and signalled to the other three players that the game was over. He leaned on the table and concentrated on

Shorty's words. When the information was finished he sat back in his chair deep in thought. Everyone remained quiet. They knew better than to incur his wrath by intruding on his private world.

Suddenly he hit the table hard with his fist. 'The bitch!' he snarled, his eyes darkening with hate. 'She'd sell me out.' His voice, cold with threat, went quiet. 'Well, we'll see. Her days are numbered. How the hell did that detective find her?'

'Luck, most likely,' Shorty suggested.

Midge's lips tightened. 'I should have done for him when he came here enquiring for Annie. Fooled us with his disguise as an American sailor.'

Things had gone wrong since he tried to pin a murder on James Walton so that he would have no competition for Annie's affection. Now the only way to recoup would be to eliminate her and so save his own skin.

'Bramwell House,' he said thoughtfully. 'Shorty, I want you out there right away. Take Patch with you.' He indicated a medium-built man who had a black patch covering one eye, lost in a fight which saved Midge from a knife. Midge had shown his appreciation ever since. 'Scout the area. Report its layout to me. Watch the movements of those living there, especially those of Annie if she leaves the house. A couple of days should enable me to make plans.'

Shorty and Patch left immediately. They could certainly survey the house and its position before dark.

Reaching Bramwell House, Emily, after making introductions, quickly informed Sylvia about the danger

Annie was in, of what their father had said, and of their plans to trap Midge, the details of which would be explained by Thomas.

'You think he'll come here?' she asked a little doubtfully.

'To save his own skin, yes,' said Thomas.

'Very well. You have my support but none of you must be put in any danger which cannot be counteracted.' She looked at Annie and Ed. 'Welcome to you both. I'll tell the staff to get your rooms ready.'

'You are most kind, Miss Thornton,' said Annie, grateful appreciation in her eyes.

'Annie is a friend of Meg's sister so maybe Meg could be available to help her,' suggested Emily.

Sylvia nodded. She started across the hall but stopped and turned to Annie. With a serious expression of concern she said, 'Don't let them talk you into doing anything you don't want to do. It is you who will be at risk.'

'I won't,' said Annie, aware of her mounting doubt about the whole affair.

Thomas hid his annoyance at Sylvia for sowing disquiet in Annie's mind, and said, 'Emily, will you look after Annie? I want to show Ed what I have in mind before the light fades. If he doesn't agree that my plan is feasible it's no good wasting time on it.'

'Very well,' she concurred. She turned to Annie. 'Let's go in here and await Sylvia's return.' As she led the way to the door to the drawing room, her thoughts troubled her. Were they putting Annie at too much risk? Endangering her life? They entered the pleasant room and, before sitting down, she said with sincerity, 'Annie, I want you to feel at home here. And I must reiterate my sister's concern. If you don't like Thomas's idea say so and we'll not pursue it.'

'You have doubts about it?' queried Annie nervously.

'Not about Thomas's ability and I am sure he will take the utmost precautions to see that you come to no harm, but there's always the chance that things could go wrong. I don't want to undermine Thomas, I only want you to be sure you know what the consequences could be.'

Annie looked uneasy. 'And I know Midge, he can be crafty and unpredictable.' Her lips tightened. She was beginning to view the whole scheme with misgivings. If only they hadn't gone to Portland Place, Midge would not have known where she was. Why hadn't she been more insistent on leaving Hull and going to America? If only— She shouldn't entertain those words. What was done was done. But there was time to pull back. There must be some other way of bringing Midge to justice.

These thoughts were still in her mind when Sylvia returned. She and Emily showed her the room she could use while she was at Bramwell House.

'Meg will bring you some warm water. I expect you'd like to wash,' said Sylvia. 'I've brought you two of my dresses, which I think will suit you. We are about the same size, and I thought you might like a change.'

'You are both most kind. I cannot thank you enough,' said Annie, tears in her eyes.

'When you are ready come down to the drawing room and have a cup of tea,' said Emily.

When the door closed behind the two sisters Annie surveyed her room. A dressing table with mirror stood against one wall so that the light from the two windows came from the left. A washstand with marble top held a floral-patterned bowl and ewer of cold water. A small table with an oil lamp stood beside the oak bed with its colourful patchwork quilt. An easy chair was placed near the windows and a stool was positioned in front of the dressing table. The walls were covered with a paper patterned in small yellow roses.

A lump came to her throat as she was transported to a similar room in Whitby, one in which she had spent many happy hours. She crossed the room to the windows, brushing her fingers across the patchwork quilt. She started. The habit of something she had done at home was still there. It brought Whitby closer.

She swallowed hard, subduing the sentimentality which threatened to bring tears. She reached the window and looked out.

Well-manicured lawns spoke of tender care and indicated a man who liked everything to be neat and tidy, a reflection of what she had sensed in the house. To the right Annie looked down on an area of small enclosures, each with its own lawn surrounded by thick hedges of yew, standing about six feet high. Even from here she could sense the seclusion of each tiny area yet each had access to its neighbour.

She shivered. A sense of threatening mystery reached out to her. For a moment she stared unseeingly at the scene. Nonsense! The feeling could have come because she knew the threat hanging over her. She focused her attention again. One side of the area of secluded lawns and yew hedges abutted on to a small area of chestnuts and oaks. As she was looking at this she became aware of a movement among the yew hedges. She cast her glance in that direction and saw Ed and Thomas deep in conversation, moving from lawn to lawn. What were they up to? What were they planning? She was to be the bait to catch Midge. Could she trust them to keep her safe? She knew what he would not hesitate to do to anyone who threatened his world. She was such a person, and, if Shorty had picked up their conversation outside 7 Portland Place, Midge would know it. Grave doubts flooded her mind.

'Well, Ed, you've seen the layout of this garden; do you think I'm right that we can use it to our advantage?' Thomas put the question as they strolled into the main lawn among the yews, a square slightly bigger than the others. A stone sundial stood at the centre and two stone seats, each large enough for three people, were positioned opposite each other close to the hedges.

Ed looked around, judging, estimating, just as he had done while listening to Thomas's ideas as they had passed from one enclosure to the other. He had satisfied himself that the hedges were thick enough to allow entry to each area only through one gap cut just wide enough to admit one person at a time. The exception was the central lawn, on which they were standing. Here there were two entrances on opposite sides of the square.

He rubbed his chin thoughtfully. 'I suppose so. But I'm deeply concerned for Annie's safety. We must have her under surveillance all the time.'

'If you have second thoughts about what we are going to do, say so,' said Thomas, understanding Ed's dilemma. 'We can cancel the whole thing and get you and Annie back to Hull without Shorty knowing, but that would mean Midge getting away with murder.'

Ed nodded. 'I know.' His words were slow and deliberate as he considered the options. Then, a decision made, he said more firmly, 'If Annie is willing we'll follow your plan. Let's go over it once again and then tomorrow we'll take Annie through it.'

Thomas did so and at the end of it Ed said, 'This presupposes that Shorty or some other of Midge's blackguards will be watching the house.'

'I'm certain of it. If Shorty overheard what we said, and I'm sure he would do, he'd report to Midge and knowing we'd brought you to Bramwell House, Midge would send him out here.'

'And you reckon if Annie carries out the routine you propose that will get back to Midge who'll act upon it?'

'I think there's nothing more certain. If he feels threatened by Annie, and he must do after what Shorty will have told him, he's not going to sit back and watch her talk, he's going to try to stop her.'

'Very well, but it depends on Annie. I've still got an uneasy feeling about this, so it has to be her decision. I won't try to force her.'

'That I can understand. We'll see what she says after I tell her my plan tomorrow. Come on, let's get back to the house. Mr Thornton will soon be arriving home.'

When Jonas arrived home he greeted Annie and Ed

amiably, but Emily sensed a coolness towards Thomas, before he excused himself to remove the dust of the day and change his clothes for an evening at home. He returned to the drawing room where he found Sylvia dispensing refreshing drinks.

'Sir, I would like to thank you for allowing Annie and me to stay here,' said Ed.

'After what my daughter told me I thought you needed help,' returned Jonas, then he added a note of caution. 'But I cannot approve any more than that until I know what Thomas has in mind.' He shot an icy look at him. 'I think you and I should have a word in private first.'

Thomas raised an eyebrow at Emily as he followed Jonas from the room, but she made no response.

As Thomas closed the door of the study, Jonas turned to face him. 'Young man, I do not approve of the way you have been conducting this matter.'

'Sir, if you'll let me explain, I think you will understand.'

'Hear me out first.' The snap in Jonas's voice aroused discretion in Thomas.

'Sir?'

'Firstly I agreed to Emily taking an interest in your agency because she was keen to do so, but, if you remember, I said she must not be put in any danger. Now what do I find? This is exactly what is likely to happen.'

'Sir, I think you exaggerate,' Thomas protested.

Jonas, fired by Thomas's rebuff, drew himself up as anger darkened his face. 'Indeed I do not. I know Miss Newmarch is probably in greater danger as it will be her against whom Midge Whitley is likely to act, but you are all courting danger. All right, you men, I hope, can look after yourselves, but have you the right to subject the ladies to what could have fatal consequences?'

'I am sure there will be no fatality, so I believe my means are justified to catch a murderer. Sir, I think too much of Emily to put her life in danger.'

'I suppose you see that as justification of your actions?' He gave a little shrug of his shoulders as if he held a differing opinion. His voice hardened, his eyes narrowed threateningly. 'I can't stop Miss Newmarch agreeing to go along with your plan, whatever it is. But if anyone is harmed you'll have me to answer to. And another thing, I am seriously considering telling Emily that she should have nothing more to do with your agency.'

Thomas was startled by the harshness of these last words. This was something he did not want to happen, for he felt it would be the beginning of Jonas driving a wedge between them.

'Sir, I am deeply sorry if I have offended you, and if I have given you cause to doubt my integrity. Believe me, I meant neither. Indeed I am grateful to you for allowing us the use of Bramwell House.'

'You have Emily to thank for that. If you had had the gall to presume you could use my home and my family for your own ends I would have been deeply shocked and my refusal would have been accompanied by a ban on seeing Emily again. As it was her idea, well—' Jonas left his meaning unsaid, but he had made his point pretty obvious.

'Sir.' Thomas was humble in his apology without being subservient. He would not retrieve his position with a faint-hearted approach and he made sure there was no mistaking the genuineness and sincerity of his words. 'I think highly of your daughter and I would never do anything to jeopardise our friendship or put her in danger. Nor would I ever want to offend you, and I hope this matter can be put behind us without marring our relationship.'

Jonas was struck by his straightforward approach. 'Very well. I am not one to keep grudges alive once the air has been cleared. I like to forget the points of disagreement and continue relationships as if nothing had happened.'

'Thank you, sir. I too do not keep animosity ongoing. I cannot afford to in the work I pursue.'

Jonas nodded. 'There is one other thing I want to say. You were engaged by me to find Mrs Ainslie, now this attempt to clear James Walton's name seems to have taken precedence. I hope it is not jeopardising your chances of finding her.'

'Sir, I detected a connection between all three cases for which I was engaged. There was a common denominator in James.' He held up a hand stopping Jonas's query. 'Please, sir, I would rather not go into details until I know more, but I hope I will be able to give you some news before long.'

'By next Wednesday, I trust. I must reveal the existence of the second will to James then.' There was a finality about his statement, to bring this meeting to an end. That was confirmed when he added 'Now, will you ask Emily to bring Annie and Ed to see me?'

'Don't be nervous,' whispered Emily as she escorted Annie and Ed to the study. 'Father really has no bite, though he can make his views perfectly clear and will stand no nonsense.'

'Please do sit down,' said Jonas amiably. 'You are most welcome to my home.' He indicated two chairs and he eyed his guests with an assessing look as he watched them sit down. Emily took a chair beside Annie. 'I have just made my views known to Thomas and I would like to point out a few things to you.'

'Sir, if you think we should not be here,' started Ed, only to have his words silenced by a dismissive wave of Jonas's hand.

'I don't think that at all,' he returned. 'But I am concerned for all your safety, especially Annie's, who is without doubt putting herself at grave risk.'

'Sir, Thomas has told me his plan and I think it will work. We are going to finalise the details with Annie tomorrow morning.'

'What do you think, young lady?' he asked.

Annie gave a wan smile. 'I'm not sure. I want to see this man get what he deserves but—' Her voice trailed away in doubt.

Jonas gave her an understanding fatherly smile. 'If you have any fear at all, you should not go ahead. On the other hand if this is the only way to trap this rogue then you may feel the risk is worth it. I only wanted to point these things out so that you would fully under-stand the situation. I am sure no one would hold it against you if you decided not to take part in this escapade. And you, young man,' he turned his gaze on Ed, 'you must not bring any pressure to bear on her. It must be her decision and hers alone after she knows exactly what is entailed. I want your promise on that just as Thomas has agreed.'

'Very well, sir,' replied Ed.

Jonas recognised a man who would not break his word. He was glad that Annie had such an ally. From what Emily had disclosed he reckoned Annie deserved someone like Ed with whom to make a happy future. He only hoped that nothing would go wrong with whatever it was that Thomas had planned, and he was determined to be privy to those plans.

'Now,' said Jonas rising from his seat, 'let us join Sylvia and Thomas, enjoy a pleasant evening and forget what lies ahead.'

Chapter Thirteen

Annie didn't find sleep easy. It was penetrated by past scenes with Midge. He had been there, kind, when she was at a low ebb, and in her distressed state she had been blind to his ruthless nature. By the time she had recovered her normal state of health and had got over the loss of Ed and later the betrayal by James, Midge's talons were well and truly in her and she saw no future but to go along with his rule. Then Ed had returned, and with him a chance of the life which should really be hers, but now the wrath of Midge hung over her. She knew if anything went wrong with the plan to trap him into admitting his part in the murders of Captain Ainslie and Nobby Carson she would experience the vicious consequences she had seen meted out to those who crossed him. Visions of what might happen haunted her.

She had drawn the curtains back before getting into bed and now moonlight streamed through the windows. It refocused her mind and she was thankful that it brought more pleasant thoughts. This room was so much like the one she had had at home that she felt comfortable in it. The moonlight added to that feeling, for in Whitby she had loved to experience its delicate, silvery light adding an ethereal atmosphere. She would get out of bed and go to the window where she became enrapt in the moon playing on the roofs of Whitby, casting beams across the sea which would shatter them into a myriad sparkling jewels.

Memory was driving Midge's haunting face away. Happy with the thought of something much more pleasant, she folded the bedclothes back and swung out of bed. She glided across the floor to the window expecting to see the scene she had just recalled. She received a jolt. It was not there. Instead there were gardens and lawns and, to the right, tiny lawns enclosed by thick yew hedges casting dark shadows across the grass, creating hidden corners which could contain assassins. Her eyes widened in fright. Her hand flew to her mouth, stifling the cry of fear lest it gave her presence away to watching eyes. An owl hooted, the sound eerily penetrating her room. A black form flew across the moon, its slow wingbeat menacing. She tried to turn away but she was transfixed, her legs would not answer her brain. Then with a superhuman effort she tore herself away from the window and with a cry flung herself across the room and on to the bed where she buried her head in the pillow. Her frightened sobs gradually turned to ones of pity for herself for having got entangled in such a web.

Sleep came and with it the morning.

Emily too had a restless night. In her drowsy state her

mind played havoc and, at three o'clock, it brought her wide awake, struck by the immensity of what they were doing – putting Annie's life in jeopardy to catch a murderer who might easily outwit them and claim another victim, leaving no one able to prove positively what he had done.

Their plans did not look as easy now as they had done in Portland Place. Remembering how she had hidden her annoyance when Thomas had disclosed the presence of Shorty raised her ire again. She had been hurt that he had not revealed this information to her before their arrival. Shouldn't Annie and Ed have been warned before they set out for Portland Place? Had he deliberately used them to put his plan into action, knowing that they would be in an impossible position to withdraw? Emily was disappointed in Thomas. And that upset her further, for until now she had seen no blemish in him and had looked forward to an ever-strengthening relationship built on mutual trust, sharing common interests and being drawn closer by what he had mentioned as a partnership.

Eventually she also slept.

Neither of the young women mentioned their disturbed nights when they were having breakfast.

Emily noted the way Annie conducted herself throughout the meal just as she had done yesterday evening. The conclusion she had come to then was confirmed this morning – Annie had been, at one time, used to living in similar circumstances to those enjoyed by the Thornton family. Maybe one day she would learn

271

where. And she hoped that if ever Annie returned to that life it would be with Ed, for she recognised the love he had for this girl and would be ready to adapt to whatever life she wanted. But before that could happen there was Midge to deal with and, though her sincerest wish was that Thomas's plan would succeed and Annie would be rid of the threat that hung over her, the reservations about putting Annie at risk still lingered. She had hoped that daylight would bring an easing of her mind, but doubts about trying to trap Midge here, at Bramwell House, were still strong.

'After breakfast I suggest you all accompany me so that you can understand what I propose to do,' said Thomas, leaning back against his chair, his mind alert for their reactions. He saw no dissensions but recognised that everyone around the table had varying degrees of nervousness.

'Can I be party to whatever you plan?' queried Jonas from the head of the table.

'Indeed, sir. I had hoped you would.'

'Very well, let's say we all meet on the terrace in fifteen minutes.' Seeing nods of agreement from everyone, Jonas rose from his chair and left the room.

The sun, having driven away the early morning mist, bathed the terrace with warmth. Thomas had come out a few minutes before the others to survey the landscape.

'I see no sign of anyone watching the house, but I feel sure that Midge will have arranged for that. He wants to know when Annie leaves here.'

'Am I to do that?' she asked, puzzled that leaving had been mentioned.

'No,' Thomas smiled and shook his head. 'But I expect that is what Midge will be hoping for. However, we want to lure him into coming here, so I propose that Annie should establish a routine walk each morning. It must take place at the same time and it must be such that it seems sufficiently enjoyable to her to repeat it every day. I hope it will be noted by Midge's watcher so that, when he reports his observations, Midge will know where Annie is at any precise moment.'

'And you expect, knowing this, he will confront her? And you want her to get him to talk and admit to the murders?' said Ed. He looked incredulous as if he thought this could not happen.

'But even if he does come—' started Emily.

'WHEN! NOT if.' Thomas showed his annoyance that doubts were being paraded.

'IF he comes,' went on Emily, the touch of sarcasm in her tone expressing displeasure at Thomas's snap, 'there may be no talking. He could murder Annie without a word passing between them.'

Thomas saw alarm come to Annie's expression. He needed to retrieve the situation. As he saw it, Emily and Ed were going against their agreement that no pressure, either to approve or discard his idea, should be put on Annie.

'We'll be prepared for that. Ed and I will be close at hand all the time.'

'If you are as close as you will need to be to protect Annie, won't Whitley know you are there?' Emily's sarcasm was not lost on Thomas.

He bit back the retort which sprang to his lips. What had got into her? She had been enthusiastic for this detective work, now it seemed she was deliberately putting objections in the way. 'I'm proposing to use the area of small lawns and yew hedges. With so many enclosures and such thick hedges we should be free from observation.'

'And won't they work the other way too, enabling Midge to approach unseen?' Emily pointed out, much to Thomas's chagrin.

'We'll be alert to every possibility,' returned Thomas, an edge to his voice. 'Look,' he went on quickly to forestall any more remonstrations, 'if we don't go through with this Midge will remain free and who knows who else may be murdered?'

Jonas, who had remained on the periphery of the group but had taken in every word, stepped forward. 'I would suggest that before any more opinions are expressed, which may lead to regrettable things being said, Thomas explains his ideas further.'

'Thank you, sir.' He was obviously relieved by what he took to be Mr Thornton's support. Emily felt irritated by the note of triumph directed at her. 'If you will come with me, and in case we are being watched, please act as if we were out for a pleasant morning's stroll, I'll explain what I believe will work. I'll follow the walk I want Annie to take each morning from now on.'

He started towards the steps which led from the terrace to the main lawn in front of the house. The others followed and, at his instigation, appeared to any observer to be chatting casually and taking an interest in the gardens, pausing now and then to smell a rose, point out a colourful display of lupins, or admire the glossy leaves of a shrub.

'Annie should pause every now and then to admire the garden and its flowers and take in the view, just as we are doing now. All the time she will be strolling casually towards the area of yew hedges.' As they neared this section of the garden Thomas went on. 'Annie, I would like you to use this entrance. It is the one nearest the wood so you cannot confuse it with any of the other three entrances on this side.'

They reached the opening and from then on he followed a route he had prearranged in his mind after exploring the area with Ed the previous evening. All the time he chatted to Annie making it clear what he wanted her to do.

'Don't all look at once,' he added when they reached the centre lawn, 'but if you look at the house I think you will agree that from the corner bedroom you would be able to observe this whole area and the wood.' He made his statement with the inflection of query.

'It's my bedroom,' said Sylvia. 'And, yes, you can see most of what you describe. Obviously the angle of vision is restricted in some cases by the hedges.'

'So we could use that as an observation point?' asked Thomas.

'But that would mean someone being there all the time.' There was a touch of objection in Sylvia's voice.

'Only throughout Annie's walk.'

'What would be the purpose?' asked Jonas.

'They could warn any of us below of any stranger

approaching by drawing the curtains; we'll arrange certain signals, say fully drawn and left closed if it is Midge.'

No one made any comment and Thomas got an uneasy feeling that his plan was not being received too well. He glanced at Emily who certainly did not bear an expression of approval. He went on quickly to finish by explaining to Annie that he wanted her to come to this central lawn and sit for a quarter of an hour before returning to the house by the same way that they had come.

'You expect—' started Emily.

'Yes,' he rapped sharply, wanting no more objections.

Emily glared at him, betraying her annoyance at being interrupted.

Jonas, sensing the growing irritation, brought the matter to a close. 'Is that it, Thomas?'

'Yes, sir.' He looked round everyone expectantly, but they were prevented from comment as Jonas went on quickly, 'I want you all to go to the house and leave me to have a private word with Annie.'

They were all surprised at this request, but Annie more so than the others. What could Mr Thornton want with her? Though little had passed between them, she had observed him throughout the previous evening and was drawn to the father-figure he presented. She wished her own father had been more like Mr Thornton, whom she thought ruled his household in a firm but gentle way, offering advice more often than giving orders, whereas it had been the other way round with her father. Though she loved him and appreciated all he did to bring them secure well-being, the rebel in her eventually kicked against his authority. That rebellion had brought her to the situation in which she found herself now.

When the others had gone Mr Thornton said, 'Shall we sit down?' and started towards the stone seat against one of the yew hedges. He did not speak again until they were comfortable. 'Annie, you must make up your own mind about this affair. You've heard Thomas's plan and other opinions, but ultimately it will be you who will be in danger. Thomas cannot guarantee that Whitley will come alone, indeed he may not come at all. He may be prepared to wait until you leave here as he knows you must at some time. Then he could strike.'

'I think he will come here. I know him. He's impatient. Once he has his mind set on something, he wants it done. And I know he'll want to find me and, believing I know that he instigated the murders, he will want to make sure I cannot bear evidence against him at a trial. Oh, he'll come here all right but he will be suspicious and he'll plan carefully.'

'Then you must consider what you want to do, being aware of what might happen.'

Annie looked anxious. 'I want to do the right thing, but I am at a loss as to what that is.'

The eyes he had admired during dinner the previous evening, when the talk had been of pleasant things, and today, with its threatening realities, had seemed so far away, were now troubled and seemed to be asking for his help.

'You must consider your own safety first.'

'Then I should leave here secretly at night so that if anyone is watching they wouldn't know I had gone.'

'That is true.' Jonas looked at her with understanding. 'But the way you said it tells me that you doubt if it is the right thing to do.'

'There are other people to consider, and a possibility of what could happen in the future if Midge is not caught and made to pay now.' Her brow furrowed as she awaited comment from him.

'That is a noble attitude – not born in the back streets of Hull – nor were your manners last night. Your deportment tells me you have known better surroundings than you have experienced in Hull.'

'You are a shrewd man, Mr Thornton.' Annie gave a smile. 'I came from Whitby.' She went on to tell him her story. She found him easy to talk to and a sympathetic listener.

When she finished he nodded understandingly. 'Then you want freeing of this blackguard, Midge. He may have helped you when life was running against you but he did it for his own ends, to satisfy his desires, and then wield his evil influence to force you into helping him in his life of crime. Oh, I've heard a lot about him. Never met him, but Hull would be better rid of him.' He pulled himself up short. 'Oh, dear, I told the others not to pressure you and here I am seeming to do just that.'

Annie smiled at his confession. 'That's all right, Mr Thornton, I had already made up my mind.'

He patted her hand. 'Then have faith in those who help you. Maybe when it is all over you should return to Whitby and make peace with your family. Take Ed with you. He must love you very much to have returned from America hoping to find you again. He'll have no worries finding work in Whitby, he being a sailor. I'm sure your father would help.'

Annie smiled her appreciation of his advice. 'Thank you, Mr Thornton, for listening so patiently. It has done me good to talk. Maybe Ed will see Whitby as an opportunity.'

'I'm sure he will. Come, let us join the others.'

Thomas and Emily were a little behind Sylvia and Ed when they reached the terrace and, when he saw them go straight into the house, he took hold of Emily's hand and held her back.

She cast him a sharp glance of vexation and glanced down disapprovingly at his hand which gripped hers.

He released his hold as he said, 'Emily, what has got into you? Yesterday and again this morning you seem to me as if you don't agree with what I'm doing.'

'I saw Father as you suggested and smoothed the way for you using Bramwell House, doesn't that show you I approve?'

'Up to a point. It's your attitude to everything else. You seem to want to put obstacles in the way, I even thought you might persuade Annie not to go through with it.'

'I haven't, have I?' she replied haughtily.

'No, but there were a few moments when I thought you might and that you had Ed as an ally. So what is wrong? There have been times when your words have been strong with sarcasm at my suggestions. There were moments, during my interview with your father, that I thought you might have said things against me, but it was clear that you had told him it was your suggestion that we use Bramwell House, and for that I am grateful. If it had been my suggestion I'd have been out on my ear and banned from seeing you.'

Emily looked startled. 'Father said that?'

'Yes. So what are you holding against me? What have I done to upset you?' He took hold of her hands. He felt resistance, but he held them firmly. Looking earnestly into her eyes he said, 'I wouldn't for the world do anything to offend you. I love you too much to risk losing you.' She looked down. 'Emily, we cannot go on in this atmosphere, please tell me what is wrong so that I can put it right, no matter what it takes.'

She raised her eyes to his. 'You did not trust me,' she said quietly.

'What? When was this?' Disbelief was written all over his face.

'You knew Portland Place was being watched but you did not tell me.'

'But I did.'

'Not until Annie and Ed were there. You thought if you told me before, I would persuade you to tell them and they would not come. But you wanted Annie to be seen so that she would be forced into your scheme.'

Thomas stared at her. She had seen through him. 'I'm so sorry,' he muttered.

'You should have told me. You should have trusted me.' Behind her accusations was a plea for him to put this right between them.

280

He recognised it and grabbed his chance. 'Emily, believe me I am sincerely sorry for this. I can't have been thinking straight. My reasoning was fogged by the desire to set Midge up and it blinded me to the fact that I would be offending you. I did not mean anything by it. Please, please forgive me. I promise it won't happen again.'

'It better hadn't. If we are to be partners then we should trust each other.'

'I love you, Emily.' His hands slipped to her waist and he drew her close. He looked down into her eyes. 'I'm humbly sorry, my love. Forgive me?'

She nodded and met his kiss with equal fervour.

'Please don't let anything mar our relationship again,' he said as their lips parted.

'It mustn't,' she said and slipped her arm through his as they started towards the door to the house. 'Was Father hard on you last evening?'

Thomas gave a little laugh. 'He was until he knew you had suggested coming here. Then he toned down his attitude, but he gave me fair warning about endangering you and indicated that if I gave him the slightest cause for complaint he would veto your helping me and ban me from seeing you altogether.'

She laughed. 'Then you'd better be careful.'

'I trust you can weave him round your little finger.'

'You are sure of this?' Midge snapped the query at a confident Shorty. Confidence in his subordinates irritated him even though he was dependent on it for accurate information.

'We've watched for four days now. The pattern is always the same, except on two occasions Ann—' Shorty saw anger flare in Midge's eyes – 'er ... Miss Newmarch,' no one dare be familiar with her Christian name in his presence, 'was accompanied by one of the Miss Thorntons, the one whom I saw with the detective.'

'Alternate days?'

'Yes.'

'So if they keep to that Annie will be alone tomorrow?'

'Yes.'

'Always at the same time?'

'Yes.'

'And she remained sitting in this central area?' He pointed at the plan of the gardens at Bramwell House which Shorty had drawn for him.

'Always. For fifteen to twenty minutes.'

'Was there anyone else keeping an eye on her?'

Shorty gave a smile. 'Yes. Two gardeners work here.' He pointed to a spot close to the hedged area. 'But they weren't gardeners. We rumbled them – Ed and the detective.'

Midge gave a chuckle. 'Good work, Shorty. Has anyone ever seen you or Patch?'

'No. Certain of it.' Shorty gave a smile of cunning. 'I got us both a spyglass so we were able to watch from a distance, and Patch is a good tree climber.'

Midge laughed. 'Well done. I'll come with you today, see the area for myself and then you needn't keep watch any more after today.'

Shorty was surprised by this order but he knew better than to question it.

After Shorty had left, Midge sat in a thoughtful mood. His dismissal of Shorty and Patch from their mission had been a sudden decision. He had planned to use them as a backup to his scheme, but he had suddenly felt the urge to see this through himself. Annie was a threat to his liberty, and he wanted to make sure she was no longer that. The only way to make absolutely certain was to do the job himself; besides, the desire to see her look of horror, to hear her plead and beg, had become almost overwhelming.

Reaching the vantage point half an hour before Annie would appear, Midge studied the surrounds of Bramwell House carefully. Shorty had done well in choosing this position for there was little of the area which could not be seen. From their place on the edge of the wood the far side of the area of lawns and yew hedges was not visible, but Midge judged that to be of little consequence especially when he saw Ed and Thomas emerge with rakes and spades and head for the section which Shorty had told him about. He watched Annie and Emily come out of the house and saunter through the garden, chattering as if they hadn't a care in the world. He smiled to himself thinking of the moment the next day when he would have Annie at his mercy. By the time the two friends had returned to the house Midge had formulated his plan of action.

'You saw my signal, half-drawn curtains?' queried

Sylvia anxiously when everyone had returned to the house.

'Perfect,' replied Thomas. 'So there were three of them today?'

'Yes. The two who have always been here plus a third man. They used the same vantage point, a good one for them.' She gave a little smile. 'But they never thought we had a better one from my bedroom.'

'Can you describe the third man?' asked Ed.

Tension came to the room as Sylvia hesitated. Would her description fit the man they all expected? 'Well, as you already know they are using the cover of trees at the far side of the wood so it is not too easy to be precise about anyone, except that the man with the eye-patch does the climbing and the short one moves around, scouting the area. The newcomer was of medium build but gave the impression of power, seemed to have authority in the way he was addressing the other two. He was in earnest conversation with the short one, pointing here and there as if he was querying.'

'It must be Midge. But why didn't he face me today?' said Annie, wishing the confrontation had been concluded.

'Remember this is the first time he's been. No doubt he's had reports from the other two and wanted to see the lie of the land for himself so that he could finalise his course of action,' said Thomas.

'And I was with you today,' added Emily. 'It will have been noted by his two men that I have done that on alternate days.'

'And tomorrow you won't be with me.' There was a

tremor in Annie's voice as the magnitude of what might happen then raised a threatening head. Her look, pleading for the burden of responsibility to be taken from her, was shot with terror.

'Then the trap will be laid,' Thomas hastened to reassure her. 'It seems to me that tomorrow might be the day, so we'll be extra vigilant.'

'Don't forget Midge can be cunning,' warned Ed, 'and the regular routine we have adopted may have made him suspicious.'

'And don't you think your role as gardeners might have been recognised? If so Whitley might have ideas to outwit you.' Emily added doubt to everyone's mind about the feasibility of Thomas's plan.

'I don't think we'll have been recognised. But if we have it won't matter because once we are in our positions we are hidden from his view. We can see your bedroom windows and once we receive your signal that Midge has moved into the area bound by the yew hedges we move too.' Thomas tried to reassure everyone but he knew he had not been totally convincing.

It was something that worried him for the rest of the day, though he kept this to himself. He had been warned about Midge's cunning and Emily's point could be right. Maybe there was something else he could do?

He was no nearer an alternative when they all met at breakfast the next morning. But something niggled at him, something which seemed to have come into his mind when he had been out walking alone the previous day, trying to make sure that he had thought of every possibility and banish the fear that plans could go wrong.

Jonas offered to stay at home but, recognising Thomas's desire for normality, he departed for his office in Hull.

At precisely ten o'clock Annie left the house by the front door. It was a pleasant day. The early morning clouds were breaking up and, shorn of its cover, the sun was beginning to warm the earth. Annie breathed deeply, enjoying the feeling as the air filled her lungs. She strolled to the balustrade and leaned on it, taking her weight with her hands. She gazed across the lawns to the fields beyond, dotted with trees, oaks, chestnuts, elms and a line of poplars. She felt the peace and tranquillity and wondered how terror and violence could exist alongside it. She stiffened at the thought, for with it came the realisation that it was she who had brought possible upheaval to the untroubled world of Bramwell House. Should she leave immediately and let Emily's home resume its restful ways? She half-turned back to the house but stopped. If she did would she be letting her friends down? She had come so far with their plans shouldn't she continue and in doing so perhaps catch a criminal who should pay for his misdeeds? She stiffened her resolve and walked casually towards the steps leading to the lawn knowing that others would be moving in accordance with Thomas's plan.

Sylvia entered her bedroom at ten o'clock and, from her window, discreetly surveyed the area on two sides. The main lawn was empty. Annie had not yet reached it from the terrace. The area of small lawns and yew hedges was also quiet, at least as far as she could see.

A slight movement in the wood to her right caught her eye and she stepped quickly to the other part of the corner window to get a better view. Her eyesight was sharp and she relaxed with a sigh when she saw two squirrels racing up a tree. The only other motion came from the topmost branches caressed by the gentle breeze. She drew up her chair and positioned it for her best view without being obvious to anyone outside.

When Thomas and Ed left the house by the back door, Thomas was still trying to recall what had lodged in the back of his mind the previous day and lain there unrevealed. They were picking up their spades when he straightened. 'Leave them, Ed. We are going to change our tactics.'

'What?' Ed was taken aback by the suggestion, though he knew from the firmness in Thomas's voice that he would brook no questioning. 'Why didn't you say so at breakfast?'

'We are expecting Midge to strike today. Remarks about the possibility that our disguise had been uncovered worried me. You'll recall that I took a walk on my own yesterday: something niggled in my mind and I've only just realised what it was.'

'Let's go back and tell the others.'

'No, Annie will have left the house, so there isn't time to tell anyone. We'll have to hope I'm right. Come on.'

'What are we doing?' asked Ed, lengthening his stride to keep up with Thomas as they strode across the cobbled yard towards the stables.

'You'll see. No time to explain now.' They hurried into the stables, where Thomas instructed two grooms to get the trap ready as quickly as possible.

The two men, recognising haste in Thomas's voice, soon had a horse between the shafts.

As they were doing so Thomas explained quickly what he wanted them to do. 'You two lie on the floor of the trap covered by some rugs. When I stop, we change coats and hats. We leave and you drive on as if you are going to Hull. Return only in an hour and go straight to the stables. Keep your hats well pulled down so that you will not be recognised except close by.'

Ed, wearing a puzzled frown, was about to say something when he caught a glance from Thomas warning him to ask no questions.

Thomas saw the mystified looks on the grooms' faces and offered an explanation. 'We are playing a little trick on the ladies in the house and we want them to think we have gone to Hull.'

The grooms smiled and nodded their understanding, only too pleased to oblige the men in their escapade.

Thomas drove the trap out of the yard and set off at a brisk pace down the drive.

'You want Midge, if he's there, to think that we've left Bramwell House and gone to Hull?'

Thomas nodded. 'Yesterday I noticed a dip in the land forming a hollow which runs towards the area where Annie will be. The drive passes through the hollow and at that point we will be hidden from the house and from the wood.'

'And that's where we change clothes with the grooms, they take over and when the trap is visible again from the wood and the house it will look as if we have continued on to Hull,' said Ed, his voice becoming charged with excitement as he saw the possibilities behind Thomas's plan, but then he added a caution, 'Will the hollow give us cover to get back to Annie?'

'Yes. That was the point which had been niggling at me and only dawned on me when we left the house this morning.'

Thomas kept a wary eye on their position and, as soon as the drive dipped into the hollow and he judged them to be protected from prying eyes, he pulled the trap to a halt. Swiftly they exchanged clothes with the grooms and jumped from the trap. Immediately the groom who had taken the reins sent the horse on its way.

'Come on.' Thomas set off at a crouching run keeping to the bottom of the hollow until he decided to check their position. 'Wait here,' he instructed Ed, and crept up the side of the hollow. He quickly surveyed the land and saw that they were still about a hundred yards from the nearest opening in the yew hedge. He slid back to Ed and the two of them moved swiftly away to achieve their goal.

Midge narrowed his eyes thoughtfully when he saw the trap emerge from the stableyard. He recognised Ed but not his companion. Could it be the detective? If so where were they going? He watched the trap proceed down the drive and was surprised to see it turn in the direction of Hull. There would be no watch on Annie. They must think he wasn't going to take any action. He smiled to himself. He could forget his plans to outwit them. Now he could move on Annie unhindered. He looked towards the house. Annie was already in the garden following the routine described by Shorty which he had witnessed yesterday. He watched from his hiding-place.

She reached the entrance to the first small enclosed lawn and passed from his sight. Now it was time for him to move. Using every possible cover he edged his way carefully towards the north-west gap in the yew hedge. He paused at the edge of the wood and glanced in the direction of the house. There was no sign of anyone. He only had a short open space to cross before he would have the shelter of the yews. He checked again, but there was no one to be seen. He left his cover at a run and slipped through the entrance to the first small lawn. He paused, caught his breath, and then started to walk with slow deliberate steps towards the place where he knew Annie would be sitting.

Sylvia started and sat upright in her chair. She couldn't believe her eyes. Thomas driving a trap with Ed beside him, heading away from the house. What were they doing? Where were they going? Why hadn't they taken up their usual role as gardeners? They had not mentioned a change of plan at breakfast. Sylvia was

290

worried. They were leaving Annie unprotected! She watched their progress for a few moments and was shocked to see the trap leave the grounds of Bramwell House and head for Hull. What should she do? She checked quickly on Annie and saw that she was about to enter the area bounded by the yew hedges. Too late to shout a warning to return to the house; she must let Emily, on standby in the hall, know what had happened, and then they must get to Annie as quickly as possible. She started to turn away from the window when a movement caught her attention. He was there! The third man she had seen yesterday, the man Annie had identified as Whitley. Alone? She quickly cast an all-seeing glance across the wood and saw no one else. She watched him straighten, look round, then leave the wood and cross the short open space to the far side of the yew trees at a quick run. He reached them and disappeared from view.

Panic gripped her. Annie was alone! Thomas and Ed were not in their prearranged places but were heading for Hull! Why? Oh why had they altered their arrangements, this day of all days? Annie would be at Midge's mercy. In a state of dread she started for the door, then she stopped and ran back to the window. Her orders had been to draw the curtains and leave them closed if she saw Midge make a move which would threaten Annie. Meant primarily for Thomas and Ed it would be useless, but Annie would be forewarned, though she wouldn't realise her protectors were not close by. Sylvia pulled the curtains closed, thankful that the wooden rings ran smoothly on the poles.

She raced from the room and down the stairs, her unexpected appearance and haste bringing Emily to her feet from her chair in the hall.

'To Annie, quick!' called Sylvia before she reached the bottom of the stairs.

'Why?' The query sprang from Emily, wide-eyed at the alarm on her sister's face.

'Whitley's there!' screamed Sylvia.

'What!' Emily's mind was shocked by the expression of panic. 'You made the signal?'

Sylvia raced for the door as she yelled an irritated, 'Of course!'

'Then Thomas and Ed will know and—'

'They aren't there!'

'What?' Shocked disbelief marked Emily's face and she was galvanised into action to catch up with Sylvia.

'I saw them in the trap heading for Hull.' Her hand was on the doorknob.

'Stop!' The word crashed with authority demanding instant adherence.

Sylvia stared at her sister. Hadn't she grasped the gravity of the situation? 'Annie's in danger!' She started to pull the door open but Emily slammed it shut. 'What are you doing?' snapped Sylvia, her temper rising.

'Wait. If we race out there Whitley will hear us and disappear, maybe kill Annie first!' Emily kept her hand firmly on the door, while the words poured out as she realised that all the preparations to trap a murderer would be for naught. 'If the men aren't there then we must be the witnesses to what we hope will be Midge's confession.'

The impact of the forcefully delivered statement nullified what had been foremost in Sylvia's mind. Her lips tightened and she nodded.

Relieved, Emily said with staccato precision, 'The centre entrance into the small garden which leads to the main one.'

Sylvia opened the door. They ran across the terrace, down the steps on to the lawn and moved easily across the grass to the opening in the hedge, knowing they could not be seen by Midge.

Annie resignedly followed her usual route, walking casually from one small enclosure to the next. She was past admiring the beautifully cut grass, the neat edges to the lawns which came close to the yew trees, thick, trimmed with precision to a height which made each area secluded and closed to prying eyes. The only view into each area was by two narrow openings cut so that only one person could pass through at a time.

Previously she had been able to relax knowing that it would take Midge a few days to make his plans, but that time had passed and today an uneasy feeling had begun to seep into her nerves. It was one of those days when it felt as if routine could be broken.

Her step faltered. The hedges were thick, protective, and wasn't it said that yew, she asked herself, warded off evil spirits? Convinced, she started her stroll again, but she seemed to be taking it more slowly as if she was reluctant to reach her destination where she knew her life could be imperilled. Could she not turn round, retrace her steps and walk away from it all? The temptation was strong. She steeled herself, counteracting her negative thoughts with more positive ones.

If she retreated she would not only be letting other people down but also herself, for would she be able to live with the knowledge that she had enabled Midge, a murderer, to maintain his freedom and ruthless rule over others?

She continued on her way to the central lawn. She crossed it to the seat, which she knew was nearest to the place where Ed and Thomas would be hoeing. She settled herself in the corner of the seat from which she could just see Sylvia's bedroom window. She glanced in its direction. The curtains were drawn! The signal! Midge was close at hand! Her body tensed. Her heart beat faster. Her fists clenched tight as if to control her urge to run.

Thomas signalled Ed to stop. He crept to the top of the slope and peered cautiously over the edge. As he had estimated from his last survey, they still had about thirty yards to go to the opening close to the east corner, but from here he had his last chance to see Sylvia's bedroom window. One swift glance was enough to send his blood coursing through his veins. The curtains were drawn! Their quarry was in the yew tree enclosure! Annie's life was in danger!

He turned and slithered back down the slope, his speed expressing concern to Ed, whose alarm was raised even further by the desperate look on Thomas's face.

'Come on! Midge is here!' he called with quiet urgency and continued on his way at a swift run.

He cut up the slope with Ed on his heels. They topped the rise close to the east corner. They moved silently and quickly to the hedge and peered cautiously into the first enclosure. No one. Thomas nodded and they ran without a sound across the grass to the opposite corner where the opening would give them access to the grassed path which ran all the way round the central area where Annie should be.

They paused. With the utmost care Thomas surveyed the lengths of path he could see. No sign of Midge. He started to step forward when he froze. A man's voice! Coming from the south entrance to the central lawn, the one they would use. He inclined his head trying to pick up the words, but they were too far away to distinguish them sufficiently to make sense. Midge must be confronting Annie. He gave a signal to Ed to follow the prearranged plan to block any escape route by covering the entrance on the north side. Ed nodded and was silently away, while Thomas moved towards the southern opening.

As they neared the yew hedge Emily grasped Sylvia's arm. She didn't want her rushing headlong to Annie. They must have the evidence they wanted. They reached the hedge close to an entrance on the north side. Seeing no one in the immediate area they slipped quietly across the grass towards the opening which would give them access to the path which surrounded the area where Annie would be. Emily signalled to her sister to be careful and guided her to one side of the opening so that they would not be seen by anyone within the main enclosure. Emily's heart was racing. She hoped they were not too late. Then, although the moments were tense, relief swept over her. A man's voice! Midge? It must be. There was no other male about. She and Sylvia inched towards the opening. They had to hear what passed between Midge and Annie and they needed to be close at hand if Midge attempted to strike.

Annie forced herself to sit quietly. After all if she had seen the signal so would Ed and Thomas and they would be alert to what was happening. Nervously she glanced at the two entrances, the one she had used on the right and the other to her left. No one.

The air was still. The sun shone brightly. On the surface the day was normal. There was no hint of the violence that might erupt in this idyllic setting.

'Hello, Annie!'

Even though the words were quietly delivered they startled her. She sat upright, her gaze swinging to the left entrance. Midge stood there, a broad grin on his face showing pleasure at the way he had frightened her, but his eyes bore an expression of hatred. She swallowed hard, trying to draw strength to face him and carry out the inquisition by which she hoped he would convict himself.

'Tongue-tied, my sweet?' he said mockingly. 'Did you think you were safe from me here at Bramwell House?' He took three steps towards her. No need to hurry this. There were no men about. No one to interrupt them. He might as well enjoy watching her squirm.

Annie took a grip of herself. 'What do you want with

me?' she asked. 'You've no right to me. You never had.'

His eyes narrowed. 'Oh yes I had. I was good to you, picked you up when you needed someone.'

'And I was grateful, and you know it. But that gives you no right to me now.'

'Rights?' he snapped. 'Rights don't matter any more.' He was walking slowly towards her, his eyes concentrating on her, frightening in the way they pierced to the very soul. 'After all I did for you, you are ready to betray me.'

'Betray you? I don't know what you mean.'

'I think you do. You know too much. How you got the information I don't know. Eavesdropping no doubt. Maybe I should never have trusted you. But I did, more fool me for giving way to my desires. But whatever, you've signed your own death warrant.'

Annie's eyes widened as if mystified. 'What are you talking about?'

'You may have told these new-found friends of yours, but without you there'll be no evidence against me, no one to testify to the truth.'

'What am I supposed to know?'

Midge gave a grunt of contempt. 'As if you needed telling that I arranged the murder of Captain Ainslie and then when things went wrong I had to get rid of Nobby in case he talked.'

'You had Captain Ainslie murdered?' She appeared surprised. 'Why?'

'Because of you. I'd given you a home when Ed left you. Everything seemed right between us, then you took up with James Walton. Jealousy burns deep. You were mine and I meant it to stay that way. I knew he was having an affair with a married woman, remember how it hurt you Annie, how you were thankful to be able to come back to me. Well, I was frightened that you would turn to him again when his affair ended. When you let slip the knowledge of his debt I saw an opportunity to get rid of him so you would not leave me.'

Emily gripped Sylvia's arm. They had the evidence. Midge had confessed. Should they press forward now? The decision was taken out of her hands as Ed appeared, hurrying along the path on their left. Surprised, relief swept over the sisters. Questions poured into their minds but these would have to wait. Ed winked and held his hand in a signal to keep quiet.

'Why didn't you just kill him?' asked Annie.

'I wanted you to forget him and I thought you would if you saw him as a thief and a murderer.'

'Then things went wrong for you.' She gave a little laugh of mockery.

'Yes, but even though Walton was acquitted I thought I had won you back, then Ed turned up and you disappeared. The rest you know. But this is where it all ends.' His right hand flashed to his belt and in the same movement he pulled out a knife.

Annie stared in horror at the vicious blade. She cringed back on the seat. 'I'll not talk. Your secret's safe with me.' Her heart beat faster. Where were Thomas and Ed? Surely they had heard enough.

'Daren't risk it, Annie. No one will know who killed you. No one knows I've been here.'

'But I will!'

The voice cut sharply into Midge's mind. He spun round, his face masked with the horror of discovery and the realisation that he had condemned himself out of his own mouth. Thomas was walking towards him. Midge crouched ready to strike for the entrance behind Thomas.

'And we will.'

The chorus from behind him jerked him round to face the other direction. Ed was running towards Annie who, once Midge's attention had been diverted, had slid off the seat and put it between herself and Midge.

Midge sized up the situation in a flash. Ed was too concerned about Annie, only two females stood between him and escape. He lunged towards them, expecting the knife to frighten them into opening a path for him. But they held firm until the last moment when Emily pushed her sister aside. Midge struck. The knife ripped Emily's dress. She felt a sharp pain in her arm. She flung herself at Midge as he tried to get past her. He heaved her aside and, as she staggered, unable to defend herself, his knife came up to strike again.

'Emily!' The cry came as Thomas hurled himself at Midge. His shoulder crashed into Midge's back and both men hit the grass. Thomas rolled over, scrambled to his knees and threw himself on Midge, grasping the hand which held the knife. He twisted viciously. There was a crack and Midge could do nothing but release his hold. He squirmed with the pain. His eyes blazed with hate but he was helpless to resist. Thomas jerked him to his feet and thrust him hard against the hedge, pinning him there with a tight grip on his throat. His eyes dared him to try to make a break.

'Is Annie all right?' he called over his shoulder.

'Yes,' shouted Ed.

'What about you two?' Thomas shot Emily a glance of concern.

Sylvia, who was picking herself up from the ground, reassured him she was all right, and, worried about her sister, turned to her to examine her wound.

'It's only a slight cut,' said Emily. 'There's no need to fuss.'

'She's not too bad,' Sylvia called to Thomas, 'but it had better be attended to as soon as possible.'

'We'll get on up to the house,' he said. He jerked Midge from the hedge, grasped his good arm, forced it up his back, and held it there as he propelled him towards the opening in the hedge.

Ed, with a comforting arm around Annie, had joined them. 'The nightmare's over, love. You did so well.'

'You certainly did,' said Emily with an encouraging smile.

Annie swallowed hard, forcing herself to hold back the tears of relief which threatened to overwhelm her. 'I thought no one was ever coming.'

'The delay is another story for when we have all recuperated and this blackguard is under lock and key,' said Thomas. 'But we were close and we heard every word. There couldn't have been a better confession. Whitley will never be able to deny it.'

Chapter Fourteen

The following morning, Thomas's step was brisk as he made his way to the Curzon Club. It gave out that this young man was *au fait* with the world, that he was pleased with life and, had the people who went about their daily business been able to read his thoughts they would have known that he was looking forward to revealing good news to a friend.

Events after seizing Midge had developed rapidly. Leaving the three young women at Bramwell House to recover their composure and relax in the knowledge that Midge would no longer be a threat to anyone, Thomas, accompanied by one of the grooms, had taken him into Hull. There they had handed him over to the police, making formal charges, and leaving the names of witnesses to his confession. The authorities were only too pleased to have the real culprit to stand trial for the murder of Captain Ainslie and to know that the killing of Nobby Carson was linked to the same person.

Thomas was full of good humour and looking

forward to seeing James, to whom he had sent a message asking him to meet him at the Curzon Club at ten o'clock. As he handed his coat and hat to the footman he glanced at the clock in a prominent position in the spacious hall. Seeing that he had arrived at the appointed time, he enquired if Mr James Walton was in the club.

'Yes, sir. He's in the main lounge.'

'Thank you. Will you have hot chocolate for two served as soon as possible, please.'

'Mr Walton has already ordered it, sir, to be brought when you arrived.'

'Ah, good, very kind of him.'

Thomas crossed the hall and when he entered the members' lounge James rose from his seat near a window.

'Good morning, James.' Thomas greeted him breezily, but in a quiet tone so as not to disturb the three elderly men absorbed in their newspapers.

'And to you, Thomas.' James extended his hand in greeting and felt excitement in Thomas's grip. 'My, you look like the kitten that's just been given cream instead of milk.'

Thomas laughed and surveyed the room quickly. 'Let's sit over there.' He nodded in the direction of a corner, well away from the other three occupants of the large room. As they sat down a footman came with a tray bearing the hot chocolate and home-made biscuits for which the club was renowned. He placed them on a table in front of the two men, who had chosen to sit opposite each other.

302

'Civil of you to order this,' said Thomas after the footman had poured their first cup of chocolate.

'A pleasure,' returned James. He eyed Thomas with enquiring curiosity. 'Your message gave me an unsettled night.'

'I'm sorry about that,' replied a contrite Thomas. 'You should have had no worries.'

'Well, you had made me wonder why you wanted to see me. Naturally I kept coming back to the possibility that you had made some progress towards finding who set me up.'

'Progress?' Thomas smiled knowingly. 'My dear fellow, we've not just made progress, we have the answer.'

'What?' James sat upright, leaning forward slightly, his concentration all on Thomas, the chocolate forgotten. He must not miss one word. 'Who?'

'I should begin at the beginning.'

'No! Who was it? I must know that first, then you can tell me all.'

'Midge Whitley.'

'Whitley? That bastard.' James's face darkened at the mention of his name. 'Why set me up?'

'Because of Annie.'

'Annie?' James looked puzzled for a moment then something of the reason began to dawn on him. 'Because he had heard of our association?'

Thomas nodded. 'And that bred jealousy.'

'And he wanted rid of me,' mused James. 'So why not murder me? It was known that I used to haunt the less salubrious parts of Hull on occasions. I could have

303

ended up in the river. It would have been put down to my misfortune and no one would have been any the wiser.'

'That would have been easy for him,' agreed Thomas, 'but he was afraid that Annie's affection would have still been with you, whereas if he could paint you a thief and a murderer she would want to forget you.'

'Why Captain Ainslie?' queried James.

'He was unlucky to put into port at the time Midge was looking for a likely victim.'

'No other reason?' asked James cautiously. He was not sure if Thomas was aware of his liaison with Elizabeth Ainslie.

'None that I know of,' said Thomas, not wanting to reveal the full extent of his knowledge at this time.

Thomas noticed James relax a little at this news, reaching for his cup and taking a sip of his chocolate as if that put a stop to his misgivings.

'Midge? Have you taken this information to the police?'

'I've taken Midge!'

James relaxed even more. A problem had been lifted from his mind. 'So there'll be no more trouble from him?'

'Certainly not.'

'He'll stand trial?'

'Of course. And he's not likely to get off. I've too many witnesses to his confession.'

'Confession?' James looked puzzled. 'Midge confessed to the murder?'

'Yes. And I have four witnesses apart from myself.'

'Good grief, man, how did you do it?'

During the next half hour, while enjoying his chocolate, Thomas related the reasoning and sequence of events which had led to the unmasking and arrest of Midge Whitley.

James's attention was intense. No word was missed. He absorbed every fact. As the story came to an end, he leaned back in his chair, the tension visibly draining from him. 'Thomas,' he said with heartfelt sincerity, 'I have a great deal to thank you for. The relief I feel is immense. I was acquitted but I know there are those who still think that maybe I had something to do with it. Now even they will have to admit that their continued suspicion is wrong.' He paused a moment and then went on, 'To think Whitley was so jealous over my association with Annie that he resorted to murder. What a good job I paid that debt, and thank goodness Jeremy arrived home before the trial finished. And now my name is completely cleared because of you, and of course because of Emily, Annie, Sylvia and Ed. I owe them all a deep debt of gratitude, but probably Annie most of all. She risked her life for me.' He turned a thoughtful gaze on Thomas. 'Do you think it would be wise for me to see her?'

'You doubt it because of your previous relationship with her?'

'Yes. I don't want to cause her any more upset and pain.'

'You won't do that. Annie is a strong person. And I don't think anyone or anything will destroy her love for Ed. As a matter of fact she asked if it would be possible to see you. Emily said she would arrange it at some time in the future when certain matters concerning you were cleared up. That has happened so I see no objection of my doing so now.'

'But will Ed protest?'

'He was there when Annie made her request and he gave his approval. He is deeply in love with her. It may have rankled with him that she refused to go to America with him, but he never stopped thinking about her. He gave up the chance of a good career and returned to Hull to find her, hoping that she still had feelings for him. He'll not stand in the way of anything she wants.'

'Then tell me where I can find her.'

James's knock on the door in Bourne Street later that day was answered by Ed, who looked questioningly at the well-dressed stranger.

'Ed Berriman?'

'Yes.'

'James Walton. I understand Miss Annie Newmarch is here. May I have a word with her? Just a few moments. I believe you know I am in her debt and I would like to thank her for what she has done.'

'Come in.' Ed made no more comment as he stood to one side to allow James to enter the house. He closed the door and led the way down the passage. 'Annie, there's someone to see you,' he said as he entered the room on the right.

'James!' Her gasp of pleasure carried memories of a past friendship from which she would recall only the happy moments. She jumped to her feet and held out her hand.

Ed had started for the door. 'Ed don't go. We have no secrets,' she said.

'Please stay.' James added to Annie's request. 'I'd like you to hear what I have to say.'

Ed gave a pleasant nod, closed the door and indicated a seat to James who took it gratefully.

'I'm sorry to intrude on you both but, Annie, after what you have done for me I could not wait to express my thanks.'

'James, I have done nothing but bring you trouble. If I hadn't taken up with Midge, if I hadn't let it slip about your debt—'

'No.' James shook his head. 'None of it was your fault. It was all of my own making. I've heard the whole story from Thomas Laycock, of how you trapped Midge into making a confession. I can never show my appreciation of what you did to find the person behind Captain Ainslie's murder. You risked your life and in so doing you have cleared my name completely. And that is important to me.' He glanced at Ed. 'You have a wonderful girl here. Take care of her.'

Ed smiled his appreciation of James's assessment. 'I know, I am a lucky man.'

'What are your plans now? Are you thinking of returning to America?'

Ed shook his head. 'No. Annie has a yearning to make peace with her family and so I think before long we will go to Whitby. I'm sure there will be plenty of opportunity there for a sailor.'

'Then I wish you both well.' James stood up. 'And I hope that the three of us can remain friends.'

'I'm sure we can,' replied Ed, and extended a hand to seal a friendship.

Annie had risen from her chair. 'Just one thing before you go, James.' She crossed the room to a table in front of the window. She opened a small teak box, took something from it and when she turned to James she held out the locket. 'James, I shouldn't have this.'

'But I gave it to you. It is yours. Who deserves it more after what you have done?'

'And I give it back, for your true love, the person who finds a special place in your heart.'

'Ah, James, you got my message.' Jonas looked up as the young man entered the attorney's office. 'Thank you for coming.'

The two men shook hands and James turned to acknowledge Emily and Thomas. When he looked back at Jonas he said, 'Sir, you are all looking rather grave when really you should all be happy that my name has been completely cleared of being involved in that frightful case.'

'Do sit down, James.' Jonas indicated the chair which had been left vacant and resumed his seat behind his desk. 'Indeed we are all truly pleased at the outcome of Thomas's investigation and the events at Bramwell House.'

'Good, good. Then let's wipe those solemn looks away with a bit of good news. You must remember that I soon come into my full inheritance, so I'm going to throw a big party for all my friends to celebrate that and having my name finally cleared.'

No one spoke; Emily and Thomas waited for her father to speak in his official capacity, while he was wondering how to break the news to this young man so obviously in high spirits. He wasn't going to like what he was about to hear.

'What, still no smiles at that idea?' cried James. 'What has got into you all this morning?'

Jonas cleared his throat. 'James, I am afraid I am the bearer of bad news.'

James's smile gradually faded as he looked from one to the other, seeking an explanation, but their expressions gave nothing away. He could sense something was drastically wrong. His exuberance was deflated. What was the matter? Why were Emily and Thomas here? What had Jonas to say to him that concerned them?

'Bad news?' James frowned. The words came slowly and deliberately with an enormous query behind them.

Jonas nodded solemnly. 'I'm afraid so. It concerns your mother's will.'

'Which will soon have to be implemented.'

'I'm afraid the will you know about won't be executed.'

'Won't?' His eyes widened in bewilderment. 'Why not?' He gave a small irritated shake of his head.

'A second will, dated later than the one which was read to you, has been found.'

'What?' James was shaken by the thought of what might lie behind the attorney's bald statement. He was incredulous. 'Another will? Why didn't you produce it before?' Annoyance was rising in his voice.

'Because I did not have it.'

'But you were mother's attorney. You must have had it. She dealt with no one else.'

'It is true that she engaged no other attorney, but that did not preclude her making another will. She signed it before witnesses and dated it two days before she died. It is a legal document relating to how she wished her estate to be disposed of, and being of a later date to the other supersedes it.'

'If she did not lodge it with you then—?'

'I can only surmise that she intended to, but doing so must have been overlooked by everyone in the aftermath of her death. If you had not been in such a big hurry to leave Shaken Hall and had taken time to go through your mother's papers you might have found it.'

'If it was at Shaken Hall how do you come to have it now?' James frowned with suspicion.

Jonas looked to his daughter. 'Tell him, Emily.'

Emily told her story calmly and precisely. When she had related all the facts she went on, 'I thought I was doing the right thing making sure that the intruders had not damaged the house. It was by accident that I saw the will and thought it should be brought to Father.'

'And you kept all this to yourself all this time? Why wasn't I told immediately?'

'I deemed it wise to keep it to ourselves until we could look further into the matter,' explained Jonas.

'And what was there to probe? Surely I—' His voice tailed away. His suspicions about the contents of the new will deepened quickly. 'Well?' he scowled.

'I think I had better read this new will to you.'

'I certainly think you should,' snapped James. His thoughts were in a turmoil. He had an awful feeling that he was going to hear something he would not like.

Jonas picked up the papers from his desk and read the contents clearly so that James could not misunderstand their meaning.

He listened in stunned silence. When Jonas had finished James gave a slight shake of his head as he said, 'I just don't believe it,' his voice scarcely above a whisper.

'I'm afraid it's true,' returned Jonas firmly.

Those words bit deep and unrolled an unexpected future before James, one in which he would have none of the luxury he had expected. A wild, haunted look came to his eyes as if he were searching for a solution which would be beneficial to him. 'My mother must have been out of her mind,' he said half to himself, then his voice became louder as he cried, 'That's it! She made this second will when she was deranged!' He stared hard at Jonas. Seeing no expression of agreement, he said, 'She must have been. Don't you see? My mother wouldn't cut me off like that. You saw what she really meant in that first will.' He still saw no approval in Jonas. 'All right, I'll contest it on the grounds that my mother was unstable when she made it.' The fever of dispute gripped him and words poured from him without reasonable thought behind them. 'I can give examples of other eccentricities in her latter days. There's no one to contest what I say. Mrs Sugden is dead. I'll make out—'

'Young man!' cut in Jonas harshly with such power that James's tirade was cut short. 'You don't know what you are saying. I certainly hope you don't mean it.'

'Mean it? Of course I mean it! That money, all the property, everything is rightly mine. You try and stop me!'

The challenge had been thrown down but Jonas knew he would never have to accept it. He said as kindly as he could, 'James, you had better forget what you have said. Everyone here will do so. Mrs Sugden may be dead but your mother had other servants who will verify that she was of sound mind right up to her death. Mrs Sugden was a witness to your mother's signature just as she was to the first will. As you say, she is dead, but the other witness is very much alive and he will confirm that your mother was of sound mind when she signed the second will.'

James saw his world crumbling around him. 'Who was he?' he demanded.

Jonas glanced at Thomas.

'Thomas?' gasped James.

Jonas nodded.

'So that's why you are here.' James gave a small laugh, accepting the trick fate had played on him. 'You save my reputation one day and condemn my future another.'

'Sorry, James, but I cannot do other than to verify that your mother's mind was as clear as crystal when I saw her put her name to that piece of paper.' Thomas's words carried a finality with them.

James shrugged his shoulders resignedly. Then he

started as an even more horrifying aspect of what he would have to live with hit him. 'Good God, my mother went to her grave thinking I was a murderer!'

'Surely not,' said Emily, though she knew that James must be near the truth.

'Of course she did,' rapped James. 'She left her money to Elizabeth Ainslie as a sort of compensation for the wrong she thought I had done her. Why else would she do so? Oh why, oh why didn't she live until after the trial?' There was anguish and genuine love in his cry and it mingled with regret that his wild side had caused her heartache and had now brought him to a point where his future was not as bright and carefree as it could have been.

'That is regrettable,' said Jonas.

'Regrettable? It's more than regrettable. What must she have thought of me?' His voice trailed away to a whisper. 'Maybe I am a murderer. Maybe I killed my mother. Maybe she died of a broken heart and that was my fault.' His voice choked with emotion. His eyes were damp. His recollections were of a kindly lady who had loved him and had given him every chance to fulfil his ambitions.

'You can't blame yourself,' said Emily gently, but with each word emphasised to pierce James's condemnation of himself. 'You did not kill Captain Ainslie.'

'But Mother didn't know that. She didn't live long enough to know I was innocent of what I was accused, but the fact that I was arrested, charged with this heinous crime with all the evidence stacked against me was enough to kill her.' He looked at Thomas. 'My God, it's a good job you got Whitley under police custody or I'd have done for him myself, revenge for the hell my mother must have gone through.' The words were spat with such venomous hate that they left no one in any doubt what the outcome would have been had Whitley still been free.

'James, your mother would not have wanted you to do that,' said Emily. Jonas and Thomas left her to do the talking. In James's agitated state he would be more receptive to the soothing tones of Emily's gentle voice. 'Nor would she want you to go through life with hate in your heart, not even for the man who caused it all.'

'Me.' He shook his head in a gesture of regret.

'No. Not you. You cannot always be looking back, saying if only. She would want you to look ahead now.'

'Look ahead? Yes, I did just that. I had plans for my inheritance. Oh, not the spendthrift life everyone would expect me to lead. The trial taught many lessons. Oh, I'll still seek some pleasure in the odd wager but not to the extent I have done in the past.' He turned to Thomas. 'You know that. You saw me at Briar Manor. I had plans to make certain investments which would have made my mother proud of me, but now that chance has gone.'

'Not as bad as that, surely,' put in Emily. 'Your mother has left you something, and, as she says in the will, she hopes that the money gives you a chance to establish yourself in some worthwhile occupation.'

'It will, but not in the way I had planned if I had received what is rightly mine.' His voice went quiet and he said almost as if he were speaking to himself, not wanting anyone else to hear. 'If only I could find

Elizabeth Ainslie.' Then he raised his voice again as he glanced at Emily. 'Why did you find this damned will? I suppose Mrs Ainslie's smiling, though she has no need of it. That old skinflint of a husband would leave plenty.'

'We don't know what Mrs Ainslie thinks. She doesn't know about the will. We have been unable to find her.'

'So?'

'That was one reason for not revealing the existence of the second will to you until now,' said Jonas. 'We had hoped to find her first. That is why I engaged Thomas.'

'And what have you done? Have you any idea where she is?' James's voice still held a snap.

Thomas shook his head. 'I have made little progress in that direction. It seemed to me that all the three cases on which I was engaged might be linked. Having solved two of them appears to have weakened any connection to finding Mrs Ainslie. There is however one possible avenue to explore – the one common denominator to all three cases.'

'And what is that?'

'You.'

'Me? What could I know of Mrs Ainslie's whereabouts?'

'When I was telling you about our unmasking of Whitley I omitted to tell you, because it had no bearing on that episode, that we know that you met Mrs Ainslie on several occasions when her husband was away.'

James was startled, but he realised there was no point in denying it. 'How do you know that?'

'That doesn't matter.' Thomas saw no reason to reveal Annie's evidence. That she had followed James to his liaison with Elizabeth Ainslie was better left undisclosed. 'The fact is that it is true.' No denial came from James, so he went on. 'Now, it is possible that you know where she is.'

James gave a contemptuous laugh. 'I have no idea. She left Hull immediately after the trial, she was never in court and must have been kept informed what was happening, for when I tried to contact her the day following my acquittal I was told she had gone and none of her household knew where. Within a couple of days they had all left Hull too, so it looked as though she was not returning, a point which seemed to be borne out by the fact that she hasn't even contacted her husband's attorney about a will. I never even received a word from her after my arrest, so you see what she really thought of me.' The bitterness had returned and deepened but this time it revealed that he thought he had been duped.

'Did you learn anything from her that might give us a clue to her whereabouts?' asked Emily.

'I know nothing about her past, nor where she came from, nor how she came to marry Captain Ainslie, a man much older than herself. It was the last fact that brought us together, but it doesn't matter how we met, the fact is that she used me – a sap to ease the life she had to spend with an older, reclusive man.' He gave a grunt of disgust. 'Used me and now she's got what is rightfully mine.'

'But she would not expect that,' said Emily, her voice holding a touch of urgency to dispel the antagonistic attitude to Mrs Ainslie from a man she must have admired, to risk scandal and the wrath of a husband.

James gave a sarcastic smile. 'Whether she did or not, she's got it.' His lips tightened into a grim line. 'If I ever see her again—' His eyes darkened and he stood up. 'I suppose there's nothing more to be said.'

No one spoke. He turned for the door and without a word left the office.

James's thoughts were filled with the blows he had been dealt in those few minutes. A fortune had been taken from him. The future had suddenly become gloomy. His mother had died thinking him a murderer. And he had been reminded that the woman he had come to love had never communicated with him from the moment of his arrest for the murder of her husband, and that her silence had remained even though he had been absolved of the crime.

He needed to think, to reassess his life, to tune in to possibilities in the future. His thoughts were still in a turmoil when he entered the Curzon Club, knowing that there would be few members there at this hour of the day. He ordered a whisky to be brought to him in a quiet corner, and that suited him, for he wanted no company to intrude on his time.

He had done some planning expecting to have a good inheritance with which to work. He knew many people had judged him a squanderer and expected that the fortune he would inherit would be frittered away in gambling and high living, but James had had other plans. He knew that the money had not come easily to his adoptive parents and had resolved to use it to the best possible advantage. Money makes money and he would see that it did, while still enjoying himself. But now that was all gone. Now he would have to work hard to make something of his life, something of which his mother would be proud and make up for the opinion she had taken to the grave.

Unless he could find Elizabeth!

Jonas shrugged his shoulders as the door closed behind James. 'I don't like that young man's attitude.'

'What could you expect?' said Emily, inclined to be sympathetic towards James. 'He's just had great wealth snatched from him.'

'I detected an animosity towards Mrs Ainslie which could erupt with serious consequences.'

'You can't mean violence?' gasped Emily. 'That would get him nowhere.'

'Your father could be right,' put in Thomas. 'I've seen cases like this in America.'

'But he wouldn't—' Emily's protest was interrupted by Thomas.

'I'm not saying that he would resort to killing or even physical abuse. As you say, that would serve no purpose because, for all we know, Mrs Ainslie may have made a will and the Walton money would be passed on by that. But James could seriously threaten her to such an extent that Mrs Ainslie revokes her will in James's favour.'

'Then we must find her quickly,' said Jonas. 'It is imperative, especially if James tries to find her. This will must be made known to her as soon as may be and she must be warned against any possible actions by James.

Have you any idea where you might start?'

'Let's go over the few points we have,' suggested Emily. 'What do we know of the mysterious Elizabeth Ainslie?' She took a sheet of plain paper and a pencil and wrote across the top, 'Elizabeth Ainslie'. She continued to speak as she wrote. 'Age.' She looked up. 'How old do you both think she is?'

'Late twenties?' suggested Jonas.

'Possibly a little younger,' said Thomas.

'I'll put twenty-five.'

She continued to write, 'Height five feet eight. Shortish hair, brown, with a natural wave. Pretty. Married Captain John Ainslie when she was twenty and he was forty-five. Wedding took place five years ago.'

'We don't know where,' put in Thomas, 'so you had better note the ports of call.'

Emily nodded and wrote, 'London, Newcastle and Middlesbrough.'

'Could he have met her in some foreign port?' asked Jonas.

'It is a possibility,' Thomas admitted. 'The banker, Mr Smith, with whom Captain Ainslie was working, told us that the *Fauconberg* was shipping wine from Spain, calling to dispose of some of its cargo at those three places before returning to Hull.'

'Do you know anything about Mrs Ainslie's origins?' Jonas put the question again.

'No, Father,' replied Emily. 'Mr Smith said that Captain Ainslie told him she was from good stock but that the family had fallen on hard times and that she had nothing and no one.'

'A marriage out of pity on his part?' mused Jonas. 'And the seizure of a chance to escape poverty on hers? Who knows?'

'Captain Ainslie appears to have been a very private man and seems to have imbued her with the same attitude.' Emily wrote 'Recluse', voicing the word at the same time.

'But she did go out occasionally,' corrected Thomas. 'We have the evidence of her groom and of course of Annie who saw her with James.'

'Meetings with James. Shopping expeditions.' Emily spoke deliberately as she wrote each word.

'Did she do all the shopping?' asked Jonas, somewhat surprised that this might be so.

'No,' said Emily. 'When we talked to her groom he told us that she left the purchase of household goods to the housekeeper. The few times she ventured on such outings she bought dressmaking goods and materials.' She noted 'purchased dress material' and added, as she explained to her father, 'We found no evidence of her engaging a dressmaker. Her dresses were immaculately made. Did she make them herself? If so where had she learned her skill? Her home town?'

'Could her skill offer a starting point for your enquiries?' suggested Jonas. He made his query as if he had not thought its implication through.

'But we'd have to know where she came from and we don't know that,' objected Thomas.

'And if we knew where she came from the dressmaking aspect would be irrelevant.' Emily's voice tailed away as she was speaking. Her words had been slowly dominated by a contradictory thought. 'Maybe you are right, Father.' Her eyes brightened and she looked excitedly from one man to the other. 'Suppose she is a dressmaker, the quality of her skill would be well known. We could make enquiries about dressmakers in the places where Captain Ainslie may have married her.'

'You mean we should try and trace if she was known as a highly skilled dressmaker in London, Newcastle or Middlesbrough? An impossible task when you think how many there will be, besides we are talking about someone who would be there five years ago. Would anyone remember a dressmaker that long?' Thomas answered his own question, 'I doubt it.'

Emily looked crestfallen. Thomas had dampened her suggestion. Her lips tightened, annoyed that what had appeared, at first, a good idea, should be viewed as something which couldn't be achieved.

She started to turn her attention to another point, but when she glanced down at her notes the word dressmaking seemed to spring at her. She looked up, her thoughts racing ahead of her. 'Suppose,' she said, 'Elizabeth Ainslie was not born in one of those ports, suppose she had gone there already trained as a dressmaker and had done so because she saw opportunities there.' She paused.

Before she could go on, Thomas put in, 'That could be, but I think you are taking a lot for granted.'

'Maybe I am, but I believe in exploring all angles and this one could give us a starting point.' She saw both men were about to say something but she held up her hand saying, 'Hear me out.' She moistened her lips.

'Let's take this idea, that she moved to one of those places, a stage further. Put yourself in her place – a skilled dressmaker, seeking an opportunity to develop and expand a trade at which you were exceptional, which of those three places would you choose?'

At first Thomas had been mystified, but, by the time Emily had finished, his expression had changed to one of understanding, and admiration for the way she had directed her thoughts. He saw that by following her theory there was a chance of tracing Elizabeth Ainslie.

'Well?' prompted Emily, a little irritated that the men weren't enthusiastic about her ideas.

Jonas pursed his lips and shrugged his shoulders.

'Thomas?' She broke into his thoughtful hesitation as he weighed up the possibilities. 'Which one would you choose?'

'There would be customers in all those places, but if I had been in her situation I would have gone to Middlesbrough.'

'But that's only a new town, really came into being in 1832,' Jonas pointed out. 'There would be far more likelihood of customers in either of the other two places.'

'But that's precisely why I would choose Middlesbrough,' went on Thomas enthusiastically. 'Because it is new. It will expand on the back of the iron industry and that means more and more people coming to the area and that would mean a better chance to establish a new business.'

'Right. Exactly what I thought,' Emily enthused. 'So we begin there.'

'You mean that's where *I* will start,' said Thomas,

with emphasis so that Jonas would realise he was not condoning her suggestion.

She shook her head. 'No. I mean we.' She saw Thomas shoot a look at Jonas. She gave a little chuckle. 'You needn't look for Father's reaction. I'll tell you what it is, "she can't possibly be serious about going to Middlesbrough".' She turned her compelling eyes on him. 'I'm going, Father, and that is an end to it.'

'Now see here, young lady,' blustered Jonas, 'you cannot possibly go gallivanting—'

'No, you see here, Father. Thomas and I are partners and as such we should share everything about this business. I know you warned him about getting me into danger, but what danger is there in enquiring about a dressmaker?'

Jonas, caught in an awkward situation, pursed his lips in irritation for a moment. Then his expression softened and he looked at Thomas with a wry smile. 'She's got me there. How can I object?' As he turned his eyes on his daughter they took on a more serious expression, one which would brook no objections to what he was about to say. 'Sylvia must go with you.'

Emily knew the signs and merely said, 'A chaperone.'

Fearing that she might say more than was wise, Thomas intervened quickly. 'Quite right, sir. It could look very amiss if we booked accommodation together even though we had separate rooms.'

Chapter Fifteen

Emily, Sylvia and Thomas prepared to leave for Middlesbrough the following day, Thursday. Not knowing how long it would take to locate Mrs Ainslie, if indeed they ever could, they took sufficient personal belongings to last them a week.

Jonas was at the station to see them leave, wishing them speedy success with their enquiries.

Thomas was solicitous about the sisters' comfort for they had never taken a train journey before and indeed had never been further than the local countryside around Hull. So it became somewhat of an adventure to them and they were attentive to everything around them as befitted enquiring minds.

They changed trains at Selby where they took the Newcastle train as far as Darlington. After a short wait they caught the train for Middlesbrough, where Thomas hired a cab to take them to a hotel, leaving the choice to the cabbie's recommendation.

The bedrooms were comfortable and the public

rooms spacious and well appointed. They learned that the hotel had only been built a year ago and was looking to attract a moneyed clientele who appreciated luxury and good food. Over the evening meal they toasted the cabbie's choice of accommodation, and Jonas's advice to live well without overspending as all expenses would be met by Mrs Walton's estate once the investigation was completed.

The following morning, Emily enquired from the staff at the hotel if they could direct her to any good dressmakers, and finished up with a list of six.

Armed with a pencilled map of the town, the streets they wanted highlighted with thicker lines, Emily and Thomas started their search, leaving Sylvia to have a leisurely time on her own.

Not knowing Elizabeth's name before she was married proved a stumbling block, but Thomas's description of her, which he had gained from her ex-groom, helped somewhat, or more precisely enabled the person being questioned to say they knew no one like that. They were given the names of five other dressmakers but by mid-afternoon they were footsore and weary and decided to leave them until the following day. Feeling a little despondent they returned to their hotel where a bath, a rest and Sylvia's company over an appetising evening meal revived their spirits.

At the same time in Hull James was dining alone and still trying to identify a starting point for his search for Elizabeth Ainslie. He had considered a number of possibilities but had rejected them all. He began to wonder if

325

he might find a clue in their past association that would lead him to her. He carried his mind back to the times he had spent with her.

There had been an empathy between them from their first meeting when he had caused her to fall when she was leaving a haberdashery shop in Hull. He had subsequently discovered her name and had called at Westfold to offer further apologies. From then on they had sought each other's company away from Westfold whenever possible. He had declared his understanding when she had refused to do anything which would hurt her husband and had agreed to terminate their liaison whenever she wished.

But these recollections brought him no nearer solving the puzzle of her whereabouts, for he had never pried into her past, deeming it unwise and impolite to do so.

He frowned. Where could she be? It was vital to his future to find her and he must do that before Thomas was successful.

He wondered if Thomas had made any progress. After what had been said during their last encounter at Mr Thornton's office he could ask him for a report.

An idea halted his attempt to fork a piece of meat. Maybe he could find out something from Simon. It was possible that Sylvia had picked up some news from Emily and mentioned it to Simon.

It was with some hope that he sought Simon on Saturday morning only to have it dashed when he learned that his friend was out of Hull for the weekend and would not return until Monday afternoon.

*

'You have no regrets at leaving Hull?' Annie turned her gaze from the town to Ed who was standing beside her as the *Mary Jane* plied her way down the Humber towards the open sea.

'None, my love. Wherever you are I will be happy.' He smiled and took her hand.

They leaned on the rail with the canvas cracking above them as it took the breeze. Ropes creaked, timbers groaned and water swished along the side of the vessel as the bow cut through the sea.

Annie snuggled close to him, thankful to be leaving a town where she had undergone ecstasy and heartache, danger and security, and, among them all, had made friends, good and bad. She thanked God that the good ones had prevailed and now she faced a future as a better person for her experiences, and in the knowledge that she wanted to spend it with the man beside her. As the ship rounded Spurn Point it was as if this was the new beginning, and she sent a silent message of thanks to Jonas for advising her to return to Whitby and make peace with her family.

Once the vessel was tied up at a quay on Whitby's east side, Annie and Ed were quickly ashore. Ed tossed a coin to two urchins, pay to carry their worldly possessions crammed into two bags. They weaved their way through the flow of people to cross the bridge to the west side.

Her step was brisk with excitement as, holding his hand, she guided him along Bagdale and up the hill until she turned in front of a row of imposing houses known as New Buildings.

A long path led alongside a well-kept garden to a door reached by three steps. Ed took the bags from the boys and, as he followed Annie, he felt as if the house was watching him, trying to size up a stranger.

Annie tugged at the iron bell-pull. A few moments later the door opened. The maid's eyes widened as she exclaimed, 'Miss Annie!'

'Yes it really is me, Lilian.'

Lilian fussed as she moved out of the way and held the door open while Annie and Ed stepped inside.

'Mother and Father?' queried Annie.

'In the drawing room, miss.' The maid started towards a door on the right.

'Wait.' Annie's crisp tone brought Lilian to a halt. 'Don't announce us. We'll give them a surprise.'

'Very good, miss.' Lilian gave a little curtsy and, with a quick glance of curiosity at Ed, hurried away to the rear of the house, no doubt to convey to the rest of the servants that the prodigal Miss Annie had returned, bringing with her a tall, rugged but good-looking young man.

Annie paused at the drawing room door, glanced at Ed, and tried to instil confidence in him with a smile. She drew a deep breath and opened the door. As she walked into the room she said with a steady voice. 'Hello, Mother. Hello, Father.'

Sarah and Stanley Newmarch were so startled by the unexpected intrusion that Sarah, who was knitting, dropped a stitch, and Stanley spluttered on his cigar and dropped the *Whitby Gazette*, the newspaper he was reading.

'Annie!' they both gasped together.

Annie, her face broad with a smile of greeting, rushed to her mother and kissed her on both cheeks.

'Oh, my dear.' Sarah, overwhelmed by the joy of seeing her daughter home again, was at a loss for firmer words of welcome.

Annie kissed her father on both cheeks. 'I'm home, Father,' she said firmly and then added contritely, 'I'm sorry for the way we parted and I hope that we can forget all that happened.'

Delighted to have Annie home, his stern countenance softened. 'Welcome home, daughter.' He gave a little cough. 'I'm ready to let bygones be bygones if you will settle down, with your wild streak under control.'

'Of course I will, Father.' She kissed him again, a token of agreement. 'And I want you to meet the reason why.' She held out her hand to Ed. 'This is Ed Berriman.' Her introduction bubbled with enthusiasm, for she wanted her parents to have no reservations about her feelings for him. 'I want you to welcome him warmly, for at some time in the future I mean to marry him.'

Her parents, taken aback by her forthright attitude, which had thrown the usual convention aside, turned to the young man.

His doubts about the reception he might receive were back after the unexpected announcement she had just made. 'I'm pleased to know you, sir, and you, ma'am.'

'Welcome to our home,' returned Stanley. 'My daughter is surprising us in more ways than one.' He glanced at his wife who nodded her agreement and then flashed a worried gaze at Annie.

Ed gave a little smile. 'She surprised me too. She pre-empted me, sir. Once I had settled in Whitby and ascertained my prospects I would have approached you to seek your permission to marry her.'

Stanley stiffened. He would have liked to know more about Ed Berriman before being put in this situation. But this was typical Annie. He had tried to curb her impulsive urges before and what had it led to? A terrible disagreement, harsh words and Annie leaving home. Now she was back and it appeared as if she was as impulsive as ever. Though he would not let it break his outward façade, he secretly admired her spunk and the fact that she knew her own mind. She was stubborn. If she had her mind set on marrying this young man, he knew that there was little he could do about it. Opposition would only antagonise her and there would be every likelihood of her walking out again. He did not want that to happen. He loved her too much to cause a rift which might never heal.

'Young man,' Stanley said gravely, 'I think you and I should go into my study and have a talk about your prospects.'

'There's no need, Father,' put in Annie quickly. 'Ed has no work at the moment. He has recently returned from America where he went on being offered a very good position as mate on a coastal vessel trading between the New England ports, Canada and New Orleans.'

Stanley nodded but made no comment. He looked sharply at Ed. 'Why did you return?'

'Sir, because of Annie. I met her when she first came

330

to Hull. She seemed in need of help because she did not know the place nor anyone living there.'

'Hull!' The thought of her daughter arriving there with no one to turn to brought a gasp of horror from Sarah.

'I was all right, Mother. Ed took me home and he and his mother were very good to me,' explained Annie.

Stanley prompted Ed. 'Go on, young man.'

'When I got this offer to go to America I asked Annie to come too, but she didn't want to leave England. It's my belief that she did not want to be far from her family. I know she missed you. But I had a contract to fulfil and had to go. I hoped that some day she might be reunited with you and then come to America, for I saw the prospects there to be good and expected to be able to extend my contract when it ran out. But I couldn't get Annie out of my mind so I didn't take up the offer of an extension and returned to Hull hoping to find her again.'

'And he did,' said Annie with a smile.

Stanley still held his serious expression. 'Very commendable. You must have thought a great deal about her.'

'I did and still do, sir.'

'But a young man without employment – what is a father to say?'

'Yes,' whipped in Annie breezily. 'And then help him to find a job.'

Stanley raised his eyebrows. 'As easily as that?'

'For you, yes,' pressed Annie.

Her father grunted, flattered by the esteem in which his daughter held him.

Keen to have her daughter near, Sarah said in a no-nonsense voice, 'Of course you'll help him.'

It was shortly before midday that Emily and Thomas entered an establishment over a shop in Linthorpe road. They found themselves ushered into a small office at one end of a large room in which four young women were making dresses.

'Miss Vallely?' enquired Emily tentatively of the middle-aged woman who stood imperiously behind her desk.

'Mrs,' she said drawing herself up straight.

'My apologies,' returned Emily humbly. 'We were wondering if you could help us trace a dressmaker whom we need to contact.'

For a moment the woman seemed suspicious, but Emily put it down to disappointment because they were not customers. 'Do sit down.' She indicated two chairs on the opposite side of the desk.

'You employ the girls as dressmakers?' asked Thomas.

'Yes. I train them, and though I say it myself no girl leaves here who is not competent enough to earn a living on her own.' Mrs Vallely was delighted to indulge in praising her own ability. 'I will not let any girl leave until she can turn out a well-made dress. And I might add that there are some who are brilliant, but they are few and far between.' She glanced out of the window which gave her a view of the girls at work. She shook her head sadly. 'I'm afraid I haven't one in that category at the moment.'

'It is one such person for whom we are looking,' said Emily eagerly, now that Mrs Vallely had talked about experts. 'Maybe she trained under you, though we aren't at all sure that she even came from Middlesbrough.'

'Before we go any further, may I enquire if this is a personal quest or on what authority do you seek her?' Mrs Vallely judged these people to be respectable but she exercised a need for caution.

Thomas hesitated to introduce himself as having a detective agency in case it made her cautious about imparting information. Instead he said, 'We are acting on behalf of an attorney in Hull who needs to trace this person in connection with a legacy.'

Satisfied, Mrs Vallely nodded. 'What is her name?'

Emily gave a gesture of regret. 'We only know her as Mrs Ainslie. We don't know her maiden name.'

'Then how can I help you?' Mrs Vallely emphasised the words to impart a note of disgust. It was obvious that she would soon regard this encounter as a waste of time. 'Do you have a drawing or a picture from one of those glass plates I've heard about?'

'You're a knowledgeable lady,' commented Thomas, deeming that a little flattery would not go amiss.

'I like to keep abreast of things,' she replied, preening herself.

'Very commendable indeed,' said Thomas. 'But I'm afraid we do not have a picture. I will describe her to you. Maybe you will recognise her.'

As he made his points emphasising Elizabeth's salient features, Emily saw a faint light of recognition in Mrs Vallely's eyes.

'You know her?' cried Emily strongly when Thomas had finished.

Mrs Vallely was silent. She seemed to be looking beyond them as if her mind was carrying her back to a time she had relished. Suddenly she started and said quietly, 'Elizabeth Riches. And how that name fitted her. She was the prettiest girl I ever employed, oh she'd turn every man's head, but she held them off. She had sense. I knew nothing of her background, except that she came from Northumberland and, as far as I could learn, had no family. It was not my place to pry, though I am particular about my girls. But this one I could tell came from a decent home. She came to Middlesbrough looking for work. She met Mrs Bellam whose daughter, Ivy, worked here. She brought Elizabeth to me and, liking the look of the girl, I agreed to give her a trial. It was obvious that she had been taught the basic skills. She was a good worker, had a nimble brain and was quick to learn. She progressed rapidly. I soon realised I had a gem. Her work was exquisite, the best I have ever seen, better than mine and that's saying something.'

Excitement gripped Emily and Thomas. Questions were forming on their lips but they did not want to interrupt Mrs Vallely for she was pouring out information that could be valuable to them. They were sure Elizabeth Riches was Elizabeth Ainslie.

'I don't think I will ever have another girl like her. I tried to encourage her to set up on her own but she was content to stay with me; not that I minded, for her work became known and more and more customers came to me. Then one day, she sent word to me that she was not

334

coming to work, that in fact she was leaving my employment and leaving Middlesbrough. She did not even come to say goodbye. I was devastated, especially as it was obvious that she must have known for a couple of days, for, when I went to her workplace, everything she had been working on had been completed. She had left nothing unfinished.'

'I think this is the person we are looking for. She is an expert dressmaker,' said Emily.

'You say she is married?' Mrs Vallely raised an astonished eyebrow. 'But I never had any evidence of her interest in men.'

'How long ago since she left you?' queried Thomas.

'I have no need to think about that. Losing a girl of her calibre, and she was only twenty at the time, sticks in the mind. Five years ago.'

'I'm sure it's her,' said Emily with a keen glance at Thomas who, with a smile of satisfaction, nodded his agreement.

'When did you last see her?' asked Thomas.

Mrs Vallely showed surprise at the question. 'When she left five years ago.'

'You've not seen her recently?' queried Emily, disappointment rising in her for she felt sure that if Elizabeth had returned to Middlesbrough she would have come to her old workplace.

Mrs Vallely shook her head. 'No. Why? Were you expecting her to be here?'

'We did not know what to expect,' said Thomas.

'If this is the person we want, and I feel sure it is, where do you think she might be?' prompted Emily.

Mrs Vallely looked mystified. 'With her husband, of course.' She glanced suspiciously from one to the other. 'Isn't she?'

'No, you see her husband is dead and she has disappeared.'

'Oh.' Mrs Vallely did not know what else to say. She sounded concerned and bewildered.

'All we had to go on was that she was a very good dressmaker and we thought she might have married in Middlesbrough. We are lucky to have found you and you have been able to identify her but we are still a long way from finding her. We had hoped that she might have returned to her origins which we suspect may have been in Middlesbrough, but you say she came from Northumberland.'

'Yes, but I do not know where.'

'Maybe Mrs Bellam will know. Does her daughter still work for you?'

'No. She left to start her own business with my blessing, then after two years she went to Whitby where I believe she has done very well. A thriving port has well-off merchants, ship-owners, captains and others whose wives require the best.'

Emily cast her disappointment aside and said, 'Maybe Mrs Bellam can help, can you direct us to her home?'

'I can do better than that. Ivy's sister, Jill, works here.' She rose from her chair and went to the door. She called, 'Jill, come here for a minute.'

A young girl stopped sewing and left her chair with only a cursory glance at the other two girls who, knowing Mrs Vallely was watching, did not display their curiosity.

Jill looked worried and kept her head down. As she reached the office door her steps faltered as if she was unsure of what she should do next.

'Come in, come in,' said Mrs Vallely impatient at the girl's hesitation. Jill entered the office and Mrs Vallely closed the door. 'This lady and gentleman would like to ask you a few questions, Jill,' she said, tempering her tone a little. 'They concern Elizabeth Riches. You'll remember her, she lived with you and she and Ivy were very good friends.'

Jill looked up and nodded.

'We need to find her,' explained Emily, her voice deliberately friendly to try to put the girl at ease. 'We have some important news for her. Do you know where she came from?'

Jill shook her head as she muttered a low, 'No.' Then her eyes sharpened. 'But I know where she is.'

'What?' Both Emily and Thomas exclaimed disbelievingly, their eyes widening with doubt. They glanced questioningly at Mrs Vallely, wondering if this girl could be trusted, and saw she was equally surprised.

'How could you know that?' demanded Mrs Vallely. Her tone did not disguise the fact that Jill would be in trouble if she was lying.

'I do, Mrs Vallely. She called at home a few nights ago and when Mother told her our Ivy was in Whitby she said she'd go there.'

'And did she?'

'Yes. Left us the next day.'

Emily and Thomas exchanged glances of triumph. They felt sure they would find Elizabeth Ainslie in Whitby.

James was an early caller at Simon's office on Monday only to be told that Mr Sutcliffe would not be there until two o'clock. He instructed the clerk to keep that time clear for him as it was most urgent for him to see Mr Sutcliffe as soon as possible.

'I'm sorry to intrude on your time so soon after your return, but it is important to me,' apologised James as he shook hands with Simon on the stroke of two.

'Think nothing of it, James,' replied Simon, dismissing the apologies with a wave of his hand. 'My clerk said you seemed to be rather agitated. You're not in trouble again?'

James gave a wry smile. 'Not in the way you mean.' He frowned. 'I have something to ask you.'

Simon leaned back in his chair, spread his hands and said, 'Ask away.'

James hesitated, then said sheepishly, 'I'm embarrassed to ask you this.'

'Embarrassed? You?' Simon's grin showed mocking doubt.

'Well, I could be asking you to betray a confidence, so if you don't want to answer, I'll understand.'

Simon cocked a curious glance at him. 'I can only judge when I hear what you have to say.' He concentrated his gaze on his friend.

'You may have heard that my mother left the greater part of her fortune to Mrs Ainslie.'

'What?' Simon jerked forward with surprise. Now he knew why James was looking long-faced when he came in.

'Never mind the whys and wherefores. I don't know the reason. You'll have to speculate like me. But as you'll know, Mrs Ainslie has disappeared.' Simon nodded. 'Mr Thornton wants to find her to implement the will and he has engaged Thomas to find her.'

'Sylvia mentioned that Thomas had been given the job of finding Mrs Ainslie but naturally she didn't tell me why. At this stage that would be confidential.' He frowned with curiosity. 'So what do you want to ask me?'

'I wondered if you had heard if Thomas had made any progress.'

Simon hesitated a moment. 'You mean has Sylvia told me anything?'

'Well, I suppose so—' James's delivery betrayed his feeling of unease.

'This can't be easy, but I'm afraid I know nothing of what Thomas has done. I think you knew that would be my answer. You wouldn't expect me to disclose what could be confidential information, but I can say with all truth that I know nothing.'

James experienced some measure of relief that he had not forced his friend into an embarrassing position, but at the same time he was disappointed that he had learned nothing to further his search for Elizabeth. His mind had drifted but came back sharply when he realised that Simon was still speaking.

'. . . but I don't suppose it will be a secret that Sylvia

has accompanied Emily and Thomas to Middlesbrough.'

'Middlesbrough? Why? What would take them there?'

Simon shrugged his shoulders. 'I don't know. She told me she might be away for a few days but wasn't sure how long. Whether it has anything to do with the search for Mrs Ainslie I couldn't say.'

Simon had no more to offer but that snippet of information occupied James's thoughts as he returned home.

Middlesbrough? It was an unlikely place for them to visit. A new town, about thirty years old. He had never heard them mention having friends there, so the most likely explanation was that they had discovered a clue as to Elizabeth's whereabouts.

Should he go there too? If he did where would he start looking? He hadn't even the slenderest of leads. He would be relying on sheer luck, and he needed something more substantial than that.

When Mr Newmarch came in from a business meeting on Monday evening he announced, 'I have arranged an interview for Ed, tomorrow morning, with a great friend of mine, Captain O'Rourke, master of the *Northern Star*. His mate has broken his leg and won't be fit to sail for Spain next week. I hope I did right, for I judged you would not be happy away from the sea.'

'You are a perceptive man, sir, and I thank you for your thoughtfulness.'

Stanley looked at his daughter. 'I am sorry to be the one to take him away from you so soon.'

She came to him with a grateful look in her eyes. 'I

340

know the sea has to be Ed's life and I embrace it for him.'

'With that understanding you can be a happy couple.' He kissed his daughter fondly.

'And I've a surprise for you too,' announced her mother. 'As a welcome home present I will buy you a new dress.'

'Oh, thank you, Mother.' Annie ran to her, flung her arms round her and hugged her with great affection.

'I'll send word to my dressmaker to come here when Ed goes for his interview. She paused and then added as an afterthought, 'And while she is here I'll order a new one for myself.' She glanced at her husband who shrugged his shoulders resignedly, but he was pleased that his beloved wife and daughter were happy.

The following morning excitement heightened in the Newmarch household as, with the two men despatched to meet Captain O'Rourke on board the *Northern Star*, the time drew near for the appointment with Mrs Newmarch's dressmaker.

Annie and her mother were sitting in the drawing room when they heard the distant sound of a bell. Annie, her eyes bright, jumped to her feet.

'Lucy will answer it,' said Sarah.

Annie subsided back on to her chair and fidgeted impatiently with the sleeves of her dress.

Voices in the hall were followed by a tap on the door. Lucy opened it and announced, 'Miss Ivy Bellam, ma'am.'

'Please show her in,' returned Sarah.

The girl stood to one side, her back to the door, and

341

her smile and nod, directed at the visitors, indicated that Mrs Newmarch was ready to receive them.

Sarah and Annie rose from their chairs as two young women walked briskly into the room.

'Mrs Newmarch,' greeted the first one brightly. 'How kind of you to seek my services again.'

'Miss Bellam, a good dressmaker is like precious gold and once I found you I knew I had found that gold.'

'You flatter me, ma'am.'

Annie was hardly hearing the conversation. She was in a trance, hardly able to believe her eyes, as she looked beyond Miss Bellam to the young woman who stood a few paces behind. Elizabeth Ainslie! What was she doing in Whitby in the company of a dressmaker?

'And I'd like you to meet my new partner, Elizabeth Ainslie,' continued Miss Bellam.

'Pleased to meet you.' Sarah extended her greeting. 'And may I introduce my daughter, Annie.'

Annie quickly recovered her wits. Outwardly she was composed and returned the greeting, while her mind was giving thanks that she and Elizabeth Ainslie had never met face to face in Hull.

'Where are you from, Elizabeth?' asked Sarah.

'Middlesbrough. Ivy and I were friendly there in our early days of learning dressmaking.'

'And may I say that she is the best dressmaker that I have ever seen,' put in Ivy, to Elizabeth's embarrassment.

'I have been admiring the workmanship in your dress,' said Sarah. 'Did you make it yourself?'

'Yes, ma'am.'

342

'Admirable. Don't you think so, Annie?'

'Perfect.'

'Then Elizabeth will make yours.' She glanced at Ivy. 'I want one for Annie as well as for myself, so you shall make mine.'

'Very good ma'am.'

Ivy and Elizabeth took sample materials from the two bags they had brought, and the four ladies got down to discussing and choosing the cloths and the patterns for the dresses. They paused for hot chocolate brought to the drawing room by Lucy at precisely the time ordered by Sarah.

Ivy and Elizabeth were meticulous in taking measurements and when they parted all four were delighted with the way the morning had gone.

Annie thanked her mother, made her excuses and retired to her room to write to James.

Chapter Sixteen

Emily, Thomas and Sylvia, excited at the prospect that their search for Elizabeth could be nearing its end, had to curb their desire to get to Whitby quickly. A coach would leave Middlesbrough to connect with one at Guisborough. This would reach the coastal town late on Tuesday afternoon.

Two miles out of the market town they felt an alteration in the movement of the coach. A few moments later it began to slow. Puzzled, the passengers looked anxiously at each other. They had all settled down for the journey and did not want it interrupted.

'What's happening?' Emily asked Thomas.

'Don't know,' he replied with a shake of his head and a grimace which indicated he feared trouble.

The coach lurched and came to a halt as the coachman applied the brake.

Thomas, who was sitting near the door, lowered the window and looked out. 'What's wrong?' he called, seeing the coachman jump to the ground.

'Horse gone lame, sir.' He hurried to join the second coachman who had already gone forward.

Thomas glanced round his fellow passengers. 'I expect you all heard that. I'll go and see what it means.' He opened the door, climbed out and hurried over the rutted trackway, thankful that the rain which had threatened earlier in the day had come to nothing. He reached the two men who were examining one of the lead horses. 'Is it bad?' he asked.

'Aye,' the coachman grunted without looking up from the leg he was handling gently.

Taking note of the men's concentration, Thomas did not speak again as he awaited their verdict.

Another three minutes passed before they straightened.

'There's nowt else for it, Jim. Thee'll have to take her back and bring another,' said the driver. He looked at Thomas. 'Sorry about this, sir, but these things happen.'

Though the implication made him seethe at the delay, the men were not to blame, so he nodded and asked, 'How long will it take?'

The coachman scratched his cheek. 'Jim's got to walk the horse back and he can't hurry it with a leg like that, but he'll be able to ride the fresh mount back.' He paused and pursed his lips thoughtfully. 'Maybe an hour or an hour and a half before we are under way again. You and your lady friends and the other passengers will just have to make yourselves as comfortable as possible.' He turned away to help the other man who had started to unfasten the harness.

Thomas returned to the coach to impart this information to the passengers, who accepted the situation, resigned to the fact that they could do nothing about it. The only shaft of annoyance at the delay came from Thomas when he informed Emily and Sylvia that it was possible that they would now be too late to find Ivy Bellam's workplace still open.

'But we'll try,' countered Emily, attempting to revive their optimism.

When the second coachman returned, the horse was soon hitched to the rest of the team. The coachman made his apologies to the passengers once again as he saw them seated comfortably for the rest of the journey.

Although the driver urged the horses to make up lost time there was little he could do to counteract the roughness of the terrain as he followed the trackway which lay between the moors and the sea.

Emily and Sylvia were thankful that Thomas knew Whitby from his earlier days and did not express any worry when they enquired of him about where they could find accommodation.

'This coach uses the Angel Inn in Whitby. It is an efficient coaching house and from what I remember it has the reputation of being the best hostelry in Whitby. I'm sure we'll find comfortable rooms there.'

Immediately the coach pulled in there was hustle and bustle everywhere. The landlord appeared, shouting greetings to the coachman as he threw the reins to a stableman, while another ran to steady the sweating team of horses and two other men started to unhitch them. The landlord received news of the delay and extended sympathies to the passengers, while keeping a supervisory eye on the three youths who were attending to the luggage.

Two passengers were met by relatives and a third collected his one bag and hurried away from the yard. Thomas helped Emily and Sylvia from the coach and approached the landlord.

'Good day, sir,' greeted the rotund and florid-faced innkeeper. 'I hope you are not too tired after the delay.'

'Thank you for your commiseration,' acknowledged Thomas. 'It was more of a nuisance than tiring. Now, I hope you have three rooms available for myself and my travelling companions.'

'Indeed I have, sir. Please follow me.' He cast a look across the active scene, caught the eyes of two of his youths and signalled with a raised finger.

One of them turned to Sylvia, 'Your baggage, ma'am?'

Sylvia indicated which was theirs and started after Thomas and the innkeeper. He escorted them up the stairs having gathered three keys on the way.

'The rooms are very similar,' he said on opening the first door. 'I hope they are satisfactory.'

They stepped inside the room to find a comfortable-looking bed covered by a brightly coloured patchwork quilt. The pillowcases looked as if they had just been washed and ironed. A wardrobe stood against one wall. A marble-topped washstand with ewer and bowl stood against another. A small dressing table and stool were placed close to the four-paned window. There was also a small table on the right of the bedhead and an easy chair positioned to the left of a fireplace with black surround.

347

'These will suit very well,' said Emily having received an approving nod from Sylvia.

'Thank you, ma'am. If you require fires, please say so and I will have them lit.' He handed the two remaining keys to one of the youths and sent them off to open the other rooms. He turned to Thomas. 'How long will you be wanting the accommodation?'

'That is difficult to say. May we take the rooms on a daily basis?'

'Certainly, sir. I like to know the position in case I have other people seeking accommodation.'

'Of course. I will let you know the moment we know we must move on.'

'Very good, sir. Will you be dining here this evening?'

'Yes.'

'Would the ladies like a refreshing cup of tea now?'

'It would be most acceptable,' said Emily in a voice that anticipated the enjoyment.

Once the innkeeper and his staff had gone and Emily and Sylvia had decided which rooms they would have, Thomas made his suggestion. 'When you have refreshed yourselves I think we should go to the address Jill Bellam gave us.'

After they had washed away the dust of travel and revelled in the reviving cup of tea, the three friends left the Angel Inn. They spoke little as Thomas escorted the sisters along Baxtergate to the bridge.

Neither Emily nor Sylvia had been to Whitby before and they were entranced by the seaport with its narrow streets and red-roofed houses, climbing the opposite cliff towards the ruined abbey, their tiles flamed by the lowering sun. They would have liked to view the town at a more leisurely pace, but at this moment their mission of utmost urgency precluded that. Even though the town was vibrant with people leaving work; hurrying home; rushing to catch a shop before it closed; or running to deliver a document before work was finished, an atmosphere of calm, engendered by the onset of evening, was settling over it. Housewives made a final purchase before doors were locked and shutters fastened, or sought a shop which remained open late. Children made one last chase before running home to avoid a mother's wrath.

'Let's hope we find Ivy Bellam still working,' said Thomas.

As they crossed the bridge, they were exposed to the fresh breeze funnelling between the cliffs. It rippled the river and sent folk scurrying for the shelter of the narrow streets.

They quickened their pace along the short length of Bridge Street and turned into Church Street. Now their search for the dressmaker's premises began in earnest. Their stride slowed as they looked for the necessary sign announcing the ownership and designation of the shop, or it quickened to pass to the next one for scrutiny.

They had nearly reached the turning to the market place when Emily called, 'Here it is.' The dress in the window had caught her eye and directed her attention to the notice that announced, 'Ivy Bellam, Dressmaker.'

Thomas was quickly beside her, hoping that their quest was about to be fulfilled. He tried the door but it was locked. His lips tightened with annoyance and

Emily saw the frustration she felt reflected in the look he gave her. They pressed their faces to the window but saw no flicker of light inside the building, nor any sign of life. Thomas backed across the narrow street gazing at the section above the shop, but his hopes of seeing some sign of habitation were dashed.

'The upstairs windows are shuttered,' he said on rejoining Emily. 'The rooms are probably only used for storage. We'll have to come back tomorrow.'

'If you have had sufficient breakfast I think we should be getting to the other side of the river,' suggested Thomas.

'Very well,' agreed Emily. 'Are you coming, Sylvia?'

'You couldn't keep me away. I'm just dying to see Mrs Ainslie's face when you tell her about her legacy from Mrs Walton.'

'Thank goodness we've found her before James, though I don't think he can possibly have any idea where she is,' said Emily with a sense of relief as she pushed herself from the table.

'I hate to think what he might have done to get his hands on the legacy,' said Sylvia.

Within a few minutes they had left the Angel Inn and were heading for the bridge, Church Street and 'Ivy Bellam, Dressmaker.'

A bell tinkled in the rear of the shop when they opened the door. The room was neatly laid out with a patterned carpet, two easy chairs, a rack with several dresses hanging from it and two tailor's dummies on which there were dresses which brought admiration

350

from Emily and Sylvia. Several sheets of paper, two ledgers, measuring tapes, scissors, two boxes of pins and tailor's chalk were neatly arranged on a desk. The whole atmosphere was one of an efficient business and good workmanship.

A young woman appeared from the room at the back from which there came the sound of low voices and clipping scissors.

'Good morning,' the young woman said with a friendly smile. She was smartly dressed in a plain frock which Emily judged to be her working attire for she had several pins in her left sleeve, handy for use. 'Can I help you?'

'Good morning,' returned Emily pleasantly, acting as spokeswoman for the others who nodded their greeting. 'Are we speaking to Miss Ivy Bellam?'

'I'm sorry, but she is out at the moment. She'll be back in about ten minutes. If you want to see her particularly, please take a seat, or maybe I can help you?'

'In actual fact we are looking for Mrs Elizabeth Ainslie,' said Emily. 'We were told that we might find her here.' Even as she was speaking she realised the identity of the young woman for she fitted the description they had gained from her ex-groom: the short hair, the fine features which, moulded together, gave her an ethereal air. Her beauty was still evident even though her face had drained of its colour and her eyes had taken on a look of suspicion and were touched with fear.

Elizabeth's heart pounded. Her mouth was dry. Who were these people who knew she was here? They had

351

used her married name! They must be from Hull, yet she had left there without taking leave of anyone, hoping that she would not be traced, that her past in that town could be wiped from her memory by a new life. How had they found her?

Her instinct was to deny her identity but she already appreciated that that would be useless. Her outward reaction to hearing her name from these strangers had given her away, as was evident from the look on Emily's face.

'You? You are Mrs Ainslie?' There was as much statement as question in Emily's words.

Elizabeth nodded and shot questioning glances at each of the people in turn. 'Who are you?' Her voice was scarcely above a whisper as if she feared the answer.

Emily recognised the misgivings and made her introductions lightly. 'I'm Emily Thornton, this is my sister Sylvia, and the gentleman is Thomas Laycock. We are here on behalf of a Hull attorney.'

The mention of Hull confirmed her suspicions but it still struck hard at Elizabeth's mind. She had to take a firm grip on herself to stop her anxiety from pouring out. Hull had brought her little happiness. She had clutched at the promise of a comfortable life, of never wanting again, but had not reckoned that the price would be to lead a life which was almost that of a recluse. And when she had found some solace in a love which could never be fulfilled it had turned against her with murder. By leaving Hull she thought she could leave it all behind and find some happiness in a life and with people she should never have left.

'How did you find me?' she asked quietly.

'Miss Bellam's sister in Middlesbrough. We found out that you used to work for Mrs Vallely.'

Elizabeth bit her lip. Jill. Why hadn't she sworn her to secrecy about her visit to Middlesbrough? But she had never expected anyone to come looking for her, let alone trace her through her past connections with Middlesbrough.

'And what do you want with me?' She feared the worst, that the whole sordid past of murder and deceit would be brought up again. Her hands were clammy. She wiped them down the sides of her dress but it did nothing to alleviate the dread which was closing round her heart. If these people could find her, so could James. Her dread deepened into terror. They could be working for him, finding her so that he—

'We have some important news for you.' Her thoughts were broken by the sound of the man speaking.

'Something important? For me?' There was a touch of derision in the disbelief in her voice.

'Yes. You are a rich woman – the beneficiary of the large portion of the estate of Mrs Harriet Walton.'

'What?' Elizabeth was incredulous. 'Nonsense.'

'It is true,' interposed Sylvia.

Elizabeth gave a little laugh of contempt. 'I don't believe you. I never met the woman. She didn't know me.'

'Oh, I assure you, Mrs Ainslie, that you are well known in Hull,' said Thomas, and immediately wished he had never made that statement.

Elizabeth's eyes flared with fiery anger. 'No doubt! As

the mysterious widow of a murdered sea-captain. Oh, yes everyone will know me for that. You don't fool me. There is no will with my name on it, only that left by my husband. Mrs Walton had no reason to leave me her money.' Her voice rose. Her agitation heightened. 'Will?' she snorted. 'The real reason you are here is to find me for James. He's frightened. Scared stiff that I will betray the truth behind Captain Ainslie's murder. Oh yes, he was tried and got acquitted, but I wonder if he would have escaped the noose if the real reason for the killing had been known.' Her voice was strident, on the verge of hysterics. 'I'd hoped for peace here. Now you've ruined all that. Now I'll have to move on, find somewhere where you or James can never find me.' She gave a wild laugh. 'Go back to him. Tell him you found me. That once again he's ruined my life. Why couldn't he have left well alone? We could have gone on as we were but, oh, no, he wanted something—'

She choked on her words and Emily seized the opportunity to get a word in. 'What we are telling you is the truth. You are all wrong about us working for James. We came because—'

'Get out,' screamed Elizabeth. 'Out, out, out!' She stepped towards them with a wild menace in her eyes. 'Out!'

The door of the shop opened.

'Ivy!' yelled Elizabeth with relief.

Ivy sized up the situation in a flash. Elizabeth was in a dreadful state and it could only have been caused by these three strangers. They can't have been customers and therefore in her eyes had no right to be in the shop. She gave them a withering look. 'I think you had better leave,' she said coldly. 'I will not have my partner upset, no matter what it is about.' She had her arm protectively round Elizabeth's shoulder. Sobs started to rack her friend's body, sobs filled with relief that she now had trusted help beside her, yet tinged with fear of these people. 'Please leave.'

'Miss Bellam, I presume,' started Thomas.

'You suppose correctly. Now, leave, or do I have to call the law?' Her look was fierce and Thomas knew that this was no idle threat, something which was confirmed when she called over her shoulder, 'Jenny,' to one of the two young girls who were standing wide-eyed in the doorway to the back room.

'We had better leave,' suggested Emily.

'A wise decision,' said Ivy. She held on to Elizabeth in a defiant attitude.

'James is innocent,' Thomas called out.

Ivy felt Elizabeth's body tighten. 'Go!' she snapped forcefully, leaving no doubt that there would be considerable trouble if they stayed.

Emily gripped Thomas's arm. 'Come,' she said. 'Say no more now.'

Thomas accepted her judgement and they filed quickly from the shop.

When the door closed, Ivy said, 'Jenny, mash some tea. Grace, lock the door, put the closed sign up and then help Jenny.' As the two girls started to obey she added, 'Wait. The pair of you must say nothing about what you have heard today. If I learn you've been blabbering you'll have no job and you'll bring dire consequences on yourselves.'

'We'll say nothing, miss.' They made their promises. 'Cross our hearts.'

'All right. See that you don't utter one word about it. Now off with you.'

The two girls scurried away about their tasks.

'Come, sit down,' said Ivy, easing Elizabeth to one of the chairs. 'Calm yourself. There will be no upheaval, I'll see to that.' Her voice was firm and reassuring.

Elizabeth sank slowly on to the chair. Ivy signalled to Grace, who had seen to the closure of the shop, to draw the other chair near Elizabeth.

Once the door to the back room was closed she sat down and took Elizabeth's hand in hers. She was deeply concerned, for she had never seen her friend so wrought up and dejected.

'Now, tell me who those people were and why they were here?' she said gently.

A great sob racked Elizabeth's body. Her world, in which she thought she had found stability, had been turned upside down again.

'They were from Hull.' The words choked in her throat.

'Hull?' Ivy was puzzled. 'But you told me that you knew no one there; that your husband expected you to live the life of a recluse, and that you had done so.'

'That's true,' said Elizabeth with a small nod.

Ivy, seeking confirmation of the facts she had been given, went on, 'You told me that when your husband died you decided there was no future for you in Hull and that you left.' Elizabeth nodded. 'You told me you went to Northumberland hoping that you might find some

356

trace of your family, remote as it might be.'

Elizabeth nodded again. 'Yes,' she whispered.

'You never went back to Hull?'

'No.'

'You were in Northumberland all the time until you turned up at Mother's in Middlesbrough?'

'Yes. As I told you, I found a great-aunt and she kindly gave me a home provided I promised to look after her until she died. I had nowhere else to go.'

'And after she died, three weeks ago, you came to Middlesbrough when her affairs had been taken care of. You hoped that the life you had known there could be taken up again.'

'Yes. I didn't know what else to do. Your mother told me you were in Whitby so I came here knowing you to be the only real friend I had.' Tears came to her eyes. 'And now your kindness in welcoming me and making me a partner has been thrown in your face. I'm sorry, Ivy, I truly am.'

'Think nothing of it. What are friends for?'

'I'll move on. You shouldn't have to bear my troubles.'

'You'll do no such thing,' snapped Ivy indignantly. 'Running away will solve nothing. These people have found you once and they'll find you again.' She then added more lightly. 'Besides I don't want to lose such an expert dressmaker. And we have those dresses to make for Mrs Newmarch and her daughter Annie.'

Elizabeth gave a wan smile. 'You are so kind. I will never—'

A knock on the door from the back room interrupted

357

her. Jenny and Grace came in with the tea and placed the tray on the desk. Ivy thanked them and, after they had left, poured the tea. She handed a cup to Elizabeth.

'Drink that, good and sweet.' She watched her friend spoon the sugar into her cup and then said, 'Elizabeth, why were those people looking for you after all this time? I think there is more to your story than you have told me.'

Elizabeth hesitated, wondering how much she should reveal.

Ivy, recognising what was behind the pause, said, 'I think you had better tell me everything. Those people will be back.'

'Oh no!' Alarm clouded Elizabeth's face.

'I'm sure of it. If they have been looking for you for so long they are not going to give up easily. Now tell me everything so I can help you.'

Elizabeth waited a moment then said, 'My husband was murdered.'

'Murdered!' Ivy gasped. 'But you told me he died and I took that to mean of natural causes.'

'I saw no reason to go into the sordid story. I thought it would never come up again. How wrong I was.'

'Go on,' Ivy prompted.

Elizabeth told her how her husband had been killed; that it appeared to be a straightforward case of robbery; that James Walton had been tried and acquitted. 'If he hadn't been I would have come forward as a witness for I could prove where he was when my husband was murdered.'

Ivy's eyes widened at the implication. 'With you?'

Elizabeth nodded.

'Why didn't you tell the authorities straight away?'

'To prevent any scandal for me and for him.'

'And he never mentioned you at the trial?'

'No.'

'Then he must have loved you very much.'

'That's what I thought, but I began to think he was guilty of arranging the crime so that we could marry.'

Ivy looked astounded. 'Had he ever intimated this to you as a likely solution to your problem?'

Elizabeth shook her head. 'No, but the more I thought about it the more I saw it as possible and that the murder was made to look like a robbery, the accusation by a witness was arranged knowing that at the right moment a friend would come forward with proof that James was innocent. I couldn't live with that so I left Hull.'

'You never spoke to James about it?'

'No. I didn't want to face him.'

'So what have these people to do with it?' asked Ivy cautiously.

'Don't you see?' Elizabeth's voice was agitated. 'James must have employed them to find me. He's frightened I've guessed the truth. They came with some cock-and-bull story that his mother had left me her fortune.' She gave a grunt of contempt. 'A ruse to lure me back to Hull.'

'And you think he would harm you?'

'I'm frightened!'

By Wednesday James was no nearer solving the problem

of the possible whereabouts of Elizabeth. As improbable as it might seem, he was coming to the conclusion that he would have to go to Middlesbrough and hope to pick up some clue as to what his three friends were doing there. What else could he do? If he waited in Hull for their return it might be too late; his plans could be thwarted.

He was in this uncertain frame of mind when he heard the letter-box squeak. He pushed himself from his chair with a despondent sigh, annoyed that he could see no certain way forward to find Elizabeth, and went into the hall. An envelope lay on the mat beside the front door. He picked it up and returned to the room he had just left, took a letter opener from his desk and slit the top of the envelope. He drew out a sheet of paper and started to read. After the first few words he scanned the rest quickly. As their meaning struck home tension gripped him and he sank on to a chair beside the desk to read them more slowly.

Whitby

My dear James,

Ed and I are in Whitby with my family – a wonderful reconciliation.

But this letter is not about me, it is about you. The lady to whom I believe you want to give the locket is here in Whitby. I do not know where she is living. You should be able to trace her by calling at Ivy Bellam, Dressmaker, in Church Street.

Always your friend,

Annie

360

James was consumed with excitement. Annie had given him a solid lead. He nodded and his lips tightened in a grim smile of satisfaction. She could not know about the will, and had unwittingly delivered Elizabeth to him. Deciding that it would be quickest to make the journey on horseback, he made the necessary preparations speedily. As it was now late afternoon and there was no possibility of reaching his destination before dark he decided to stay somewhere overnight and arrive in Whitby early the next day.

He found accommodation at an inn on the outskirts of Scarborough, enjoyed a meal of game pie with a tankard of ale. He retired early, but sleep did not come readily, for his mind was occupied with his quest.

He was awake early and he swung out of bed and went to the window from which there was an uninterrupted view to the east, beyond the cliff. The faint streaks of dawn were beginning to bring a distinguishing mark between sea and sky. The waning moon still left a silvery wash to compete with the stars soon to be overpowered when the sun rose above the horizon. The inn sign creaked on its iron supports as a gentle dawn breeze swung it to and fro.

James stretched, driving away the last remnants of stiffness. Wide awake, there was no point in waiting here. He dressed quickly and was pleased when he heard movement somewhere below.

When he reached the bottom of the stairs the innkeeper appeared from a room on the left.

'Good morning, sir,' he greeted him amiably, though

James would not have blamed him if he had been grumpy at being disturbed so early. 'Heard you moving about. Thought you might want an early start. I've breakfast nearly ready for you.'

James smiled his appreciation of the landlord's thoughtfulness. 'That's very perceptive and kind of you. And that smell is more than appetising.'

'Sit yourself down, sir. I'll bring it through in a moment.'

James sat down at a table which had been laid with knife, fork, cup, saucer and a board on which there was a loaf of bread and a knife. He had just settled himself when the innkeeper appeared with a plate on which sizzled two fried eggs, three rashers of bacon and two slices of fried bread.

'That will fortify you for your ride.'

'It certainly will,' agreed James, and lost no time in savouring the meal while the landlord brought him a pot of tea.

Feeling highly satisfied, he paid generously and expressed his appreciation when he stepped outside and found his horse ready saddled.

He kept the animal to an easy pace for half a mile and then, with the sky brightening gradually from the east, he put it into a canter, breaking every now and then into a gallop. This morning there was no need to conserve energy. His eagerness to complete his mission was conveyed to his mount and he encouraged it to respond.

It was about eight o'clock when he began the descent into Whitby on a track which brought him to the east bank of the river. The quays were beginning to come alive as daily routine was embraced by sailors, dockers and fishermen. Not knowing Whitby, James halted a man who stepped out of a house on his right.

'Sir, can you tell me the way to Church Street and where I can find a good hostelry with suitable stabling for my horse?'

'You're in Church Street now,' the man explained. 'It stretches all the way to the steps leading up to the parish church. Keep on as far as the White Horse. Landlord there will see to your needs.'

James thanked the man and sent his horse forward at a walking pace, keeping it under his strict control, so as not to fall foul of pedestrians, carts, pack-horses and wagons with goods for ships bound for foreign ports. He turned into the yard beside the White Horse. At the sound of hoofs on the cobbles a youth ran out of the inn and took the bridle to steady the horse.

'Stabling, sir?' he called.

'Yes,' answered James swinging from the saddle. 'Good rub down and feed.'

'Yes, sir.' The youth led the horse towards the stable.

James entered the inn and very soon was ensconced in his room, refreshing himself after the ride. Feeling more comfortable he went to the window, which overlooked Church Street, and his attention was drawn to a dress in a window two shops further along on the opposite side of the street. Could that be the shop he was looking for? He shrugged himself into his coat and hurried down the stairs excited at the prospect that soon he could be in possession of the exact whereabouts of Elizabeth.

He left the inn and crossed the street and in a few

363

moments he was staring at the notice in the window confirming that this was the shop he was looking for. He tried the door but it was locked. Disappointed, he glanced along the street and saw that many of the shops were still closed. He was too early. Deciding that he would be too conspicuous if he waited outside the shop he decided he would return to his room from where he could keep watch.

He had been doing so for twenty minutes when he was brought upright in his chair and focused his concentration on two young ladies approaching the shop.

Elizabeth! A strange feeling gripped him. Knowing she was to get what was rightfully his hung heavily in his mind, yet his heart was touched by the memory of what he had shared with her. His eyes narrowed as he watched them deep in earnest conversation, their expression serious. They reached the door of the shop and stopped. The other young woman searched in her small cloth bag and withdrew a key, from which he deduced she must be Ivy Bellam. She unlocked the door and turned to go. Elizabeth stopped her with a restraining hand on her companion's arm. Elizabeth looked worried and when she spoke it looked as if she was making a gesture of pleading. Ivy shook her head and appeared to be remonstrating with Elizabeth, then, with a final forceful word, Ivy departed along Church Street. Elizabeth watched her for a few seconds, glanced back along the street and then dejectedly entered the shop and closed the door.

'Perfect!' said James to himself. Elizabeth would be alone. He left his room and hurried down the stairs.

He strode out of the inn with his mind set on the

imminent face-to-face encounter with Elizabeth. In his haste he was oblivious of other people on the street and collided with a housewife, basket over her arm. Winded, she gulped and shot James a withering look, but banished it quickly under the spell of his charm as he uttered profuse apologies.

Satisfied that she was all right, he opened the door to the dressmaker's, stepped inside and waited as the sound of the bell faded into silence. His heart beat a little faster and his body tensed at the sound of footsteps coming from the back room. The door swung open and Elizabeth appeared.

She stopped as if frozen to the floor. She was dumbstruck with shock, hardly able to believe her eyes. Her face paled. A shiver ran down her spine and dread tightened around her heart. 'James!' The name came out as a drawn-out incredulous exclamation. 'What are you doing here?'

'I came to see you, Elizabeth.' He kept his voice even. 'There are things we should talk about.'

'I have nothing to say to you.'

James sensed hatred creeping into her tone. 'But, Elizabeth—'

She was quaking, afraid of what he might do. Oh why hadn't Ivy stayed, she knew she would be leaving her alone? Delivering some sample materials to three customers, Jenny and Grace would be at least another half hour before they came to start work. She clenched her fists in a determined effort to control her fear and forced her voice to be strong. 'I don't know how you dare after what you did,' she cut in viciously.

'I did nothing,' he protested.

She gave a grunt of disbelief. 'Nothing? You call murdering my husband nothing?'

'You know I was acquitted, and you know I wasn't there – I was with you.'

Contempt burned in her eyes. 'Ah, but you arranged it and I know the real reason why you did and you weren't tried for that.'

'I had no part in it. I had no reason to have your husband murdered.' James's words came strongly as he tried to pierce the barrier in her mind.

'I don't believe you. Now get out of here!' Her eyes narrowed with loathing and then she turned her head away as if she could not bear to look at him. 'I want nothing to do with you.'

'Elizabeth, I love you.' With desperation in his voice he hoped this declaration would make her think again.

Instead they brought a fierce look of disgust and hate. 'You planned John's murder to look like a robbery, knowing you could rely on Jeremy Loftus to prove your innocence, while all the time it was murder so you could marry me. I thought you truly loved me, but that was no way to prove it.'

James was devastated to hear such a condemnation come from her lips. 'It's not true,' he cried, aghast at the accusation. 'As much as I love you I would never stoop to murder. Surely you know that, after what we meant to each other?'

'I loved you.' Sadness had crept into her voice. 'You brought a new life to me. I had someone my own age who cared for me. But you also knew that I would not bring scandal to my husband's name, you knew I would not leave him. He had been too kind to me. I could not desert him.' The sadness was superseded by a rise of anger. 'But our arrangements were not good enough for you. You wanted me all to yourself and were prepared to murder for it. Well, I want nothing to do with you ever again!'

'You're wrong, Elizabeth, so very wrong. I loved you, I still do. It's true I wanted you to myself but I would never instigate a murder to achieve what I wanted.'

She shook her head and clamped her hands over her ears. 'I don't want to hear this,' she cried.

He sprang forward and grasped her by the shoulders. 'You will listen.' His eyes were ablaze with determination. 'You'll come back to Hull with me and hear what really happened.' Frightened by his fierce tenacity, she shrank back and tried to escape his hold.

'I'm innocent!' James tried to drive the truth into her mind with the power of his voice.

She strove harder to free herself from the clutches of the man she regarded as a murderer. She was in danger. She knew it. If only someone would come into the shop.

'Stop struggling,' he yelled. 'And listen to me.'

She shook her head angrily. 'I don't want to hear your excuses. I won't—'

He pushed her hard against a wall making it harder for her to tussle with him. Her eyes widened with deeper fear as his penetrating look bore into her, seeking to make her succumb so she would hear the truth.

She opened her mouth to scream but the sound froze on her lips with the tinkle of the shop bell. Relief flooded over her. Help was here.

'James!' The name slammed through the air jolting him with the bitter accusation that lay behind it.

His grip on Elizabeth slackened. He swung round. 'Emily!'

A deep groan came from Elizabeth. The sight of Emily drained any hope from her and she sank against the wall. 'You.' The word came long and slow. 'I knew you were in league with him, I knew it was all a plan to lure me back to Hull.' She started to sob hysterically.

'Leave her be,' snapped Emily as she rushed past James and, supporting Elizabeth to a chair, said soothingly, 'It's all right, Mrs Ainslie. Everything will be all right.'

'Not if you take me back to Hull.' She looked round wildly. 'Where's Ivy? Why doesn't she come?'

'Thank goodness I got here in time before you could harm her.' An accusing glance accompanied Emily's words thrown at James with contempt.

He was bewildered. 'Harm her? I had no intention of hurting her.'

'It didn't look like it to me.' Emily gave him a look of disgust. 'Don't tell me you weren't trying to force her to rescind the will in your favour?'

'I wasn't!' he stormed. 'I'll admit it crossed my mind immediately after you told me about the second will but I dismissed it. I realised that, even though I had no word from Elizabeth since she left Hull, I still loved her.'

'He doesn't. He can't.' Elizabeth screamed through her sobs. 'He had my husband murdered.'

'I didn't,' yelled James. 'Believe me, I didn't!'

'What he says is true,' said Emily gently but with

conviction. She looked deep into Elizabeth's eyes. 'Believe me no one means you any harm. The murder of your husband was arranged by Midge Whitley. You gave us no chance to tell you this yesterday. See, I have a newspaper cutting which will prove it.' She withdrew a piece of paper from her bag and handed it to Elizabeth.

She read it through tear-stained eyes. It was a report of Midge's confession to the police and mentioned nothing about Bramwell House nor the way in which he had been caught, merely stating that the arrest had been made in the country near Hull.

As she realised the implications of these printed words, she looked at James with a humble contrite expression. 'Oh, James, can you ever forgive me for the way I have wronged you?'

'Elizabeth, you did not wrong me, you only wronged yourself. It was only natural for you to think what you did.' He held out his hands and she took them as she stood up. 'I can see now why you left Hull without seeing me, why you never even sent a word after you had gone. And all the time I thought it was because you didn't care.'

Engrossed as they were in their concern for each other they hardly heard the bell, but became aware of Emily slipping quietly out of the shop.

James drew her closer. 'I condemned you in my mind and I was furious when I learned that Mother had left practically everything to you. But it's a good job she did otherwise I might never have attempted to find you.'

'And the hate in my heart would have been there for ever. We have a lot to thank your mother for.'

369

'We have. And I wish she could know, but now we must look to the future.' Recalling Annie's words he took the locket from his pocket and slipped it over her head as he said, 'For the one I love.' He took her gently in his arms. His eyes expressed the love which came from his heart and the joy of being with her again.

She fingered the locket with gentle affection. 'It's beautiful.' She looked up at him. 'I hope it can be a symbol of a renewal of the love we once shared.'

'I'm sure it will be,' he said. 'We must forget the ill-construed feelings we had for each other over the last few months and look forward to a life of love together, which I'm certain will be the stronger because of what we have been through.' His lips met hers softly and then, as his arms tightened around her, she felt them move into a passion to which she responded eagerly.

The door opened and Emily peeped in. 'Are you two ready to receive visitors?' she asked with a knowing smile.

There was a touch of embarrassment to their nod.

'Sylvia and Thomas were waiting for me outside and we've just met Miss Bellam returning to the shop. We've calmed her immediate reaction on seeing us and I've explained that James was here when I arrived and that everything is all right now.'

As Ivy came in she still had a look of concern, but she quickly dismissed that when she saw the radiant happiness on her friend's face. 'And this is James?' she said.

'Yes. And I'm pleased to meet you, Ivy. I hope you will come to Hull and join the rest of us when Elizabeth and I marry.'

Elizabeth's eyes brightened. 'May I take that as a proposal?'

'Of course,' laughed James. 'What else could it be? Though this may not be the romantic setting you deserve.'

'What does the setting matter?' She smiled. 'And the answer is, yes.'

When the excitement bound up with congratulations died down, Elizabeth said, 'But I can't return to Hull just yet, I have a dress to complete for a Miss Annie Newmarch.'

James made no comment. Emily, Sylvia and Thomas exchanged knowing looks as to how James had come to be in Whitby, but, realising that Annie's surname had never been mentioned during any explanation, they kept quiet about her identity. Maybe James wanted it that way.

'And when you have done that I expect that will mean the end of our short partnership,' said Ivy with disappointment and regret. 'Together again after so long, now to part again.'

'That needn't be,' said James. 'A partnership can operate in both towns.'

'You mean I could open a business in Hull connected with Ivy's here?' asked Elizabeth eagerly.

'If that is what you would like. You'll have enough money to do so. Why not design clothes as well as make them? Then you'll have to meet more often to exchange ideas.'

Elizabeth and Ivy looked questioningly at each other, then they smiled broadly and said together, 'Why not?'

Their embrace cemented their desire for a future in which they would work together.

James stayed behind after Emily, Sylvia and Thomas made their goodbyes and returned to the Angel Inn to make preparations for their return to Hull.

'I'm afraid you'll have to amuse yourself for the rest of the morning,' said Elizabeth. 'Ivy and I have to visit Mrs Newmarch and her daughter to take the first measurements for their dresses.'

'I think I'll come with you,' declared James.

Elizabeth gave a little chuckle. 'But you'll be bored stiff.'

He shrugged his shoulders. 'I can always leave, but if you are in a partnership I think I should take an interest in what you are doing.'

Elizabeth looked wryly at Ivy. 'What do you think, should we take him along?'

Ivy smiled. 'Why not?'

Arriving at the Newmarch residence they were shown into the drawing room where Mrs Newmarch and Annie were waiting.

Although Annie had thought James would come to Whitby looking for Mrs Ainslie, she had not expected to see him under these circumstances. 'James!' Surprise automatically brought his name to her lips.

'Hello, Annie,' he returned quietly.

'You know each other?' asked Elizabeth, taken aback just as Ivy and Mrs Newmarch were by this unexpected acquaintance.

James nodded. 'This is the Annie whom Thomas

spoke about when he explained how my innocence was proved. She also wrote to me to tell me you were in Whitby.'

Elizabeth looked incredulously from one to the other, then as the full meaning of James's statement made its impact she let grateful eyes rest on Annie. 'I owe you a great deal for risking your life to prove James not guilty. And I thank you for letting him know where I was. But how did you know me? I led a reclusive life in Hull. And how did you know that James would want to know where I was?'

There was no need to tell Elizabeth about her relationship with James and so she merely said, 'I knew James and I knew he was in love with you. I saw you together in Hull. I think both you and I could have borne witness to his whereabouts at the time of your husband's murder if it had been absolutely necessary to do so.'

Elizabeth flushed at the implication but only said, 'Thank goodness you did.'

Seeing her mother was becoming more and more bewildered by this exchange Annie gave her a brief but satisfactory summary of what it was all about.

When she had finished, Elizabeth said, 'Shall I start taking your measurements, Miss Newmarch?'

Annie nodded. 'Very well, but I think circumstances have drawn us close enough to be on first name terms.'

Elizabeth smiled. 'I believe you are right, Annie.'

James saw Annie's eyes rest on the locket and then turn to him. He saw approval in them and in the almost imperceptible nod she gave him.

The *Amelia* left the calm of the river and the protection of the piers to meet the swell of the sea. Orders were shouted and instantly obeyed so that the sails caught the breeze and the ship was brought on a course for Hull.

Emily and Thomas stood by the rail enjoying the sharp air, the sunshine and relaxing in each other's company which needed no words to emphasise the empathy between them. It had grown stronger during their search for Elizabeth. There had been times when each seemed to be able to read the other's thoughts and anticipate opinions and reactions.

Sylvia had discreetly made excuses to leave them to themselves, sensing that this departure by sea from Whitby, though their stay had been short, would be memorable to them. She had sauntered towards the bow and was now in relaxed conversation with two passengers who had also boarded at Whitby and were bound for London, the ship's final destination.

Emily and Thomas watched in shared silence as the *Amelia* slipped away from the port and the picturesque scene of cliffs and red-roofed houses.

Thomas's hand slipped into hers. 'A satisfactory conclusion to the first case of our partnership,' he said.

'And Whitby, where it was all solved, will always have a special place in our hearts,' she replied.

'It will,' he agreed and then added, 'would you like to spend our honeymoon there?'

Her eyes smiled at him. 'Whitby seems to be the place for proposals. I'd like nothing better.'

He took her into his arms and, oblivious of the sailors about their work and the passengers taking their last glimpse of Whitby, he kissed her. As their lips parted he said, 'You have made me a happy man.'

'And I hope I will always do so.'

When the *Amelia* arrived in Hull they took a carriage straight to Bramwell House.

The cabby was asked to wait while Emily wrote a brief note for him to deliver to her father's office. She wanted him to know that they were home and that he should not delay in Hull after he had finished work. Sylvia also wrote to Simon inviting him to a special meal that evening.

Jonas, eager for news, returned home early, but apart from informing him that they were the bearers of good news refused to tell him any more until they were all settled around the dining table.

He listened intently as Emily and Thomas each took up parts of the story, with Sylvia putting in some brief explanations for Simon's benefit.

When they had finished Jonas sank against the back of the chair. 'Just one thing. The locket which gave you your first lead to Annie – what happened to it?'

'Ed had come back into Annie's life and, knowing where James's love lay, she gave the locket back to him, telling him to give it the one he really loved.'

'And he did?'

'Yes. He gave it to Elizabeth.'

'So the locket has returned to the Walton inheritance.' His look of deep satisfaction also held

375

admiration for their efforts. 'What do you think of them, Simon?'

'Sir, I think we have a very good detective agency in Hull and that should be of benefit to your business and my father's.'

Jonas nodded. 'I agree.' He put on a serious doubting countenance when he added, 'But do you really think a young woman should be involved in such investigative enquiries which may be, at times, unsavoury?'

Emily knew this was directed at her but she said nothing as she waited on tenterhooks for Simon's reply.

'Sir,' said Simon in all seriousness, though he got in a sly wink at Emily without anyone else seeing, 'the way the world is moving, women are going to take more and more interest in many things still regarded as man's domain, but I believe they can bring much good judgement. And so in the case of a detective agency,' he paused as if making a careful consideration, 'I think their deductive powers and common sense can help a great deal. And they can be protected from the seedier side of the work if they so desire.'

Jonas nodded while his lips tightened as if he disapproved. Seeing Emily expecting an unsatisfactory statement from him, he decided to keep her wondering. He looked at Thomas. 'Have you anything to say?'

'Well, sir, I was hoping you would agree with Simon's views.'

'You still think a partnership with my daughter in your detective agency will be a good thing?'

'Most certainly, sir. And I hope you will approve and

376

then extend that approval to a partnership beyond the detective agency.'

Jonas allowed his relaxation to be obvious. He smiled. 'I take it Emily has already said yes to you on both counts?'

'I have, Father,' put in Emily with an unmistakable firmness.

'Then may both partnerships have a long and happy future.'